*With tall, handso[me]
like these it's easy t[o ...]
the passion of th[e ...]
up unexpec[tedly ...]
shockingly pregnant!*

bombshell
for the
BOSS

Liz Fielding

Nicola Marsh

Jackie Braun

bombshell
for the
BOSS

Liz Fielding

Nicola Marsh

Jackie Braun

All the characters in this book have no existence outside the imagination of the author, and have no relation whatsoever to anyone bearing the same name or names. They are not even distantly inspired by any individual known or unknown to the author, and all the incidents are pure invention.

All Rights Reserved including the right of reproduction in whole or in part in any form. This edition is published by arrangement with Harlequin Enterprises II B.V./S.à.r.l. The text of this publication or any part thereof may not be reproduced or transmitted in any form or by any means, electronic or mechanical, including photocopying, recording, storage in an information retrieval system, or otherwise, without the written permission of the publisher.

This book is sold subject to the condition that it shall not, by way of trade or otherwise, be lent, resold, hired out or otherwise circulated without the prior consent of the publisher in any form of binding or cover other than that in which it is published and without a similar condition including this condition being imposed on the subsequent purchaser.

® and ™ are trademarks owned and used by the trademark owner and/or its licensee. Trademarks marked with ® are registered with the United Kingdom Patent Office and/or the Office for Harmonisation in the Internal Market and in other countries.

Mills & Boon, an imprint of Harlequin (UK) Limited, Eton House, 18-24 Paradise Road, Richmond, Surrey TW9 1SR

BOMBSHELL FOR THE BOSS
© Harlequin Enterprises II B.V./S.à.r.l. 2012

The Bride's Baby © Liz Fielding 2008
Executive Mother-To-Be © Nicola Marsh 2007
Boardroom Baby Surprise © Jackie Braun Fridline 2009

ISBN: 978 0 263 89775 3

025-0612

Harlequin (UK) policy is to use papers that are natural, renewable and recyclable products and made from wood grown in sustainable forests. The logging and manufacturing processes conform to the legal environmental regulations of the country of origin.

Printed and bound in Spain
by Blackprint CPI, Barcelona

The Bride's Baby

Liz Fielding

Liz Fielding was born with itchy feet. She made it to Zambia before her twenty-first birthday and, gathering her own special hero and a couple of children on the way, lived in Botswana, Kenya and Bahrain—with pauses for sightseeing pretty much everywhere in between. She finally came to a full stop in a tiny Welsh village cradled by misty hills, and these days mostly leaves her pen to do the travelling. When she's not sorting out the lives and loves of her characters, she potters in the garden, reads her favourite authors and spends a lot of time wondering 'What if...?' For news of upcoming books—and to sign up for her occasional newsletter—visit Liz's website at www.lizfielding.com

CHAPTER ONE

SYLVIE SMITH checked the time. Her appointment had been for two o'clock. The time on her laptop now read two forty-five—because she hadn't just sat there in the luxurious reception of Tom McFarlane's penthouse office suite twiddling her thumbs and drinking coffee.

Chance would have been a fine thing.

The message couldn't have been plainer.

She was the enemy and so she'd been left to twiddle her thumbs without the courtesy of a cup of coffee to help fill the time.

Not a problem. Her nerves were already in shreds without adding a surfeit of caffeine to the mix. And she hadn't twiddled her thumbs either. She didn't have time to waste thumb-twiddling. Didn't have time to waste, full stop.

Instead she'd occupied herself finalising the details of an Indian-style wedding she was coordinating for a supermodel. She'd even managed to track down an elephant that was for hire by the day.

She'd also soothed the nerves of a fading pop diva who was hoping to revive her career with a spectacular launch party for her new album.

All of which had helped to keep her from dwelling upon the approaching meeting. When—if—it ever happened.

She knew she was the last person in the world Tom McFarlane wanted to see. Understood why he'd want to put off the moment for as long as was humanly possible. The feeling was mutual.

The only thing she didn't understand was why, when he'd been so obviously avoiding her for the last six months, he was putting them both through this now.

She checked the time again. Ten to three. Enough was enough. Her patience might be limitless—it was that, and her attention to detail, that made her one of the most sought-after event planners in London—but her time was not.

This meeting had been Tom McFarlane's idea. The very last thing she'd wanted was a meeting with a man she hadn't been able to get out of her mind since she'd first set eyes on him. A man who had been about to marry her old school friend, and darling of the gossip mags, Candida Harcourt.

All she wanted was his cheque so that she could settle outstanding bills and put the whole sorry nightmare behind her.

She closed down her laptop, packed it away, then crossed to the desk and the receptionist who had been studiously ignoring her ever since she'd arrived.

'I can't wait any longer,' she said. 'Please tell Mr McFarlane that I'll be in my office after ten o'clock tomorrow if he has any queries on the account.'

'Oh, but—'

'I should already be somewhere else,' she said, cutting short the woman's protest. Not strictly true—her staff were more than capable of dealing with any crisis involving the album launch party, but sometimes you had to make the point that your time—if not quite as valuable as that of a billionaire—was still a limited commodity. And maybe, on reflection, he'd be as glad as she was to avoid this confrontation and just put a cheque in the post. 'If I don't leave now—'

The receptionist didn't answer but a prickle of awareness as the woman's gaze shifted to somewhere over her right shoulder warned her that they were no longer alone.

Turning, she found her view blocked by a broad chest, wide shoulders encased in a white linen shirt. It was open at the neck and the sleeves had been rolled back to the elbow to reveal brawny forearms, strong wrists.

A silk tie had been pulled loose as if its owner had been wrestling with some intractable problem. She didn't doubt that, whatever it was, he'd won.

Despite the fact that she'd spent the last six months planning Tom McFarlane's wedding, this was only the second time she'd actually seen him face to face.

Make that forehead to chin, she thought, forced, despite her highest heels, to look up. She'd known this was going to be a difficult afternoon and had felt the need to armour herself with serious clothes.

The chin was deeply cleft.

She already knew that. She'd seen photographs long before she'd met the man. Tom McFarlane wasn't much of a socialite, but no billionaire bachelor could entirely escape the attention of the gossip magazines, especially once his marriage to the daughter of a minor aristocrat—one who'd made a career out of appearing in the glossies—had been announced.

The cleft did nothing to undermine its force; on the contrary, it emphasised it and, for the second time, her only thought was, What on earth was Candy *thinking*?

Stupid question.

From the moment she'd bounced into her office demanding that SDS Events organise her wedding to billionaire businessman Tom McFarlane, Sylvie had known *exactly* what Candy had been thinking.

This was the fulfilment of her 'life plan'. The one with which, years ago, she'd enlivened a school careers seminar by announcing that her 'career plan' was to marry a millionaire. One with a house in Belgravia, a country estate and a title. The title was negotiable; one should apparently be *flexible*—the size of the bank account was not.

Why waste her time sweating over exams when she had no intention of going to university? Students saddled with overdrafts and loans held no interest for her. All her effort was going to be put into perfecting her natural assets—at which point she'd performed a pouty, cheesecake pose—and making the perfect marriage.

Everyone had laughed—that was the thing about Candy, she always made you laugh—but no one had actually doubted that she meant it, or that she was capable of achieving her goal.

She'd already looked like coming close a couple of times. Maybe, rising thirty, she'd realised that time was running out and she'd jettisoned everything but the core plan although, inflation being what it was, she'd upgraded her ambition to billionaire.

A better question might have been, What on earth had Tom McFarlane been thinking?

An even dumber question.

It was a truth universally acknowledged that a smile from Candy Harcourt's sexy mouth was enough to short-circuit the brain of any man who could muster more than one red blood cell. She might have bypassed her exams but she hadn't stinted on the midnight oil when it came to enhancing her career assets which were, it had to be admitted, considerable.

Gorgeous, funny—who could possibly resist her? Why would any man try?

And while Tom McFarlane might give the impression that he'd been rough-hewn from rock—and eyes that were, at that moment, glittering like granite certainly added to the impression of unyielding force—she had absolutely no doubt that he was a male with red blood cells to spare.

Something her own red blood cells had instantly responded to with the shocking eagerness of a puppy offered something unspeakable to roll in.

As their eyes had met over Candy's artfully tumbled blonde curls, the connection had short-circuited all those troublesome hormones which had been in cold storage for a decade and they'd instantly defrosted.

She was not a puppy, however, but a successful businesswoman and she'd made a determined effort to ignore the internal heatwave and stick to the matter in hand. Fortunately, the minute he'd signed her contract, Tom McFarlane—who obviously had much more important things to do—had made his excuses and left.

Just thinking about those ten long minutes left the silk of the camisole she was wearing beneath her linen jacket sticking to her skin. But she'd got through it then and she could do it again.

It was part of the job. As an event planner she was used to handling awkward situations—and this certainly came under the heading of 'awkward'. She just needed to concentrate on business, even if, feeling a little like the space between the rock and the hard place, it took all her composure to stiffen her knees, stand her ground, keep the expression neutral.

'If you don't leave now?' he prompted.

'I'll be in trouble…' Wrong. She was already in trouble, but with the hardwood reception desk at her back and the rock blocking her exit she was stuck with it. Reminding herself that drooling was a very bad look, she summoned up a professional smile and extended a hand. 'Good afternoon, Mr McFarlane. I was just explaining to your receptionist—'

'I heard.' He ignored the hand. 'Call whoever's expecting you and tell him he'll have to wait. You're mine until I say otherwise.'

What? That was outrageous but the glitter in those eyes warned her that provocation had been his intent. That he was waiting for the explosion. That he would welcome it.

Not in this life, she thought, managing a fairly creditable, 'She. Delores Castello,' she added, naming the pop diva. 'So you'll see why your request is quite impossible.' She wanted this over and done with, not dragged out, but when a man started tossing orders around as if he owned the world, it was a woman's duty to stand her ground and prove to him that he did not.

Even if the knees had other ideas.

'I do have a window in my diary,' she began, flipping open the side pocket of her bag.

If she'd hoped to impress him with her client list the strategy signally failed. Before she could locate her diary he said, 'What's impossible, Miss Smith, is the chance of you getting another chance to talk me into settling your outrageous account.'

Sylvie grabbed her bottom lip with her teeth before she said something she'd regret.

The man was angry. She understood that. But her account was not outrageous. On the contrary, she'd worked really hard to negotiate the best possible cancellation deals, pushing people to the limit. She hadn't had to do that but she had felt just the smallest bit *responsible* for what had happened.

She would have told him so if her lip hadn't been clamped between her teeth.

'Your call, Miss Smith,' he prompted, apparently convinced that he'd proved his point. 'But if you walk away now I promise you you're going to have to sue me all the way to the House of Lords to get your money.'

He had to be kidding.

Or, then again, maybe not.

Glacial, his voice went with the raw cheekbones, jutting nose, a mouth compressed into a straight line. It did nothing to cool her. Like a snow-capped volcano she knew that, deep beneath the surface, molten lava bubbled dangerously. That if she wasn't careful the heat would be terminal.

Tom McFarlane was made from the same stuff that centuries ago had driven men across uncharted oceans in search of glory and fortune. He was their modern equivalent—a twenty-first-century legend who'd worked in the markets as a boy, had been trading wholesale by the time he'd been in his teens, making six-figure deals by the time he'd left school. His first million by the time he'd been twenty. The expression 'self-made man' could have been invented just for him.

He was the genuine article, no doubt, but, much as she admired that kind of drive and tenacity, his humble beginnings had made him a very odd choice of mate for Candy.

He might be a billionaire but he had none of the trappings of old money. None of the grace. He wasn't a man to sit back and idle his time away playing the squire.

There was no country estate or smart London town house. Just a vast loft apartment which, according to an exasperated Candy, was on the wrong side of the river.

Apparently, when she'd pointed that out to him, he'd laughed, ridiculing those who paid a fortune for a classy address to look across the river at him.

She'd been forced to hide a smile herself when Candy had told her that. Had thought, privately, that there had to be billionaires out there who would be less abrasive, easier to handle.

But maybe not quite so much of a challenge.

The chase might have been chillingly calculated but Sylvie was pretty sure that when the quarry had been run to earth and the prize claimed, the result would have been hot as Hades.

Maybe Candy was, when it came right down to it, as human as the next woman and had fallen not for the money, but for the testosterone.

The fact that Tom McFarlane had exactly the same effect on her, Sylvie thought as, not waiting for her answer, he turned and walked across reception to the wide-open doors of his office—leaving her to follow or not, as she chose—did not make her feel one whit better.

On the contrary.

But if Candy had thought she'd got him where she wanted him, she'd been fooling herself.

She might have momentarily brought him to heel with her silicone-enhanced assets but he wasn't the man to dance on her lead for long.

Unlike his bride, however, Sylvie wasn't in any position to cut and run when the going got tough. This wasn't 'her' money. Her account was mostly made up of invoices from dozens of small companies—single traders who'd done their job. People who were relying on her. And, sending a stern message to her brain to stay on message, she went through the motions of calling her very confused assistant and explaining that she would be late.

The call took no more than thirty seconds but, by the time she'd caught up with him, Tom McFarlane was already seated at his desk, a lick of thick, dark brown hair sliding over the lean, work-tempered fingers on which he'd propped his forehead as he concentrated on the folder in front of him.

An exact copy of the one that must have arrived in the same post as his bride's Dear John letter. The one he'd returned with the suggestion that she forward it to the new man in his ex-bride-to-be's life.

Except he hadn't been that polite.

She'd understood his reaction. Felt a certain amount of sympathy for the man.

She might honestly believe that he'd had a lucky escape, but obviously he didn't feel that way and he had every right to be hurt and angry. Being dumped just days before your wedding was humiliating, no matter who you were. Something she knew from first-hand experience.

She and Tom McFarlane had that in common, if nothing else, which was why she understood—no one better—that an expression of sympathy, an 'I know what you're going through' response, would not be welcome.

If she knew anything, it was that no one could have the slightest idea what he was feeling.

Instead, she'd tucked the account and the thick wad of copy invoices into a new folder—one of the SDS Events folders rather than another of the silver, wedding-bells adorned kind she used for weddings—and had returned it with a polite note reminding him that it was his signature on the contract and that the terms were payment within twenty-eight days.

She hadn't bothered to remind him that five of those days had already elapsed, or add, After which time I'll place the account in the hands of my solicitor...

She'd been confident that he'd get the subtext. Just as she'd been sure that he would understand, on reflection, that coordinating a wedding—even when you were doing it for an old school friend—was, like any other commercial enterprise, just business.

She'd hoped for a cheque by return. What she'd got was a call from the man himself, demanding she present herself at his office at two o'clock the next day.

She hadn't had a chance to tell him that her afternoon was already spoken for since, having issued his command, he'd hung up. Instead, she'd taken a deep breath and rescheduled her appointments. And been kept waiting the best part of an hour for her pains.

When she didn't immediately sit down, Tom McFarlane

glanced up and she felt a jolt—like the fizz of electricity from a faulty switch—as something dangerous sparked the silver specks buried in the granite-grey of his eyes. The same jolt that had passed between them on their first meeting. Hot slivers of lightning that heated her to the bone, bringing a flush to her cheeks, a tingle to parts of her anatomy that no other glance had reached since…no, forget since. She'd never felt that kind of response to any man. Not even Jeremy.

What on earth was the matter with her?

She'd never done anything at first sight. Certainly not love. She'd known Jeremy from her cradle. Actually, that might not have been the best example…

Whatever.

She certainly didn't intend to change the habits of a lifetime with *lust*. Mixing business with pleasure was always a mistake.

But it meant that she understand *exactly* what Candida had been thinking. Why she hadn't settled for some softer billionaire. Some malleable sugar daddy who would buy her the country estate and anything else she wanted…

'I'd advise you to sit down, Miss Smith,' he said. 'This is going to take some time.'

Usually, she and her clients were on first name terms from the word go but they had both clung firmly to formality at that first meeting and she didn't think this was the moment to respond with, *Sylvie, please…*

And since her knees, in their weakened state, had buckled in instant obedience to his command, she was too busy making sure her backside connected securely with the chair to cope with something as complicated as speech at the same time.

He watched as she wriggled to locate the safety of the centre of the chair. Continued to watch her for what seemed like endless moments.

The heat intensified and, without thinking, she slipped the buttons on her jacket.

Only when she was completely still and he was certain that he had her attention—although why it had taken him so long to realise *that* she couldn't possibly imagine; he'd had her absolute attention from the moment she'd set eyes on him— did he speak.

'Have you sacked him?' he demanded. 'The Honourable Quentin Turner Lyall.'

She swallowed. Truth, dare... She stopped right there and went for the truth.

'As I'm sure you're aware,' she said, 'falling in love is not grounds for dismissal. I have no doubt that the Employment Tribunal would take me to the cleaners if I tried.'

'Love?' he repeated, as if it were a dirty word.

'What else?' she asked. What else would have made Candy run for the hills when she had the prize within days of her grasp?

She had Tom McFarlane, so presumably she had the lust thing covered...

But, having dismissed her question with an impatient gesture, he said, 'What about duty of care to your client, Miss Smith? In your letter you did make the point that I am your client.' He regarded her stonily. 'And I imagine Mr Lyall did go absent without leave?'

Oh, Lord! 'Actually, he... No. He asked me for some time off...'

He sat back, apparently speechless.

'Are you telling me you actually gave him leave to elope with a woman whose wedding you were arranging?' he said, after what felt like the longest pause in history.

This was probably not a good time to give him the 'dying grandmother' excuse that she'd fallen for.

When Candy had borrowed Quentin for bag-carrying duties on one of her many shopping expeditions it had never crossed Sylvie's mind that she'd risk her big day with the billionaire for a fling with a twenty-five-year-old events assistant. Even one who'd eventually make her a countess. He came from a long-lived family and the chances of him succeeding to his grandfather's earldom before he was fifty—more likely sixty—were remote.

And, while she'd been absolutely furious with both of them, she did have a certain sympathy for Quentin; if a man like Tom McFarlane had succumbed to Candy's 'assets', what hope was there for an innocent like him?

But, despite what she'd told Tom McFarlane, when Candy had finished with Quentin and he did eventually return, she was going to have explain that, under the circumstances, he couldn't possibly continue working for her. Bad enough that it would feel like kicking a puppy, but Quentin was a real asset and losing him was going to hurt. He had a real gift for calming neurotic women. He was also thoroughly decent. It would never occur to him to go to a tribunal for unfair dismissal.

Maybe it was calming Candy's pre-wedding nerves—she had gone into shopping overdrive in those last few weeks—that broad sympathetic shoulder of his, that had got him into so much trouble in the first place.

Tom McFarlane, however, having fired off this last salvo, had returned to the folder in front of him and was flicking through the invoices, stopping to glance at one occasionally, his face utterly devoid of expression.

Sylvie didn't say a word. She just waited, holding her breath. Watching his long fingers as they turned the pages. She could no longer see his eyes. Just the edge of his jaw. The shadowy cleft of his chin. A corner of that hard mouth…

The only sound in the office was the slow turning of paper

as Tom McFarlane confronted the ruin of his plans—marriage to a woman whose family tree could be traced back to William the Conqueror.

That, and the ragged breathing of the woman opposite him.

She was nervous. And so she should be.

He had never been so angry.

His marriage to the aristocratic Candida Harcourt would have been the culmination of all his ambitions. With her as his wife, he would have finally shaken off the last remnants of the world from which he'd dragged himself.

Would have attained everything that the angry youth he'd once been had sworn would one day be his.

The good clothes, expensive cars, beautiful women had come swiftly, but this had been something else.

He hadn't been foolish enough to believe that Candy had fallen in love with him—love caused nothing but heartache and pain, as he knew to his cost—but it had seemed like the perfect match. She'd had everything except money; he had more than enough of that to indulge her wildest dreams.

It had been while he was away securing the biggest of those—guilt, perhaps for the fact that he'd been unable to get her wedding planner out of his head—that she'd taken to her heels with the chinless wonder who was reduced to working as an events assistant to keep a roof over his head. How ironic was that?

But then he was an *aristocratic* chinless wonder.

The coronet always cancelled out the billions.

When it came down to it, class won. Sylvie Smith had, after all, been chosen to coordinate the wedding for no better reason than that she'd been to school with Candy.

That exclusive old boy network worked just as well for women, it seemed.

Sylvie Smith. He'd spent six months trying not to think

about her. An hour trying to make himself send her away without seeing her.

As he appeared to concentrate on the papers in front of him, she slipped the buttons on her jacket to reveal something skimpy in dark brown silk barely skimming breasts that needed no silicone to enhance them, nervously pushed back a loose strand of dark blonde hair that was, he had no doubt, the colour she'd been born with.

She crossed her legs in order to prop up the folder she had on her knee and for a moment he found himself distracted by a classy ankle, a long slender foot encased in a dark brown suede peep-toe shoe that was decorated with a saucy bow.

And, without warning, she wasn't the only one feeling the heat.

He should write a cheque now. Get her out of his office. Instead, he dropped his eyes to the invoice in front of him and snapped, 'What in the name of blazes is a confetti cannon?'

'A c-confetti c-cannon?'

Sylvie's mind spun like a disengaged gear. Going nowhere. She'd thought this afternoon couldn't get any worse; she'd been wrong. Time to get a grip, she warned herself. Take it one thing at a time. And remember to breathe.

Maybe lighten things up a little. 'Actually, it does what it says on the tin,' she said.

His eyebrows rose the merest fraction. 'Which is?'

Or maybe not.

'It fires a cannonade of c-confetti,' she stuttered. Dammit, she hadn't stuttered in years and she wasn't about to start again now just because Tom McFarlane was having a bad day. Slow, slow… 'In all shapes and sizes,' she finished carefully.

He said nothing.

'With a c-coloured flame projector,' she added, unnerved by the silence. 'It's really quite…' she faltered '…spectacular.'

He was regarding her as if she were mad. Actually, she thought with a tiny shiver, he might just be right. What sane person spent her time scouring the Internet looking for an elephant to hire by the day?

Whose career highs involved delivering the perfect party for a pop star?

Easy. The kind of person who'd been doing it practically from her cradle. Whose mother had done it before her—although she'd done it out of love for family members or a sense of duty when it was for community events, rather than for money. The kind of person who, like Candy, hadn't planned for a day job but who'd fallen into it by chance and had been grateful to find something she could do without thinking, or the need for any specialist training.

'And a "field of light"?' he prompted, having apparently got the bit between his teeth.

'Thousands of strands of fibre optic lights that ripple in the breeze,' she answered, deciding this time to take the safe option and go for the straight answer. Then, since he seemed to require more, 'Changing colour as they move.'

She rippled her fingers to give him the effect.

He stared at them for a moment, then, snapping his gaze back to her face, said, 'What happens if there isn't a breeze?'

Did it matter? It wasn't going to happen...

Just answer the question, Sylvie, she told herself. 'The c-contractor uses fans.'

'You are joking.'

Describing the effect to someone who was anticipating a thrilling spectacle on her wedding day was a world away from explaining it to a man who thought the whole thing was some ghastly joke.

'Didn't you discuss any of this with Candy?' she asked.

His broad forehead creased in a frown. Another stupid question, obviously. You didn't become a billionaire by wasting time on trivialities like confetti cannons.

Tom McFarlane had signed the equivalent of a blank cheque and left his bride-to-be to organise the wedding of her dreams while he'd concentrated on making the money to pay for it.

No doubt, from Candy's point of view, it had been the perfect division of labour. She'd certainly thrown herself into her role with enthusiasm and there wasn't a single 'effect' that had gone unexplored. It was only the constraints of time and imagination—if she'd thought of an elephant, she'd have insisted on having one, insisted on having the whole damn circus—that had limited her self-indulgence. As it was, there had been more than enough to turn her dream into what was now proving to be Tom McFarlane's—and her—nightmare.

A six-figure nightmare, much of it provided by the small specialist companies Sylvie regularly did business with—people who trusted her to settle promptly. Which was why she was going to sit here until Tom McFarlane had worked through his anger and written her a cheque. Even if it took all night.

Having briefly recovered her equilibrium, she felt herself begin to heat up again, from the inside, as he continued to look at her and she began to think that, actually, all night wouldn't be a problem...

She ducked her head, as if to check the invoice, tucking a non-existent strand of hair behind her ear with a hand that was shaking slightly.

Tidying away what was a totally inappropriate thought.

Quentin wasn't the only one in danger of losing his head.

The office was oddly silent. His phone did not ring. No one put their head around the door with some query.

The only sound for what seemed like minutes—but was

probably only seconds—was the pounding beat of her pulse in her ears.

Then she heard the rustle of paper as Tom McFarlane returned to the stack of invoices in front of him and started going through them, one by one.

The choir.

'They didn't sing,' he objected. 'They didn't even have to turn up.'

'They're booked for months in advance,' she explained. 'I had to call in several favours to get them for Candy but the cancellation came too late to offload them to another booking...'

Her voice trailed off. He knew how it was, for heaven's sake; she shouldn't have to explain!

As if he could read her mind, he placed a tick against the list to approve payment without another word.

The bell-ringers.

For a moment she thought he was going to repeat his objection and held her breath. He glanced up, as if waiting for her to breathe out. Finally, when she was beginning to feel light-headed for lack of oxygen, he placed another tick.

As they moved steadily through the list, she began to relax. She hadn't doubted that he was going to settle; he wouldn't waste this amount of time unless he was going to pay.

The 1936 Rolls-Royce to carry Candy to the church. Tick.

It was just that he was angry and, since his runaway bride wasn't around to take the flak in person, she was being put through the wringer in her place.

If that was what it took, she thought, absent-mindedly fanning herself with one of her invoices, let him wring away. She could take it. Probably.

The carriage and pair to transport the newly-weds from the church to their reception. Tick.

The singing waiters...

Enough. Tom raked his fingers through his hair. He'd had enough. But, on the point of calling it quits, writing the cheque and drawing a line under the whole sorry experience, he looked up and was distracted by Sylvie Smith, her cheeks flushed a delicate pink, fanning herself with one of her outrageous invoices.

'Is it too warm in here for you, Miss Smith?' he enquired.

'No, I'm fine,' she said, quickly tucking the invoice away as she shifted the folder on her knees, tugging at her narrow skirt before re-crossing her long legs. Keeping her head down so that she wouldn't have to look at him. Waiting for him to get on with it so that she could escape.

Not yet, he thought, standing up, crossing to the water-cooler to fill a glass with iced water. Not yet...

Sylvie heard the creak of his leather chair as Tom McFarlane stood up. Then, moments later, the gurgle of water. Unable to help herself, she pushed her tongue between her dry lips, then looked up. For a moment he didn't move.

With the light behind him, she couldn't see his face, but his dark hair, perfectly groomed on that morning six months ago when he'd come to her office, never less than perfectly groomed in the photographs she'd seen of him before or since, looked as if he'd spent the last few days dragging his fingers through it.

Her fingers itched to smooth it back into place. To ease the tension from his wide shoulders and make the world right for him again. But the atmosphere in the silent office, cut off, high above London, was super-charged with suppressed emotion. Instead, she forced herself to look away, concentrate on the papers in front of her, well aware that all it would take would be a wrong word, move, look, to detonate an explosion.

'Here. Maybe this will help.'

She'd been working so hard at not looking at him that she

hadn't heard him cross the thick carpet. Now she looked up with a start to find him offering her a glass of water, presenting her with the added difficulty of taking it from his fingers without actually touching them.

A difficulty which something in his expression suggested he understood only too well. Maybe she should just ask him to do them both a favour and tip it over her…

'Thank you,' she said, reaching for it and to hell with the consequences. His were rock-steady—well, he was granite. Hers shook and she spilt a few drops on her skirt. She probably just imagined the steam as it soaked through the linen to her thighs as he folded himself down to her level and put his hand round hers to steady it.

Someone should warn him that it didn't actually help. But then she suspected he knew that too and right now she was having enough trouble simply breathing.

'I've got it,' she managed finally. He didn't appear to be convinced and she looked up, straight into his eyes, at which point the last thing she wanted was for him to let go. 'Really,' she assured him and instantly regretted it as he stood up and returned to his chair, lean and lithe as a panther.

And twice as dangerous, she thought as she gratefully took a sip of the water. Touched the glass to her heated forehead. Told herself to get a grip….

CHAPTER TWO

'SHALL we get on?' Tom McFarlane prompted as he returned to his desk.

Sylvie silently fumed.

Why on earth was he putting himself through this? Putting *her* through it?

It couldn't be about the money. The amount involved, though admittedly large, had to be peanuts to a man of his wealth.

It was almost, she thought, as if with each tick approving payment he was underlining the lesson he'd just been handed— the one about never trusting the word of someone just because they said they loved you. Presumably Candy *had* told him that she loved him. Or maybe, like Candy, he thought of marriage as a business deal, a mutually satisfying partnership arrangement. That love was just a lot of sentimental nonsense.

Maybe it wasn't his heart that was lying in shreds, but his pride. Or was it always pride that suffered most from this most public declaration that you weren't quite good enough?

'The singing waiters?' he repeated, making sure they were on the same page.

'I'm with you,' she said, putting the glass down. There was a dangerously long pause and she looked up, anticipating some sarcastic comment. But he shook his head as if he'd thought better of it and placed a tick alongside the figure.

Her sigh of relief came a little too soon.

'Doves? Are they in such demand too?' he enquired a few moments later, but politely, as if making an effort. He couldn't possibly be interested.

'I'm afraid so. And corn is not cheap,' she added, earning herself another of those long looks. She really needed to resist the snappy remarks. Especially as the gifts for the bridesmaids came next.

Candy had chosen bracelets for each of them from London's premier jeweller. No expense spared.

The nib of his pen hovered beside the item for a moment, then he said, 'Send them back.'

'What? No, wait.' He looked up. 'I can't do that!'

'You can't? Why not?'

Was he serious? Hadn't he taken the *slightest* interest in his own wedding?

'Because they're engraved with your names and the date.' This was cruel, she thought. One of his staff should be dealing with this. Pride was a killer... 'They were supposed to be a keepsake,' she added.

'Is that a fact?' Then, 'So? Where are they? These keepsakes.'

Could it get any worse? Oh, yes.

'Candy has them,' she admitted. 'She was having them gift-wrapped so that you could give them to the bridesmaids at the pre-wedding dinner.' He frowned. 'You *did* know about the pre-wedding dinner?'

'It was in my diary. As was the wedding,' he added. Caught by something in his voice, she looked up. For a moment she was trapped, held prisoner by his eyes, and it was all she could do to stop herself from reaching out to squeeze his hand. Tell him that it would get better.

As if he saw it coming, he gathered himself, putting himself mentally beyond reach.

She tried to speak and discovered that she had to clear her throat before she could continue.

'There are cufflinks for the ushers too,' she said, deciding it would be as well to get the whole jewellery thing over at once. 'And for you.'

'Were they engraved with our names too?'

'Just the date,' she replied.

'Useful in case I ever manage to forget it,' he said and, without warning, something happened to his mouth. She thought it might be a smile. Not much of one. Little more than a distortion of the lower lip, but Sylvie reached for the glass and took another sip of water.

It sizzled a little on her tongue, turning from ice-cold to lukewarm as it trickled down her throat. If he could do that with something so minimal, what on earth could he achieve when he was actually trying?

No. She didn't want to know. It didn't bear thinking about.

'I'm sure she'll return them,' she said in an effort to reassure him. Once she came back from wherever she was hiding out. She'd be eager to negotiate the sale of her story to whichever gossip magazine offered her the most to spill the beans on the break-up and the new man in her life before the story went cold.

Billionaireless, she would need the money.

'How sure?' he asked, holding the look for a full thirty seconds. 'And, even if she did, what would I do with them? Sell them on eBay?' She opened her mouth but, before she could speak, he said, 'Forget it.'

And, placing a tick against the item, he moved swiftly on.

It was only when they reached the cake that the cracks began to show in his icy self-control.

Candy, to her surprise, hadn't gone for some modern confection in white chocolate, or the witty little individual cakes that were suddenly all the fashion, but an honest-to-goodness traditional three-tier solid fruit cake, exquisitely iced by a master confectioner with the Harcourt coat of arms and Tom McFarlane's company logo in full colour on each layer.

The kind of cake where the top tier was traditionally put aside to be used as the christening cake for the first-born.

Until that point she'd almost felt as if Candy had been playing at weddings, more like a little girl let loose with the dressing-up box and her mother's make-up—or in this case a billionaire's bank account—than a woman embarking on the most important stage of her life. But that cake had suggested she'd been serious.

Maybe she'd just been trying to convince herself.

'Where is this monstrous confection?' Tom McFarlane asked.

'The cake?'

'Of course the damn cake!' he said, finally snapping, proving that he was made of more than stone. 'Did she take that with her too? Or has it already been foisted on some other unsuspecting male?'

'That's an outrageous thing to say, Mr McFarlane. The people I deal with are honest, hard-working businessmen and women.' She should have stopped then. 'Besides, no one wants a secondhand wedding cake.' Particularly one with someone else's coat of arms emblazoned on it.

'They don't? What a pity the same can't be said about brides.' For a moment she thought he was going to let it go. But not this time. 'So?' he demanded, glaring at her. 'What will happen to it?'

Desperate to get this over with, she was once more tempted to ask him if it mattered.

The words were on the tip of her tongue but then, for a split second, she caught a glimpse of the man beneath. A man who'd worked himself up from labouring in the markets to the top floor of a prestigious office building but had never forgotten how hard it had been or where he'd come from and was just plain horrified by such profligate waste and realised that, yes, to him it did matter.

'That's for you to decide,' she said.

'Then call the baker. He can deliver it to my apartment this evening.'

This was her cue to suggest that he was joking.

Had he any idea how big it was?

She restrained herself, but when she hesitated he sat back in his chair and gestured for her to get on with it.

'Do it now, Miss Smith.'

About to ask him what he'd do with ten pounds plus of the richest fruit cake—not including the almond paste and icing—she thought better of it. Maybe he liked fruit cake.

And when he got tired of it he could always feed the rest to the ducks.

It was all downhill from there with a mass of personalized stuff—all of it now just so much landfill. Menus, seating cards, table confetti in their entwined initials, candles, crackers with their names and the date on them, filled with little silver gifts for the guests—she'd managed to negotiate the return of the gifts. Every kind of personalized nonsense, each imprinted with their names and the date of the wedding that never was.

There wasn't a single thing that Candy had overlooked in her quest for the most extravagant, the most talked-about wedding of the season.

The list went on and on but the only other invoice to provoke a reaction was the one for the bon-bonnière.

'Well, here's something different,' he said, stretching for a touch of wry humour. 'A French tradition for wasting money instead of a British one.'

Seeing light at the end of the tunnel, she was prepared to risk a smile of her own but instead she caught her breath as, his guard momentarily down, she caught a glimpse of the grey hollows beneath his eyes, at his temple.

Maybe he heard because he looked up, a slight frown puckering his brow.

'What?' he demanded.

She shook her head, managed some kind of meaningless response that appeared to satisfy him, but after that she kept her head down and finally it was all done but for the last invoice. The one for her own fee, which she'd reduced by twenty per cent, even though the cancellation had caused nearly as much work as the actual day would have done.

'It's as well you don't offer a money back guarantee,' he said.

'My company's services carry a guarantee,' she assured him.

'But not one that covers parts replacement.'

Which was almost a joke but this time she didn't even think about smiling. 'I'm afraid not, Mr McFarlane. The bride is entirely your responsibility.'

'True,' he said, surprising her. 'But maybe you're missing out on a business opportunity,' he continued as, finally, he wrote the cheque. 'It would be so much simpler if one could pick and choose from a list of required qualities and place an order for the perfect wife.'

'Like a washing machine? Or a car?' she asked, wondering what, exactly, had been his specification for a wife. And whether he'd adjust it in the light of recent events.

Go for something less glamorous, more hard-wearing.

'Performance, style, finish...' She had been dangerously close to sarcasm but he appeared to take her analogy seriously. 'That sounds about right.' Then, as he tore the cheque from the book, 'But forget economy. Fast women and fast cars have that in common. They're both expensive to run. And you take a hit on the trade-in.' He didn't hand her the cheque but continued to look at it. 'Good business for you, though.'

'I'm not that cynical, Mr McFarlane,' she assured him as, refusing to sit there like a dummy while he made her wait for him to hand it over, she set about gathering her papers.

She tucked them back into the file and stowed them in her case, taking all the time in the world over it, just to prove that she was cool.

That nothing was further from her mind than a speedy exit from his office so that she could regain control over her breathing and her hormones, both of which had been doing their own thing ever since she'd been confronted at close quarters by whatever it was that Tom McFarlane had in such abundance. And she wasn't thinking about his money.

When everything was done she looked up and said, 'No one, no matter who they are, gets more than one SDS wedding.'

'Speaking personally, that's not going to be a problem.'

And he folded the cheque in two and tucked it into his shirt pocket.

No...

'Once has been more than enough.'

He stood up and hooked his jacket from the back of the chair before heading for the door.

No... Wait...

'Shall we go, Miss Smith?' he prompted, opening it, waiting for her.

'Go?' She stood up very slowly. 'Go where?'

'To pick up all this expensive but completely useless junk that I'm about to pay for.'

Oh. No. Really. That was just pointless. Besides the fact that she was now, seriously, running out of time as well as breath. Her staff didn't need her to hold their hands, but the pop diva was paying for that kind of service.

Sylvie was really annoyed with herself about that. Not the time—that was all down to Tom McFarlane. But the breath bit.

It wasn't even as if he'd *tried*. Done a single thing to account for her raised pulse rate or the pitifully twisted state of her hormones.

Apart from looking at her.

It was, apparently, enough.

'I'm qu-quite happy to dispose of it for you,' she said quickly. She could at least spare him the indignity of having to haul it to the recycling centre. Then, when that offer wasn't leapt on with grateful thanks, 'Or I can arrange to have it delivered.'

It wasn't as if he could be in a hurry for any of it.

'If that's more convenient for you,' he said. Her relief was short-lived. 'I assume you're not planning to charge me for storage?'

'Er, no…'

He nodded. 'I'm leaving the country tonight—my diary has been cleared, the honeymoon villa paid for—but I can hold on to the cheque until I get back next month and we can finish this then.'

What?

'I'll give you a call when I get back, shall I?'

Give her a call…?

Everyone had their snapping point. His had been the wedding cake. This was hers.

'You have got to be joking! I've already rearranged my afternoon for you and been kept waiting nearly an hour for my trouble. And I've got a party this evening.'

'Your social life is not my problem.'

'I don't have a social life!' she declared furiously.

'Really?' His glance was brief but all-encompassing, leaving her with the feeling that she'd been touched from head to foot in the most intimate way. And enjoying every moment of it.

Then he lifted one brow the merest fraction as if he knew...

'Really,' she snapped. Every waking moment of her life was spent making sure other people had a good time. 'This is business. And my van, unlike me, can't do two things at once.'

For some reason, that made him smile. And she'd been right about that too. Something about the way one corner of his mouth lifted, the skin crinkled around his eyes. The eyes heated...

'No problem,' he said, bringing her back to earth. 'For a reasonable fee, I'll hire your company one of mine.'

Beneath the riotous collage of balloons, streamers and showers of confetti with which Sylvie's van—the one presently engaged elsewhere—was painted, you could just about make out that its original colour was, like her mood, black.

Tom McFarlane's van was an identical model. Equally glossy and well cared for and equally black. In his case, however, the finish was unrelieved by anything more festive than his company's gold logo—TMF enclosed in a cartouche—so familiar from that wretched cake.

They'd ridden in his private lift down to the parking basement in total silence. With no choice but to go along with him, she was too angry to trust herself to attempt small talk.

Her sympathy was history. Sylvie no longer cared what he was feeling.

Smug self-satisfaction, no doubt, at putting her to the maximum possible inconvenience just because he could.

He led the way past an equally black and gleaming Aston Martin that was, no doubt, his personal transport. Fast and classy with voluptuous cream leather upholstery, it fitted his specification perfectly.

For a car or a wife.

Shame on Candy for dumping him; he *deserved* her!

They reached the van. He unlocked it, slid open the driver's door and held out the keys.

She stared at them.

She'd been tempted to insist on driving the van herself, if only to reclaim a little of the control which he'd wrested from her the moment she'd arrived at his office. If he was really serious about charging her for using it—and nothing about him so far suggested he had a sense of humour; his smile, when he'd finally let it go, had been pure wolf—it seemed eminently reasonable.

She'd had Tom McFarlane up to the eyebrows; he'd used up every particle of goodwill and she didn't want to spend one more minute with him than was absolutely necessary.

But she also wanted this over and done with as quickly as possible and had been counting on the fact that macho man wouldn't be able to stand by and watch her load and unload the thing by herself.

She might, of course, be fooling herself about that. It was quite possible he'd enjoy watching her work up a sweat as she earned every penny of her—reduced—fee. She was already regretting that twenty per cent. She'd earned every penny of it this afternoon.

Too late now. She'd just have to think of the eighty per cent she would be paid. The money for all those suppliers who'd put their heart and soul into making Candy's dream come true. And her reputation for being the kind of solid, dependable businesswoman whose word, in a business that was not short on flakes, meant something. Trust that had taken time to garner when her centuries-old name had, overnight, become a liability...

'I'd come and give you a hand but I have to take delivery of a cake.' Then, 'Do you need a hand up?'

'No, thanks,' she snapped back, snatching the keys from him

and tossing her bag on to the passenger seat. 'I've got one of these and I frequently drive it myself.'

'Not in that skirt or those heels, I'll bet.'

Oh, terrific!

That was where anger and speaking before your brain was engaged got you. But it was too late to change her mind because he didn't give her the chance to do so and back down gracefully. Instead he gave one of those I'm-sure-you-know-best shrugs— the ones that implied it was the last thing he thought—and stood back, leaving her to get on with it.

Unfortunately, getting on with it involved hoisting her narrow skirt up far enough to enable her to step up into the cab. Which was far enough for Tom McFarlane to get the full stocking tops and lace underwear experience.

The up side—there had to be an up side—was that it would be his breathing under attack for a change.

'Not that I'm complaining,' he assured her, apparently perfectly in control of his breathing.

And a good thing too, she decided. One of them ought to be in control of their bodily functions. Not that she bothered to dignify his remark with an answer, but let her skirt drop, smoothing it primly beneath her as she sat down, before placing the key in the ignition.

'What kept you?'

She'd had to buzz him so that he could let her through into the basement parking garage and by the time she'd pulled into the bay by the private lift that would take her directly to the penthouse loft apartment he was there, waiting for her.

His impatience touched a chord deep within her. Despite her very real, her *justifiable* anger with Tom McFarlane, her own impatience with every interruption, every traffic delay had been driven not by her need to be with an important client in Chelsea but by some blind, completely insane desire to get back to him. To renew the edgy, heat-filled connection.

He might make her angry but for the first time in years she felt like a woman and it was addictive...

'I can manage,' she assured him as he opened the door, offered her a helping hand. The default reaction of the modern woman. When did that happen?

It didn't matter; he took no notice. 'I've seen you manage once today. Since I've already seen your underwear, this time we'll do it my way.'

'A gentleman wouldn't have looked,' she gasped, outraged. *Outraged by the fact that he obviously thought her legs not worth a second look.*

'Is that a fact? I guess that just proves that I'm not a gentleman.' His eyes gleamed in the dim light of the underground garage. 'Didn't your old school chum tell you that it was one of the things she liked most about me? After my money. The risk. The realisation that for once in her life she wasn't in control.' He leaned close enough for her to feel his breath upon her cheek. For every cell to quiver with heightened awareness. Her skin to get goose-bumps. 'That she was playing with fire.'

Sylvie's mouth dried.

It worked for her.

'But then again,' he said, straightening, 'you're no lady, Miss Smith, or you'd have accepted my offer of assistance. So shall we try it again? Need a hand?'

'The only help I need is with the boxes,' she declared angrily. She certainly didn't need to hitch up her skirt to get down. All she had to do was swing her legs over the side and drop to the floor but, then again, Tom McFarlane was going out of his way to rile her, so why make it easy for him?

It wasn't as if she'd wanted to organise this wedding in the first place—especially not once she'd met the groom—but Candy had begged and when she wanted something, no one could deny her anything.

Except, it seemed, Tom McFarlane.

And maybe the house in Belgravia and the country estate were, after all, non-negotiable if you weren't marrying for love…

In retrospect, Sylvie thought, it was easy to see why she'd left so much of the detail to Quentin, but it really was too bad that, when all her instincts had been proved right, she was being punished by this man, not just for her bad judgement but for his too.

And her body seemed intent on joining in.

Maybe that was why, instead of jumping down, she put her hands flat against the seams of her skirt in a deliberately provocative manner, as a prelude to sliding it back up her legs.

To punish him—punish them both—right back.

Tom McFarlane couldn't believe the way he was behaving. He was already calling himself every kind of a fool. He'd cleared his desk in preparation for a month away and all he'd had to do was get on a plane. Instead, he'd demanded Sylvie Smith's presence in his office to explain her invoice. And then, as if that hadn't been sufficient misery for both of them, he'd made a complete fool himself by demanding she deliver a pile of useless junk to his apartment.

He'd already put himself through an afternoon of torment, looking at her long legs as she'd crossed and re-crossed them, her sexy high-heeled shoes highlighting the beauty of slender ankles.

They were the kind of legs that could give a man ideas—always assuming he hadn't got them the minute he'd set eyes on her. Hadn't had the best part of two hours, while she'd kept him waiting, to think about them.

But enough was enough and, before she could repeat the

move with the skirt, he snatched back control, seizing her around the waist to lift her down.

Taken by surprise, she gasped as she grabbed for his shoulders, bunching his shirt in her hands as she clung to him. She was not the only one short of breath. Close up, by the armful, Sylvie Smith's figure more than lived up to the promise glimpsed when she'd unbuttoned that sexy little jacket. All soft curves, it was the kind of figure that would look perfect in something soft and clinging. Would look even better out of it.

For a moment they were poised, locked together, just two people, holding each other, heat sizzling between them with only one thing on their minds—and it sure as hell wasn't wedding stationery.

A wisp of her streaky blonde hair brushed against his cheek and, as naturally as breathing, his hand slipped beneath the chocolate silk to cradle her ribcage, his thumb teasing the edge of a lace bra that he knew would exactly match the trim on what could only be French knickers.

There was no exclamation of outrage. Instead, as his thumb swept up over the aroused peak of her nipple, Sylvie Smith's lips parted, her breathing grew ragged and the look in her eyes was pure invitation as she seemed to melt against him, clinging to his shoulders as if they were the only thing keeping her on her feet.

It would be impossible to say whether it was the shudder that ran through her, her tongue moistening her hot, full lower lip or the tiny moan low in her throat that precipitated what happened next.

Or maybe it was none of those things. Maybe this had been in his mind from the very beginning, from the minute he'd first set eyes on her six months ago when he'd walked into her office and had instantly wanted to be anywhere else in the world.

Why he'd provoked today's meeting.

Because this raw, atavistic connection between two strangers, rather than a wedding that had lain like lead in his gut for weeks, was what today had been all about and the connection between them was as inevitable as it was explosive.

Control? Who did he think he was kidding...?

As his lips touched hers it was like oxygen to a fire that had been smouldering, unseen for months. One minute there was nothing. The next it was wildfire. Unstoppable...

Somehow they made it to the lift and he groped back for the key that closed the doors, sending it silently upward as they tore at the fastenings on each other's clothes, desperate for skin against skin. Just desperate.

A ping announced the arrival of an email from his office. Tom McFarlane bypassed the trip to Mustique, driven by a woman's tears to take the first long haul flight out with a vacant seat, and he'd hit the ground running the moment he'd touched down in the Far East. Work. Work had always been the answer.

He opened it. Read the note from his secretary and swore. Then he picked up the picture postcard of Sydney Opera House lying beside the laptop. Read the brief message—'Wish you were here'—not a question but a statement, before tearing it in two.

'I'll be fine...'

Famous last words, Sylvie thought as she regarded the pregnancy test. But then, when she'd said them, she hadn't been talking about the fact that she'd just had unprotected sex with a man with whom, despite the fact that he'd taken up residence in her brain, she'd never made it to first name terms.

She'd hoped, expected, that he'd call from Mustique, if only to make sure that there had been no consequences to their moment of madness. Maybe, even better, just to say hello. Best of all to say, I'd like to do that again...

Apparently he wouldn't. No doubt he thought that she'd have dealt with the possibility of any unforeseen consequences without a second thought. It was true; she had momentarily thought about emergency contraception while she'd been walking past a pharmacy the day after Tom McFarlane had made love to her. Then, just like some teenage kid buying his first packet of condoms, she'd come out with a new toothbrush.

Not because she was embarrassed, but because she had given it a second thought.

She was nearly thirty and a baby would not be bad news. She smiled as she lay her hand over her still perfectly flat abdomen. Far from it. It was wonderful news. Totally right. For her, anyway.

Quite what her baby's father would make of it was another matter altogether. She'd given up hoping for any kind of a call from him when she'd received a freshly drawn cheque in the post, clipped to a compliment slip with 'settlement in full' typed on it, followed by someone's indecipherable initials. Not his. Well, no, he was taking time out in the fabulous villa that Candy had chosen for their honeymoon.

He'd reinstated the twenty per cent she'd deducted and couldn't have made his point more succinctly. He'd known exactly what he was doing. Had regained control…

She returned the twenty per cent with a brief note, reminding him that she had deducted it from her bill. Stupid, no doubt, but pride had its price and it had been essential to make the point that she did not.

A secretary replied to thank her for pointing out the error, assuring her that Mr McFarlane had been informed.

She wasn't going to risk that this time. Or a formal letter from a lawyer demanding a paternity test. He had a right to know he was about to become a father, but she was going to make it plain that this was something he'd have to deal with himself and steeled herself to call his office.

She doubted that holidays came easily to him and fully expected that he would have returned early, but was informed that he was still away and did she want to leave a message?

She declined. A letter would be easier. That way she could keep it cool. She pulled a sheet of her personal notepaper from the rack, uncapped her pen.

An hour later she was still sitting there.

How did you tell a man you scarcely knew that he was about to become a father? Especially since Candy had shared her joy that ruining her figure to provide him with an heir had not been part of the deal.

How could she tell a man who apparently had no desire for children of his own that this was the most magical thing that had ever happened to her? Share just how amazing she felt, how happy she was? How life suddenly had real meaning?

She knew he'd hate that and, since she didn't want him angry, she'd keep it businesslike. Strictly to the point. Give him room to look past a moment of sizzling passion and see what they'd created together so that he could, maybe, find it in his heart to reach out to his child without any burden of liability to get in the way.

Finally, she began.

Dear Tom,

No. That wouldn't do. She blotted out the memory of crying his name out as he'd brought her body humming to life and scratched out *Tom* and, clinging instead to the memory of that twenty per cent, she wrote:

Dear Mr McFarlane—that was businesslike.

I'm writing to let you know that as a result of our recent...

She stopped again.

What? How could she put into words what had happened. His unexpected tenderness. The soaring joy that had brought the tears pouring down her face...

He hadn't understood the tears, how could he? She just kept saying, 'I'm all right...' Blissfully, brilliantly, wonderfully more than 'all right'. And she would have told him, but then Josie had rung in a panic because Delores was out of her head on an illegal substance half an hour before everyone was due to arrive and the baker had turned up with the cake and there had been no time. And all she'd said was, 'I have to go.'

She'd expected him to ring her. Kept hoping he would. But when she'd rung his office using the excuse of reminding him about the cheque—they'd somehow forgotten all about that— she'd been told he was away. He had, apparently, taken her at her word and caught his plane...

Come on, Sylvie. Get a grip. Keep it simple.

...as a result of our recent encounter, I am expecting a baby in July.

Businesslike. To the point. Cool. Except there was nothing cold about having a baby. When she'd seen the result of the pregnancy test there had been a rush of an emotion so powerful that she could hardly breathe...

Please believe me when I say that I do not hold you in any way responsible. It was my decision alone to go ahead with the pregnancy and I'm perfectly capable of supporting both myself and my son or daughter. My purpose in writing is not to make any demands on you, but obviously you have a right to know that you are about to become a father. Should you wish to be a part of his or her life, I would welcome your involvement without any expectation of commitment to me.

She crossed out *without any expectation of commitment to me*. You could be too businesslike. Too cool…

You have my assurance that I won't contact you again, or ever raise the subject in the unlikely event that our paths should cross. If I don't hear from you, I'll assume that you have no wish to be involved.
Yours
Sylvie Smith

What else could she say? That she would never forget him? That he had broken down the protective wall that had been in place ever since Jeremy had decided that he wasn't up for the 'worse' or the unexpectedly 'poorer'—at least not with her—leaving her with everything in place for a wedding except the groom.

That she would always be grateful to him for that. And for the precious gift of a baby.

A new family. The chance to begin again…

No. That would be laying an emotional burden on him. Any involvement must not be out of guilt, but because he wanted to be a father. If he didn't, well, at least that way, her child would be spared the bitter disillusionment she'd suffered at the hands of her own father.

Something dropped on to the paper, puddling the ink. Stupid. There was no reason for tears, absolutely none, and she palmed them away, took out a fresh sheet of paper and wrote out her letter minus the crossings out. Then she drove across to the other side of the river and placed her letter in Tom McFarlane's letter box so that she wasn't tempted to write again if he didn't reply, just in case it had been lost in the post. Could be sure that no one else would open it, read it…

Then, since there was nothing else to be done, she went home and started making plans for the changes that were about to happen in her life.

Tom managed to get the last seat on the flight back to London. Four months. He hadn't stopped travelling for four months. Like a man on the run, he'd been in flight from the memory, burned into his brain, of Sylvie Smith, silent tears pouring down her face.

For a moment, in that still, totally calm space, when he'd spilled his seed into her, he'd felt as if the entire world had suddenly been made over for him, that he was the hunter who'd come home with the biggest prize in the world.

Then he'd seen her tears and realised just what he'd done. That while she kept saying 'I'll be fine...' she was anything but. 'I have to go...' when all he wanted was to keep her close.

And work, he'd discovered, was not the answer, which was why he was going back to face her. To beg her to forgive him, beg her for more...

About to go through passport control, he paused at a book shop—with a twelve hour flight ahead of him, he'd need something to read—and found himself confronted by the face that haunted his dreams, both waking and sleeping. Not crying now, but smiling serenely out at him from the latest copy of *Celebrity*.

Saw the story flash—*'Sylvie's Happy Event!'*

He didn't need an interpreter to decipher 'happy event' and for a moment he felt a surge of something so powerful that he felt like a man with the world at his feet. She was wearing something soft and flowing and there was nothing to show that she was pregnant. Only the special glow of a woman who had just told the world that she was having a baby and was totally thrilled about it.

His baby...

He picked up the magazine. Opened it and came crashing back to earth as he saw that the cover photograph had been cropped. Inside, the same photograph showed that she was posed with a tall, fair-haired man and the caption read:

'Our favourite events organiser Sylvie Smith, who has just announced that she's expecting a baby later this summer, is pictured here with her childhood sweetheart, the recently divorced Earl of Melchester. Their marriage plans were put on hold when Sylvie's grandfather died and, as Jeremy put it, "life got in the way". It's wonderful to see them looking so happy to be together again and we confidently predict wedding bells very shortly.'

He read it twice, just to be sure, then he tossed the magazine in the nearest bin and went back to the desk to change his ticket.

'Where do you want to go, Mr McFarlane?'

'It doesn't matter.'

CHAPTER THREE

JOSIE FOWLER flung herself full length into the sofa that had, at considerable expense, been provided for the comfort of their clients. With her feet dangling over the arm and her arm shielding her eyes, she groaned.

'Late night?' Sylvie asked.

'Late and then some. I have to tell you that you are, without doubt, a world class fantasy wedding planner.'

'*Event* planner,' Sylvie said, pulling a face. She was so *off* weddings. 'We are SDS *Events,* Jo. Fantasy or otherwise, weddings are no different from any other job.' *Cue, hollow laughter...* 'I take it from your reaction that everything went according to plan yesterday?'

In other words, please tell me that the bride didn't have second thoughts...

'Pleease!' Josie, in full drama queen mode—despite her eighteen-hole Doc Martens and punk hair-do, both of them purple—clutched both hands to her heart. 'What SDS *event* would dare to deviate from "the plan"?'

'According to my grandfather,' she said in an effort not to think about the Harcourt/McFarlane debacle—she'd promised herself she wouldn't think about that nightmare, or the Tom

McFarlane effect, more than three times a day and she was already over budget— 'the first casualty of battle is always "the plan".'

She laid her hand over the child growing beneath her heart—living proof of that little homily.

'That would be your Colonel-in-Chief of the regiment grandfather, right?'

'It certainly wasn't my party-throwing playboy grandfather. His idea of "a plan" was to order enough champagne to float a battleship and leave everything else for someone else to worry about.' Including the final bill. And the sweetest man on earth. 'As you'll learn, when emotions are involved anything can happen,' she continued as, letter in hand, she carefully placed a tick on one of the plans that decorated every available inch of wall space.

This one was for a silver wedding celebration. She felt safe with a silver wedding. Then, hand on her back, she straightened carefully.

'Are you okay?' Josie asked. Then, 'Sit down, I can do that.'

'It's done,' she said, waving away her concern. 'Don't fuss.' Then, 'Tell me about the wedding.'

'I *have* told you. It was fabulous.' Then, 'You're not *still* smarting over the bride who got away, are you?'

'No!' Her legendary calm slipped a notch and not just because of the wedding that never was. 'No,' she repeated, getting a grip. 'The one thing I can't be held responsible for is the bride getting cold feet. Even if she chose to warm them on one of my staff.'

'You are not responsible! For heaven's sake, it was more than six months ago. Even the groom will have got over it by now.'

'I couldn't say.' All she knew was that he hadn't responded to her letter. 'Can we please just concentrate on yesterday's wedding?' she said, jerking her mind away from that long afternoon she'd spent with Tom McFarlane. The solidity of his shoulders beneath her hands. The way his hands had felt against her skin. That raw, overwhelming need as he'd looked down at her, touched her…

The only thing on his mind had been instant gratification with the first woman to cross his path. It had been nothing more than a reaction to being dumped, she knew. A wholly masculine need to have his ego restored. With maybe a little tit-for-tat payback thrown in for good measure. Just in case she needed to feel any worse about herself.

'Look, if you don't trust me, Sylvie, maybe you should find someone—'

Jerked back from the danger of slipping into self-pity, she said, 'Oh, Josie… Of course I trust you! I wouldn't leave such a major event to anyone in whom I didn't have the utmost faith. Besides, I knew you'd rather be coordinating a wedding in the Cotswolds than babysitting a women's rights conference in London. Sensible woman that you are.' Then, with determined brightness, 'So, not a single hiccup, then? There'll be no comebacks when I send the bride's papa the final account?'

'Anyone who didn't know you better, Sylvie, would think you only cared about the money.'

'I promise you, I don't do this for fun,' she replied.

'Oh, right. As if you didn't work yourself to a standstill to ensure that every little detail was perfect so that the bride has a day she'll never forget.'

'That's just good business, Jo. I apply exactly the same standards to every event.'

'You're a perfectionist, no doubt about it. But you do always seem to go the extra mile for weddings.'

'I just worry more. It's not quite like a conference or some company event, is it? For the two people involved it's a once in a lifetime occasion. If it goes wrong they aren't going to say, "Oh, well, never mind. We'll have the fireworks next time." At least I hope not!'

'I knew it! You're just like the rest of us. Beneath that ice-cool exterior beats a heart of pure mush.'

'Rubbish. Mush, let me tell you, doesn't pay the bills,' she said crisply. It certainly hadn't been 'mush' she'd felt…

No. She was overdrawn on thinking about Tom McFarlane. Overdrawn and heading for bankruptcy.

'So?' she continued a touch desperately. 'Did we do good?'

'We did great,' Josie said, lowering her feet to the floor and joining her at the wall plan. 'It was perfection from the moment the bride arrived in her fairy tale coach until the last firework faded in the midnight sky.' She sighed. 'You were absolutely right, by the way, to resist the bride's plea for bows on the tails of the horses.'

'You didn't say that when she had hysterics in the office,' Sylvie reminded her. 'As I recall, your exact words were, "Give the silly cow what she wants…"'

'I just don't have your class, Sylvie.'

'It's easy to get carried away.' To lose sight of what a wedding actually meant in the pressure to indulge in every over-the-top frill. 'When in doubt just think of it as a feathers-and-curls situation. If you have feathers in your hat, who's going to notice the curls?'

'You see? I would go for both every time. I guess that's the difference between Benenden and a sink estate comprehensive school…'

'Not necessarily.'

It certainly hadn't stopped Candy Harcourt from going for the feathers, the curls and every other frippery known to woman-kind. But then she'd had a big empty gap to fill, one that had taken all the frippery she could get her hands on, and it still hadn't been enough.

When it had been the real thing, Candy had only needed the man she loved and a couple of witnesses. Of course that might have been because his family would have done everything they could to stop it if they'd had advance warning.

They'd sent her a photograph that someone had taken of them after the ceremony, along with a note from Candy apologising for leaving her to deal with the fallout and one from Quentin tendering his resignation.

It had been plain that he was hoping that she'd beg him to come back but she'd managed to resist the temptation and, to her relief, he'd already been snapped up by one of her competitors.

'Besides,' she said, doing her utmost to banish Candy and Quentin and their somewhat unexpected happy ever after from her memory, 'you have the street smarts, Jo. One look from you and everyone thinks twice about giving us the run-around.'

Tom McFarlane wouldn't have given Josie a moment's trouble, she thought.

'And no one is better at keeping everything running behind the scenes on the big day,' she continued. 'Taking you on was the best day's work I ever did.'

Which was, despite the many warnings she'd received to the contrary, absolutely true.

Josie looked at her, swallowed and muttered, 'Thanks.' And, in an attempt to cover her confusion, bent to see what she'd been doing. 'Hey, you've found another piper!'

'Let's hope this one doesn't take a notion to do a spot of mountaineering and break something vital before the big day.' She stood back. 'Now all I need is for the happy couple to finalise the menu and, since the Rolling Stones are a little out of the budget for this affair, an RS tribute band so that the guests can revisit their ill-spent youth in a night of rock and roll.' Then, 'Did those new caterers do the business?'

'For goodness' sake, Sylvie! I told you it was perfect!'

'There's no such thing as perfect,' she said, but with a smile. 'Just find me some little thing and I'll stop worrying.'

'Idiot.' Then, 'Okay, the horses pooped in front of the church, hence my change of heart about the ribbons. Will that do?'

'That is perfect,' she said. Sylvie knew it was stupid, but there was always *something;* it was like waiting for the other shoe to drop. 'You made sure it was cleaned up?'

Josie grinned. 'I got lucky. The church warden was hoping for a donation for his roses and he was all ready with a bucket and shovel.'

'You both got lucky, then.'

'Too right. And, to put your mind totally at rest, the flowers were out of this world,' Josie said, holding up her hand and ticking the items off one by one. 'The choir were angelic. The food was amazing, those caterers are definitely a find. The string quartet, as far as I could tell—that is *soooo* not my kind of music—played in tune. Even the sun shone.' Having run out of fingers, she shrugged. 'What else is there?'

'You want a list?' Sylvie held up her own hand, ready to tick off the five legendary worst ever wedding disasters that every planner dreaded. Apart from the bride changing her mind days before the wedding.

Or the wedding planner losing it with the forsaken groom, she thought, forgetting the list as she placed her hand on the growing bulk of the baby she was carrying.

That was an item of gossip that would have made the *story* into a *STORY* and she came out in a cold sweat just thinking about what a meal *Celebrity* would make of it if they ever found out whose baby she was carrying.

Not that they hadn't tried. Jeremy had been less than amused to be lined up as a possibility and had called her demanding she deny the rumours.

It was cruel not to, and maybe if he hadn't behaved like such a pompous ass she'd have done it. Not that he'd actually changed, she realised. She was the one who'd done that, but only after wasting ten years…

'The list?' Josie prompted, looking at her a little oddly. She might not have believed the official version, that the single mother pregnancy had been planned using a 'donor'. She hadn't elaborated and Josie hadn't pushed it. And, rising thirty with no partner and a ticking biological clock, even her closest friends had let it go without more than a slightly raised eyebrow.

'Oh, right, the list…'

Before she could begin, the phone rang.

She reached back, glanced at the caller ID and, picking it up, said, 'Hi, Laura. How are you?'

'Pretty good, thanks, Sylvie, but, as always, I'm in need of a favour.'

'Let me guess. You want an "SDS Event" for the silent auction at this year's Pink Ribbon Club lunch?'

'No…' Then, 'Well, yes, obviously, if you're offering. We raised a bundle on that last year.'

'Then it's yours.'

'That's very generous. Thank you. I'll just write that in…' She paused, presumably to make a note of it.

'So?' Sylvie prompted. 'What's the favour?'

'Oh, yes! It is a big one, although on this occasion I'm in a position to offer you something in return for your efforts.'

'Oh?' Laura sounded really excited but not missing the fact that she would be making an 'effort', Sylvie sat down and, pulling her notebook towards her, said, 'Okay, let's hear it.'

'You're not going to believe this, but I've just had a phone call from *Celebrity* magazine. They want to do a feature on the charity and they're using the Spring Wedding Fayre we're holding as a backdrop. They've even offered us a generous donation for our co-operation.'

'They have?' No wonder she was excited. 'They usually only pay for exclusive coverage,' she warned. 'That won't win you any friends with the local press. Willow Armstrong has been very supportive.'

'I know, but this won't affect local coverage. *Celebrity* are prepared to be generous because we're pulling out all the stops for the Club's tenth anniversary. That's why I approached them in the first place. Your mother was always one of their favourites. All those wonderful parties…'

'Yes…'

Throwing parties was something of a family tradition. Experience she'd put to profitable use when everything had gone belly-up.

'So what do you want from me?'

'Well, your mother founded the charity…'

'Yes.'

'And you are our Honorary President.'

Laura's slow build-up was beginning to make her uneasy. 'And?'

'Well, it all just fits together so perfectly, don't you see? Your mother's parties. And now you're the wedding planner at the top of every bride's wish list.'

'Event planner, Laura. Weddings are just one part of our business.'

'I know, I know, but honestly they've come up with the most brilliant idea. One that I know you're going to love.'

'Really?'

When it came to some 'brilliant idea' concocted by the features editor of a gossip magazine, 'love' was unlikely to be her first reaction but Sylvie reserved judgement until she heard what it was.

'Really. They're going to feature a fantasy wedding, using our exhibitors. That's going to be their exclusive.'

'Oh, I see...' Actually that *was* a good idea... 'Well, well done, you.' Then, 'You want me to give you some ideas for the fantasy thing, is that it? I'll be happy to—'

'No, Sylvie, I want a little bit more than that.' Laura could scarcely contain herself. 'A lot more than that, actually. What they want is for you to use the Fayre's exhibitors to create your *own* fantasy wedding!'

'Mine? But I'm not getting married.'

Laura gave a little tut as if she were being particularly dim. 'No, no, no... Don't you see? You've organised so many fabulous weddings for other people that everyone will be agog to know what you'd choose for yourself.'

Oh, confetti!

The *Celebrity* features editor must have spotted her name on the letterhead and thought all her birthdays had come at once.

'Bride, groom, two witnesses and the local register office?' she offered hopefully.

Laura laughed, confident she was being teased. 'I think *Celebrity* will want something a little more fairy tale than that!'

Oh, yes. *Celebrity* would want everything, up to and including her heart on her sleeve, which they were apparently ready to extract with a blunt knife. They couldn't have been more obvious.

'Just think what fun it will be,' Laura continued. 'Gorgeous clothes, fabulous food, all those special touches you're so famous for. We've got some truly wonderful local exhibitors and you can totally let yourself go—'

'Laura,' she said, cutting in before this went any further. 'I'm sorry, really, but I can't do that.'

There was a moment of stunned silence. Then Laura, stiff now, said, 'I realise that there won't be any big London names, Sylvie, but there's no need to be quite that dismissive.'

Oh, good grief, she'd misunderstood. It wasn't the exhibitors she was turning down. It was the whole nightmare scenario.

'No...' she began, but it was too late.

'Your mother, if she were still with us—'

Sylvie lowered her head into her hand, knowing what was coming and helpless to stop it.

'Lady Annika would be very disappointed to think that you'd let us down.'

No! No! No! Sylvie stuffed her fist into her mouth to stop the scream leaking out.

Josie, staring at her, mouthed the word, 'Trouble?'

She just shook her head, unable to answer. This wasn't trouble; this was the old girl network in full working order and, if nothing else would do it, the 'old girls' would play the guilt card without a second's thought.

'You may be an important businesswoman these days, but people still remember your family. Remember you. You're a local girl and you have a duty to fly the flag for your town.' As if aware that her attention was drifting, Laura pitched her voice at a level capable of cutting cold steel. 'Forget your mother's charity...' *oh, low blow!* '...these people should be able to count on your support.'

The guilt card swiftly followed by the demands of *noblesse oblige*. Because, even when the *noblesse* had gone well and truly down the pan, the *oblige* just refused to quit.

Guilt and duty. The double whammy.

'This feature wouldn't just be fabulous PR for you, it would give some small designers a real chance to get noticed—'

Okay! Enough!

There was no need to lay it on with a trowel. Once the 'your mother would be disappointed' gambit had been played, Sylvie knew it was all over bar the shouting and, pulling herself together, she attempted to stem the flow.

'Laura...'

'Of course I don't suppose *you* need PR these days—'

'*Laura!*'

'And, as for the fee *Celebrity* are offering the charity, well—'

'Laura, don't you ever read *Celebrity?*'

'Well, no. It's not my kind of thing. You won't tell them, will you?'

'No, but that's not the point. If you ever read the thing, you'd know that the reason I can't possibly do this is because I'm six months pregnant.'

'Pregnant?' Then, 'I didn't realise. When did you get married?'

Sylvie added 'hurt' to the range of expressions in Laura's voice.

'I didn't, Laura. I'm not.'

'Oh, *well,* that's even better. You can really—'

'No,' she said quickly, anticipating what was coming next. 'I can't. I'm not getting married.' Could this get any worse? 'I just wanted a baby.'

Or better.

Because it was true.

Once she'd got over the shock, she'd realised that she did want this little girl. Desperately.

Laura, momentarily stumped, quickly recovered. 'Oh, well, it doesn't actually matter, does it? You don't have to appear in the feature. No one would expect you to actually model something you'd chosen for yourself. Not before the wedding. Bad luck and all that? I'm sure *Celebrity* can organise a lookalike model.'

'Do they have to? Couldn't they find someone a little taller, a little thinner,' she said, making a joke of it. Trying not to think what Tom McFarlane would make of it.

She'd expected him to call her. What she expected him to say, she didn't dare think about. But she'd given him the option to walk away and he'd apparently taken it.

'How much are *Celebrity* offering?' she asked, refusing to dwell on it. Ignoring the hurt. And, certain that she'd won, Laura gave her the figure.

For a clutching-at-straws moment she'd hoped she might be able to cover the sum herself, buy her freedom. But, even as she'd clutched, she'd known that it was never going to happen.

This was about more than money.

It was about raising the profile of the charity that her mother had founded. A chance to show a national audience what they'd achieved, maybe even encourage women to set up branches in other areas; charities, like every other organization, had to grow or die. About giving local artists and craftsmen a national stage on which to air their talent.

And it was for her too. Refusing to hide.

Settled in her mind, Sylvie drew a deep breath and, burning all her boats, said, 'Actually, Laura, that's not enough.'

'What isn't enough?'

'The fee *Celebrity* are offering you. It isn't enough.'

'It isn't?' Laura asked, surprised out of her disapproval as she was thrown on the defensive. 'I thought it was very generous.'

'I'm sure they told you that, but for this feature…' for Sylvie Duchamp Smith giving a wedding master-class, for another excuse to rake over old bridal coals and speculate on the identity of the father of her child '…they'll pay twice that.'

'No!'

'Oh, yes!' The magazine had picked up the tabs for a couple of the weddings she'd organised and she knew what she was talking about. If they wanted to fill their pages with her personal fantasy, the charity her mother had founded was going to be paid the going rate. 'You can take my word for it.'

'Oh, I do,' Laura assured her, suddenly catching on to the fact that she'd hooked her fish. 'Maybe, as our Honorary President, you could talk to them? Since you seem to know so much about it.'

She fought down the temptation to remind the charity's Chairman that the post of 'Hon Pres' was supposed to be just that, an honorary one, and said, 'Leave it to me.' She could, if nothing else, use the opportunity to ensure that the features editor focused on the fantasy wedding and, for her full co-operation, leave old stories buried. 'So where is this all going to take place?'

'I've been saving the best until last,' she said. 'We've been offered the use of Longbourne Court for the Fayre. Back where it all began.'

Longbourne Court.

Sylvie, expected to respond enthusiastically, discovered that her tongue was refusing to connect with the roof of her mouth.

'Isn't that just perfect?' Laura said when Sylvia failed to say it for her.

There was no such thing as perfect...

A slightly flat, 'Great,' was the best she could manage.

'It was bought several months ago by some billionaire businessman and we've all been agog, as you can imagine.'

Oh, yes, she could imagine. It would have been the talk of coffee mornings and bridge parties across the county.

'Obviously, we all hoped he was going to live in it, but he's instructed Mark Hilliard, the architect...?' She paused, waiting for her to acknowledge the name.

'Mmm...'

'He's instructed Mark to draw up plans to convert the house into a conference centre.'

'Oh?'

'It's a shame, of course,' she said, finally cottoning on to a lack of enthusiasm from her audience. 'It's such a beautiful house. But there you are.'

Yes, indeed, there she was.

'Since it's "listed" it's going to take a while to sort out, but the *Celebrity* feature will give it one last outing and it's fitting that its swansong will honour your mother. And that you'll be part of it.'

'I hope the planning people won't be too difficult,' she said, without commenting on the fittingness or not of her participation in its final moments as a country house. 'Longbourne has been empty for much too long.'

The rock star who'd bought it originally hadn't spent more than a weekend or two there and since he'd fallen from the balcony of his New York penthouse, leaving his affairs in a mess, several years ago there had been nothing but gossip and rumour about what would happen to the estate.

Not that she'd been listening. That was all in the past. History.

'Well, whatever is planned isn't going to happen until English Heritage have had their say on the subject,' Laura said. 'That's how I heard what was happening; George is on the local committee, you know. That's when it occurred to me that in the meantime our billionaire might like the opportunity to demonstrate his credentials as a good neighbour.'

'And he agreed?'

'I suppose so. I actually spoke to some woman who appears to be in charge of the day-to-day running of the company and she was really enthusiastic about helping the charity. Well, everyone has been touched, haven't they?'

Woman at the helm or not, she doubted that sentimentality had much to do with the decision.

'The fact that the proposed conference centre will get acres of free publicity in *Celebrity* wouldn't have anything to do with that, I suppose?'

'Oh, Sylvie! Don't be so cynical.'

Why, just because she had a reputation for planning fantasy parties and weddings, did everyone think she should be sentimental? It was just *business*...

'And even if his company does get something out of it, well, what of it? I know it was your home, Sylvie, but times have changed and the conference centre will provide jobs locally. It's a win-win-win situation.'

'I suppose so.' Sylvie had made a point of staying well clear of her family home since it had been sold lock, stock and barrel, to pay off her grandfather's creditors, but Laura was right. The publicity would be good for everyone.

The Pink Ribbon Club charity founded by her mother; local designers; the tradesmen who would be employed to work on the conversion as well as local businesses.

In fact, when it came right down to it, the entire Melchester economy apparently rested on what frock she'd choose to wear to her own fantasy wedding.

Fantasy being the operative word. One fantasy in a lifetime was enough and she hadn't been kidding about the register office.

But, with Longbourne Court in the equation, *Celebrity* was going to have to stump up vastly more than their original offer. This was big and if they wanted to make themselves look good by clinging on to the trailing pink ribbons of her mother's charity, they were going to have to pay for the privilege.

Tom McFarlane drew up in front of the tall wrought iron gates of Longbourne Court.

Two things were wrong.

They were standing wide open.

And, decorating each of the central finials, was a large knot of pink ribbons.

He picked up his cellphone and hit fast dial.

'Tom?' Unsurprisingly, his CEO was surprised to hear from him. 'Isn't it the middle of the night where you are?'

'Right at this moment I'm at the gates of Longbourne Court, Pam, and I'm looking at pink ribbons. Please tell me that I'm hallucinating.'

'You're back in the UK?' she responded, ignoring his plea. Then, 'At Longbourne?'

A long blast on an air horn drowned out his reply, which was probably just as well.

'I'm sorry if I've returned in time to spoil the party,' he said, not stinting on the sarcasm, 'but I've got pink ribbons in front of me and an irate trucker with his radiator an inch from my rear. Just tell me what the hell is going on.'

'Hi, Pam,' she prompted, ignoring his question. 'I'm sorry I'm being a grouch but I'm jet lagged. As soon as I've had a decent night's sleep I'll hand over the duty-frees, along with the big fat bonus I owe you for taking care of—'

'I'm not in the mood,' he warned.

'No? Well, it's a lovely day and maybe by the time you reach the house you'll have remembered where you mislaid your manners,' she replied, completely unperturbed. 'When you do, you'll find me in the library running your company.'

'You're here?' he demanded. Stupid question. Pink ribbons and trucks didn't appear without someone to organise them. Pam obviously thought so too, since her only response was the dialling tone.

The truck driver sounded off for the second time and, resisting the temptation to swear at the man—he was only trying to do his job, whatever that was—he tossed the phone on the seat beside him and drove through the gates.

The trees were breaking out in new leaf and the parkland surrounding Longbourne Court had the timeless look of a set for some boobs-and-breeches costume drama, an illusion rudely shattered as he crested the rise.

The house was standing golden and square in the bright sunshine, just as it had for the best part of three centuries, but the only horsepower on show was of the twenty-first century variety. Trucks, cars, vans.

The nearest belonged to a confectioner who, according to the signage on her faux vintage vehicle, proclaimed to the world in copperplate script that she specialized in bespoke wedding cakes. One glance confirmed that there were caterers, photographers, florists—in fact, anything you could think of—ditto.

The kind of scene he'd so narrowly avoided six months ago, when Candy had decided that mere money wasn't enough to compensate for his lack of breeding and had traded up to a title. Not that 'Hon' was that big a deal but if she hung in there she'd make it to Lady eventually.

She could, with advantage, have taken lessons from her good friend Sylvie Smith. She hadn't messed about, she'd gone straight for the big one; she'd made damn sure that the 'childhood sweetheart', the one who'd make her a countess, didn't get away a second time.

CHAPTER FOUR

TOM parked his Aston in the coach house, alongside Pam's zippy BMW coupé and a black and silver Mini that he didn't recognise, but which presumably belonged to one of her staff. Inside the house it was all noise and chaos as the owners of the vehicles milled about, apparently in the process of setting up shop in his house.

He didn't pause to enquire what the devil they thought they were doing, instead hunting down the person responsible. The woman he'd left to keep his company ticking over while he put as much distance between himself and London as possible.

He found her sitting behind an antique desk in the library, looking for all the world like the lady of the manor.

'What the hell is going on?' he asked.

She peered over the top of her spectacles. 'Nice tan,' she said. 'Shame about the manners.'

'Pink ribbons,' he countered, refusing to be diverted.

'Maybe coffee would help. Or would you prefer tea? Better make it camomile.'

He placed his hands on the desk, leaned forward and, when he was within six inches of her face, he said, 'Tell me about the ribbons, Pam.'

'You are supposed to grovel, you wretch,' she said. 'Six

months! You've been away six months! I had to cancel my trip to South Africa and I've totally missed the skiing season—'

'What's to miss about breaking something vital?'

She almost smiled.

'Come on, Pam, you're the one who made the point that the honeymoon was booked so I might as well give myself a break.'

'What I had in mind was a couple of weeks chilling out on a beach. Or raising hell if that's what it took. As I recall, you weren't that keen.'

'I wasn't and I didn't. When I got to the airport I traded in my ticket for the first flight out.'

'And didn't tell a soul where you were. You did a six-month disappearing act!'

'I wish. You can't hide from email.'

She shrugged. 'I kept it to the minimum.'

'You're not fooling me, Pam Baxter. You've had absolute control while I've been away and you've loved every minute of it.'

'That's not the point! Have you any idea how worried I've been?' Then, presumably to distract him from the fact that she'd backed down before he'd apologised, she said, 'And, as for the ribbons on the gate, I don't know anything about them. But if I had to make a guess I'd suggest that the Pink Ribbon Club put them there.'

Okay.

He was distracted.

'What the hell is the Pink Ribbon Club when it's at home?' he asked, but easing back. He'd known she'd worry, but hanging around to offer explanations hadn't been appealing. 'And, more to the point, why are they hanging the damn things from my gate?'

She offered him a brochure from a stack on the desk. 'I've given them permission to hold a Wedding Fayre here—that's

Fayre with a y and an e—so I imagine they're advertising the fact to passing traffic. That's why I'm here this week,' she explained. 'The couple who are caretakers of the place do a good job, but I can't expect them to be responsible for the house and its contents with so many people coming and going.'

'Why?' he asked.

'Why did I give the PRC permission to stage the Fayre here? It's a local charity,' she said. 'Founded by Lady Annika Duchamp Smith?'

He stared at the wedding bell and horseshoe bedecked brochure for a moment before dropping it and subsiding into an ancient leather armchair.

'The Duchamp family owned the house for generations,' she prompted when he didn't respond. 'It's their coat of arms on the gate.'

'Really. Well, that covers the Duchamps. What's the story on the Smiths?' he asked, remembering a Smith with that hallmark English aristocratic cool and a voice that told the world everything they needed to know about her class, background.

A Smith with silvery-blue eyes that not only looked as if they could cause chaos if they had a mind to, but had gone ahead and done it.

Pam shrugged. 'Presumably Lady Annika married a Mr Smith.'

'For his money rather than his name, apparently, since she chose not to relinquish her own.'

For a moment there, when the word *charity* had been invoked, he'd found himself on the back foot but he quickly rallied. These people stood for everything he loathed.

Privilege, inherited wealth, a belief in their own innate superiority.

People for whom charity meant nothing more than another social event.

For a while he'd been dazzled too. Then completely blinded. But he had both feet firmly back on the ground now.

'It'll take more than playing charity queen to get Lady Annika back inside Longbourne Court,' he said.

'Well, actually Lady Annika—'

'I mean it,' he cut in, not interested in her ladyship. 'Give the Ribbon mob a donation if you think they're doing a good job, but get rid of her. And her Fayre with a y and an e.' He snorted with disgust. 'Why do they spell it like that?'

'Beats me,' she replied, 'but I'm afraid you're stuck with it. Even if it wasn't far too late to ungive permission, I wouldn't. *Celebrity* magazine are covering the event—which is why we need a dress rehearsal so that they can get photographs. Your conference centre is about to get the kind of publicity that money just can't buy.'

'You didn't know I was planning a conference centre.'

'Oh, please! What else are you going to do with it? Live here? On your own? Besides, our favourite architect, Mark Hilliard, sent me a sheaf of forms from the Planning Department.'

'He didn't waste any time!' Then, realising that Pam was looking at him a little oddly, 'Which is good. I stressed the need to get on with it when I spoke to him.'

'Oh? You managed to find time to *speak* to your architect.'

'It was a matter of priorities. The sooner we get started on this, the better.'

'In that case, the publicity is good news.'

'You think? This may come as a surprise to you, Pam, but the people—the *women*—who read gossip magazines, who go to Wedding Fayres, spelled with a y and an e, do not organise conferences.'

'I arrange conferences,' she pointed out.

'You are different.'

'Of course I'm not. And I never miss an edition of *Celebrity*.'

'You're kidding?'

'Am I?' She didn't bother to reassure him, just said, 'You're nothing but an old-fashioned misogynist at heart, aren't you, Tom?'

'You can't get around me with compliments—'

'And maybe the teeniest bit of a snob?'

'A snob!' On the contrary, he was the self-made man whose bride-to-be had decided that, once spending his money—egged on by her old school chum, Miss Smith—had lost its novelty, and the mists of lust had cleared, he wasn't good enough to marry.

'An inverted one,' she elaborated, as if that was any better.

'I'm a realist, Pam.'

'Oh, right, that would be the realist who fell off the edge of the earth six months ago, leaving me to hold the fort?'

'Which disproves your misogynist theory. If I disliked women, why would I leave you in charge while I took some much needed time out? Unlike you, I don't take three holidays a year. And why would I have appointed you as my CEO in the first place? Besides, I kept in touch.'

'Because I'm damn good at my job,' she said, answering the first two parts of his question. 'But, for your information, the occasional email to keep me up to date with the real estate you've been vacuuming up on whichever continent you happened to be at the time so that I could deal with the paperwork, is not keeping in touch.'

'I'm sure I sent you a postcard from Rio,' he said. The only one he really remembered was the one he hadn't sent.

'"Wish you were here"? Chance would have been a fine thing. Besides, I wanted to know how you were.' Then, 'You've lost weight.'

'I'm fine, okay!' She didn't look convinced. 'Truly. But I

decided that since I was taking a break I might usefully expand my empire while I was about it.'

'That's not expanding your empire, it's called displacement activity,' Pam said, giving him what his grandmother would have described as an old-fashioned look. 'If you were a woman, you'd have bought shoes.'

'Which proves my point about women,' he said. 'Real estate is a much better investment.'

'And, assuming you were thinking at all, which I take leave to doubt,' Pam continued, ignoring that and returning to the third part of his question, 'I'd suggest it's because you don't think of me as a woman at all.'

'Which is the highest compliment I could pay you.'

'Is that right? And you're surprised that Candy Harcourt dumped you?'

Surprised was not actually the first word that had come to mind. Relieved... Evading the question, he said, 'So, is this Wedding Fayre your idea of payback for leaving you to do your job?'

'Well, if I'd known you were going to be here, that would definitely have been a bonus. As it is, like you, I was being realistic. This is business. I *am* doing my job. Looking after your interests in your absence.' She gave him a long, hard look. 'And, as my last word on that subject, I suggest you go down on your knees and thank Candida Harcourt—or should I say The Honourable Mrs Quentin Turner Lyall—for letting you off the hook.'

'She actually married him?'

'It's true love, according to *Celebrity.*' Then, when he scowled at the mention of the magazine, 'Be grateful,' she said, misunderstanding his reaction. 'Divorce would have cost you a lot more than the fancy wedding she ran out on.'

'Thanks for the vote of confidence.' He dragged his hair back from his forehead. It immediately flopped over his forehead again. It needed cutting...

'It's not you that I doubt.' She shrugged. 'Impoverished aristocracy are always a risk. Marrying for money goes with the territory. In the old days they had no choice but to stick with the deal, but these days divorce is just as profitable. Not that I'm suggesting your only attraction was fiscal.'

'In other words, she was just amusing herself with a bit of rough? Got carried away for a moment...'

Something else she had in common with her old school chum, Sylvie Smith. No wonder she'd cried. He'd only lost Candy while her indiscretion could have lost her the ermine and the guaranteed seat at the next coronation...

Pam raised her hands in a gesture that could have meant anything but, taking the opportunity to change the subject, he indicated the noises off in the entrance hall.

'I appear to have no choice but to accept that this is a done deal. How long is it going to last?'

'The Fayre? It'll all be over by Monday.'

'A week? I've got to put up with pink ribbons on my gates for a week?' he demanded.

'Be glad this isn't Italy—everyone would be congratulating you on the birth of a daughter.'

'That's not remotely funny,' he declared. Anything but.

'For heaven's sake, Tom, lighten up.' Then, more gently, 'If you'd given me some indication that you were coming home I'd have warned you what was happening. Why don't you go back to London? Catch up with everyone. Longbourne Court will still be here next week.'

'Nice idea, but I've arranged to meet Mark Hilliard here this morning.'

'I could put him off until next week.'

'No,' he said, hauling himself out of the chair and heading for the door. 'I want to get started.' He wanted to subject the house to his will; making it entirely his would draw a line under the whole affair. 'Give me twenty minutes to take a shower and you can bring me up to date. There is hot water, I take it?'

'Plenty. I'll get Mrs Kennedy to make up the bed in the master suite.'

'Thanks. And if you were serious about the coffee, that would be good too.'

'I'll get on to it.' Then, as he opened the door, she called, 'Oh, Tom! Wait! Before you go, I should warn you—'

'Twenty minutes,' he repeated, closing it behind him, then stood back as two men manhandled a large sheet of plywood through the hall and into the ballroom.

He'd been away for months; there wasn't a thing that wouldn't wait another twenty minutes.

He fetched his overnight bag from the car, then headed for the stairs.

His foot was on the first step when the sound of a woman's voice drifting from the drawing room riveted him to the spot.

'I like to start with the colours, Lucy.'

He dropped the bag, moved closer. Heard someone else say, 'This is going to be a spring wedding, so… what? Primroses, daffodils… Yellow?'

'No.' The word was snapped out. Then, more gently, 'Not yellow. April is getting late for daffodils. I did see violets as I drove in through the wood, though. Why don't you take a tour of the exhibitors and bring me anything and everything you can find from deepest violet through to palest mauve? With just a touch of green, I think.'

'Anything special?'

'Ribbons, jewellery, accessories. Ask the florist what he'll have available. And don't forget to make a note of where everything came from…'

She had her back to him, standing shadowed by the deep embrasure of the door as she quietly absorbed everything that was going on but, long before she turned, stepped forward into the sunlight streaming in through front doors propped wide open for workmen carrying in a load of steel trestles, he knew exactly who that voice belonged to.

He'd spent an entire afternoon listening to it as they'd gone, item by item, through her account. Watching her unbutton her jacket. Moisten her lips.

All the time he'd been away it hadn't been Candy's last-minute change of heart that had kept him from sleeping.

It had been the flush on Sylvie Smith's cheeks. The memory of long legs, a glimpse of lace.

Her hot body moulded to his.

Her pitiful tears.

Her tears had haunted him, plaguing him with guilt, but now he understand that her tears had not been for what he'd done to her, but because she'd just risked everything she had in a momentary rush of lust. No wonder she couldn't wait to get away…

Sylvie smiled encouragingly at the youthful journalist, the advance guard from *Celebrity* whose job it was to research background and photo opportunities so that when the photographer arrived on Sunday there would be no waiting. And to encourage her to give her imagination free rein when it came to the fantasy wedding.

Full of enthusiasm, the girl immediately set about hunting down anything she could find in the chosen colour scheme.

Sylvie, not in the least bit enthusiastic, dropped the face-aching smile that seemed to have been fixed ever since she'd arrived at Longbourne Court and looked around at the chaos in what had once been her mother's drawing room.

The furniture had been moved out, stored somewhere to leave room for the exhibitors. But it wasn't the emptiness that tore at her. It was the unexpected discovery that, despite the passing of ten years, so little had changed. It was not the difference but the familiarity that caught at the back of her throat. Tugged at her heart.

The pictures that had once been part of her life were still hanging where they had always been. Velvet curtains, still blue in the deep folds but ever since she could remember faded to a silvery-grey where the light touched them, framed an unchanged view.

There was even a basket of logs in the hearth that might have been there on the day the creditors had seized the house and its contents nearly ten years ago, taking everything to cover the mess that her grandfather, in his attempt to recoup the family fortunes, had made of things.

But driving in the back way through the woods at the crack of dawn, walking in through the kitchen and seeing Mrs Kennedy standing at the sink, her little cry of surprised pleasure, the hug she'd given her while they'd both shed a tear, had been like stepping back in time.

She could almost imagine that her mother had just gone out for an hour or two, would at any moment walk through the door, dogs at her heels...

She swallowed, blinked, reminded herself what was at stake. Forced herself to focus on the job in hand.

She'd already decided that the only way to handle this was to treat herself as if she were one of her own clients. Just one more busy career woman without the time to research the endless details that would make her wedding an event to remember for the rest of her life.

Distancing herself from any emotional involvement.

It was, after all, her job. Something she did every day. Nothing to get excited about. Except, of course, that was just what it should be. Something to be over-the-moon excited about rather than just a going-through-the-motions chore.

She shook her head. The quicker she got on with it, the quicker it would be over. She had the colour scheme, which was a start.

'I'll be in the morning room,' she called out to Lucy, already busily talking to exhibitors, searching out anything useful. It was time she was at work too, hunting down a theme to hang the whole thing on, something original that she hadn't used before.

And the even bigger problem of the dress.

She turned to find her way blocked by six and half feet of broad-shouldered male and experienced a bewildering sense of *déjà vu*.

A feeling that this had happened before.

And then she looked up and realised that it was not an illusion. This *had* happened before, except on that occasion the male concerned had been wearing navy pin-stripe instead of grey cashmere.

'*Some billionaire...*' Laura had said, but hadn't mentioned a name. And she hadn't bothered to ask, pretending she didn't care.

She cared now because it wasn't just 'some' billionaire who'd bought her family home and was planning to turn it into a conference centre.

It was Tom McFarlane, the man with whom, just for a few moments, she'd totally lost it. Whose baby she was carrying. Who'd grabbed her offer to forget it had ever happened. She'd expected at least an acknowledgement...

'Tell me, Miss Smith,' he said while she was still struggling to get her mouth around a simple, Good morning, using exactly the same sardonic tone with which he'd queried every item on her invoice all those months ago. The same look with which he'd reduced her to a stuttering jangle of unrestrained hormones.

Despite everything, she hadn't been able to get that voice, the heat of those eyes, his touch, the weight, heat of his body, out of her head for weeks afterwards.

Make that months.

Maybe not at all...

The man she most wanted to see in the entire world. The man she most dreaded seeing because she'd made a promise and she would have to keep it.

'What?' she demanded, since they were clearly bypassing the civilities, but then there had never been anything civil between them. Only something raw, almost primitive. 'What do you want?'

Stupid question...

He didn't want anything from her.

'To know what you're doing here.' Then, presumably just to ram the point home, because he must surely know that it had once been her home, 'In my house.'

'It's yours?' she said, managing to feign surprise. 'I was told some billionaire had bought it but no one thought to mention your name. But then I didn't ask.' And because she had nothing to apologise for—she'd not only been invited here, but was taking part in this nonsense at great personal inconvenience and no little expense—she said, 'If you'll excuse me, Mr McFarlane?'

She'd been so right to keep it businesslike.

He didn't move, but continued to regard her with those relentlessly fierce eyes that were apparently hell-bent on scrambling her brains.

The man she'd dreaded seeing. The man she'd longed more than anything to see, talk to. If he would just give her a chance, let her show him a scan of the baby they'd made. His daughter. But maybe he understood the risk, the danger of being sucked into a relationship he'd never asked for, never wanted.

She'd given him that get-out-of-jail-free card and could not take it back. And, since he was studiously avoiding the subject, clearly he had no intention of voluntarily surrendering it.

'I have a lot to get through today,' she said, unable to bear it another moment and indicating that she wanted to pass. She'd meant to sound brisk and decisive but the effect was undermined by a slight wobble on the 'h-h-have'.

She might have a lot to get through but the dress would have to wait until she'd had enough camomile tea to drown the squadron of butterflies that were practising formation flying just below her midriff.

Except that it wasn't butterflies but her baby girl practising dance steps.

His baby girl…

'I don't think so,' he responded, not moving.

Well, no. She hadn't for a moment imagined it would be that easy. Trapped in the doorway, she had no choice but to wait.

'What are you doing here?' he repeated.

A man came through the front door carrying a pile of chairs and Tom McFarlane moved to let him pass, taking a step closer so that she was near enough for the warmth of his body to reach out and touch her.

The warmth had taken her by surprise the first time; she would have sworn that he was stone-cold right through until he'd put his hands around her waist, slid his palms against the bare skin of her back and his mouth had come down on hers, heating her to the bone.

Not cold. Anything but cold. More like a volcano—the kind with tiny wisps of smoke escaping through fumaroles, warning that the smallest disturbance could bring it to turbulent, boiling life.

Her only escape was to retreat, take a step back. His eyes, gleaming dangerously, suggested it would be the safe move, but she knew better.

She wasn't the naïve girl who'd left this house nearly ten years ago. She'd made a life for herself; had used what skills she had to build a successful business. She hadn't done that by backing away from difficult situations, but by confronting them.

She knew he'd take retreat as a sign of weakness so, difficult as it was, she stood her ground.

Even when he continued to challenge her with a look that sent the butterflies swerving, diving, performing aerial loop the loops.

'In the middle of a Wedding Fayre?' he persisted, when she didn't answer.

He didn't sound particularly happy about that. He'd be even less so if he knew why she was part of it. They were in agreement about that, anyway. Not that it helped.

'I'm, um, working. It's a *Celebrity* thing,' she said, offering the barest minimum in the hope that he wouldn't be interested in the details. 'They're covering this event.'

'I'd heard,' he said, leaning back slightly, propping an elbow in one hand while rubbing a darkly stubbled chin in urgent need of a shave with the other as he regarded her with a thoughtful frown. 'So what kind of feature would a wedding planner be working on for a gossip magazine?'

Of course he was interested.

Men like Tom McFarlane—women like her—did not succeed by glossing over the details.

'I don't just coordinate weddings,' she replied. 'SDS, my company, organises all kinds of events. Celebrations. Bonding weekends for company staff. Conferences…'

At this point she would normally offer to send a brochure.

She fought the temptation, but only because she'd have to explain to Laura how she came to be thrown out of what had once been her family home.

'And which of those events is being featured by *Celebrity?*'

He spread his fingers in a gesture so minimal that it made the word redundant but which, nevertheless, perfectly expressed his meaning. 'At a Wedding Fayre.'

She shifted her shoulders, sketching an equally minimal shrug while she tried to come up with an answer that wouldn't send him through the roof.

Rescue came in the form of Pam Baxter, approaching from the kitchen.

'Tom?' she said, evidently surprised to see him. 'You're still here. I've just asked Mrs Kennedy to make you some breakfast.' Then, looking to see who he was talking to, 'Oh, hi, Sylvie,' she said, spotting her in the shadows of the doorway. 'Have you introduced yourself to—'

'There was no need—' Tom McFarlane cut short her introduction '—Miss Smith and I have already met. In her professional capacity.'

'Oh?' Then, belatedly catching on to his meaning, 'Oh.' She might have added something else under her breath. Neither of them asked her to speak up. In fact no one said anything for what seemed like a very long time until Pam broke the silence with, 'Have you settled in, Sylvie? Got everything you need?'

'Settled in?' Tom McFarlane demanded before she could reply, never taking his eyes off her.

'Sylvie's wedding is being featured by *Celebrity* magazine,' Pam said, which saved her the bother of having to give him the bad news.

'Her wedding?'

The silver specks in the rock-grey eyes turned molten. He was angry. Well, of course he was angry. He probably thought she'd arranged the whole thing, had brought it to his doorstep in an attempt to force his hand.

'They're giving Sylvie's charity a vast amount of money for the chance to feature it,' Pam said before she could do anything, say anything to reassure him. 'She was going to stay in Melchester, but it seemed so much more sensible to have her stay here. It's not as if we're short of rooms.'

'Her charity?' He turned away to look at Pam and for a moment Sylvie was assailed by a curious mixture of emotions. Relief, largely. But something else. Something almost like *loss*...

As if being looked at by Tom McFarlane brought her to life. Which would explain why, ever since she'd had to leave him, taking delivery of that damn cake, she'd felt something had been missing.

'The Pink Ribbon Club? Sylvie's mother, Lady Annika Duchamp Smith, founded it.'

'Your father was *that* Mr Smith?' he said.

For a moment Tom McFarlane had been distracted, but now he regarded her with, if that was possible, even more dislike.

Something missing? That would be her common sense, obviously.

'Yes,' she said shortly. 'He was that Mr Smith.'

'And now the charity is yours.'

'I took my mother's place as the Honorary President, that's all. I help with fund-raising when I can. Like now.'

'So you used to live here?'

She'd misjudged him over that. He hadn't known. But he did now.

'Well, yes,' she said, doing her best to imply a good-heaven's-that-was-years-ago carelessness. As if it didn't matter. Adding, with polite interest, 'I understand that the plan is to turn the place into a conference centre.'

'And where did you hear that?'

'From someone who lives locally who's involved with English Heritage.' She gave a little shrug. 'You can't keep secrets in the country, Mr McFarlane.'

'No?'

There was something almost threatening in the word. A warning.

Ignoring it, striving for casual, as if it *really* didn't matter to her what he did with the house, she said, 'Are you telling me it isn't true?'

'Oh, it's true,' he assured her, with what could only be described as a satisfied little smile—nowhere near big enough to get anywhere near his eyes—which suggested that she needed to work on her 'carelessness'. 'Do you have a problem with that?'

'Not at all—'

'A rare moment of agreement—'

'—in fact I was going to offer my company's conference services. I'll ask my office to send you a brochure, shall I?'

That, at least, got a reaction. A glowering, furious reaction but Pam stepped in before it boiled over with a swift interjection.

'I'd better go and put your breakfast on hold for another twenty minutes. Sylvie? Can I get you something?'

'Thanks, but I don't need waiting on, Pam,' she said. 'I know my way about.' Which was probably exactly the wrong thing to say but she doubted that there was anything she could say that was right.

Realising that this was a conversation going downhill fast, Pam took charge. 'It's no trouble. Camomile tea, isn't it?' And, before she could say anything else calculated to irritate her boss, 'You're okay in the morning room? It's warm enough?'

'It's perfect. Thank you.'

Pam waited, evidently planning to escort her out of harm's way, but, still trapped in the doorway by Tom McFarlane's rock-like figure, she was unable to escape so, with a meaningful look at him, she said, 'Shout if you need anything, Sylvie.' And left them to it.

'So, Miss Duchamp Smith—'

'Just Smith. Sylvie,' she added with a touch of desperation—

how ridiculous was that? It didn't elicit an invitation to call him Tom and, since she was the one in the wrong place, she said, 'I promise you that I had no idea that it was your company that had bought Longbourne Court, Mr McFarlane.' She emphasized the Mr McFarlane, making the point that she wasn't here to put in a plea for her baby. Or for herself. 'If I'd known—'

He didn't wait for her to tell him that she wouldn't have accepted Pam's invitation to stay. He simply leaned close and, speaking very softly, said, 'Well, you do now, so you won't get too comfortable in the morning room, will you? Or upstairs. I've had my fill of your kind.'

She didn't have to ask what kind of woman he thought she was. Twenty per cent told her that and how could she protest when the last time they'd been this close he'd had one hand on her naked back and the other had just found the gap between stocking and the lace of her Agent Provocateur French knickers and nothing about her response had suggested she was anything but happy about it…

'I promise you,' she snapped back, her cheeks flaming, 'getting comfortable is the last thing on my mind.' Then, lifting her hand in a gesture that indicated she'd like to move and that she wanted enough space to do it without the risk of physical contact, she said, 'If you'll excuse me, the sooner I get started, the sooner I'll be out of here.'

And, finally, she'd managed to say something right because, without another word, he stepped back, allowing her to escape.

CHAPTER FIVE

Tom watched as, head held high, Sylvie Smith walked quickly away.

At their last meeting she'd arrived buttoned up for business in a designer suit, hair coiled up in some elegant style, make-up immaculate, but it hadn't taken her long to start unbuttoning, loosening up. For those big silvery-blue eyes, smoked with heat, to be sending out an unmistakable message, apparently as incapable as him of resisting the attraction between them.

Today he'd caught her unawares, casually dressed in soft dusky-pink layers that all but disguised her condition, her hair caught back with a matching chiffon scarf. Not a button in sight.

She'd been less obviously flirtatious and yet the look had still been there, he thought, his gaze drifting down over hips that were curvier than he remembered, wide-legged trousers that flapped a little as she strode briskly in the direction of the morning room, drawing attention to her comfortable flat shoes.

But he didn't need the short skirt and high heels to feel the same tug of heat that had caught him on the raw a year ago, when he'd walked into her office behind Candy.

When his marriage plans had fallen apart he'd responded by giving her a bad time. Not that she hadn't deserved it.

Then, stupidly, he'd just responded.

He'd done his best to kill the flame, but six months on, his body, driven, denied for months, was on fire again.

The only difference was that this time she was the one getting married.

Concentrate...

Forget Tom McFarlane. Forget that she'd jumped every time the phone rang for weeks after she'd had to race away to save her client from wrecking her own party.

After she'd gone back to find his flat empty. That, after the passion, he'd still gone on his honeymoon for one...

Cold. He was cold...

Beneath the fire there was only ice, she reminded herself.

The raw sexual attraction that had been so unexpected, so new to her, had, for him, been no more than an instinctive male response to a situation charged with tension. An atavistic need to prove his masculinity in the face of rejection.

It hadn't been *personal*.

If she hadn't believed it then, had clung to that hope despite reality, he'd certainly gone out of his way to make sure she understood his feelings this morning.

I've had my fill of your kind...

Her kind being women like Candy Harcourt. Two of a kind. Not.

The truth of the matter was that he didn't know a thing about her. Didn't want to know. Wasn't interested.

Sylvie dragged her gaze away from the familiar distant view of the old village, nestled in the valley bottom alongside the river. The square Norman tower of the church. Forced herself, instead, to look at the photographs provided by the designer who was going to pull out all the stops to provide her with her dream dress.

There was just one problem.

No dream.

Not one with a possibility of coming true, anyway.

She was going to have to be content with the one she had. The one she'd already fulfilled when she'd taken control of her own destiny, refusing ever again to allow her fate to be dictated by circumstances over which she had no control. Or thought she had. She laid a hand against her belly as her baby moved as if to remind her that fate had a way of mocking those who thought they'd beaten her, turning the pages of the album with the other, hoping for something, anything.

A gut response that said 'this one'.

It shouldn't matter, but stupidly it did. If she was going to lay out her fantasy for the world to judge, it had to be real. Perfect.

There's no such thing as perfect...

The 'gut response' wasn't working. It was fully occupied coping with her unexpected confrontation with Tom McFarlane. He looked thinner. Tanned, but thinner. Harder, if that was possible. His features chiselled back to the bone...

She shut her eyes in an attempt to block out the image. Concentrate on the dress. Style... She should stick with style because the wedding dress, as she always reminded her brides, should be an extension of your natural look.

Your wedding day was not a moment to experiment with a fashion statement.

Especially if the result was going to be splashed, in full colour, across the pages of *Celebrity*.

Geena Wagner, the designer showing at the Fayre, was incredibly talented and her gowns were all, without exception, beautiful.

Something like the flowing, beaded and embroidered silk chiffon kaftan-style dress might well have been her choice if she'd been thinking of a beach wedding.

She paused to make a note on her PDA for Josie. She had a bride who was considering that option.

Unfortunately, while the idea of a runaway wedding for two on some deserted beach might be deeply appealing, her task—and she'd had little choice but to accept it—was to include as many exhibitors as possible, which meant it would have to be a traditional wedding.

The whole village church, bells and choir job, with bridesmaids, ushers, fancy transport, a marquee fit for a maharajah and more flowers than Kew Gardens.

It should have been a piece of cake. She'd done it before. Sitting in this room, making lists, her mother offering suggestions. She wasn't that girl any more...

At least she'd made a start with the flowers, she thought, reaching out for the tiny posy of violets that Lucy—taking her task very seriously—had gone out into the park to pick for her. Sweet-scented purple velvet flowers, heart-shaped leaves, tied with narrow purple ribbon. She lifted it to breathe in the scent and for a moment smiled.

Her bridal flowers would be a simple posy of violets. Maybe she could set a new trend for simplicity, she thought, returning to the photographs. A minimalist wedding. Very classy.

The strapless cleavage-enhancing dresses were almost too minimalist, but while perfect for a civil ceremony in some glamorous setting, wouldn't work in the village church. Or maybe it just wouldn't work for her.

And yet the look would have to be show-stopping.

She needed a theme, something that would tie everything together, or the feature risked being no more than a series of photographs of things...

She sighed, poked amongst the collection of goodies Lucy had found for her. Held a long amethyst earring against her neck. A scrap of smoky mauve chiffon. Ribbons, dried flower petals, invitation cards with envelopes lined with lilac tissue.

All utterly gorgeous, but she'd done all that love's young

dream, happy ever after, fairy tale thing ten years ago. Had seen it crumble to dust the minute there was trouble.

Maybe that was why she'd been hit so hard by the Candida Harcourt/Tom McFarlane debacle. It had been too close to home. Had brought back too many painful memories. Despite Tom McFarlane's move on her, it was obvious that he hadn't been over it, he'd just been hurting.

Her response had been to shift the hands-on wedding stuff to Josie, using her pregnancy as an excuse. Not that the clients were getting second-best. Josie was brilliant at making things run on oiled wheels behind the scenes. In fact, if she wasn't very careful, her rivals would be headhunting her, offering her all kinds of incentives to come and work for them.

She made a note on her PDA to do something about that. Which was just another way of putting off the task in hand.

'Come on, Sylvie,' she muttered, taking a couple of long, slow, calming breaths. 'You can do this.'

And then, avoiding the dresses, she picked up one of a pair of embroidered and beaded purple silk shoes.

'Anything catch your eye?' Geena said from the doorway.

'These shoes?' she offered.

'You're finding it difficult?'

She indicated her shape. 'Just a bit. But I've definitely ruled out the vestal virgin look,' she said, indicating the photograph in front of her. 'Not that it isn't lovely,' she added quickly. 'They're all lovely but, to be honest, I'm finding it hard and it's not the bump. It's just not real, you know?' She tried to think of some way to explain. 'I find most of my brides are thinking about their groom when they choose their dress.' Most of them. 'When they find the dress of their dreams they always say something like, "He'll just melt when he sees me in this…"'

Candy, on the other hand, had said, 'Everyone I know will die of envy when they see me in this...' But then that had been the standard by which she'd judged everything about her wedding. Not what Tom would think but how envious everyone else would be.

Maybe that was the difference between marrying for money and marrying for love. Candy hadn't needed any of the trappings when she'd married Quentin. Just the two of them had been enough.

She'd read all about it in their 'true love' story in *Celebrity*.

'You know it's going to be perfect when they say that, don't you?' Geena agreed, breaking into her thoughts. But then, dressing brides was her business so clearly she understood better than most.

'It does help,' Sylvie said. Then shrugged. 'I don't know. Maybe I've planned too many "perfect" weddings that didn't last.'

'Think about the ones that have,' she said, taking the shoe, looking at it. 'This is totally gorgeous.' She tried it on but it was too small and she handed it to Sylvie. 'Go on, your feet are smaller than mine. Try it.'

Anything was better than looking at wedding dresses and the shoe *was* fabulous. She slipped it on and extended her foot. The colour glowed. A few small beads set amongst the rich embroidery caught the light and sparkled.

They both sighed.

'I think we have a bit of a Cinderella moment here,' Geena said with a grin. 'Try the other one. Walk about...' Then, after a moment, 'Are you getting anything?'

'A total reluctance to take them off, give them back,' she admitted, laughing, 'but honestly, purple shoes!'

'Colour is making a big impact in wedding gowns these days,' she said thoughtfully. 'It might work. Embroidery? Appliqué? I have a woman who is brilliant at that.' Then, getting no encouragement, 'What we really need to get you in the mood is a man.'

'I'm sorry, I can't help you there,' she said, concentrating on the shoes.

'No? Really? But what about—'

'Believe it,' Sylvie swiftly cut in. 'The infant is the result of a...a...sperm donation.'

'At a clinic?' She did not sound convinced.

'Not quite, but the man wasn't included in the deal.'

'Oh, well, not to worry. He doesn't have to be "the one",' she said, making little quotation marks. 'Just someone hot enough to get you in that dreamy, this-will-make-him-melt mood.' Then, when she shook her head, 'A this-will-make-him-want-to-tear-it-off-and-take-you-to-bed mood would do,' she assured her.

Which fired up all those visions of Tom McFarlane that she'd been doing her best to smother.

'Not possible, I'm afraid.'

'No? Shame. But there are some seriously hunky blokes putting up a marquee out there. I'll go and drag one of them in, shall I?'

She turned as someone cleared his throat behind her.

'Oh, hi, Mark. What are you doing here?' Then, before he could answer, she glanced at Sylvie, a wicked little gleam in her eye. 'Sylvie, have you met Mark Hilliard, very hot architect of this parish? Mark, Sylvie Smith.'

'You've been misinformed, Sylvie. I live in Upper Haughton with my wife and our three children, so whatever Geena has in mind I regret that the answer is no.'

'My sentiments exactly,' Sylvie said quickly.

But he wasn't finished. 'For this parish you need Tom McFarlane, Geena. The new owner of Longbourne Court.'

And, as the man himself appeared in the doorway, he left them to it while he took his notebook on a tour of the morning room.

'Tom?' Geena said, offering her hand. 'Geena Wagner.' Then, she stood back to admire the view. 'Oh, *yes*. You're perfect.'

'I am?' he asked, confused but smiling. A natural smile, the kind any man would bestow on an attractive woman at their first meeting. The kind he'd never given her.

He hadn't caught sight of her—yet.

Sylvie struggled to protest, but only managed a groan—enough to attract his attention. The confusion remained, but the smile disappeared as fast as a snowball tossed into hell.

'Absolutely perfect!' Geena exclaimed in reply to his question, although he didn't appear to have heard. 'You're not married, are you?' Geena pressed, apparently oblivious to the sudden tension, unaware of the looming disaster.

'Why don't you ask Miss Smith?' he replied while she was still trying to untangle her vocal cords. Stop Geena from making things a hundred times worse.

The mildness of his tone belied the hard glitter in his eyes as he looked over Geena's head and straight at her. As if the fact that he wasn't was somehow *her* fault.

Along with global warming, the national debt and the price of fuel, no doubt.

'You know each other! *Excellent*. The thing is, Tom, Sylvie needs a stand-in fantasy man. Are you game?'

'Nnnnnn…' was all she could manage, since not only were her vocal cords in a knot, but her tongue had apparently turned into a lump of wood.

'That rather depends on the nature of the fantasy,' he replied, ignoring her frantically shaking head. His expression suggested that he harboured any number of fantasies in which she was the main participant…

'Well, all I need is for you to stand there looking hot and fanciable.' She smiled encouragingly. Then, before he could move, 'That's it. Perfect.'

'I didn't do anything,' he protested.

'You don't have to,' she said, grinning hugely at her own cleverness. 'Right, Sylvie. Get your imagination into gear.'

'Geena, I think…'

'Thinking is the last thing I want from you. This is all about feelings. The senses,' she said bossily, stepping from between them and, taking her by the shoulders, lined her up so that she was facing him.

The sun was streaming into the morning room and she'd shrugged off the loose knee-length cardigan-style wrap that had become a permanent cover-up since her pregnancy had begun to show and her condition was unmistakable.

And his expression left her in no doubt as to his feelings. He was angry…

'Forget that sweater, those pants, excellent though they are,' Geena said. 'For this exercise he's wearing a morning suit…' she glanced down at the purple shoes '…a grey morning suit with a purple waistcoat and violets in his buttonhole.'

Tom McFarlane made a sound that suggested 'not in this life'.

'He's standing at the altar and he's—'

'What altar?' Tom demanded, having been finally jerked out of his own private fantasy world in which, no doubt, all wedding coordinators were fed on wedding cake—the kind with rock-hard royal icing—until their teeth fell out.

What had he done with that wedding cake…?

'Good point, Tom. Village church, Sylvie?' she asked, breathing into her thoughts.

Sylvie opened her mouth, determined to put an end to this nightmare, but it was apparently a rhetorical question because Geena swept on without waiting for an answer.

'Where else? But you don't have to worry about that, Tom.'

'I don't?' he said, apparently unconvinced, but Geena was in full flow and nothing, it seemed, was going to stop her.

'Absolutely not. We're doing all the work here.'

Sylvie shrugged helplessly as Tom McFarlane lifted a brow in her direction, putting them, for the briefest moment, on the same side.

Not possible.

In the middle of the night she might have succumbed to the impossible dream. The happy ever after. But that was all it had ever been—a dream.

'Okay, Sylvie. The church doorway is decorated with evergreens and flowers. Your bridesmaids are waiting. All adults?' she asked. 'Or will you be having children too?'

Concentrate on the wedding. Just make the most of this fantasy moment...

'One adult,' she said. If this were real, she'd want Josie in the rear, running things. Parting her from her boots might be difficult, but at least her hair already matched the colour scheme. 'Assorted children. Four girls, one boy.'

Her fantasy should, after all, be close to reality as possible and she had four god-daughters who would never forgive her if they were excluded from the big day. And a five-year-old godson who would probably never forgive her if he was expected to appear in public in a pair of satin breeches. But he'd look sweet and his sisters could use the threat of posting the photographs on the Internet to keep him in order when he was at that difficult age—the one between five and ninety-five.

Girls needed all the edge they could get, she thought, as she stopped fighting a deep need for this and just let herself go.

'Okay, here's the scene,' Geena said. 'The organ strikes up, your father takes your arm...'

'No!' Last time that had been her grandfather's role. This time there was no one. 'I'll be on my own,' she said, doing what Geena had said. Not thinking. Just feeling.

Realising that both Geena and Tom were looking at her a little oddly, she said, 'I'm an adult. I don't need anyone to give me away.'

'Oh, right... Well, whatever. It's your wedding. So you're poised to walk up the aisle.' Geena picked up the violets, pressed them into her hand. 'Okay, the organ strikes up, you hear the rustle as everyone in the church gets to their feet. This is it. Da da da-da...' she sang. 'You're walking up the aisle. Walk, walk,' she urged, pushing her towards Tom. 'Everyone is looking at you. People are sighing, but you don't see them, don't hear them,' she went on relentlessly. 'Everything is concentrated on the only two people in the church who matter. You, in the dress of your dreams,' she said. 'And him.'

She met Tom McFarlane's gaze.

Why was he still there? Why hadn't he just turned around and walked out? He didn't have to stay...

'What does it feel like as you move, Sylvie?' Geena murmured, very softly, as if they were truly in church. 'Cool against your skin? Can you feel the drag of a train? Can you hear it rustle? Tell me, Sylvie. Tell me what you're feeling. Tell me what he's seeing...'

For a moment she was there in the cool church with the sun streaming in through the stained glass. Could feel the dress as it brushed against her legs. The antique lace of her grandmother's veil...

Could see Tom McFarlane standing in the spangle of coloured light, looking at her as if she made his world whole as she walked down the aisle towards him, a simple posy of violets in her hand.

'Tell me what he's seeing that's making him melt,' Geena persisted.

His gaze dropped to the unmistakable bulge where his baby was growing beneath her heart and, shattering the illusion, said,

'Sackcloth and ashes would do it.' Then, turning abruptly away, 'Mark, have you got everything you need in here?'

He didn't wait for an answer but, leaving the architect to catch up, he walked out, as if being in the same room with her was more than he could bear.

Mark, his smile wry, said, 'Nice one, Geena. If you need any help getting your foot out of your mouth I can put you in touch with a good osteopath.' Then, 'Good meeting you, Sylvie.'

Geena, baffled, just raised a hand in acknowledgement as he left, then said, 'What on earth was his *problem?*'

Sylvie, reaching for the table as her knees buckled slightly, swallowed, then, forcing herself to respond casually, said, 'It would have been a good idea to have asked where we met.'

When she didn't rush to provide the information, Geena gestured encouragingly. 'Well? Where did you meet?'

'I went to school with the woman he was going to marry, so I was entrusted with the role of putting together her fantasy wedding. I did try to warn you.'

'But I was too busy talking. It's a failing,' she admitted. 'So what was with the sackcloth and ashes remark? What did you do—book the wrong church? Did the marquee collapse? The guests go down with food poisoning? What?'

'The bride changed her mind three days before the wedding.'

'You're kidding!' Then, glancing after him, 'Was she crazy?'

'Rather the opposite. She came to her senses just in time. Candy Harcourt?' she prompted. Then, when Geena shook her head, 'You don't read the gossip magazines?'

'Is it compulsory?'

Sylvie searched for a laugh but failed to find one. He knew and she'd seen his reaction.

While there had been only silence, she had been able to fool herself that he might, given time, come round. Not any more.

It couldn't get any worse.

'No, it's not compulsory, Geena, but in this instance I rather wish you had.'

'I still don't understand his problem,' she said, frowning. 'You can't be held responsible for the bride getting cold feet.'

'She eloped with one of my staff.'

'Ouch.' She shrugged. Then, as the man himself walked across the lawn in front of the window, 'I still think that taking it out on you is a little harsh and if I didn't have my own fantasy man waiting at home I'd be more than happy to give him a talking to he wouldn't forget in a hurry. Although, to be honest, from the way he looked at you—'

'I believe the expression "if looks could kill" just about covers it,' Sylvie cut in quickly, distracting Geena before she managed to connect the dots.

'Only if spontaneous combustion was the chosen method of execution. Are you sure it was only the bride who fell for the wedding planner?' she pressed. Then perhaps realising just what she was saying, she held up her hands, in a gesture of apology. 'Will you do me a favour and forget I said that? Forget I even thought it. How bad would it be for business if brides got the impression they couldn't trust you with their grooms?'

'What? No!' she declared, but felt the betraying heat rush to her cheeks.

Geena didn't pursue it, however—although she had an eyebrow that spoke volumes—just said, 'My mistake.' But not with any conviction—she was clearly a smart woman. Her sense of self-preservation belatedly kicked in, however, and she said, 'Okay, forget Mr Hot-and-Sexy for the moment and just tell me what you saw.'

'Saw?'

'Just now. I was watching you. You saw something. Felt something.'

What she'd seen was the image that Geena had put into her head. Her nineteen-year-old self dressed in her great-grandmother's wedding dress, the soft lace veil falling nearly to her feet.

The only difference being that in her fantasy moment it hadn't been the man she'd been going to marry standing at the altar.

It had been Tom McFarlane who, for just a moment, she'd been certain was about to reach out and take her hand...

'Sylvie?'

'Yes,' she said quickly. 'You're right. I was remembering something. A dress...'

Concentrate on the dress.

'Are you really going to be able to make something from scratch in a few days?' she asked a touch desperately. 'Normally it takes weeks. Months...'

'Well, I admit that it's going to be a bit of a midnight oil job, but this is the world's biggest break for me and everyone in the workroom is on standby to pull out all the stops to give you what you want.' Then, 'Besides, since you're not actually going to be walking up the aisle in it—at least not this week—it wouldn't actually matter if there was a strategic tack or pin in place for the photographs, would it?'

'That rather depends where you put the pins!'

'Forget the pins. Come on,' she urged. 'This is fantasy time! Indulge yourself, Sylvie. Dream a little. Dream a lot. Give me something I can work with...'

Those kind of dreams would only bring her heartache, but this was important for Geena and she made a determined effort to play along.

'Actually, the truth is not especially indulgent,' she said with a rueful smile. 'Or terribly helpful. I did the fantasy for real when I was nineteen. On that occasion the plan was to wear my great-grandmother's wedding dress.'

'Really? Gosh, that's so romantic.'

Yes, well, nineteen was an age for romance. She knew better now...

'So, let's see. We're talking nineteen-twenties? Ankle-bone length? Dropped waist? Lace?' She took out a pad and did a quick sketch. 'Something like that?'

'Pretty much,' she said, impressed. 'That's lovely.'

'Thank you.' Then, shaking her head. 'You are so lucky. How many people even know what their great-grandmother was wearing when she married, let alone still have the dress? You *have* still got it?'

About to shake her head, explain, Sylvie realised that it was probably just where she'd left it. After all, nothing else seemed to have been touched.

But that was a step back to a different life. A different woman.

'I'm supposed to be displaying your skills, Geena,' she said. 'Giving you a showcase for your talent. A vintage gown wouldn't do that.'

'You're supposed to be giving the world your personal fantasy,' Geena reminded her generously. 'Although, unless it's been stored properly, it's likely to be moth-eaten and yellowed. Not quite what *Celebrity* are expecting for their feature. And, forgive me for mentioning this, but I don't imagine your great-grandmother was—how do they put it?—in an "interesting condition" when she took that slow walk up the aisle.'

'True.' The dress had been stored with care and when she'd been nineteen it had been as close to perfect as it was possible for a dress to be. Life had moved on. She was a different woman now and, pulling a face, she said, 'Rising thirty and pregnant, all that virginal lace would look singularly inappropriate.'

'Actually, I've got something rather more grown-up in mind for you,' she replied. 'Something that will go with those shoes.

But I'd really love to see your grandmother's dress, if only out of professional interest.'

'I'll see what I can do.'

'Great. Now, hold still and I'll run this tape over you and take some measurements so that we can start work on the toile.'

CHAPTER SIX

MARK HILLIARD didn't say a word when Tom joined him, but then they'd known one another for a long time. A look was enough.

'I'm sorry about that. As you may have realised, there's a bit of...tension.'

'Sackcloth and ashes? If that's tension, I wouldn't like to be around when you declare open war.' Mark's smile was thoughtful. 'To be honest, it sounded more like—'

'Like what?' he demanded, but the man just held up his hands and shook his head. But then, he didn't have to say what he was thinking. It was written all over his face. 'It was a business matter,' he said abruptly. Which was true. 'Nothing else.' Which was not.

Sackcloth and ashes.

That wasn't like any business dispute he'd ever been involved in. It was more like an exchange between two people who couldn't make up their minds whether to throttle one another or tear each other's clothes off.

Which pretty much covered it. At least from his viewpoint, except that he hadn't wanted to feel that way about anyone. Out of control. Out of his mind. Racked with guilt...

She had clearly wasted no time in putting him out of her mind. But he could scarcely blame her for that. He'd walked away, hadn't written, hadn't called, then messed up by asking his secretary to send her a cheque for the full amount of her account. Paid in full. No wonder she'd sent the money back.

And then, when he'd been ready to fall at her feet, grovel, it had been too late.

But six months hadn't changed a thing. Sylvie Smith still got to him in ways that he didn't begin to understand.

And he was beginning to suspect, despite the fact that she was expecting a baby with her childhood sweetheart—and he tried not to think about how long that relationship had been in existence, whether it was an affair with her that had wrecked the new Earl's marriage—it was the same for her.

The truth of the matter was that, even in sackcloth, she would have the ability to bring him to meltdown. Which was a bit like getting burned and then putting your hand straight back in the fire.

But as she'd stood there while that crazy female went on about the village church, about walking up the aisle, about someone standing at the altar—about *him* standing at the altar—he'd seen it all as plainly as if he'd been there. Even the light streaming through a stained glass window and dancing around her hair, staining it with a rainbow of colours.

He'd seen it and had wanted to be there in a way he'd never wanted that five-act opera of a wedding, unpaid advertising in the gossip magazines for Miss Sylvie Duchamp Smith that Candy had been planning.

A small country church with the sweet scent of violets that even out here seemed to cling to him instead of some phoney show-piece. A commitment that was *real* between two people who were marrying for all the right reasons.

So real, in fact, that he'd come within a heartbeat of reaching out a hand to her.

Maybe Pam was right. He should go back to London until this was all over. Except he knew it wouldn't help; at least here he would be forced to witness her making plans for her own wedding. The 'blooming' bride. Blooming, glowing…

Euphemisms.

The word was *pregnant*.

If nothing else did it, that fact alone should force him to get a grip on reality.

Realising that Mark was looking at him a little oddly, he turned abruptly and began to walk towards the outbuildings.

'Let's take a look at the coach house and stable block,' he said briskly.

Pregnant.

'I think we could probably get a dozen accommodation units out of the buildings grouped around the courtyard,' Mark said, falling in beside him.

'That sounds promising. What about the barn?'

'There are any number of options open to you there. It's very adaptable. In fact, I did wonder if you'd like to convert it into your own country retreat. There's a small private road and, with a walled garden, it would be very private.'

If it had been anywhere else, he might have been tempted. But Longbourne Court was now a place he just wanted to develop for maximum profit so that he could eradicate it from his memory, along with Sylvie Smith.

The last thing Sylvie had done before she'd left Longbourne Court was to pack the wedding dress away where it belonged, in a chest in the attic containing the rest of her great-grandmother's clothes.

Not wanted in this life.

It was going to be painful to see it again. To touch it. Feel the connection with that part of her which had been packed away with the dress.

Always supposing the chests and trunks were still there.

There was only one way to find out, but Longbourne Court was no longer her home; she couldn't just take the back stairs that led up to the storage space under the roof and start rootling around without as much as a by-your-leave.

But as soon as she'd talked to Josie, reassured herself that everything was running smoothly in her real life, she went in search of Pam Baxter, planning to clear it with her. Get it over with while Tom McFarlane was still safely occupied with the architect.

She'd seen him from the window. Had watched him walking down to the old coach house with Mark Hilliard.

He'd shaved since their last encounter. Changed. The sweater was still cashmere, but it was black.

Like his mood.

And yet he'd had a smile for Geena. The real thing. No wonder the woman had been swept away.

It had been that kind of smile.

The dangerous kind that stirred the blood, heated the skin, brought all kinds of deep buried longings bubbling to the surface.

Not that he'd needed a smile to get that response from her. He'd done it with no more than a look.

But then there had been that look, that momentary connection across Geena's head when, for a fleeting moment, she'd felt as if it were just the two of them against the world. When, for a precious instant, she'd been sure that everything was going to be all right.

No more than wishful thinking, she knew, as she watched a waft of breeze coming up from the river catch at his hair. He dragged his fingers through it, pushing it back off his face before glancing back at the house, at the window of the morning room, as if he felt her watching him.

Frowning briefly before he turned and walked away, leaving Mark to trail in his wake.

She slumped back in the chair, as if unexpectedly released from some crushing grip, and it took all her strength to stand up, to go and find Pam.

The library door was open and when she tapped on it, went in, she discovered the room was empty.

She glanced at her watch, deciding to give it a couple of minutes, crossing without thinking to the shelves, running her hand over the spines of worn, familiar volumes. Everything was exactly as she'd left it. Even the family bible was on its stand and she opened it to the pages that recorded their family history. Each birth, marriage, death.

The blank space beneath her own name for her marriage, her children—that would always remain empty.

The last entry, her mother's death, written in her own hand. After all her mother had been through, that had been so cruel. So unfair. But when had life ever been fair? she thought, looking at the framed photograph standing by itself on a small shelf above the bible.

It was nothing special. Just a group of young men in tennis flannels, lounging on the lawn in front of a tea table on some long ago summer afternoon.

She wasn't sure how long she'd been standing there, hearing the distant echo of her great-grandfather's voice as he'd repeated their names, a roll-call of heroes, when some shift in the air, a prickle at the base of her neck, warned her that she was no longer alone.

Not Pam. Pam would have spoken as soon as she'd seen her.

'Checking up on me, Mr McFarlane?' she asked, not looking round, even when he joined her. 'Making sure I'm not getting too comfortable?'

'Who are these people?' he asked, his voice grating as, ignoring the question, he picked up the photograph and made a gesture with it which—small though it was—managed to include the portraits that lined the stairs, the upper gallery, that hung over fireplaces.

She waited, anticipating some further sarcasm, but when she didn't answer he looked up and for a moment she saw genuine curiosity.

'Just family,' she said simply.

'Family?' He looked as if he would say something more and she held her breath.

'Yes?' she prompted, but his eyes snapped back to the photograph.

'Didn't they have anything better to do than play games?' he demanded. 'Laze about at tea parties?'

Her turn to frown. Something about the photograph disturbed him, she could see, but she couldn't let him get away with that dismissive remark.

Laying a finger on the figure of a young man who was smiling, obviously saying something to whoever was taking the photograph, she said, 'This is my great-uncle Henry. He was twenty-one when this was taken. Just down from Oxford.' She moved to the next figure. 'This is my great-uncle George. He was nineteen. Great-uncle Arthur was fifteen.' She leaned closer so that her shoulder touched his arm, but she ignored the *frisson* of danger, too absorbed in the photograph to heed the warning. 'That's Bertie. And David. They were cousins. The same age as Arthur. And this is Max. He'd just got engaged to my great-aunt Mary. She was the one holding the camera.'

'And the boy in the front? The joker pulling the face?'

'That's my great-grandfather, James Duchamp. He wasn't quite twelve when this was taken. He was just short of his seventeenth birthday four years later when the carnage that they call The Great War ended. The only one of them to survive, marry, raise a family.'

'It was the same for every family,' he said abruptly.

'I know, Mr McFarlane. Rich and poor of all nations died together by the million in the trenches.' She looked up. 'There were precious few tennis parties for anyone after this was taken.'

Tom McFarlane stared at the picture, doing his best to ignore the warmth of her shoulder against his chest, the silky touch of a strand of hair that had escaped her scarf as it brushed against his cheek.

'For most people there never were any tennis parties,' he said as, incapable of moving, physically distancing himself from her, he did his best to put up mental barriers. Then, in the same breath, 'Since we appear to be stuck under the same roof for the next week, it might be easier if you called me Tom. It's not as if we're exactly strangers.' Tearing them down.

'I believe that's exactly what we are, Mr McFarlane,' she replied, cool as the proverbial cucumber. 'Strangers.'

He nodded, acknowledging the truth of that. The lie of it. 'Nevertheless,' he persisted and she glanced up, her look giving the lie to her words as she met his gaze, as if searching for something... 'Just to save time,' he added.

'To save time?'

She didn't quite shrug, didn't quite smile—or only in self-mockery, as if she'd hoped for something more. What, for heaven's sake? Hadn't she got enough?

'Very well,' she said. 'Tom it is. On the strict understanding that it's just to save time. But you are going to have to call me Sylvie. My time may not be as valuable as yours, but it's in equally short supply.'

'I think I can manage that. Sylvie.'

Divorced from 'Duchamp' and 'Smith', the name slipped over his tongue like silk and he wanted to say it again.

Sylvie.

Instead, he cleared his throat and focused on the photograph.

'Why is this here?' he asked. 'Didn't you want it?' Then, because if this had been a photograph of his family, he would never have let it go, 'It's part of your family history.'

Sylvie took the photograph from him. Laid her hand against the cold glass for a moment, her eyes closed, remembering.

'When the creditors moved in,' she said after a moment, 'all I was allowed to take were my clothes and a few personal possessions. The pearls I was given by my grandfather for my eighteenth birthday. And my car, although they insisted on checking the log book to make sure it was in my name before they let me drive away.'

It should have mattered. But by then nothing had mattered...

'You'll understand if I save my sympathy for the people who were owed money.'

She looked up at him. So solid. So successful. So scornful.

'You needn't be concerned for the little men,' she said. 'We always paid our bills. Our problems were caused by two lots of death duties in three years and the fact that my grandfather, after a lifetime of a somewhat relaxed attitude to expenditure, had decided to think of the future, the family and, on the advice of someone he trusted, had become a Lloyds "name" a couple of years before everything went belly-up.'

A fact which, when he realised what it meant, had certainly contributed to the heart attack that had killed him and, indirectly, to the death of her mother.

'The irony of the situation is that if he'd carried on throwing parties and letting the future take care of itself we'd all have been a lot better off,' she added.

'But this photograph doesn't have any value,' he protested. 'Beyond historical interest. Sentimental attachment.'

'Yes, well, they did say that once a complete inventory had been taken I would be allowed to come back, take away family things that had no intrinsic value. But then a world-famous rock star who'd visited the house as a boy was seized by a mission to conserve the place in aspic as a slice of history.'

Tom McFarlane made a sound that suggested he was less than impressed.

'I know. More money than sense, but he made an offer that the creditors couldn't refuse and, since he was prepared to pay a very large premium for his pleasure, he got it all. Family photographs, portraits, all the junk in the attic. Even Mr and Mrs Kennedy, the housekeeper and man of all work, were kept on as caretakers, so it wasn't all bad news.'

'Could they do that? Sell everything?'

'Who was to stop them? I didn't have any money to fight for the rights to my family history and, even if I did, the only people to benefit would have been the lawyers. This way everything was settled. Was preserved.'

And she'd been able to move on, make another life instead of every day being reminded of things she'd rather forget.

Jeremy putting off the wedding—just until things had settled down. Her mother's determination to confront the people who were draining everything out of her family home. Her father... No, she refused to waste a single thought on him.

'I'd moved into a flat share with two other girls by then and had barely enough room to hang my clothes, let alone the family portraits.' She took the photograph from him and replaced it on the shelf where it had been all her life. All her mother's life. All her grandfather's life too. 'Besides, you're right. This isn't just my history. As you said, it was the same for everyone.'

Had he really said that? he wondered as he looked around him.

Longbourne Court was a gracious minor stately home, but from the moment he'd walked through the door Tom had recognised it for what it was. A *family* home. A place where generations of the same family had lived, cradle to grave, each putting their mark on it.

It wasn't just the portraits or the trees in the parkland. It was the scuffs and wear, the dips in the floorboards where countless feet had walked, the patina of polish applied by a hundred different hands. Scratches where dogs had pawed at doors, raced across ancient oak floors.

He realised that Sylvie was frowning, as if his question was beyond her. And it was, of course. How could she know what it was like to have no one? No photographs. No keepsakes.

'Not everyone has memories, a place in history, Sylvie.'

'No memories?' He hadn't mentioned himself and yet she seemed to instantly catch his meaning. 'No family?' Then, 'How dreadful for you, Tom. I'm so sorry.'

She said the words simply, sincerely, his name warm upon her lips. And, for the second time that day, Tom regretted the impulse to speak first and think afterwards. Betraying something within him that he kept hidden, even from himself.

'I don't need your pity,' he said sharply.

'No?' Maybe she recognised the danger of pressing it and, no doubt trained from birth in the art of covering conversational *faux pas,* she quickly moved away and, looking around, said, 'I was hoping to find Pam. I don't suppose you know where she is?'

'Why? What do you want her for? If you're in a hurry, maybe I can help.'

She hesitated, clearly reluctant to say, which no doubt meant it had something to do with this wretched Wedding Fayre. He thought he was hard-nosed when it came to business, but using her own wedding as a promotional opportunity seemed cold even to him.

But, choosing to demonstrate that he was quite as capable as her when it came to covering the awkward moment—at least when he wasn't causing them—he said, 'The truth is I was looking for you in order to apologise for my "sackcloth and ashes" remark. It was inexcusable.'

'On the contrary. You had every excuse,' she said quickly. 'I really should have made more of an effort to stop Geena before she got totally carried away.'

'You might as well have tried to stop a runaway train.'

'True, but even so—'

'Forget it,' he said. 'I should have done it myself, preferably without the crash barrier technique. I'm not normally quite so socially inept, but I'm sure you will understand that you were the last person I expected to see at Longbourne Court.'

And, confronted with the growing evidence of her impending motherhood which, two months on from seeing her on the cover of that hideous magazine, was now obvious, he was trying hard not to think about just how pregnant she was.

Trying not to wonder just how soon after that lost moment with him she'd found the man she wanted to spend the rest of her life with. Someone who was a world away from him. Someone she'd known for ever...

'That makes two of us,' she said. 'You were the very last person I expected to see. Candy told me you disliked the country.'

'I dislike certain aspects of the country. Hunting, shooting,' he added.

'Me too. My great-grandfather banned all field sports from the estate. He said there had been too much killing...' She paused for a heartbeat and then said, 'You did get my letter?'

He nodded and turned away. He should apologise, explain that he hadn't meant it the way she'd taken it. She'd earned every penny of her fee. But what would be the point?

In truth, six months spent thinking about what had happened, about her—whether he'd wanted to or not—had left him with a very clear understanding of his responsibility for what had happened.

He'd known what he was doing when he'd called her to his office.

Had known what he was doing when he'd kept her there, forcing her to go through that wretched account, when, in truth, it had meant nothing to him.

Convinced that she had somehow sabotaged his future, he'd wanted to punish her. The truth was he'd sabotaged his own plans, had become more and more distant from Candy as the wedding had grown nearer, using the excuse of work when the only thing on his mind had been that moment when he'd walked into Sylvie Smith's office and she'd looked up and the smile had died on her lips…

And he'd blamed her for that too.

Then, for just a moment, instead of being a man and woman locked in an ongoing argument, they had been fused, as one, and the world had, briefly, made complete sense—until he'd seen the tears spilling down her cheeks and had known, without the need for words, that he'd got it wrong, that he'd made the biggest mistake of his life.

What good would it do to say any of that now? She had her life mapped out and to tell her how he felt would only make her feel worse. Better that she should despise him than feel sorry for him.

'I'm sorry,' he said. 'For everything.'

She turned away, a faint blush of pink staining her cheeks as, no doubt, like him, she was reliving a moment that had fired not just the body, but something deeper—the mindless heat of two people so lost to sense that nothing could have stopped them.

Or maybe he was just hoping it was that. It was, in all likelihood, plain guilt.

The fact that just six months later she was visibly pregnant with another man's child demonstrated that as nothing else could and he'd done his level best to forget her.

From the first moment he'd set eyes on her he'd done his best to put her out of his mind.

That he'd felt such an immediate, powerful attraction to this woman at their first meeting when Candy, the woman he was about to marry, was standing next to him, had been bad enough and he'd kept his distance, had avoided anything to do with the wedding plans. Had buried himself in work and done his best to avoid thinking about her at all.

He'd made a fair fist of it until she'd waved her presence in front of him with that damned invoice.

If she hadn't added that handwritten 'Personal' to the envelope—no doubt in an attempt to save him embarrassment—his PA would have opened it, dealt with it, would have put through the payment without even troubling him.

Instead, it had been left on his desk to catch him on the raw when he'd opened it. Raw, angry, he had been determined to look her in the eye and challenge her. Challenge himself.

Well, he'd won. And lost.

Twice. Because, face to face with her now, he knew that she was the one. The One.

Then, because that was the last thing he wanted to think about, he said, 'What did you want Pam for?'

She stared at him for a moment, then raised a hand, swiping at the air as if to clear away something he couldn't see, then crossed distractedly to the desk as if she might find her.

'I just wanted to ask her if I could go up into the attics to look for something that belonged to my great-grandmother. To borrow for a little while.'

'Your great-grandmother?' he repeated, grateful for the distraction. 'How long has it been there?'

'Since I put there. Before I left.' She turned back to face him. 'Unless you've already started to clear things?' She made it sound as if he was destroying something beyond price.

Maybe, for her, he was.

'Apart from instructing Mark Hilliard to put in an application for outline planning, I've done nothing,' he assured her, 'and, as far as I can tell from my tour of the place with Mark this morning, nothing appears to have been touched.'

'Oh. Well, that's hopeful.'

She'd begun to soften as they'd talked about her family and for a moment he'd forgotten the barrier between them as, apparently, had she. It was back in place now and it wasn't that edgy barrier with which she'd fought the attraction between them but something colder. Angrier.

'Was this the great-grandmother who married the boy in the photograph?' he asked, using what he'd learned about her. That people, her family, were more important than possessions. Hoping, against all reality, to draw her back to him.

'James. Yes. The other lot, the Smiths, were a soldiering clan so they were constantly on the move and by comparison travelled light.'

She said it dismissively, clearly not a big fan of the Smiths. She hadn't wanted her father at her wedding, at least not walking her down the aisle, he remembered. What was that about?

'From the clutter upstairs, I'd say that's probably a good thing,' he said, making no comment. Then, as if he didn't have another thing in the world to occupy him, 'Do you want to take a look up there now?'

'It is a bit urgent,' she said and glanced, a touch helplessly, at Pam's desk. 'Will Pam be back soon?'

'Not in time to be of any help to you.' For a moment he waited, his intention to make her ask for his help, to need him just once, but his curiosity got the better of him and, more interested in her urgent desire to examine the contents of an old trunk than in scoring points, he stood back and, inviting her to lead the way, said, 'Shall we go?'

Neither of them moved, both remembering the last time he'd said those words.

Then, abruptly, Sylvie said, 'There's really no need to bother yourself.' Which did nothing to allay his curiosity. 'Honestly. I know the way.'

'I'm sure you do, Sylvie, but it's no bother,' he assured her. 'I'm going to have to clear the attics very shortly and it will be useful to have someone who can tell me what, exactly, is up there before it gets tossed into a skip.'

'You wouldn't!' she declared, her eyes widening in a flash of anger. So Miss Sylvie Duchamp Smith wasn't quite as detached about her family's belongings—even the ones left to rot in the attics—as she would have him believe.

'I might,' he said carelessly. 'One family's treasures are another man's junk.'

'No doubt,' she said, that quick flash of fire back under control.

'Unless you can prove me wrong.'

'It's your junk. You must do with it as you wish.'

'True.' But having her acknowledge that fact gave him rather less pleasure than he'd anticipated which was, perhaps, why he said, 'I should warn you that it's pretty dusty up there so you might want to change your shoes. It would be a pity to spoil them.'

'What?' She looked down, let slip a word that somehow didn't sound quite as shocking when spoken in those crisp consonants, perfectly rounded vowels.

'Is there a problem?' he enquired.

'Yes!' Then she wiggled her toes and, with an unexpected smile that turned the silvery-blue to the colour of a summer sky, she looked up and added, 'And, then again, no. It just means that, having worn them most of the morning, I'm going to have to buy them.'

'Is that a problem?' he asked, recalling Pam's earlier comments on the subject. 'I understood shoe-buying was the antidote to all feminine ills.'

'You shouldn't believe everything that Candy told you,' she snapped. 'And I'm not here for recreational shopping.'

'No?' Obviously wedding planning was her livelihood but, even so, he'd have thought she'd have been a little less matter-of-fact about it. 'I thought that was what weddings were invented for.'

'If you believe that, Tom, I suggest you familiarise yourself with the words of the marriage service,' Sylvie said, regarding him with a long cool look that made him wish he'd kept his mouth shut. Then, with an unexpected blush, she shook her head and said, 'The truth is that this wedding is more about recreational borrowing. But once you've worn the shoes, they're yours.'

'You'll never regret it,' he said, finding it easier to look at her feet than her face.

'I will if I don't change them. Why don't you go on and I'll catch you up?' she suggested, losing the tigerish protectiveness she'd shown when she'd thought he was prepared to throw the contents of all those trunks away. That touch of hauteur when she'd chastised him for his lack of respect for the marriage service. Instead, snapping back into a defensive attitude as she turned and walked quickly away, not waiting for him to answer her.

He did anyway, murmuring, 'No hurry,' as, for the second time that morning, he watched her retreat as fast as her pretty purple shoes would carry her. 'I might get lost.'

Too late. He already was.

CHAPTER SEVEN

SYLVIE took a few moments to splash water on her face. Regain her composure.

She shouldn't have asked him. She'd promised, but she had to be sure. She didn't want to believe him so incapable of feeling...

She blew her nose, tucked a wayward strand of hair back into her scarf. Regarded her reflection in the glass. 'Serves you right, my girl,' she said, then laid her hand against her waist. 'Be thankful for what you've got.'

And with that she changed into sensible shoes and rejoined Tom McFarlane at the foot of the stairs. Neither of them spoke but she was intensely conscious of him at her side, then at her back as she led the way up the last flight of narrow stairs to the attics.

Why on earth had he waited?

It wasn't as if he didn't know the way...

She reached for the light switch but he was a fraction faster and, as their hands connected, her mind was filled with the image of long fingers holding his pen, ticking off invoice after invoice, on that endless afternoon. The memory of their strength as he'd lifted her down from the van, the way they'd felt against her skin.

Demanding, tormenting, sensitive...

'I've got it,' he said pointedly and she yanked her hand back as if stung.

The tension between them was drawn so tight that she half expected the bulb to blow as he switched it on, but only the dust burned as, throwing a dim glow over the abandoned detritus of generations of Duchamp lives, it began to heat up.

'Good grief!' she said, more as a distraction than a genuine exclamation of surprise as she glanced around. 'What a mess!'

'I thought that was the general rule with attics? That they were a dumping ground?'

'Well, yes, but it helps if it's an ordered dumping ground.' Which it had been, mostly, and she'd hoped to be able to go straight to her grandmother's chest, grab the dress and run.

No matter what he'd said, or what she'd promised, she knew that spending any time up here picking over family history with Tom McFarlane would only underline the painful truth that he did not want to be part of it.

She'd asked him outright and he couldn't have made it plainer that he didn't want to know. Fine. Her only concern had been that he should know that he was about to become a father so that he could make a choice.

Well, he'd made it.

The last thing she wanted in her little girl's life was a father who didn't care about her. Better to stick with the myth of the sperm 'donor'. At least that way she would know she was totally wanted by her mother. Could believe that she had been planned. A joy.

That was real enough.

All she wanted to do now was get this *Celebrity* feature over and done with so that she could leave Longbourne Court and Tom McFarlane behind. Especially Tom McFarlane.

He was not good for her peace of mind under any circumstances and up here, alone, under the eaves with the belongings of generations of her family, the feeling was oddly intensified because, whether he wanted to be or not, he *was* part of it now, part of her family, no matter how much he despised them all.

'The trunks used to be lined up around the room so that you could get at them,' she explained, doing her best to keep this businesslike. 'Tidily.'

Looking around, it was obvious that things had been moved about in the recent past. Long enough ago for dust to have covered the clean spaces, but months rather than years.

'I imagine any number of surveyors have moved them over the years so that they could check out the fabric of the roof,' Tom said.

That it was an eminently reasonable suggestion did not make her feel any better.

'Yours being the latest, no doubt,' she snapped. 'Well, they should have jolly well put them back where they found them.'

'Maybe this *is* where they found them,' he pointed out, 'but I'll be sure to pass on your criticism.'

'Well…good,' she replied, lifting the lid of the trunk nearest to her, as if satisfied. Then reeled back.

'Good grief, what's that smell?'

'Camphor,' she said, flapping at the air to disperse the fumes, but only succeeding in stirring up the dust and making things worse. 'To keep away the moths,' she said, choking from the combination, 'which would otherwise have feasted…' she gasped for air '…on all this fine wool suiting.'

'And not just the moths. That smell would keep away anybody who ever thought about wearing them,' he assured her. Then, with concern, 'Are you all right? Is this okay? It won't affect the…'

The word didn't make it out of his mouth.

'Baby,' she snapped, still coughing. 'It's not a dirty word.'

'No. I'm sorry.'

'So you said.' If he'd been any stiffer he'd have cracked in two, she thought. 'But I'm not, so that's okay, isn't it?'

He closed the trunk. 'I'm happy for you,' he said, turning away to open a second trunk.

That was it? She thought the camphor had made her gasp but his carelessness left her mouthing the air like a fish out of water.

Could he really be so…indifferent?

'This is better,' he said as, with a complete lack of concern, he held out an old tinplate truck for her to see. The kind of toy that might have belonged to one of the youths in the photograph and was now worth a considerable amount of money. Then he picked up a teddy bear, dressed as a clown, which was worth a great deal more. He offered it to her. 'You'd have been better to have left your clothes behind and taken this.'

'Chance would have been a fine thing,' she said, taking it from him, feeling for the button in the ear.

Even the vintage wedding dress had been part of the estate according to the emotionless men who'd moved in to make an inventory of contents, watching her like hawks to make sure she didn't pack anything more valuable than her underwear. They'd actually taken apart the framed photograph of her mother before she'd packed it, just to be sure that nothing valuable was secreted behind the picture.

She hadn't argued with them. She'd been beyond making a scene, couldn't even be bothered to put the photograph back in the frame, but had abandoned that along with the rest of her life.

What did a picture frame matter? Or an old wedding dress, for that matter, when her groom had put the ceremony on hold until everything had been 'sorted out'. As if it ever could be.

What on earth was she doing up here looking for it now? This wasn't moving on. This was just wallowing in the past. Something you did when you had no future. She was carrying her future in her womb. His future too.

'It's definitely a Steiff,' she said, handing it back to him. 'And, because it's been shut away, the colours haven't faded, which will increase the value. I'd advise you to be very careful before you toss any of this stuff into a skip. Who knows, on a good day at auction, you might even recoup the cost of your wedding. Wouldn't that be ironic?' she pushed, desperate for a reaction of any kind.

The only indication that he'd heard was the slightest tightening of his jaw as he turned away from her.

'Is this what you're looking for?' he asked after opening another trunk to reveal more clothes, this time layered in tissue. Then, 'No camphor?' He glanced across at her. 'Don't moths attack women's clothes?'

Sylvie sighed and let it go, looking across at the chest Tom had opened. 'That's a sandalwood chest,' she said, wriggling between a couple of battered trunks to squeeze into the tiny space beside him without touching him. 'Natural moth proofing.'

Her attempt at avoidance was brought to naught by the fact that her centre of gravity had shifted and, despite the sensible shoes, she wobbled against him. In an instant his hand was around what had once been her waist and he was holding her safe. Just as he had once before.

For a moment their gazes seemed to lock, all breathing to cease, and it was that moment in the garage all over again.

'Okay?' he asked softly; his eyes in the dim light seemed to be dulled with anguish. It was just her imagination, she told herself. Or the dust...

She forced herself to turn away, look at the trunk, the dress, lying in its layers of snowy tissue.

'Oh...' Then, 'Yes...'

And the dust—or something—caught in her throat as she lifted her hand first to her lips, then out to touch the tissue paper. Curling her fingers back when she saw the state of them.

'What is it?' he asked.

'It's, um, just a dress...'

She'd wrapped it in tissue and returned it to the chest that contained her great-grandmother's clothes. The special ones. The ones she couldn't bear to part with. Designer gowns from Balenciaga, Worth, Chanel. Silk and velvet. Accessories from the art deco period. Bags, buckles, shoes. Even lingerie.

'My great-grandmother was very stylish. Very elegant. A bit of a trend-setter in her day,' she said with forced brightness. She must not cry. They were just things... 'They should have gone to the Melchester museum for their costume department. My mother had it on her list of things to do.' She blinked. No tears... 'You always think there's so much time...' Then, not wanting to think about that, she turned to him. 'What happened to your family?'

It was hard to say which of them was more shocked. Tom McFarlane, that she'd had the temerity to ask the question. Or her, for having dared pose it.

'I have no family,' he said without expression.

'That's not true!' And her hands flew protectively to the child at her waist, as if to cover her ears.

Not any more.

And she wanted to reach out, take his hand and place it on their growing child so that he could feel what it meant. Would understand.

'That's the way I like it,' he said, his expression so forbidding that, instead, she flinched. And then, before she could gather herself, speak, he gestured towards the tissue-wrapped dress in a manner that made it plain that the matter was closed.

'What's so special about this dress?'

After a long silence she turned to the trunk and, having rubbed her hands against the seat of her trousers to remove the dust, she unfolded the tissue to reveal the long lace veil.

Tom stared at the exquisite lace for a moment before turning to her and saying, 'Why am I surprised?' Then, 'Is this for your wedding?'

'Oh, please! I don't think the virginal veil is quite me, do you?' she asked, pulling a face, mocking herself. Mocking them both. Then, when he made no comment, 'Geena wanted to see it.' She shrugged. 'Embarrassing as it was, the visualisation exercise jarred loose some ideas and I think she has some thought of interpreting this dress for the new maturer, pregnant me. It won't do, of course.'

'Why don't you wait? Until after you've had the baby?'

'*Celebrity*'s copy date is fixed, I'm afraid. It's this weekend or never.' Then, looking up at him, 'Obviously they'll acknowledge that we've used it with your permission.'

'That really won't be necessary,' he replied. 'I've had more than enough of weddings to last me a lifetime. In fact, I'm beginning to feel as if I'm trapped in some nightmarish time-loop in which the word "wedding" is a constantly recurring theme.'

She finally snapped. 'Do you think you're the only one who's ever been stood up days before a wedding?' she demanded. 'Believe me, you'll get over it.'

'I have your guarantee?' Then, 'I'd forgotten. It happened to you too, didn't it?' And when, shocked, she didn't reply, 'I saw a piece about you in *Celebrity*.'

'Oh, that.' She shrugged. 'Yes, well, it was three weeks rather than three days in my case, but who's counting?'

'So tell me, Sylvie, how long did it take you to get over being left at the altar?'

'A great deal longer than you, Tom. Let's face it, you were over it the minute you put your hand up my skirt.'

The minute the words left her mouth, Sylvie regretted them. But she was angry with him, wanted to hurt him as he was hurting her. The pain that she'd felt as a nineteen-year-old, abandoned by the man she'd loved, was a world away from his hurt pride and she refused to indulge him in a session of mutual bonding over their shared experience of being dumped just before the wedding.

But, in her haste to deter his curiosity, she'd made a major mistake. Desperate to stop his thoughts—her thoughts—from dashing off in one direction, she had provoked another, equally powerful memory of that moment, inevitable as a lightning strike, when, compelled by some force outside all the norms of acceptable behaviour, they'd both totally lost it.

The searing heat of his mouth. An intimate and personal touch that had, in an instant, bypassed her will, overridden her mind, stolen everything. And, just for a moment, given her back something she'd thought lost for ever. Given her a lot more...

Equally powerful but without meaning, she reminded herself, even as his eyes seemed to darken, soften in response to the memories she'd so carelessly stirred up, as the electricity in the air raised the tiny hairs on her arms in a shiver of awareness.

She fought it, fought the need for his touch, her yearning for the soft whisper of words that she heard only in her dreams, knowing just how easy it would be to give in to the moment. Easy to say, but he was as close now as he had been then. Close enough that the scent of his wind-blown hair, newly laundered clothes, the faint musk of warm skin overrode the smell of camphor and hot dust.

Much too close.

Even in this dim light she knew her face would betray her thoughts, everything she was feeling, and he needed no more than the tiny betraying whimper of remembered joy, shatteringly loud, in the silence—an open invitation to repeat the experience, just in case his memory needed jogging—for his expression to change from thoughtful to something very different.

'Is that right?' he murmured, tightening his hold, bringing her round to face him so that his mouth was just inches from her own. 'Maybe we should try that again. So that you can explain it to me.'

Not in this world, she thought, but there was no time to object before his lips touched hers, sending a thrill of pleasure—the heat that haunted her dreams—spiralling through her.

'Step...' he said, his hand sliding beneath her long, loose top, cool against her warm skin as he leaned into her, deepening the kiss, and she shivered, but not with cold.

No...

This was wrong.

Stupid.

Inevitable.

Inevitable from the first moment he'd walked into her office. She'd known it. He'd known it. Like iron filings to a magnet. Why else would he—would she—have gone to such lengths to avoid each other? It was the only wedding she'd ever coordinated where the groom had been totally absent.

But inevitable didn't make it—

His tongue stroked her lower lip and every cell in her body responded as if to some unheard command, as if standing on tiptoe, reaching out for more.

'By...'

—right.

'Step...'

Oh... Confetti...

Her knees were water. Another minute and she'd be sprawled over one of the trunks in a rerun of that moment when that instant attraction had overcome every particle of common sense, every lesson that she'd ever learned about the fickleness of the human heart. When the heat had overcome the ice and turned it to steam.

To be overwhelmed, to forget yourself so completely might be excusable once.

Twice...

Her head felt like lead, she didn't have the strength to move it, break contact, but then his hand slid forward on its inevitable journey towards her breast and instead encountered the mound of her belly and, as if drawn to him, her baby girl turned, reached out to him. And he was the one whose head went back as if struck.

For a moment his expression was desolate, empty, but then as if, all along, it had been no more than a demonstration that she was still in his power, his to take or leave as he pleased, he let his hand drop to his side.

'Perhaps not,' he said, but with a touch of self-mockery. She didn't doubt that, as for her, the desire had been real enough, but maybe one of the reasons he was a billionaire was his ability to learn from past mistakes and never repeat them.

'Definitely not,' she said, although her mouth was dry, her voice woolly and not quite as steady as she intended. But, with the help of a steadying breath, she slowly jacked her self-control back into position. 'You don't need a step-by-step instruction manual, Tom McFarlane. You know all the moves.'

'Now, why,' he asked, looking down at her, 'do I get the impression that was not a compliment?'

'I'm sorry, but I really can't help you there,' she said as, with extreme care and ignoring the cold emptiness where for a moment his hand had rested against his growing child, she turned away and scooped up the tissue-wrapped gown, holding it across her arms in front of her. A shield. 'You're just going to have to work that one out for yourself.'

She managed a smile. If she managed to keep it light, to laugh it off as if it were nothing, staying on at Longbourne Court might, just might, be possible for the next few days.

And, pitifully, she didn't want to leave. Not yet. She'd fled in misery ten years earlier. This felt like a second chance to say goodbye properly.

And she hadn't quite given up on her baby's father.

His reaction to the baby's movement beneath his hand suggested he wasn't as immune to the idea of fatherhood as he thought. Maybe if she could somehow make him believe that she did not want anything for herself—convincing herself would be something else—he might find it in his heart to love a daughter, no matter how unexpected.

But not now. Not here. Right now, the only thing on her mind was to put some safe distance between them. Try to recover the little ground she seemed to have made when they'd been in the library.

'If you'll excuse me, I really must get this to Geena,' she said.

'The wedding must come first?'

And she thought she could do irony...

'The wedding *feature* must come first, Tom.' Then, 'Purple shoes. Purple waistcoats. I suspect Geena is already working on yours.'

'You're really going to wear them?' he said, refusing to be drawn in by the waistcoat. 'The shoes.'

'The idea is growing on me,' she admitted. 'What do you think?'

'I think it's the groom's job to colour coordinate with the bride. I also seem to recall that you promised to help me sort out the contents of the attics—'

'I will—'

'—but it seems that now you've found what you wanted you can't wait to escape.'

His tone was disparaging but she smiled nevertheless. His first reaction on seeing her had been to warn her not to get too comfortable. Now he was asking for her help, even though they both knew that auction houses would be falling over themselves for the chance to make an inventory of the contents of the Duchamp attics.

'Actually,' she replied, 'I think the deal was that I'd point out what was up here, but even that's going to take more than half an hour, which is just about all I've got right now.' Then, glancing around because it was safer than looking at him, 'What will you do with it all?'

'Is it any of your business?' he asked, reclaiming a little of the distance he'd briefly surrendered. 'Since it's all mine?'

It was in the nature of a challenge but she didn't rise to it. She'd ceased to think of any of this as hers a long time ago. 'No,' she said, shaking her head. Then, after a moment, 'None at all.'

'You don't mean that,' he said, regarding her through narrowed eyes. 'You want something. The bear? Your grandmother's clothes for the costume museum?'

Was he really capable of tempting her simply for his amusement? Or was his conscience beginning to prick him? There really was no need for him to feel bad about becoming the unwitting owner of the junk her family had stuffed up here.

'Actually, I'd quite like some of them for myself, but that's just self-indulgence,' she assured him.

Some things were lost for ever and you just had to accept it. Live with it.

'Why don't you just leave it all up here?' she suggested.

He shook his head. 'I need the room. Come on, you might as well tell me.'

She looked at him. He seemed serious enough and nothing ventured, nothing gained—she might as well ask for something that could be auctioned off to help the women her mother had cared so much about.

'Nothing for me. Truly. But if you're feeling generous, and since you thought it was all going to be rubbish anyway, maybe you'd consider giving a few things to help raise money for the Pink Ribbon Club?'

Tom McFarlane didn't know what he'd expected. But, surrounded by family treasures that she'd lost, given the opportunity to reclaim some precious memory, it had never occurred to him that she'd ask for something to give away.

'The charity your mother founded? What does it do, actually?'

'It supports women with cancer. And their families. When my mother was going through her treatment, she realised just how fortunate she was.'

'Private treatment? No waiting?'

'Cancer is like war, Tom. There are officers and there are men, but the bullets don't distinguish between them.'

'I'm sorry. That was a cheap shot.'

'Yes, actually, it was.' Then she lifted her shoulders in a barely-there shrug. 'But you're right. She had her chemo in a private room. Had the very best medical attention, every chance to recover. The thing was, Tom, she didn't take it for granted. She knew how lucky she was, which is why she took so much pleasure in being able to give something back.'

'But she still died.'

Pam had attempted to fill him in on some of the background while he'd had breakfast. He'd shut it out, concentrating on what had been happening with various projects he'd left in her more than capable hands when he'd taken to the hills, not on Sylvie Smith's family. But he had picked up the fact that Lady Annika Duchamp Smith was dead.

'Not from cancer. She was driving to London to talk to the bank in an attempt to sort out the mess.' Her gesture took in the attic, but that wasn't the mess she was referring to. 'The weather was bad, she was upset. I should have been with her instead of behaving like a bratty teenager.'

He saw her throat move as she swallowed and it was all he could do to stop himself from reaching out to her, but this time in a gesture of comfort.

Before he could make a total fool of himself—she'd finally got the Earl to provide her with every possible comfort—she gathered herself and said, 'Look, don't worry about it. You've loaned us the house. That's more than generous.' She didn't wait for an answer, but said, 'I have to go.'

'Or course. I mustn't delay you.'

With a wedding to plan and a baby on the way, she had more than enough to keep her occupied.

It wasn't a problem. He'd get someone from one of the auction houses to come and sort through the trunks. Put aside anything of value.

She paused in the doorway, looked back. 'If you like, I'll give you a hand later. If you're planning on staying?'

Was there just a hint of hope in her voice? A fervent wish that he'd make himself scarce and leave her to have the free run of the house, to be cosseted by the old family retainers for a few days so that she could pretend that nothing had changed?

Or was she expecting company?

'I'm staying,' he assured her, crushing it. Then regretted the thought.

Despite their similar backgrounds, she was nothing like Candy, who, it had to be admitted, was shallower than an August puddle.

No doubt she just wanted to forget, wipe from her memory, the moment when she'd clung, whimpering and pleading, to him. And who could blame her for that? Why on earth would she want to remember?

'Maybe, if you have some time to spare later, you could give me some clues as to what I might find,' he suggested.

'Well, there's nothing on television,' she said, 'so you've got yourself a date.' Then, almost as an afterthought, 'But do bring a brighter light bulb so that we can at least see what we're doing.'

She had that natural authority that would have had the serfs leaping to her bidding, he thought. Perfect lady of the manor material. And a smile that would have made them happy to leap.

If he wasn't careful, he'd find himself leaping right along with them.

'I'll ask Mr Kennedy to replace it,' he replied.

Just to make the point, in case she was in danger of forgetting, that this was *his* house and if anyone was going to issue orders in it it would be him.

CHAPTER EIGHT

SYLVIE watched with a certain amount of detachment as Geena and her staff went into raptures over her great-grandmother's wedding dress.

'This is so beautiful, Sylvie!' Geena said, examining the lace. The workmanship. 'French couturier?'

'Undoubtedly,' she said. 'Great-grandma Clementine started out as she meant to go on. But it's a dress for a very young bride. She was barely nineteen when she married my great-grandfather.'

She managed a shrug, as if such a thing was unbelievable.

'I agree. I've designed something much more sophisticated for you. Flowing, loose, since it's a style that suits you so well. No veil, though. I thought a loose-fitting jacket with wide sleeves, turned-back cuffs.'

She proffered her sketches.

Sylvie swallowed. 'It's absolutely gorgeous, Geena. Perfect. What's that in my hair?'

'A small tiara. Nothing over the top,' she added with a grin. 'Since you seem hooked on elegant restraint.'

'I don't know about restraint,' Sylvie said with a wry smile. 'There are the purple shoes.' She gave a little shrug. 'I forgot I was wearing them so I had to buy them.'

'If you believe that, my darling, who am I to contradict you? I'll put in an order for the purple waistcoat then, shall I?'

'Will anything I say stop you?'

'I don't know, give it a try.'

She shook her head.

'Okay, you can leave the tiara to me, if you like. The woman who makes them for me is showing at the Fayre. Can we add a touch of green to the violet? You're not superstitious?'

'No.' She'd done everything by the book the first time and it had still all fallen apart. And this time it was make-believe, so it really didn't matter. 'I'll send you over a colour sample—'

'Don't worry, I'll pick it up when I come over with my final drawings and material swatches for the appliqué first thing in the morning. Be ready to make a decision.'

'I've got the message, but now I really have to love you and leave you because I have an appointment with the caterer, the florist and the confectioner.'

Followed by an evening cosseted with the devil himself, sorting through the discarded ephemera of generations of the Duchamp family.

Not the brightest of decisions, considering the effect he had upon her. She couldn't think what had made her volunteer. Or maybe she could, which was truly dumb, even though he hadn't carried through with this morning's opportunistic pass. Despite the fact that she hadn't done a single thing to discourage him.

Somehow they'd managed to move on without sinking into terminal embarrassment, although only she knew how hard it had been to keep it light, make a joke of it.

Only she knew how torn she was between relief and regret that he'd taken a step back, rescuing her from her runaway hormones.

She might have spent the last six months yearning for the phone to ring, for him to make a move, to suggest they continue where they'd left off, but the truth was that some affairs were doomed from the start. And that was all it would ever have been for him—a tit-for-tat affair to throw oil on the fire of gossip and give him back his pride.

A lesser man would have gone for it without a second thought. Used it to bolster his shattered self-esteem. Used her to strike back.

That he hadn't seemed to prove that Tom McFarlane was made of finer stuff. He didn't need to hurt someone else to make himself feel good. Not even her, even though he couldn't have made it plainer that he despised everything that made her who she was. A reaction which only increased her curiosity about the forces that had shaped his character.

She frowned as she wondered about his lack of family memories.

His meteoric rise from teenage entrepreneur to billionaire was the stuff of legend, but where had that teenager risen from? If he had no family, it would go a long way to explaining his inability to confront emotional issues. His coldness in the face of Candy's desertion. His inability to connect physical love with anything deeper.

Maybe.

But it would have to keep, she told herself with a sigh as she pulled into the caterer's premises, trying to raise her enthusiasm for the latest twist on poached salmon—never a favourite.

'Something smells good,' Sylvie said as she tossed a folder containing menus, photographs of flowers and every style of cake imaginable on to the kitchen table and crossing to the stove where Tom, unbelievably, was beating potato into submission. 'Mrs Kennedy's spiced beef casserole?'

'It's beef and it's a casserole, beyond that I'm not prepared to hazard a guess,' Tom said. 'I'm only responsible for the vegetables.'

He offered her the pan and Sylvie dipped a finger in the

potatoes, licked it and groaned with pleasure. 'Butter, garlic. Real food.'

'There's plenty for two,' he said, apparently amused at her pleasure.

'Are you sure? I'd better warn you that I'm starving.'

'A first. A woman with an appetite,' he said, his smile fading as quickly as it had come. 'But then you're eating for two.'

'Oh, I've never been a fan of lettuce,' she said, too hungry to worry about his sudden loss of interest, instead reaching up to the warming rack above the stove for a couple of plates. 'Where's Mrs Kennedy?' she asked. 'Why isn't she mashing your spuds?'

'She's putting her feet up after being run ragged by the hordes of exhibitors and construction people tramping through the house all day, wanting tea, scones and sandwiches. You are aware that they're eating us out of house and home?'

Us?

Just a figure of speech, no doubt, but it sent a thrill of pleasure rippling through her tired limbs.

'Send the bill to *Celebrity;* this is their party,' she replied and, since emotion was off his radar, doing her best to keep the smile down and the tone chirpy.

'They're picking up the tab for everything?' he asked, glancing at her.

'Peanuts for them. You missed out, Tom. If you'd let them cover your wedding they'd have been stuck with the bill.'

'And filled their pages with the story when Candy made her break. No, thanks. It was enough of a circus already.'

Sylvie grinned. 'You got off lightly, Tom. Last month I organised a wedding where the bride arrived on an elephant—'

'Stop! Stop right there.'

'And you escaped the butterflies…'

'Give me a break,' he said, but he was grinning too.

'Okay. But only because you're being so protective of Mrs Kennedy. Although I bet she had a whale of time with an endless stream of people to fuss over for a change.'

'A stream of people taking advantage.'

'Rubbish. She didn't *have* to make scones. She didn't have to offer them anything. The workmen almost certainly brought flasks and packed lunches with them.'

Tom's only response was a noise that sounded like something a disgruntled bulldog might have made as he spooned some of the rich casserole on to a plate.

'I understood the Fayre was your party,' he said. 'Pink ribbons and all.'

'Okay,' she said, opening a drawer and finding knives and forks for both of them, before pulling out a chair and making herself comfortable at the kitchen table. 'Why don't you send the bill to me and *I'll* send it on to *Celebrity?*' Then, 'And I promise that I won't make you go through it item by item.'

'No?' he said as he put his own plate on the table, holding her attention while he fetched two glasses and a bottle of red wine that was already open. Then, as he looked up and caught her gaze, 'Maybe I'll insist.'

And Sylvie blushed. What an idiot! Anyone would think she was angling for a repeat performance...

Maybe she was.

'But tomorrow they're on their own,' he continued as he pulled out a chair and sat down opposite her.

She cleared her throat. 'Right.' Then, 'Will you tell Mrs Kennedy that you're going to spoil her fun? Or would you like me to do that?'

He shook his head, trying not to smile. 'Just tell her not to overdo it. Meantime,' he said, 'I don't expect her to wait on me.'

'Perish the thought,' she agreed as he filled both glasses

without bothering to ask her whether she wanted wine or not and he looked up, apparently catching the ironic tone.

'What?'

She shrugged. 'Well, I may be wrong,' she said, getting up and fetching a bottle of water from the fridge and another glass, 'but I suspect she's disappointed not to have had the chance to lay out everything in the dining room to show the new "master" what she can do.' Then, as he scowled, presumably at falling into her trap, 'And maybe just a little anxious about their future too. They have a pension—that was ring-fenced—but their cottage has been their home for thirty years.'

'I don't suppose anyone was worrying about that when the bailiffs were in.'

'You suppose wrong. My mother was deeply concerned. As far as she was concerned, they had tenure for life and it was one of the things she hoped to straighten out.' She dismissed that. It was past. 'I'm not trying to get at you, Tom. I'm just telling you how it is.'

For a moment he just stared at her, then he nodded. 'I'll give it some thought.'

'Thank you.' Then, 'Where's Pam tonight? Isn't she hungry?'

'She's taken the opportunity, with my presence, to go back to London for a couple of days to catch up.' He raised an ironic glass in her direction. 'It's just you, me and the ghosts.'

Okay, maybe she'd asked for that with her 'master' crack. He couldn't have made it clearer that he despised the landed gentry and everything they stood for.

Would no doubt enjoy turning this venerable old manor house into a conference centre, the stables into accommodation for bright young executives. Take pleasure in the thought of them being moulded into team leaders as they played paintball war games in the ancient woodland.

And why not?

It was a new era, meritocracy ruled and she should be using this opportunity to demonstrate her own company's experience in the field of conference coordination.

She'd relish the chance to expand her business in that direction.

Whatever Josie thought, she had, like Tom, had enough of weddings to last her a lifetime. And she was losing her taste for celebrity parties too. Maybe it was impending motherhood but she wanted to do something a little more grown-up and meaningful with the rest of her life than think of new ways to spend other people's money. When this week was over she was going to talk to Josie about a partnership, gift her the 'fun' side of the business so that she could concentrate on more serious stuff.

She didn't think that Tom McFarlane would be that impressed if she used the opportunity to pitch for his business, however, so she poured herself a glass of water and, matching his gesture, touched it to his.

'To the ghosts,' she said, 'although I have to warn you that they're all family. Protective of their own.' She swallowed a mouthful of water, put down her glass, then picked up a fork and speared a small piece of tender beef. 'I'll sleep soundly enough tonight,' she lied. How likely was that with him just yards away? 'You, on the other hand, are going to be tearing the place apart and I doubt they'll take kindly to that.'

'Then I'm glad you're here. If they come calling, I'll seek refuge with you.'

She choked as she swallowed the beef. Then, unable to help herself, laughed. 'Why on earth would I protect you?'

'Because this is all your fault.' He gestured around the kitchen with his fork. 'If you'd kept your staff under better control, Candy would have had her country estate and Longbourne Court would have been safe for another fifty years.'

She stared at him, shocked out of her teasing. Her appetite suddenly non-existent. 'You bought this for Candy?'

He didn't answer her question, but just said, 'Do you think she would have thought twice about running off with Quentin if she'd known?'

Sylvie lifted her shoulders and said, 'It was always Candy's declared ambition to marry a millionaire, Tom, and she came close more than once, as I'm sure you know.'

He shrugged. 'She could scarcely deny that there hadn't been a certain amount of history,' he admitted. 'Her romances were always given the full *Celebrity* treatment.'

'As were her break-ups. She had a habit of doing something outrageous, wrecking her chances.'

'So? What are you saying? That I'm the last in a long line to get her very individual style of brush-off?'

She shook her head. 'Not exactly.' She stirred the creamy potato with her fork. 'I always assumed it was because she thought she could do better. Had someone richer, more interesting, more exciting in her sights. But then she had you, Tom, and she still ran.'

The corners of his eyes fanned into a smile. 'I do believe you've just paid me a compliment.'

'I do believe I have,' she replied, matching his smile and raising it. Then, feeling slightly giddy, 'I've been thinking about it ever since I saw them together. When they came home.' The change in her had been extraordinary. 'She didn't leave you for someone richer or more interesting, but for sweet, adorable Quentin. A man without anything very much to offer her except love.'

'And the prospect of a title.'

'He comes from long-lived stock, Tom. No one inherits in that family until they're drawing their pension.'

'Then why?'

'Why did she marry him? I guess she finally found what she'd been looking for all this time. The missing ingredient.'

Tom frowned.

'They were in love,' she said. 'I'm sorry, but hearts trumps diamonds. Love trumps everything.'

'I'm glad for her.' Maybe she didn't look convinced, because he said, 'Truly. We both had what the other wanted, or in her case thought she wanted. But neither of us was ever so lost to reality that we believed we were in love.'

'Reality is a good basis for marriage,' Sylvie assured him, moved at his unexpected generosity. 'There's so much less possibility of disillusion setting in over the honeymoon cornflakes.'

She'd seen the mess that friends—'deeply in love' friends—had made of their marriages.

'It's a great theory but it doesn't take account of the X factor that makes fools of us all.' Then, 'You didn't answer my question.'

'Would Longbourne Court have been enough to carry Candy up the aisle?' She regarded him thoughtfully. 'Do you regret not telling her?'

'There's no right answer to that question.'

'No, but if it helps, I've known Candy since we were both twelve years old and I've never seen her so...*involved*. For what it's worth, I don't think the crown jewels would have swayed her.'

'In that case, I'm glad I didn't tell her.' He clearly didn't have quite the same faith in the power of 'the real thing' as she did. Then, obviously not wanting to pursue the matter, he said, 'How are your wedding plans coming along? Did the dress do the trick?'

'Geena is happy,' she said, not elaborating.

'What about you?'

She lifted her shoulders. 'It's her show and I'm sure the result will be stunning. To be honest, I'm getting to the point where I just want the whole thing over with.'

Tom regarded her steadily. 'Isn't this supposed to be the happiest day of a woman's life? Every fantasy she ever dreamed of?'

'Yes, well, right now, Tom, my fantasy would be to have someone else arranging all the details. I suddenly see the attraction of hiring a wedding planner; I really should have left this to my assistant.' Josie would have been great. 'Unfortunately, she's already handling both our jobs.'

Tom regarded Sylvie with a touch of real concern. There were dark hollows beneath her eyes, at her temples and, despite her assertion that she was starving, she was doing little more than push her food around the plate.

This was all too much for her.

She should be resting, not racing about trying to organise a wedding at a moment's notice when she had a demanding job, a company to run. Where the devil was her 'groom'? The father of her baby? Why wasn't he taking on some of the burden of this?

'If you don't mind me saying so, Sylvie, you don't appear to be enjoying this very much.'

'Believe me, only the fact that I'm supporting a very worthwhile charity induced me to put myself through this.'

He frowned. There was something not quite right about all this, but he couldn't put his finger on it. 'How much did *Celebrity* offer to cover this wedding of yours?'

'Nowhere near enough,' she said, finally breaking into a laugh. 'It doesn't help that it's all at such short notice.' He was staring at her. 'Because of the Wedding Fayre?' she prompted.

Was that it?

Did her Earl, so recently freed from one marriage, think he was being rushed, pressured into another, not just by her pregnancy but to support her charity?

It would take a brave man to ask a soon-to-be bride that particular question and he confined himself to, 'Above and beyond the call of duty, no doubt, but with your experience it must be little more than going through the motions.'

She sighed. 'You'd think so, wouldn't you?' she said, toying with the mash so that he wanted to scoop it up, forkful by forkful, and feed it to her in small comforting bites. 'I've done it hundreds of times for other people. The problem is that I have a reputation to maintain. My "wedding" has got to have that special wow factor,' she said, looking about as 'wowed' as a post-party balloon. 'It's got to be imaginative, different, original.'

'So what's the problem?'

'I need a theme. Normally I have a bride to drive that enthusiasm, feed me with ideas. Too many ideas, sometimes.'

'And you don't have any ideas about what you want for your own wedding?'

'Sad, isn't it?' she said, pulling a face. 'The problem is that I've done all this before. Spent months planning every last detail.'

'Not everyone gets a second chance to get it right.'

'Maybe that's the problem. It was perfect the first time.' She smiled a little sadly. 'Too perfect. I drive Josie crazy demanding she find some tiny flaw, something that went wrong…'

'The Arabs weave tiny mistakes into their carpets in the belief that only God can make things perfect.'

She looked at him, her eyes lit up. 'That's it. That's exactly it… When Jeremy was five and I was in my cradle, our families were already planning a dynastic marriage and like well-behaved children we did the decent thing and fell in love.'

'How convenient.'

'You think we were just talked into it?' she asked, less than amused. 'In love with the idea?'

'I may think that but I wouldn't dare make the mistake of saying so,' Tom hurriedly assured her.

'Of course you would. You just did. But honestly, it couldn't have been more perfect. Then my grandfather died, the creditors moved in and the wedding was put on hold.'

Then her mother had died too. While she was behaving like a bratty teen because she'd been dumped by the man she'd loved—his entire family—because they didn't want to be connected to the disaster.

'And Jeremy?' he asked. 'What happened to him?' Because something evidently had.

'Oh, he was offered a transfer abroad by his company.'

'That would be Hillyer's Bank?'

'It would.'

'Convenient. I imagine he was shipped out of harm's way so that the relationship could die a natural death.'

'Cynic.'

'But right.'

Money and land marrying money and land. He suspected that the only one who had been totally innocent was Sylvie—much too young to cope with a world of hurt. Without thinking, he reached out and wrapped his fingers around hers.

Startled, she looked up and he saw her swallow, blink back tears that she'd let flow in the aftermath of lovemaking. And, just as he had been then, he was overwhelmed with a sense of helplessness. 'I'm sorry, Sylvie,' he said, removing his hand from hers, picking up his glass, although he didn't drink from it.

'Don't be.'

No. She'd got her happy ending. Ten years late, but it had all come right in the end for her. So why were her eyes still shining with unshed tears?

How many had she wasted already on a man who was so clearly not worth a single one?

'Marriage is for better or worse and we were far too young, too immature, to handle the "worse",' she said, as if she had to explain. 'At least this way we didn't become just another statistic.'

'There's an up side to everything,' he said. 'So they say.' Even the cruellest wounds scarred over with time and Jeremy Hillyer, newly elevated to his earldom, had finally returned to claim his childhood sweetheart. And, before he could stop himself, Tom found himself saying, 'Is there anything I can do to help?'

'Excuse me?'

She might well look surprised. He'd hardly been the most welcoming of hosts.

But then, having always considered love to be just another four-letter word, he appeared to have been sideswiped by feelings that wouldn't go away. That just got deeper, more intense the more he'd tried to evade them.

It seemed that the man with a reputation for never letting an opportunity slip his grasp had, in the biggest deal of his life, missed his chance.

'With the wedding?' he said.

'You're kidding?' And, out of the blue, she laughed. A full-bodied, joyful laugh that lit up her eyes as the sun lit the summer sky. Then, 'Oh, right, I get it. You think if you can hurry things along I'll be out of your hair all the quicker.'

'You've got me,' he said, even though it had, in fact, been the furthest thing from his mind. Sitting here with her, sharing a meal, talking about nothing very much, was an experience he thought he would be happy to repeat three times a day for the rest of his life.

Well, that was never going to happen. But he had today, this week and, despite everything, he found that he was laughing too.

'So? The dress—' and she'd wanted an updated version of the original dress, he now realized '— is taken care of. What's next?'

She looked confused, uncertain, as well she might.

'It's therapy,' he assured her. 'Confronting what you fear most.'

'Oh, right.'

Was that disappointment? Not the explanation she'd been looking for? Hoping for?

'Food,' she said, accepting it. 'Something a man so wonderfully gifted with a potato masher must surely know all about.'

'A man who lives alone needs to know how to cook.'

'I wouldn't have thought that was a problem. Surely women are fighting over the chance to feed you, prove themselves worthy.'

'Not the kind of women I date,' he said.

And she blushed. He loved how she did that.

'This should be right up your street, then,' she said, ducking her head as she pushed the glossy menu brochure across the table to him. Then, holding on to it, she asked, 'What would be your perfect wedding breakfast?'

There had been something intense about the way she'd said that, about the look she gave him. As if there was some deeper meaning. As if she was trying to tell him something.

'Probably nothing in here,' he admitted, waiting—although what for he could not have said.

She shrugged as she finally released it. 'Surprise me.'

He picked it up, but couldn't take his eyes off her. She wasn't glamorous in the way that Candy had been glamorous. But she had some quality that called to him. A curious mixture of strength and vulnerability. She was a woman to match him, a woman he wanted to protect. A combination that both confused him and yet seemed to make everything seem so simple.

Except for the fact that she was carrying another man's child. A man who'd run out on her when she'd needed him most. And apparently had to do nothing more than turn up to pick up the threads and carry on as if nothing had happened.

'The deal is that I check out the menu, you eat,' he said.

For a moment he thought she was going to argue, but then she picked up her fork, using the food as a shield to disguise the fact that she was blushing again. Something she seemed to do all the time, even though she'd responded to him like a tiger. The woman was a paradox. One he couldn't begin to understand. Didn't even try. Just waited until he was sure that she was eating, rather than just pushing the food around her plate, before he gave his full attention to the simpler task of choosing a menu for her wedding, just as, twelve months ago, she'd been choosing one for his.

Sylvie, watching Tom flicking through the sample menus, rediscovered her appetite. Somehow, talking to him, she'd finally managed to bury every last remnant of the hurt that Jeremy had caused her.

Learning that he'd met someone else in America, was getting married, the arrival of each of his children, had been a repetition of the knife plunge to her heart, each as painful as that first wound inflicted on the day he'd told her that they needed 'a little space'. That he was going away for a while just when she'd needed him most.

Maybe if he hadn't been her first love, her only love, she'd have got over it sooner. As it was, no one had touched her until Tom McFarlane had walked into her office and, with just one look, had jump-started her back into life, just as the garage jump-started her car when the battery was flat.

There would be no more tears over Jeremy Hillyer. Tom McFarlane had erased every thought of him; she'd scarcely recognised him when he'd turned up at that reception. Not because he'd aged badly, far from it. But because it was so easy to see him for the shallow man he'd always been.

No more tears for the girl she'd been either.

They'd threatened for a moment, but Tom had been there and they'd dried off like a summer mist.

The trick now would be to avoid shedding any over him.

He looked up from the brochure and, with an expression of

disgust, said, 'Is this really what people are expected to eat at weddings? Fiddly bits of fish. Girl food. We've got to be able to do better than that.'

We. The word conjured up a rare warmth but she mustn't read too much into it. Or this.

'The idea is that it's supposed to look pretty on a plate,' she said.

'For *Celebrity* or for you?'

'Is there a difference?'

'Whose wedding is this?' he demanded, disgusted. 'What would you really choose? If you didn't have to pander to the whims of a gossip magazine?'

Whoa…Where had that come from? It wasn't just irritation, it was anger. As if it really mattered.

'They are paying a lot of money to have their whims pandered to,' she reminded him. 'Besides, there are the Wedding Fayre exhibitors to think of. This is their big chance.'

'It's your wedding. You should have what you want.'

That did make her laugh. 'If only, but I don't think ten minutes with the registrar in front of two witnesses, followed by a fish and chip supper would quite fill the "fantasy" bill, do you?'

'That's what you'd choose?'

'Quick, simple. Sounds good to me.' Then, because his expression was rather too thoughtful, 'That's classified information, by the way.'

'Of course. I realise how bad it would be for business if it got out that the number one wedding planner hated weddings.'

'I didn't say that!'

'Didn't you? Or are you saying that it's only your own wedding that you can't handle?'

'I can handle it!' Of course she could handle it. If she wasn't here. If he wasn't here. 'It's just that it's all been a bit of a rush. I can't seem to get a hold of it. Find my theme.'

'Why don't you wait until after the baby arrives? Isn't that what most celebrities do these days?'

'I'm not a celebrity,' she snapped. 'And the Wedding Fayre is this weekend.'

'There'll be other fayres.'

'People are relying on me, Tom, and when I make a commitment, I deliver. It's a done deal.'

'So you're going through this hoopla just for the sake of a donation to charity?'

'It's a really big donation, Tom. We'll be able to do so much with the money. And I really do want to help local businesses.'

'That's it?'

'Isn't it enough?'

'I thought we'd already agreed that it wasn't, but who am I to judge?' He sounded angry, which was really stupid. Her fault for making such a fuss, but before she could say so, apologise, he said, 'Fish and chips?'

'Out of the paper. Or sausage and mash. Something easy that you can eat with friends around the kitchen table.'

'Well, it certainly beats anything I've seen in here,' he agreed, tossing the menu brochure back on the pile of stuff she'd gathered during the afternoon. 'I didn't know there were so many ways of serving salmon.'

She groaned. 'I loathe salmon. It's just so…so…'

'Pink?' he offered, breaking the tension, and they both grinned.

'That's the word.' Then, 'Come on.' She stood up, began to gather the plates. 'Let's clear this away and then we'll go and take a look at the attics.'

'Forget the attics. Go and sit down. I'll bring you some coffee.'

She leaned back a little, pushed back a heavy strand of hair that had escaped the chiffon scarf and tucked it behind her ear. 'Excuse me?'

'You've been running around all day. You need to put your feet up. Rest.'

'Well, thanks for that, Tom. You've just made me feel about as attractive as a—'

'You *look* wonderful,' he said. 'In fact, you could be a poster girl for all those adjectives that people use when they describe pregnant women.'

'That would be fat.'

'Blooming.'

'Just another word for fat.'

'Glowing,' he said, putting his hands on the table and leaning forward. 'Apart from the dark smudges under your eyes that suggest you're not getting enough sleep.'

'Tired and fat. Could it be any worse?'

'Well,' he said, appearing to consider her question, 'maybe you're a little thinner about the face.'

About to protest, she caught the gleam in his eye and realised that he was teasing.

'Tired, fat and gaunt. Got it,' she said, but she couldn't keep the smile from her face. Teasing! Who would have thought it? 'You haven't mentioned the swollen ankles.'

'Your ankles are not swollen,' he said with the conviction of a man who paid close attention. Then, as if aware that he'd overstepped some unspoken boundary, 'Don't worry. I'm sure a skilled photographer will be able to produce pictures that won't give the game away.'

She groaned. 'The photographer. I forgot to call the photographer. It's true what they say. My brain is turning to Swiss cheese…'

'All the more reason for you to go and put your feet up now. The drawing room has been surrendered to your Wedding Fayre, but there's a fire in the library.'

'Mr Kennedy lit a fire? What bliss.'

'I lit a fire when I was working in there this afternoon. Go and enjoy it.'

'I will. Thank you.' That was the thing about living on your own. No one ever told you to put your feet up or brought you a cup of coffee. For a moment she couldn't think of anything to say. Then the word 'coffee' filtered through and she said, 'Not coffee. Tea. Camomile and honey. You'll find the tea bags—'

He closed the gap between them and kissed her, and she forgot all about tea bags.

It was a barely-there kiss.

A stop talking kiss.

The kind of kiss she could lean into and take anywhere she wanted and she knew just how right it would be because they'd done that before. But how wrong too. She wanted him just as much—more, because this time it would be her decision, one made with her heart, her head. Not just a response to that instinct to mate in times of stress that had overwhelmed them both.

But she wanted Tom involved with his baby. That was the important relationship here. Her desires were unimportant.

Maybe he understood that too, because he was the one who leaned back. Left a cold place where, for just a moment, it had been all warmth.

'—somewhere,' she finished, somehow managing to make that sound as if nothing had intervened between the first part of the sentence and its conclusion. Then, because keeping up that kind of pretence was never going to be possible, she quickly scooped up her laptop and the brochures and walked away.

Not that it helped. She could still feel his lips clinging to hers. Still feel the tingle of that kiss all the way to her toes.

CHAPTER NINE

FOR a whole minute Tom didn't move. Taking the time to regain control over his breathing, over parts of him that seemed to have a will of their own.

His heart, mainly.

For a moment there he'd been certain that Sylvie was going to kiss him back. Reach up, put her hands to his cheeks and hold him while she kissed him and he climbed over the table to get at her, show her everything he was feeling.

But this time she didn't lose it. Attuned to her in some way he didn't begin to understand, he'd sensed an almost imperceptible hesitation and he'd put a stop to it before he embarrassed himself, or her.

In fact common sense suggested that the most sensible thing he could do right now was walk out of the back door, climb into his car and head for the safety of London.

But he'd run before. There was no help for him in distance and Sylvie was locked into another relationship. She'd said it plainly enough. She'd made a commitment and she always delivered on her word.

No matter what she was feeling deep down, and he knew she had felt the same dark stirring of desire that had moved him, she wouldn't lose her head again.

As for him, the need to face himself in the mirror every morning would keep him from doing anything he'd regret. Hurting her any more than he already had.

He dragged both hands through his hair, flattening it to his head, staring at the ceiling as he let out a long, slow breath.

He'd lived without love so long that he could barely remember what it felt like, could only remember the fallout, the pain. It was an alien concept, something he could not begin to understand. And spending a lifetime watching from the sidelines as friends and acquaintances fell apart and put themselves back together again offered few clues. He had always kept his distance until, finally, he'd arranged what had seemed like the perfect marriage to the perfect trophy wife. A woman who'd neither given nor wanted deep emotional commitment.

Just the perfect trophy husband.

Then he'd come face to face with Sylvie Duchamp Smith and, from that moment on, his perfect marriage had hung like a millstone round his neck. But, like Sylvie, he'd made a commitment and, like her, he always delivered on his promises.

Yet even when he'd been granted a last-minute reprieve he'd still fought against feelings he did not understand. He'd been emotionally incapable of saying the words that would have made everything right. Had instead, for the second time in his life, reduced a woman to tears.

His punishment was to watch helplessly as she planned her wedding. A wedding that she didn't appear to be anticipating with any excitement, or pleasure, or joy.

He clung to the edge of the sink, reminding himself that she was pregnant. That whatever she was doing, for whatever reason, her baby had to come first.

He turned on the tap but, instead of filling the kettle, he

scooped up handfuls of water, burying his face in it to cool the heat of lips that still tasted of her.

And then, when that didn't help, ducking his head beneath the icy water.

Sylvie abandoned her burden on the library table and gave herself up to the comfort of one of the old leather wing-chairs pulled up by the fire and closed her eyes, but more in despair than pleasure.

The intensity of the attraction had not diminished, that much was obvious. It wasn't just her; it was a mutual connection, something beyond words, and yet it was as if there was an unseen barrier between them.

Or perhaps it was the all too visible one.

One of the things that Candy had been most happy about her 'arranged' marriage was the fact that Tom wasn't interested in children and her figure was safe for postperity.

But that was the thing about arranged marriages. There had to be something in it for both parties. This house was a pretty clear indication of what Tom had in mind. Posterity. An heir, and almost certainly a spare. Maybe two.

The family he'd never had.

So what was his problem?

If it was a business arrangement he wanted, she had the same class, connections, background as Candy and she was nowhere near as expensive. On the contrary, she was entirely self-supporting. And the heir was included.

Maybe it was her lack of silicone implants that was the deal-breaker, she thought, struggling against a yawn. Or the lack of sapphire-blue contact lenses.

'If that's what he wants, then I'm sorry, kid, we're on our own,' she murmured.

***

Tom pushed open the library door and stopped as he saw Sylvie stretched out in one of the fireside chairs, limbs relaxed, eyes closed, head propped against the broad wing.

Fast asleep, utterly defenceless and, in contrast to the hot desire he'd done his best to drown in a torrent of cold water, he was overwhelmed by a great rush of protectiveness that welled up in him.

Utterly different from anything he'd ever felt for anyone before.

Was that love?

How did you know?

As quietly as he could, so as not to disturb her, he placed the tray on a nearby table and then took the chair opposite her, content just to watch the gentle rise and fall of her breathing. Content to stay like that for ever.

But nothing was for ever and after a few minutes her eyelids flickered. He saw the moment of confusion as she surfaced, then the smile as she realised where she was.

A smile that faded when she saw him and, embarrassed at being caught sleeping, struggled to sit up. 'Oh, Lord, please tell me I wasn't drooling.'

'Hardly at all,' he reassured her, getting up and placing a cup on the table beside her. 'And you snore really quietly.'

'Really? At home the neighbours complain.'

'Oh, well, I was being kind...' He offered her a plate of some home-made biscuits he'd found as she laughed. Teasing her could be fun... 'Have one of these.'

'Mrs Kennedy's cure-alls? Who could resist?'

'Not me,' he said, taking one himself. Then, as it melted in his mouth, 'I can see how they got their name. Maybe she should market them? A whole rang of Longbourne Court Originals?'

'With a picture of the house on the wrapper? Perfect for the nostalgia market. Except, of course, that there won't be

Longbourne Court for much longer. Longbourne Conference Centre Originals doesn't have quite the same ring to it, does it?'

He didn't immediately answer. And, when he did, he didn't answer the question she'd asked.

'When you asked me if I bought the house for Candy, I may have left you with the wrong impression.'

The words just tumbled out. He hadn't known he was going to say them. Only that they were true.

'You always intended to convert it?'

'No!' He shook his head. 'No. I told myself I was buying it for her. The ultimate wedding present. But when I walked into the house, it was like walking into the dream I'd always had of what a family home should be like. There were old wax jackets hanging in the mud room. Wellington boots that looked as if somebody had just kicked them off. Every rug looked as if the dog had been sleeping there just a moment before.'

'And all the furniture in "country house" condition. In other words, tatty,' Sylvie said.

'Comfortable. Homely. Lived in.'

'It's certainly that.'

'Candy would have wanted to change everything, wouldn't she? Get some fancy designer in from London to rip it all out and start from scratch.'

'Probably. It scarcely matters now, does it?' She lifted a brow but, when he didn't respond, subsided back into the comfort of the chair. 'This is total bliss,' she said, nibbling on the biscuit. 'Every winter Sunday afternoon of childhood rolled into one.' Then, glancing at him, 'Is it raining?'

'Raining?'

'Your hair seems to be dripping down your collar.'

'Oh, that. It's nothing. I missed the kettle and the water squirted up at me,' he lied.

'And only got your hair?' That eyebrow was working overtime. 'How did you get so lucky? When that happens to me, I always get it full in the face and chest.'

'Well, as you've already noticed, I've got a damp collar, if that helps.'

'You think I'm that heartless? Come closer to the fire or you'll catch a chill.'

He didn't need a second invitation but took another biscuit and settled on the rug with his back propped up against the chair on the far side of the fireplace.

'Tell me about your winter Sundays, Sylvie.'

'I'd much rather hear about yours.'

'No, believe me, you wouldn't. They are definitely nothing to get nostalgic over.' Then, because he didn't even want to think about them, 'Come on. I want everything, from the brown bread and butter to three choices of cake.'

'We never had three choices of cake!' she declared in mock outrage. 'According to my mother, only spoilt children had three kinds of cake.'

'I'll bet you had toasted teacakes. Or was it muffins?'

'Crumpets. It was always crumpets,' she said, still resisting him. 'I will have your story.'

'You'll be sorry if you do.' But for just a moment he was tempted by something in her eyes. Tempted to unburden himself, share every painful moment. But he knew that, once he'd done that, she'd own him, he'd be tied to her for ever, while she belonged to someone else.

'Did you toast them on one of those long toasting forks in front of the fire?' he asked.

And, finally, she let it go with a laugh.

'Oh, right. I remember you, Tom McFarlane. You were the grubby urchin with your face pressed up against the window-pane.'

Her laughter was infectious. 'I wish, but I was running wild, scavenging in Docklands while you were still on training wheels. But if I had been standing at the window, you'd have invited me in, wouldn't you? Five or six years old, a little blonde angel, you'd have given me your bread and honey and your Marmite soldiers and a big slice of cherry cake.'

Then, unable to keep up the self-mocking pretence another minute, he reached for a log, using it to stir the fire into life before tossing it into the heart of the flames, giving himself a moment or two to recover. He added a second log, then, his smile firmly in place, he risked another glance.

'You'd have defied your father, even when he threatened to chase me off with his shotgun.'

Charmed by this imagined image of a family gathered around the fire at teatime, he'd meant only to tease, but in an instant her smile faded to a look of such sadness that if he'd had a heart to break it would have shattered at her feet.

'You'd have been quite safe from my father, Tom. He was never at home on Sunday afternoon. It was always tea for two.'

Beneath her calm delivery he sensed pain and, remembering how swiftly she'd cut her father out of his role at her wedding this morning, a world of betrayal. A little girl should be able to count on her father. Look up to him. That she hadn't, she didn't, could only mean one thing.

'He was having an affair?'

'My mother must have known, realised the truth very soon after the big society wedding, but she protected me. Protected him.' She looked away, into the depths of the fire. 'She loved him, you see.'

It took him a minute, but he got there. 'Your father was gay?'

'Still is,' she said. 'A fact that I only learned when his own father died, at which point he stopped pretending to be the perfect husband and father and went with his lover to live on one of the

Greek islands, despite the fact that my mother had just been diagnosed with breast cancer. He didn't care what anyone else thought. It was only his father whose feelings he cared about.'

'If she loved him, Sylvie, I'm sure your mother was glad that he was finally able to be himself.'

'She said that, but she needed him. It was cruel to leave her.'

'Are you sure it wasn't actually a relief for her too? When you're sick you need all your energy just to survive.'

She swallowed. Just shook her head.

'Do you ever see him?' he persisted. And when silence answered that question, 'Does he want to see you?'

She gave an awkward little shrug. 'He sends birthday and Christmas cards through the family solicitor. I return them unopened.'

'No...'

Touched on the raw, the word escaped him. She did that to him. Loosed emotions, stirred memories. Now she was looking at him, her beautiful forehead puckered in a tiny frown, waiting for him to continue, and he closed out the bleak memories—this was not about him.

'He doesn't know he's going to be a grandfather in a few months?' he asked. 'Are you waiting for him to read an announcement in *The Times?* To Sylvie Duchamp Smith...' he couldn't bring himself to say Hillyer '...a son.'

Or had he, too, read about it in *Celebrity?* He remembered the shock of it. The unexpected pain...

There had been a moment then, when the idea of coming home had seemed so utterly pointless that he couldn't move. An emptiness that he hadn't experienced since the day he'd realised that his mother was never coming back and he was completely alone...

'A daughter,' she said, laying a protective hand over the curve of her abdomen. 'The scan showed that it's a girl.'

'...a daughter,' he said softly.

A little girl who'd have blonde curls and blue eyes and a smile to break a father's heart.

'I wonder how he'll feel when he hears,' he said, but only because he wanted her to think about it.

He already knew.

Cut out, shut off from something he could never be a part of.

'You care?' she demanded, astonished. Looking at him as if she couldn't believe what she was hearing. 'You're actually concerned?'

'Yes, Sylvie, I'm concerned. He's your father. His heart will break.'

Under the flush of heat from the fire, she went white.

'How dare you?' she said, gathering herself, pushing herself out of the chair, swaying slightly.

'Sylvie, I'm sorry...' He scrambled to his feet, reaching out to steady her, aware that he'd strayed into a minefield but too late to do more than apologise. This was all strange to him. He'd wanted, just for a moment, to share her happy childhood memories, not drag up bad ones.

It had never occurred to him that she could have had anything but the perfect childhood.

'Sorry? Is that it?' she said, shaking him off. 'You've got some kind of nerve, Tom McFarlane.' And she was striding to the door while he was still trying to work out what he'd done that was so awful.

Abandoning him to his foolish fantasies of happy families.

'Sylvie, please...' He was at the door before she reached it, blocking her way.

She refused to look at him, to speak to him. Just waited for him to recall his manners and let her pass, but he couldn't do that. Not until he'd said the words that were sitting like a lump in his throat.

He'd already apologised for the helpless, angry insult that had spilled from his lips earlier that morning—rare enough—but now he found himself apologising again, even though he didn't know why. Would have said anything if only she'd look at him, talk to him, stay...

'I'm sorry. It's none of my business...'

She looked up at the ceiling, determinedly ignoring him, but her eyes were suspiciously bright and he wanted to take her, sweep her into his arms, hold her, reassure her. Protect her from making what seemed to him to be the biggest mistake of her life.

Marrying Jeremy Hillyer *had* to be a mistake. He'd let her down once and he'd do it again.

She didn't have to marry him just because she was having his baby.

Or was that it?

Was she so desperate to give her baby something that she felt she'd been denied? If so, she was wrong. Her father may not have been the ideal 'daddy'; her childhood may not have been quite the picture book perfect life that he'd imagined. To go with this picture book house. But she did have a father and he knew exactly how the man must feel every time one of his letters or cards came back marked 'Return to Sender'.

'You lost your mother, Sylvie. You can't bring her back, but you still have a father. Don't let anger and pride keep you from him.'

'Don't!' She turned on him, eyes blazing, and he took a step back in the face of an anger so palpable that it felt like a punch on the jaw.

For a moment he thought she was going to say more, but she just shook her head and he said, 'What?'

'Just don't!' And now the tears were threatening to spill over, but even as he reached for her, determined to take her back to the fire where he could hold her so that she could cry, get it out of her system, she took a step back and said, 'Don't be such a damn hypocrite.'

She didn't wait for a response, but wrenched open the door and was gone from him, running up the stairs, leaving him to try and work out what he'd said that had made her so angry.

Hypocrite? Where had that come from?

All he'd done was encourage her to get in touch with her father. The birth of a baby was a time for new beginnings, a good time to bury old quarrels. She might not want to hear that, but how did saying it make him a hypocrite?

He was halfway up the stairs, determined to demand an answer, before reality brought him crashing to a halt.

She might have responded to his kiss, be anything but immune to the hot wire that seemed to run between them, but she was still pregnant with Jeremy Hillyer's child.

Was still going to marry the boy next door.

Sylvie gained the sanctuary of her bedroom and leaned against the door, breathing heavily, tears stinging against lids blocking out the fast fading light.

How could a man with such fire in his eyes, whose simplest kiss could dissolve her bones and who, with a touch could sear her to the soul, be so *cold?*

How *dared* he disapprove of the way she'd shut her father out of her life when he was refusing to acknowledge his own child?

Not by one word, one gesture, had he indicated that he was in any way interested. She could live with that for herself, but what had an innocent, unborn child done to merit such treatment?

She'd accepted, completely and sincerely, that the decision to have his baby had been entirely hers. She could have taken the morning-after pill. Had a termination. She had not consulted him but had taken the responsibility on herself and because of that she'd given him the chance to walk away. Forget it had ever happened.

No blame, no foul.

It was only now, confronted with the reality of what that really meant, did she fully understand how much she'd hoped for a different outcome.

She'd hoped, believed, that by removing everything from the equation but the fact that he was about to become a father, he'd be able to love his little girl as an unexpected gift.

How dumb could she be? At least if she'd sent in the lawyers, gone after him for maintenance, he'd have been forced to confront reality, would have become engaged with his daughter if only on a financial level. He'd demand contact fast enough then.

The billionaire entrepreneur who'd checked every item on the account would want value for money.

'Damn him,' she said, angrily swiping away the dampness that clung to her lashes with the heels of her hands. Then laid them gently over her baby and whispered, 'I'm so sorry, sweetheart. I messed up. Got it wrong.'

A bit of a family failing, that. But her mother hadn't fallen apart when life had dealt her a tricky hand. She'd handled it all with dignity, courage, humour.

Her marriage. Cancer. Even the loss of everything she'd held dear.

All that and with love and understanding too. Always with love. Especially for the unhappy man she'd fallen in love with and married. A man who'd loved his own father so much he'd lived a lie rather than 'come out' and bring the old reactionary's world crashing down. Who had loved her too.

How could Tom McFarlane be so right about that and so wrong about everything else?

'What'll I do, Mum?' she whispered. 'What would you do?'

* * *

Work had always been the answer. Fingers might get burned when a deal went wrong, but the heart remained unscathed, so Tom did what he always did when nothing else made sense. He returned to the library; not to the warmth of the fire but to the huge antique desk and the package of documents and personal stuff that had piled up while he'd been away and which Pam had couriered back from the office so that he could catch up with ongoing projects and set to work.

She'd even included the 'Coming Next Month' page from the latest edition of *Celebrity,* where a photograph of Longbourne Court promoted the 'world's favourite wedding planner's personal fantasy wedding' from The Pink Ribbon Club's Wedding Fayre.

He bit down hard, pushed it away so hard that it slid on to the floor along with a load of other stuff. He left it, intent on tossing away out of date invitations, letters from organisations asking him to speak, donate, join their boards. Clearing out the debris so that he could get back to what he knew. Making money.

That had been the centre of his world, the driving force that had kept him going for as long as he could remember.

But for what? What was the point of it all?

Losing patience, he dumped the lot in the bin. Anything to do with business would have been dealt with by his PA. Anything else and they'd no doubt write again.

He scooped up everything that had fallen on the floor and pitched that in too. About to crush the sheet from *Celebrity,* however, something stopped him.

Sylvie didn't dare linger too long in the bath in case she went to sleep. Having given herself no longer than it took for the lavender oil to do its soothing job, she climbed out, applied oil to her stomach and thighs to help stave off the dreaded stretch marks, then, wearing nothing but a towelling robe, she opened the bathroom door.

Tom McFarlane was propped up on one side of her bed.

All the warm, soothing effects of the lavender dissipated in an instant.

'Don't tell me,' she said icily. 'The Duchamp ghosts are after your blood.'

'Not that I've noticed,' he said. Then, 'I did knock.'

'And when did I say "come in"?' she demanded. 'I could have been naked!'

'In an English country house in April? How likely is that?'

'What do you want, Tom?'

'Nothing. I've had an idea.' And he patted the bed beside him, encouraging her to join him.

'And it couldn't keep until morning?' she protested, but sat on the edge of the bed. 'What kind of idea?'

'For your wedding.' He held up a page from *Celebrity* and she leaned forward to take a closer look.

'It's Longbourne Court. So?'

'Turn it over.'

She scanned the page. Could see nothing. 'Do you mean this advertisement for the Steam Museum in Lower Longbourne?' she said, easing her back. Wishing he'd get to the point so that she could lie down. 'It's just across the park. Big local attraction. So what?'

'Why don't you make yourself comfortable while you think about it?' he said, piling up her pillows and, when she hesitated, 'It's just like a sofa, only longer,' he said, clearly reading her mind.

She wasn't sure she'd feel safe on a sofa with him but it was clear he wasn't saying another word until she was sitting comfortably so she tugged the robe around her and sat back, primly, against the pillows.

'Okay,' she said. 'The Steam Museum. At Hillyer House.

Jeremy's grandfather was mad about steam engines and gathered them up as they went out of use. He worked on them himself, restoring them, had open days so that the public could enjoy them. I loved the carousels—'

'They're not carousels, they're gallopers,' Tom said. 'They're called carousels on the Continent.' He made a circling motion with his hand. 'And they go round the other way.'

'Do they? Why?'

'It's to do with the fact that we drive on the left.' She stared at him. 'Honestly!'

'Don't tell me, you worked in a fairground.'

'I worked in a fairground,' he said.

'I told you not to tell me that…' she said, then looked hurriedly away. That was one of those silly things her father used to say to make her laugh.

'Okay, *gallopers,* rides, swings. It's set up just like a real old-fashioned steam fair…' She clapped her hands to her mouth. Then grinned. 'Ohmigod. Wedding Fayre… Steam fair…'

Sylvie laughed as the sheer brilliance of the idea hit her. 'It's the perfect theme, Tom,' she said as the ideas flooded in. 'You're a genius!'

'I know, but hadn't you better clear it with Jeremy first?'

'Jeremy? No. There's no need for that…' Steam engines had been the old Earl's pet obsession; Jeremy had never been interested—much too slow for him and it was run by a Trust these days. 'It even fits in with the idea of promoting local businesses.'

'Well, that's all right, then,' he said.

She glanced at him. 'What?'

He shook his head. 'Nothing. As you say, it all fits beautifully.'

'They've got everything. Test your strength. Bowl for the pig—just pottery ones, but they're lovely. And made locally too. There are even hay-cart rides to take visitors around the place.'

'I guess the big question is—does it beat the elephant?'

'Too right!' She drew up her legs, wrapping her arms around them. 'The photographer could use one of those things where you stick your head through the hole—'

'A bride and groom one.'

'—for all the guests to have their photographs taken.'

She couldn't stop grinning. 'We'll decorate the marquee with ribbons and coloured lights instead of flowers. And set up sideshow stalls for the food.' She looked at him. 'Bangers and mash?'

He grinned back. 'Fish and chips. Hot dogs.'

'Candyfloss! And little individual cakes.' She'd intended to go for something incredibly tasteful, but nothing about this fantasy was going to be tasteful. It was going to be fun. With a capital F. 'I'll talk to the confectioner first thing. I want each one decorated with a fairground motif.'

Tom watched as, swept up in the sheer fun of it, she clapped her hands over her mouth like a child wanting to hold it in, savour every minute of it.

'You like it?' he asked.

'Like it!' She turned and, anger forgotten, she flung her arms around him, hugging him in her excitement. 'You're brilliant. I don't suppose you're looking for a job?' Then, before he could answer, 'Sorry, sorry... Genius billionaire. Why would you want to work for me? Damn, I wish it wasn't all such a rush.'

'Is it even possible in the time?'

'Oh, yes.'

He must have looked doubtful because she said, 'Piece of cake. Honestly.'

Of course it was. The Steam Museum had been created by Lord Hillyer. All she had to do was ask and it would be hers for the day.

'Now I know what I want it'll all just fall into place, although I could have done with Josie to sort out the marquee. That's going to be the biggest job.'

'If it helps, you've got me.'

They were on her bed and she had her arms around him and he was telling her what was in his heart, but only he knew that. Only he would ever know that she'd got him—totally, completely, in ways that had nothing to do with sex but everything to do with a word that he didn't even begin to understand, but knew with every fibre of his being that this was it. The real deal.

Giving without hope of ever receiving back.

Sylvie's mother would have understood. Would know how he was feeling.

Sylvie… Sylvie was nearly there. Maybe his true gift to her would be to help her make that final leap…

'You'd be willing to help?' she asked, leaning back, a tiny frown puckering her brow.

He shrugged, pulled a face. 'You said it. The sooner you're done, the sooner you're out of here.'

'That's it?' She drew back as if his answer shocked her. As if she'd expected something more.

But that was it.

More was beyond him.

'I want my house back and, to get it, I'm prepared to put all my resources at your disposal,' he said with all the carelessness he could muster.

Maybe just one thing more…

'There's just one condition.' Then, as the colour flooded into her cheeks, he said, 'No!'

Yes…

'No,' he repeated. 'All I want from you is that you write to your father.'

'No…' The word came out as a whisper.

'Yes! Ask him to share the day with you. Let him into your little girl's life.'

'Why?' she demanded. 'Why do you care about him?'

More and more and more…

'Because… Because I know what it's like to have letters returned unopened. Because one day when I was four years old people came and took my mother away. I hung on to her and that was the only time I saw her cry. As she pulled away, leaving me to the waiting social workers. "I'll be all right," she said. "I have to go. These people will look after you until I come home…"' Then, helplessly, 'You said you'd have my story.'

'Where was your father, Tom?'

'Dead. She'd killed him. A battered woman who'd finally struck back, using the first thing that came to hand. A kitchen knife.' Then, more urgently, because this was what he had to do to make sure she understood, 'They took her away, put me in care. I didn't understand. I wrote to her, begging her to come and get me. Week after week. And week after week the letters just came back…'

She said nothing, just held him, as if she could make it all better. And maybe she had. Her need had dragged the story out of him. Had made him say the words. Had made him see that it wasn't his fault that his mother had died too.

'I'm sure she thought it was for the best that I forgot her, moved on, found a new family.'

'But you didn't.'

'She was my mother, Sylvie. She might not have been the greatest mother in the world, but she was the only one I ever wanted.'

Sylvie thought her heart might break at the thought of a little boy writing his desperate letters, having them returned unopened. Understood his empathy for her own father.

'What happened to her, Tom?'

'She never stood trial. By the time her case eventually came up she was beyond the law, in some dark place in her mind. She should have been in hospital, not prison. Maybe there she'd have got help instead of taking her own life.'

She reached out a hand to him. Almost, but not quite, touched his cheek. Then said, 'Are you sure you haven't been visiting with the Duchamp ghosts?'

He'd had no way of knowing how she'd react to the fact that he was the son of a wife-batterer, a husband-killer. A suggestion that he'd been communing with her ancestors hadn't even made the list and, at something of a loss, he said, 'Why would you think that?'

'Because I asked my mother what she'd do. I already knew the answer. Have always known it. Maybe she thought it was time to get someone else on my case…'

And finally her fingers came into contact with his cheek, as if by touching him she was reaching through him to her mother. And, just as they had on the evening when the connection between them had become physical, silent tears were pouring down her cheeks, but this time there was no one to interrupt them and she didn't push him away, but let him draw her close, hold her while he said, over and over, 'Don't cry, Sylvie,' even as his own tears soaked into her hair. 'Please don't cry.'

And eventually, when she quieted, drew back, it was she who wiped his cheeks with her fingers.

Comforted him.

'It'll be all right,' she said, holding his face between her hands. Kissing his cheek. 'I promise you, it'll be all right.'

'You'll write to him? Now?'

'It won't wait until morning?'

'What would your mother say?'

She sniffed and, laughing, swung herself from the bed to grab a tissue. 'Okay, okay, I'll do it.' Then, 'I'll have to fetch my bag; I left it downstairs.'

She crossed to the door, then, halfway through it, she paused and looked back. 'Tom?'

He waited.

'Don't make the same mistake your mother did.' She was cradling the life growing within her in a protective gesture. It was the most powerful instinct on earth. The drive of the mother to protect her young. His mother had done that. Had protected him from his father. Had protected him from herself...

'You're more than your genes,' she said when he didn't respond. 'You've forged your own character. It's strong and true and, I promise you, you're the kind of father any little girl would want.'

There was an urgency in her voice. A touch of desperation. As if she knew that her own baby wouldn't be that lucky...

He couldn't help her. If it had been in his power he would have stopped the world and spun it back to give them both a second chance to get things right. But he couldn't help either of them.

CHAPTER TEN

SYLVIE finally began to understand what was driving Tom's inability to make an emotional commitment. How hard it must be for him to trust not just himself, but anyone.

To understand his anger, his pain at Candy's desertion. He might not have loved her, but she'd still underscored all that early imprinting. That early lesson that no one was to be relied on...

And yet he'd trusted her enough, cared enough to stop her from hurting someone who she knew, deep down, loved her. That was a huge step forward.

She'd done her best to reassure him that he was not his father, or his mother. If she'd hoped that he'd instantly come over all paternal, well, that was unrealistic. He'd had a lifetime to live with the horrors of his early life, for the certainty that he did not want children to become ingrained into his psyche. He couldn't be expected to switch all that off in a moment.

But the longest journey started with a single step. Tonight they'd made that together.

Tom was using his cellphone when she returned to the bedroom, talking to someone about making the sideshow booths. He lifted a hand in acknowledgement and carried on, while she opened her bag, took out the small folder of notepaper she kept in there and settled at the small escritoire to write her letter. The second most difficult in her life.

It was a deliberate ploy. She wanted him to see her pen gliding across the same heavy cream paper on which she'd written to him. She uncapped her pen and smoothed a hand over her hair, lingering at the damp patch where his tears had soaked in.

And then, pushing all that from her mind, she began.

'That didn't take long,' Tom said, watching as she carefully folded the sheet into four and tucked it into an envelope. Addressed it.

'No. Sometimes things you think are impossible are nowhere near as difficult as you imagine,' she said and looked up as he joined her. 'I just invited Dad and his partner to join the festivities on Sunday. It was as simple as that.'

'Will it get there in time?'

'I'll take it to the post office first thing in the morning and send it express.'

'You'll have enough to do,' he said, holding out his hand for it. 'Leave it to me.'

'Thank you,' she said and placed the envelope in his hands. Would he remember the feel of it? How he'd felt when he'd opened it?

'I've organised a carpenter to build the stalls for the marquee,' he said. 'They'll be here first thing.'

'Fast work.' She glanced at her watch. It was barely nine. Still early enough to call some of those people who'd assured her that she could call any time, ask anything.

'What about the Steam Museum? I imagine you'll want to sort that out personally?'

'The sooner the better. I'll make that call first.'

As she picked up her cellphone Tom headed for the door. 'I'll leave you to it, then. You can leave this with me.'

He didn't wait for her to reply but, lifting the letter to indicate what he was referring to, he left her alone.

It was somewhat abrupt but it had been an emotion-charged evening. Maybe he just needed some air.

And she let it go, calling Laura, who knew everyone, and handing her the job of securing the Steam Museum for the photo shoot.

It didn't open until two on Sunday so they had plenty of time. The church was booked for early afternoon. They could finish off in the marquee in the early evening.

Tom closed the door to Sylvie's bedroom, leaned back against it for a moment while he caught his breath. While she called Jeremy to enthuse him with her excitement. Got him to call the trustees and ask them for the loan of some of his grandfather's toys for their big day.

He looked down at the letter he was holding. At least he'd managed to save one man from heartache.

His own would have to wait. He'd made her a promise and he'd keep it. But he'd leave as soon as he was sure everything was just as she wanted it. He didn't intend to be an onlooker when Jeremy Hillyer arrived to claim his bride.

'It's beautiful, Geena.'

The dress, a simple A-line shift in rich cream silk, had been appliquéd to the knees in swirling blocks of lavender, purple and green. And, instead of a veil, she'd created a stunningly beautiful loose thigh-length jacket on which the appliqué was repeated around the edge and on wide fold-back cuffs. Embroidery trailed over the silk and tiny beads caught the light as she moved—beads that matched the small Russian-style tiara Geena had commissioned to go with the gown.

'I just wish it was for real. I really hoped you were going to bring Mr Hot-and-Sexy along to try on the matching waistcoat,' she said.

'Me too,' Sylvie replied, for once letting her mask slip, her feelings show. Then, 'I meant, I wish it was for real.'

'I know what you meant, Sylvie. It was written all over your face. He is your baby's father, isn't he?'

Sylvie tried to deny it. Couldn't. Lifted her hands in a helpless gesture that said it all.

'I thought so. Men are such fools.'

'We're all fools,' she said, shrugging off the beautiful jacket.

The week had been such a roller coaster of emotions that she was almost reeling from it. Or maybe she was just exhausted.

Tom had been such a tower of strength. Organising carpenters to make the food stalls. Rounding up every set of coloured lights in the county and making sure they were fixed for maximum impact so that inside the marquee was like being inside a funfair. Finding old fairground ride cars and adapting them for seating.

And, in the evenings, he was always there, ready to talk through any problems she'd encountered and offer suggestions.

He had such a clear vision, a way of seeing to the core of things.

He only had one blind spot. There was only one subject he never mentioned. It was almost as if he was so locked into his past, his determination never to be a father, that he'd blanked it out.

It couldn't go on.

She wouldn't allow it to go on.

'Is that the dress?'

Tom was working at the kitchen table as she walked in carrying the box containing the tissue-wrapped dress and he pushed back the chair, standing up to take it from her.

'Yes. I insisted on bringing it with me, just in case.'

'In case of what?'

'In case she has a flat tyre. Or her workroom burns to the ground.' The principle that whatever can go wrong, will go wrong. 'Believe me, when you've been in this business for as long as I have—'

'Actually, Sylvie, I'm a bit concerned about the traction engines. I know you said Laura had it all in hand, but shouldn't they—'

'You don't have to worry about them. We've got all morning,' she said. 'Plenty of time.' Then, 'I'll just take this upstairs, then I want to talk to you, Tom.'

'Can you leave it for a moment?' he asked, taking the box from her, putting it on the table. 'I want you to come and see the marquee.'

'I thought it was finished.'

'It is now,' he said with the kind of smile that had become such a familiar sight over the last few days as they'd worked together. And he held out his hand. 'I've got a surprise for you.'

She laid her hand over his and he wrapped his fingers over hers. For a moment neither of them moved, then, as if jerking himself back from a dream, he headed for the door. Once they were outside, he paused for her to fall in beside him and they walked together, hand in hand, through the dusk to where the huge marquee had been erected by the hire company to display their wares, decorated at *Celebrity*'s expense for her fantasy wedding.

'Wait,' he said as they approached the entrance. 'I want you to get the full effect.' He kept tight hold of her hand as he switched on the generator. The outside was lit up with white lights along every edge—along the roof ridge, cascading from the finials, circling above the drop cloths.

Inside, the lights—smaller, more decorative, a mirror image of those on the outside—were reflecting on the polished floor. The supports were topped with huge knots of brightly coloured ribbons, the same ribbons that were plaited around them to the floor. In the corners were brightly painted stalls, offering a choice of foods. The fairground seating.

Small finishing touches had been added during the afternoon. The candyfloss machine had arrived. Bunches of balloons were straining against their strings.

And then, as she looked around, she saw it.

A fairground organ. The kind that played from printed sheets. He crossed to it, threw a switch and, as if by magic, it began to play, music filling the huge space.

'Tom! It's wonderful! The perfect finishing touch.'

Even as Sylvie said the words, she felt her skin rise in goosebumps. Nothing was ever perfect…

But then Tom said, 'Would you care to dance, Miss Smith?' And, before she could protest, he was waltzing her across the floor. And it was. Magic.

About as perfect as it was possible for something to be.

And much too brief. The music stopped. Tom held her for just a moment longer. Then he stepped away.

'Enough.'

The word had a finality about it but, before she could say anything, he turned away. 'Go in, Sylvie. It'll take me a while to shut everything down. Make sure it's all safe. I'll leave the lights until last so that you can see your way.' Then, 'Take care.'

'Yes, I will.'

For a moment neither of them moved and then, because the longer she hesitated, the longer it would be before he could join her and she could talk to him about the future, she turned and walked back to the house.

Inside, the hall was now festooned with pink ribbons in preparation for tomorrow's Fayre. The door to the ballroom stood wide open to reveal the catwalk, the tables with gilt chairs laid out in preparation for the fashion show. Mother of the bride outfits, going-away outfits, honeymoon clothes. Formal hire wear for men, including kilts. Bridesmaids and page-boy outfits. And, finally, Geena's bridal wear.

The florist had been busy all day putting the finishing touches to her arrangements. Pew-end nosegays that had been hung all along the edge of the catwalk. Table flowers.

In the drawing room all the stalls were laid out like an Aladdin's cave. Everything sparkling, fresh, lovely.

Laura was right. This was worth it, she thought. Even the weather forecast was good. It was going to be warm and sunny as it had been all week.

So why was she so cold?

She pushed open the library door, eager to get to the fire she knew would be banked up behind the guard.

But the guard was down. The room was not empty. There was someone sitting in Tom's chair. A man, who stood up as she came to an abrupt halt.

Her father.

Older, with a little less hair, a little thicker around the waistline. Deeply tanned. Still unbelievably good-looking.

Waiting. Uncertain.

She took a step towards him. He took one towards her and then she reached out, took his hand and carried it to her waist. 'You're going to be a grandfather,' she said.

'I read about it in *Celebrity*. When I saw the photograph I thought for one awful moment you were back with that piece of…' he stopped '…Jeremy Hillyer. I thought you were back with him.'

'It's not Jeremy's baby.' She covered his hand with her own. 'It's Tom's baby.' Then, 'He knew you were here, didn't he? That's why he sent me on ahead of him.'

'He said he thought we might need some time on our own.'

Then, 'I'd given up hope. When I read about the baby and you still didn't get in touch, I knew it would never happen.'

'I'm sorry. So sorry...'

'Hush. You're my little girl, Sylvie. You don't ever have to say you're sorry.' And he put out his arms and gathered her in.

Later—after they'd both cried as they'd talked about her mother, as they'd discovered they could laugh too—she said, 'Did you bring Michael with you?'

'We're staying in Melchester. He'll come tomorrow. Thank you for asking him.'

'You love him. He's part of our lives.'

'And Tom? Is he going to be part of yours?'

'I...I don't know. Just when I think that maybe it's going to be all right, I realise it isn't.' And she shivered again.

'Maybe you should go and find him, Sylvie. We can talk some more tomorrow.'

'Tom?'

She'd watched her father's tail-lights disappear over the brow of the hill and then walked through the house looking for Tom. Not just to thank him, but determined now, as never before, to make him see reason about the baby.

Mrs Kennedy was in the kitchen making a sandwich. 'Tom asked me to make sure you had something to eat.'

'I had some soup.'

'Hours ago. Did you have a visitor?'

'My father. He's coming for the Fayre tomorrow. He hopes to see you.'

'I should think so.' And she smiled. 'I'm glad you've made up.'

'Yes. Me too.' Then, 'Where is Tom?'

'As to that, I couldn't say,' she said, wiping her hands and reaching up behind a plate on the dresser to take down an envelope. 'But he called in to the cottage on his way out and asked me to come over in an hour or two and make sure you had something to eat. He said to tell you he left something upstairs for you. In your room.'

'On his way out? When?'

'A while back. Just after he turned out the lights in the marquee.'

She checked her watch. Nearer two hours. She'd thought Tom was just staying out of the way, giving them time to talk.

But she remembered the way she'd shivered. The finality in the way he'd said, 'Enough'. That he'd left something upstairs for her. Something he hadn't wanted her to find before he'd left...

She bolted up the stairs, flung open her bedroom door and saw the clown teddy propped up on her bed, just where Tom had been lying a few days ago. Looking for all the world as if he belonged there.

Because he had.

She picked up the bear, knowing that Tom had taken it from the trunk, carried it down to her room, placed it there. She buried her face in it, hoping to catch something of his scent. Trying to feel him, understand what had been going through his mind as he'd been putting things right for her. For her family.

Just as, all week, he'd been making things work for her fantasy wedding. Coming up with neat little ideas to part the visitors to the Wedding Fayre from their money. All little extras for the Pink Ribbon Club.

Then, as she looked up, she saw the letter that had been lying beneath the bear and she ripped open the flap, took out the single folded sheet of paper, then sat down before she opened it, knowing it wouldn't be good.

My dearest Sylvie

Tomorrow will be your very special day and, now you have your father to support you, I know I can leave you in his safe hands.

I'm going away for a while—but not running this time. I need to find something new to do with my life. Something bigger. Something real. My first decision is not to convert the house into a conference centre. It's a real home and I hope it will remain as such. Whatever happens, you needn't worry about Mr and Mrs Kennedy. I've made arrangements to ensure they'll never have to leave their home.

I've also asked Mrs Kennedy to see that all the clothes in the attic are donated to Melchester Museum. Everything else of value in the trunks is to be given to the Pink Ribbon Club for fund-raising purposes. The bear, however, is yours. Something belonging to your family that you can pass on to your own baby.

Finally, I want to reassure you that you can rely on my discretion. What happened between us will always remain a very special, a very private memory.

I hope the sun shines for you tomorrow and wish you and Jeremy a long and happy life together.
Yours
Tom

Sylvie read the note. Maybe she was tired; she was certainly emotionally drained, but none of it made sense.

She'd seen him just a couple of hours ago. And what the heck did he mean about her having a long and happy life with Jeremy?

She read the letter again, then went back down to the kitchen.

'What does Tom mean about you never having to leave your home, Mrs Kennedy?'

She smiled. 'Bless the man, he gave it to us. Said that's what Lady Annika would have done if she'd been able to and anyway it wouldn't be missed from the estate when it was sold.'

Sylvie sat down.

He'd given it to them. Just because she'd said... 'And the clothes? You're to send them to the Museum?'

'I believe he spoke to someone there just yesterday. He said to tell you that if there's anything you want, you should take it.'

She shook her head. 'No...'

He'd been planning this? Why hadn't he said anything?

She re-read the last paragraph again:

> *"...I hope the sun shines for you tomorrow, and wish you and Jeremy a long and happy life together."*

Jeremy?

He was always bringing up Jeremy. Had even mentioned seeing them in *Celebrity* together. Had the entire world seen that? Even her father had said...

Oh, good grief. No. He couldn't possibly think that all this wedding stuff was real. Could he?

Did he really believe that she was marrying Jeremy while she was carrying his baby? While she had been practically swooning in his arms in the attics? Was that why he'd pulled back from that kiss over the kitchen table?

"...you can rely on my discretion..."

Was that what he thought she'd wanted to talk to him about? To plead for his discretion?

'Oh, no, Tom McFarlane, you don't...'

She had his cellphone number programmed into her phone and she hit fast dial but his phone was turned off and all she got was some anonymous voice inviting her to leave a message.

'Tom? Don't you dare do another disappearing act on me—not until you've spoken to me! Ring me, do you hear? Ring me now!'

But what if he didn't?

What if he decided to head straight for the airport, put as much distance between them as possible? It was what he'd done when Candy had let him down.

She froze. Was it possible that he'd only just come back? That he'd never received her letter?

No. That wasn't possible. Despite her promise to him—to herself—she'd cracked, had asked him if he'd got it. She'd never forget his dismissive nod. And a long time later, "I'm sorry…"

None of this made sense. She had to talk to him. She dialled Enquiries for the number of his London apartment, but inevitably, it was unlisted. And there was no point in calling his office on a Saturday night. But she did that too. If he was there he didn't pick up.

There was nothing for it but to drive to London and confront him, face to face. Scooping up one of the sandwiches Mrs Kennedy had made and grabbing up her keys from the kitchen table, she ran for her car.

Tom let himself into his apartment. It was immaculate. Everything was pristine. Characterless. Empty.

As different from Longbourne Court as it was possible for it to be. In a week that rambling house had become his home. A place where he felt totally at ease.

But it would be forever linked to Sylvie. Everything he touched, every room, would bring back some memory of a smile, a gesture.

He'd never be able to walk into the morning room without remembering what he'd said to her.

Would never see violets blooming in the wood without the scent bringing back that moment when he'd come so close to reaching out to her. Betraying himself.

He tossed the keys on the table. Rubbed his hands over his face in an attempt to bring some life, some warmth back to his skin.

Picked up one of the piles of mail that his cleaner had put to one side. She'd clearly tossed everything that was obviously junk mail and had sorted the rest into two piles. The stuff she knew was important she'd put in one, anything she was doubtful about in the other.

There wasn't that much, considering how long it was since he'd been home, but all his business and financial stuff went to the office and most of his personal stuff too.

He began to shuffle through the envelopes, lost interest and tossed them back on the table, where they slithered on the polished surface and fell on the floor.

About to walk past, leave them, he saw a familiar square cream envelope, took a step back and then bent to pick it up.

It might have been coincidence that it was exactly the same as the envelope that he'd taken to the post office for Sylvie. It might have been if the handwriting hadn't been the same.

When had she written to him?

There was no stamp. No postmark. No way of knowing how long it had lain here waiting for him to return. She must have delivered it by hand. She must have come here, pushed it through his letter box, waited for an answer that had never come.

She'd asked him if he'd got her letter and he'd thought she'd meant the one returning the money but he knew that it was this letter she'd been talking about and, with a sudden sense of dread, he pushed his thumb beneath the flap and, hand trembling, took out the single sheet of paper and opened it.

Dear Mr McFarlane
I'm writing to let you know that as a result of our recent encounter, I'm expecting a baby in July...

'No!'

The word was a roar. A bellow of pain.

He didn't wait to read the rest but grabbed the phone, put a call through to the house. It rang and rang and then the answering machine picked up. 'There's to be no damn wedding tomorrow,' he said. 'Do you hear me, Sylvie? No wedding!'

Then he tried her cellphone, but only got a voicemail prompt. He repeated his message, then added, 'I'm coming right back...'

Then, in desperation, he called the Kennedys' cottage.

Her car refused to start. Her beloved, precious little car that had never once let her down, chose this moment to play dead. The lights. She'd driven through a patch of mist and had turned the lights on. And had forgotten to turn them off.

It took her ten minutes at a trot to reach the Kennedys' cottage.

'Don't you fret, Sylvie,' Mrs Kennedy said. 'You just sit down and I'll make you a cup of tea. Mr Kennedy's at a darts match, but the minute he comes home he'll get his jump-leads and fix your car for you.'

'I can't wait. I'll have to call a taxi.'

'I'll do that while you get your breath back.'

There was a half an hour wait and, while Mrs Kennedy went off to make 'a nice cup of tea', she decided to try and call Tom again, but her phone, which had been working overtime all day, chose that moment to join her car and give up the ghost.

'Stupid, useless thing,' she said, flinging it back into her bag, too angry to cry.

It was nearer an hour before she heard the taxi finally draw up outside the cottage and she didn't wait for the driver to knock but just grabbed her bag, kissed Mrs Kennedy and ran down the path to the gate.

And came to a full stop.

Leaning against the fearsome Aston, arms folded, was Tom McFarlane. And he didn't look happy.

She opened her mouth. Saw what he was holding and closed it again.

Apparently satisfied, he straightened, opened the car door and said, 'Get in.'

He didn't sound happy either and while, as recently as sixty seconds ago, she'd been fuming with impatience to see him, talk to him, that suddenly felt like the most dangerous idea in the entire world.

'You've got everything wrong, Tom,' she said, her feet apparently glued to the path.

'Nowhere near as wrong as you, Sylvie.'

'I don't actually think that's possible,' she said, finally snapping.

He was angry? Well, she wasn't exactly dancing with delight either and, freed by righteous indignation, she swept down the path and, ignoring the open car door, she walked away from him and his car. She'd rather walk...

'Sylvie!' It was a demand rather than a plea. Then, with a sudden catch in his throat, 'Sylvie, don't do it...' She faltered. 'I'm begging you. Please...'

She stopped and, when he spoke again, he was right behind her.

'Please don't marry Jeremy Hillyer.'

It was true, then. He'd really thought she was going to marry Jeremy.

'But you've been helping me all week,' she said. 'Coming up with great ideas for the wedding. This afternoon you wrote me a note wishing us all the best. What's different now?'

'Everything. I thought the baby was his. I was coming home two months ago. Coming to see you. I didn't know if you'd even talk to me but I had to try. I was in the airport, the boarding card in my pocket when I saw you smiling out of the cover of *Celebrity*. Read about your "happy event", that you were back with your childhood sweetheart.'

'But I wrote to you, Tom. I told you about the baby. I asked you if you'd got it.'

'I thought you meant the one about the money. My secretary emailed me to tell me that you'd returned it, asking me what to do with it, and I realised what you must have thought. It wasn't like that, Sylvie. I'd always intended to pay you in full. The cheque I wrote, put in my pocket, was for your whole fee.'

'Oh.'

'I told her to give it to charity, if that's any consolation.' Then, 'I didn't get this letter until this evening, Sylvie. I didn't know about our little girl…'

She blinked. 'That's impossible. I put it through your door myself. Two weeks after…' She gestured helplessly at the gentle swell of her belly.

'Which would have been perfect if I'd been there. I've been out of the country for six months, Sylvie. I only stopped to pick up my passport and then I caught the first plane with a free seat, just to put some space between us.'

'Um…I thought you were going to Mustique…'

'How could I go there after you and I…?' And he was the one lost for words. 'I hurt you, Sylvie. Made you cry. I've only made two women cry in my entire life.'

'Your mother…'

"I'll be all right. I have to go…"

His mother had said that. And so had she…

'I was crying because you'd given me something so unbelievable, Tom. I'd been frozen, held in an emotional Ice Age. Too much had happened at once. I'd lost everything and then been betrayed…' She looked up at him, wanting him to know that this was the truth. 'I spent my life making perfect weddings for other people when I was unable to even share a kiss…'

'Sylvie…'

'I came straight back, as soon as I could, but you'd gone.'

'I was in bits. I thought you couldn't wait to leave… Never wanted to set eyes on me again and who could blame you?'

She reached up, placed her fingers over his lips. 'You are my sun, Tom. You looked at me and it was instant meltdown. You held me and your heat warmed me.'

'But…'

'The tears were pure joy, Tom. And the baby…' She took his hand and placed it over the baby growing beneath her heart. '*Our* baby is pure joy too.'

'She's mine…' His face, pale in the rising moon, glowed with something like reverence. 'My little girl.'

She'd cried then and she was crying now. Silent tears that were falling down her cheeks as she said, 'You have a family, Tom.'

For a moment they just stood there and then he said, 'It's not enough. I want you, Sylvie. I tried to get you out of my mind, tried to forget you, but it was no good. I…' He stopped.

'You what, Tom?' She reached up, her palms on his cheeks, making him look at her when he would have turned away. 'Say the words.'

'I…I love you.' Then, 'I love you, but I've made a complete mess of it. It's too late…'

'Because of the wedding tomorrow? Is that the only thing standing between us?'

'Sylvie…' And this time her name was a tortured cry that rent her to the heart.

'It's a fantasy wedding, Tom. Not real. Just the "Sylvie Duchamp Smith" fantasy of what her wedding would be. If… when…she ever found a man she could spend the rest of her life with.'

She saw him wrestle with that.

'But Jeremy…'

'Is not that man. We met at a charity do. We were polite, we smiled at each other. *Celebrity* did the rest. I suspect they were hoping to provoke me into naming the real father of my child.'

'But you've been ordering cakes. Food. Flowers. You've got an updated version of the dress you were going to wear the first time…'

'The dress is nothing like the one that my great-grandma wore,' she assured him. 'I have an entirely different fantasy these days.' Then, 'I can't believe you'd think I'd sell my own wedding to the media.'

'I had the impression that you'd do anything for your mother's charity.'

'Some things are not for sale, Tom.'

Then, catching a flicker of light, the twitch of a curtain from the Kennedys' cottage, she said, 'They knew, didn't they? They knew you were coming back.'

'If you'd turned on your cellphone any time in the last two hours, so would you.'

'My battery is flat. What did you say?'

'"There will be no wedding…"'

'None?'

'Not tomorrow,' he said, reaching out and touching her cheek. 'But soon, I hope. Very soon. Because if you think you can have my baby without any expectation of commitment to her father, you've got another think coming.'

'Is that right?'

'And it's my fantasy too, remember? I want the whole works.'

'All of it?'

'All of it. Everything, everyone. Except *Celebrity*. They can have their fantasy tomorrow, but the reality will be for us alone. Not just for a day, but for always.' Then, as if realising that something was missing, he went down on one knee and, under a bright canopy of stars, he said, 'If I promise to wear a purple waistcoat to match your shoes, will you marry me, Sylvie Smith?'

Four weeks after the Pink Ribbon Club Wedding Fayre featuring Sylvie Duchamp Smith's fantasy wedding was a sell-out for *Celebrity*, Tom and Sylvie did it for real.

Sylvie arrived at the church on a traction engine that was all gleaming paintwork and brass. Geena had made her another dress—since, obviously, the groom had seen the first one. It wasn't quite the same since she never repeated her designer gowns, but it was close. And Sylvie wore the purple shoes.

Josie had added a dusting of green glitter to her purple hair and, having been bribed with an appliquéd dress with a tiny little matching jacket and a pair of pale green silk-embroidered shoes, had surrendered her boots.

The god-daughters were adorable in lavender and violet. The page scowled, but that was only to be expected. Even a five-year-old knew that purple velvet breeches were an outrage. And, as she walked up the aisle on the arm of her father, the sunlight caught the diamonds in the tiara Tom had commissioned from a local jeweller for his bride.

The fair was a riot, the food was pronounced perfect, the

children were sick on candyfloss—well, nothing was ever *quite* perfect—and Josie, now the partner in charge of weddings and parties, was overwhelmed with people demanding exactly the same for their own special day.

But, as Tom had told Sylvie, this was a one-off. For them alone.

Executive Mother-To-Be

Nicola Marsh

Nicola Marsh has always had a passion for writing and reading. As a youngster, she devoured books when she should have been sleeping, and later kept a diary whose content could be an epic in itself! These days, when she's not enjoying life with her husband and son in her home city of Melbourne, she's at her computer, creating the romances she loves in her dream job. Visit Nicola's website at www.nicolamarsh.com for the latest news of her books.

CHAPTER ONE

KRISTEN LEWIS had a thing for hotels.

She loved the luxury, the hustle and bustle, even those tiny toiletries designed to slather and splurge and make a weary soul feel like a million dollars for that split second in time.

But most of all she loved the anonymity, that people from all walks of life passed by without knowing or caring why a successful thirty-five-year-old woman would be sitting alone at a bar sipping a spritzer.

'Men,' she muttered, stabbing at the lemon wedge in her glass with a swizzle stick, wondering if their ability to blow off other people was a genetic thing.

Even as friends they couldn't be trusted.

She took another stab at the piece of lemon—which was starting to resemble Swiss cheese with the number of jabs she'd taken at it in the last five minutes—as she glanced around the Oasis bar of the Grand Hyatt hotel in Singapore.

She loved this place, with its sleek chrome lines, trendy black furniture with the occasional splash of red, and had spent many hours here with clients and work colleagues during her four-year stint working at a

Singapore TV station. The hotel's grandeur screamed 'special occasion', the reason why she'd chosen to meet Nigel here tonight, envisioning a fun evening with her best work buddy, celebrating the completion of her latest project.

Unfortunately, Nigel had had a better offer from a twenty-two-year-old temp and had given her the brush-off in the foyer.

'Buddy my butt,' she muttered, taking a sip of her favourite white-wine-and-soda combination as her gaze locked with a guy sitting at the other end of the bar.

Not bad flashed across her mind as she took in his dark eyes, dark hair, slight bump in the nose, which added character to his model-handsome face, and sardonic expression highlighted by the slight quirk of his lips.

Dropping her gaze quickly, she returned to studying coasters while mentally listing Nigel's faults, the main one being that he preferred a romantic evening with a bimbo over a night out with a long-term friend. Not that she should be surprised. If Nigel had a choice between wining and dining his latest prospective conquest or sharing a drink with a friend, she'd lose every time.

Letting her gaze sweep the room again in a general fly-by, it unerringly zeroed in on the good-looking guy, and she prepared for a quick look-away. From past experience, guys who looked like that sitting alone at a bar would still be staring at her, trying to make eye contact before moving in for the kill.

Instead, Mr Handsome was staring morosely into his drink, a sombre expression on his striking face, and crazily she sighed in disappointment. She'd never believed in fate or karma or any of that airy-fairy rubbish—yet when she'd locked gazes with the guy a second ago something intangible had zinged between them, almost like kindred spirits meeting and shaking hands before fading away.

Now he wore the same brooding, gloomy expression which matched her mood perfectly, and for an irrational moment she wondered if she should go over there and share sob stories with him.

Shaking her head, she finished off her spritzer—there had to be more wine than soda in it for her to be contemplating such an uncharacteristic action—and scrummaged in her handbag for money.

'Is this yours?'

Looking up from the giant, cavernous hole which sucked up purses, tissues, pens, make-up and everything else she needed on a daily basis, making them vanish with a flick of its clasp, she stared into the darkest eyes she'd ever seen.

A dark chocolate, they stared at her with polite interest, as if expecting something from her.

'Is this your coat?'

His voice washed over her as deep and mysterious and impressive as his eyes, and she blinked, realising he did expect something from her: an answer.

'Oh. Yes, thanks. Was it on the floor?'

She couldn't look away, lost in his hypnotic stare, floundering when she would usually have given Mr Handsome a confident smile, a polite nod and terse reply.

He was probably pulling some slick, practised move on her, and she gave guys like that short shift. Instead, she stood there like a mannequin, stiff and wide-eyed, unable to shake the feeling that this guy was on her wavelength.

Smiling, he nodded. 'Yes, you knocked it off the back of your stool while searching in that suitcase of yours.'

'Suitcase?'

If his eyes had mesmerised her, they had nothing on his smile, which had her surreptitiously leaning against the bar for support.

He pointed to her handbag. 'Looks big enough to store the odd suit and a pair of shoes or two.'

She laughed, and snapped the suitcase shut. 'I'm on the go a lot, so like to have everything at my fingertips. You know, important stuff, like pens and notebooks and all the other paraphernalia I couldn't possibly find anywhere if I left all this at home.'

His smile widened but somehow it didn't reach his eyes, a flicker of sadness darkening their depths to almost black, and she felt another twinge, an uncharacteristic urge to reach out and comfort him. 'Speaking of being on the go, I should catch some sleep. I've got an early plane to catch tomorrow.'

'Here on business?'

'Yes.'

'Ah, too bad for you that it's just a short trip,' she blurted, filled with a desperate urge to keep him talking, to find out more about the mysterious guy who saved ladies' coats from death by trampling, yet wore an invisible cloak of sadness around his broad shoulders.

'Emphasis on "for me"? By your Aussie accent, I assumed you were here on business too.'

'Not exactly. I could be on holiday,' she said, hating the stilted conversation they were having standing up, which was exactly why she didn't usually hang out in places like this.

'You're not on holiday.'

She raised an eyebrow, surprised by his matter-of-fact tone. 'How do you know that?'

'Because holidaymakers have a relaxed look about them, an excited glow, and you don't have it.'

'Gee, thanks. So I've lost my glow too,' she muttered, wondering what she was doing here, making small talk with a guy she didn't know and who'd only stopped because she was a klutz.

'You've got a glow,' he said in a tight, strangled tone which made her look up and register the fleeting interest in his eyes. 'Just not a holiday one.'

Kristen didn't know if it was her bruised ego courtesy of being stood up by Nigel, the spritzer she'd had on an empty stomach or the nebulous connection she felt for this sad stranger, but she found herself doing something completely out of character.

'If you're not too tired and can hold off on the z's a while longer, maybe you'd like to hear about my non-holiday glow?'

He didn't move, surprise mingling with something else in his eyes—regret, hope, desire?—and she wished the ground would open up as heat surged into her cheeks.

'Look, don't worry. I'm sure you have more important things—'

'I'd like that,' he said, hanging her coat over the back of the stool and holding it out for her.

'Great.'

She sat down, baffled by her behaviour and the simple pleasure derived from his acceptance.

'Would you like a drink?'

'A lemon, lime and bitters, please.'

If the splash of wine in the spritzer had been responsible for her erratic behaviour, she'd better stick to the soft stuff otherwise there was no telling what she might do.

After placing their order with the waiter—who had a knowing smile, like he'd seen this scenario a thousand times before—Mr Handsome turned to her.

'I'm Nate.'

Smiling, she held out her hand. 'I'm Kris. Non-holidaymaker. Living in Singapore and loving it.'

Warmth enveloped her hand as he shook it with a solid grip. She liked that. She hated it when guys gave her the limp-fish handshake because of her sex, though she usually showed them, turning their condescension into awe when she wowed them in the business arena.

'Family reasons?'

She shook her head, wondering if he was fishing for info about a significant other, before ditching the idea.

Nate seemed too up-front to play those sort of games. If he were interested he would've asked, and sadly she had a feeling he was sitting here chatting to her out of pity rather than desire for her as a woman. Something in the way he'd looked at her when she'd invited him to share a drink, as if he'd have liked to refuse but didn't want to hurt her feelings.

Oh well, she didn't care. Right now it felt good to talk to someone, especially with a guy who looked like Nate, regardless of his motivations for sitting here with a sad case like her.

'No, I don't have much family. Two sisters back in Sydney, that's it. I've been here working, producing one of Singapore's travel shows.'

'Sounds interesting.'

He thanked the waiter as their drinks were placed in front of them and signed the bill, giving her ample opportunity to study him.

White business shirt unbuttoned at the collar and rolled up at the sleeves revealed strong forearms, and shirt tucked into the waistband of black trousers encased long legs ending in a pair of designer shoes. However, the clothes weren't the interesting part, it was the body beneath: lean, streamlined, a physique hinting at subtle strength.

Very, very nice.

Usually, she wouldn't have given a stranger the time of day, let alone have invited him to share a drink, yet there was something so…so…*haunting* about him, an underlying vulnerability that had her wanting to cuddle him close and pat him comfortingly on the back.

'Can I ask you something?'

Her gaze snapped up from somewhere in the vicinity of his collar, where it parted to reveal a tantalising V of tanned skin, an expanse of skin she found infinitely fascinating for no other reason than what it hinted at, as the rest of his chest filled out the shirt rather well.

'Sure.'

'You were muttering into your drink earlier. Is everything okay?'

Once again, heat seeped into her cheeks. Could this get any more embarrassing, the gallant guy having a pity drink with the desperately ditched girl?

'You know what they say about talking to yourself being the first sign of madness? Well, I'm mad all right. Mad enough to want to throttle my buddy Nigel for bailing on me.'

'Ouch.'

Nate winced and she squared her shoulders, ready to rebuff his pity. Instead, she saw a glimmer of amusement lighting his eyes. 'Did he stand you up?'

'Sure did, the louse. Said he had a better offer from this girl he's been chasing for a while, so he ditches a friend for a bit of fluff. Nice.'

'Very poor form,' Nate said, his eyes twinkling beneath a mock frown. 'Friends should always come first.'

He was making light of her situation and, rather than being insulted, laughter bubbled within her at the big deal she'd made out of something pretty insignificant. 'Why did you think he stood me up?'

Nate's amusement spread to his mouth, tilting it upwards at the corners. 'Well, one look at that bag and the maniacal gleam in your eyes, any man would've made a run for it.'

She laughed, surprised the annoyance of being stood up by Nigel had receded, replaced by an unexpected need to share confidences with this guy.

'Ah, but you didn't. You're sitting here, aren't you?'

'Good point.'

He tipped his glass in her direction before taking a long sip of beer, his gaze never leaving hers.

She couldn't figure him out.

He wasn't flirting with her or making suggestive comments, or even hinting at anything untoward, but when he stared at her like that—steady, unwavering, loaded—the air between them sizzled with an invisible current, and had her reaching for her own drink which she gulped down in record time.

'You know it's his loss, right?'

Breaking the hypnotising eye contact, she said, 'Yeah, I know. The guy's got his priorities all wrong.'

'So he wasn't the love of your life?'

Kristen snorted, picturing scruffy, laid-back Nigel as anything other than a work buddy she could offload to at the end of a rough day.

'No way. Nigel and I are purely platonic.'

'Then he's definitely not worth worrying about now. You can give your friend an earful when you next see him.'

'Too right.'

Suddenly, she realised how trivial her complaint against Nigel was, and wanted to know more about the sadness she'd glimpsed in Nate when she'd first seen him. 'What about you—any life stories to tell?'

If she'd doused him with her icy drink she would've got the same response: shock combined with pain, sorrow quickly masked by an enforced blank mask.

'Not really. I'm married to my job; don't have time for anything else.'

'I know the feeling,' she said, trying to cover her monstrous gaff in prying into things which didn't concern her. 'Just call me Mrs TV Producer. So, what do you do?'

He hadn't lost his shuttered expression, and he waited before speaking, as if weighing up every word. 'I'm involved in the entertainment area too, though on the business side of things.'

'So you're one of the corporate bigwigs who control the purse strings, right?'

At last, a glimmer of a smile. 'You could say that. I'm the CEO of my own company and, apart from handling sporting rights for everything from rugby to the Olympics, we branch into other areas too.'

'Well, if I ever need a job I'll know who to come to,' she said, hating how her mind immediately latched onto his use of the word 'handling', and conjuring up startling images of him doing exactly that...with her!

'You do that.'

He drained his beer and she braced herself for the inevitable parting, totally confused by her reluctance to let him go.

She didn't know this guy.

She didn't want this to end.

She didn't have the foggiest idea what to do.

'I'm hungry after that beer. Do you want to join me for dinner?'

Trying to hide her relief—and elation—she said, 'That would be great. The buffet here is the best in Singapore.'

'So I've heard. Come on, let's try it.'

Sliding off her stool, Kristen ignored her voice of reason which yelled *What do you think you're doing, having dinner with a guy you barely know? Are you nuts?*

'I don't usually do this type of thing,' he said, handing her the infamous coat. 'Having dinner with women I just met.'

'That makes two of us.'

Happily ignoring her voice of reason, she sent him a shy smile and headed for the restaurant.

Nate forked a delicious combination of spicy black-pepper crab and fried rice into his mouth, trying to concentrate on the amazing food on his plate rather than the intriguing woman sitting across the table from him.

What am I doing here?

He'd asked himself the same question repeatedly over the last half hour and still hadn't come up with an answer. One that made sense, that was.

He didn't chat up women, he didn't accept drink invitations in hotel bars, and he sure as hell didn't have dinner with them unless it involved business, yet here he was sharing the best meal he'd had in ages with a beautiful woman he'd known for less than an hour. And enjoying it!

'Good?'

He nodded, his gaze fixed on her mouth and the way her lips wrapped around a crab claw, his groin tightening at the sheer eroticism of the movement.

This couldn't be happening.

He usually didn't have the time or the inclination. So what was he doing, fantasising about this virtual stranger's lush mouth and what it would feel like on him?

'I'm a seafood addict,' Kris said, dabbing at her glistening mouth with a serviette while he wrenched his mind out of the gutter. 'This place is famous for it.'

'Along with the roast duck, tandoori chicken, satays and the million other dishes on offer, you mean?'

She smiled, the power of that one simple action staggering in its ability to capture his interest and keep him riveted. 'Wait till you try the desserts.'

He didn't have a sweet tooth in his body, but suddenly he couldn't wait to try a chocolate mousse or lychee sorbet. In fact, he'd go along with anything this fascinating woman suggested at the moment, which showed exactly how jet-lagged he must be.

He needed to stop these two-day jaunts to Asia if this

was the result: a confused, half-drugged state which had him focussing on all the wrong cues, like the way her stunning blue eyes sparkled, how the highlights in her short, layered blonde hair shone and the way her smile lit up the room.

As for her body—tall, lithe and graceful in the slim pinstripe skirt and pale-blue shirt—he'd been struggling not to stare since he'd first seen her hunched over that gigantic bag of hers in the bar with her jacket in a pool at her feet.

She'd appeared deliciously rumpled and flustered when he'd picked up her coat, and nothing like the ice-cool blonde who'd locked gazes with him a minute before with her big, sad eyes and grim expression.

He'd watched her for a while, toying with her drink, stabbing at the lemon wedge, her mouth muttering words he couldn't hear. He would've laughed if her expression hadn't been so fragile, and, though he'd had his own problems to deal with, he'd been unable to walk past her without reaching out and giving her some indication that she wasn't alone in the world, some indication that he understood.

Boy, did he understand.

People said grief eased with time, that time healed all wounds.

People didn't know jack.

'You know, dessert is optional. You don't have to try it if you don't want.'

Hating the realisation that his mask had slipped for a moment, and she must have glimpsed some of what he was feeling, he said, 'Sorry, just thinking.'

'About something not very pleasant, by the looks of it?'

The question hung between them, softly probing but intrusive nonetheless.

'Guess being away from home has me in a mood.'

'Being homesick is the pits,' she said, replacing her serviette on the table and sitting back. 'I missed Sydney like crazy when I first came here, but you want to know the secret to getting past it?'

'Sure.'

Leaning forward, she tapped the side of her nose as if about to depart a secret lost in time. 'Orang-utans.'

Maybe the jet lag was worse than he'd thought. He could've sworn she'd just said something about homesickness being cured by great apes.

She nodded, a smile playing about her mouth. 'You heard me. Orang-utans. The biggest, goofiest guys on the planet. You can't help but love them. I was feeling pretty lousy my first week here, so I took a trip to the Singapore Zoo and spent an hour with the hairy goofballs, having breakfast with them, laughing at their antics. Suddenly, no more homesickness. Instant cure, just like that.'

She snapped her fingers and he blinked, wondering what it was about this cool yet kooky woman that had him so captivated.

'I'll keep that in mind,' he said, shaking his head in disbelief, torn between wanting to bolt from the table before she enthralled him any further and hauling her into his arms to see if she was real.

She flitted between serious and funny, sad and happy, changing emotions like the frenetic activity of the stock market on opening.

He hardly knew a thing about her, yet he wanted to know it all.

He didn't know her surname yet he knew she loved seafood, had a brain behind her beauty, and had a thing for big, orange apes.

They had little in common, yet he suddenly knew he didn't want this evening to end.

He wanted to know more, he wanted her with a staggering fierceness that clawed at him, begging to be let out and soothed by her touch, in her arms, all night.

'Uh-oh, you're having more of those unpleasant thoughts.'

She picked up the wine bottle and topped up his glass, as if a fine Shiraz would fix what ailed him. If it were that easy, he would've bought out every vineyard in Australia by now.

Direct to the point of bluntness in business, he took a deep breath, opting for the same approach now and hoping it didn't earn him a thundering slap.

'Actually, my thoughts aren't so unpleasant.'

'Oh?'

Her eyebrow kicked up, highlighting the curious glint in her blue eyes.

'I know this is going to sound crazy, and you have every right to walk away from this table when I've finished, but I was just thinking how we have a connection and I don't want this evening to end.'

Surprise flashed across her face, closely followed by—indignation?

Fear?

Hope?

He had no idea. It had been a long time since he'd spent this much time with a woman, let alone tried to fathom her emotions.

'Are you asking me to spend the night with you?'

Put like that, he tried not to cringe. It looked like he wasn't the only one who favoured the direct approach.

'I don't know what I'm asking,' he muttered, eyeing the door and wondering if it was too late to make a run for it. 'I don't do this very often. Hell, I haven't been out with a woman for years. But I know one thing—I'm attracted to you. You make me feel good. And I don't want to lose this feeling, no matter how temporary.'

Suddenly, it was as simple as that. No more, no less.

This stunning woman with her expressive eyes and lush mouth had him feeling good for the first time in a long time, and he wanted more.

'I think you do know what you're asking,' she said, her gaze locked on his, her smile uncertain as she toyed with the end of the tablecloth, twisting the damask over and over. 'I think we both do, and my answer is yes.'

'Yes?'

He exhaled, unaware he'd been holding his breath, filled with elation and anticipation and myriad emotions he couldn't describe as she stared at him with excitement glittering in her expressive eyes.

'Yes.'

From that moment everything faded into oblivion as he stood up, held out his hand, experienced an electrifying jolt as she placed hers in it, and led her from the restaurant to the lifts leading up to his room.

They didn't speak.

They didn't need to.

Words seemed superfluous as they entered his room, closed the door and fell into each other's arms like two drowning people hanging onto the last lifebuoy: desperate, frantic, caught up in a storm bigger than the both of them.

As her lips clung to his and he deepened the kiss, his arms sliding around her waist to mould her to him, a thrill shot through him.

He'd never done anything so rash, so reckless, so damn impulsive, and it felt good.

It felt great.

Thanks to the beautiful woman in his arms, he suddenly realised it was time to start living again.

CHAPTER TWO

Kristen never did anything on impulse.

She'd never understood the rash decisions people made on the spur of the moment and then lamented later. She was a thinker who weighed up options carefully for everything, from buying a pair of killer black stilettos to hiring the best grip boy.

Yet here she was lying next to the sexiest guy she'd ever met after having amazing sex. Twice!

Logical? No.

Well thought out? Uh-uh.

Satisfying, cataclysmic and exciting? Oh yeah!

Wriggling under the cotton sheet covering them, she stretched, tensing every muscle from her toes to her fingers, before relaxing, savouring the warm, sated sensation creeping through her tired body.

To say she'd never felt like this before would be the understatement of the year.

Risking a quick glance at him, she smiled, lost in delicious memories of how he'd kissed her, held her and made love to her with every inch of his body, and corny as it might sound, she knew it had been more than a physical connection.

Quite simply, they'd clicked.

For whatever reason—whether it had been his underlying vulnerability, his innate sadness or the fact he was a refined, well-mannered, genuinely nice guy—she'd thrown caution to the wind and made love with a virtual stranger.

She should be mortified, or cringing with embarrassment at the very least. Instead, she rolled onto her side and watched him sleep, filled with a calmness she'd never known.

With his lips relaxed into a half smile, and his long, dark eyelashes fanning his cheeks, he looked a lot younger than when he'd been awake and carrying around the inherent sadness like a backpack weighing him down.

What would make a successful, wealthy guy who looked like he could model underwear on billboards around the world so sad?

Guys his age with money to burn were usually chasing women, striving for the next big thing, and whooping it up in general—not necessarily in that order. She should know; she mixed in those circles and held those players at arm's length constantly.

Yet here was a guy who probably moved in that social sphere wearing his sadness like a badge of honour. He appeared to be a loner, not that she really knew anything beyond the basics about him. Heck, she didn't even know his surname!

However, there was something about him... She hadn't conjured up their connection out of thin air. It was there, it was real, and for the last few hours everything else had faded into the background while she'd linked up with a kindred spirit.

Weird, whacky, but true. No one would believe her, but then who would she tell?

'You're awake.'

Blinking away her memories she focussed on Nate, smiling at his heavy-lidded, half-asleep expression.

'Can't sleep. Guess I'm not used to sharing my bed.'

Ain't that the truth!

Not that it bothered her. She valued her independence, and hated having to fight over the duvet with a guy hogging half the bed.

'Whose bed?'

He smiled, his tone, soft and husky, washing over her like a warm spring shower and making her want to throw her arms wide and dance from the sheer beauty of it.

'Good point. Make that *your* bed,' she said, wondering how this could feel so right.

She'd expected a tense, awkward conversation on waking, perhaps the odd excuse or two. Instead they lay there, grinning at each other like a couple of goofy teenagers, barely inches apart, buck naked.

'You're okay with all this, right?'

His smile waned as the light in his eyes faded.

Uh-oh, here goes the whole 'this was a mistake, see you around' chat.

She nodded, making sure her smile didn't slip. 'Of course. I wouldn't be here if I didn't want to be. We're two consenting adults, we made a decision to spend the night together. No big deal.'

Then why the empty ring to her words? Or the hollow feeling in her heart, when she had no right to feel anything other than physical attraction for this guy?

'You're right,' he said, dropping his gaze to her hand bunching the sheet, and she relaxed with effort.

He might have just agreed with her mature, rational assessment of a rather awkward situation, but the guilty expression ripping across his face said otherwise.

She could've reached out to him, prompted him to tell her what was wrong, but she didn't have the right. In fact, apart from sharing one fabulous night of scintillating sex and an unexpected connection, she didn't even know him, at least not enough for him to share confidences with her.

Still wanting to ease the sadness now mingling with the guilt on his expressive face, she said, 'Look, I don't usually do this sort of thing, and by your reaction I'm guessing it's the same for you.'

He raised his gaze slowly upwards, remorse darkening his eyes to almost black. 'I never do this sort of thing. Why, does it show?'

Great, now he thought she'd insulted his prowess!

Reaching out to him, she covered his hand with hers, hoping the simple physical contact would convey half of what she was feeling.

'Last night was fabulous. I just meant that dealing with all this aftermath stuff is kind of icky.'

'Icky, huh?'

His lips twitched, and she silently congratulated herself for bringing a smile back to his face.

Returning his smile, she said, 'I guess what I'm trying to say is you've got nothing to feel bad about. We both wanted to be with each other last night, let's leave it at that.'

His smile flickered as something akin to shame

flashed in his eyes, and she knew she'd somehow said the wrong thing again.

'You're an incredible woman, Kris. Thank you for last night.'

He reached out and cupped her cheek, his thumb brushing her bottom lip in the slowest, most tender, barely-there movement before letting go, leaving her wanting more, craving his touch when she hardly knew it.

This wasn't good.

She was neither drunk nor stupid, so lying here lost in useless wishes of 'what may be' was pointless.

Nate had a plane to catch and a life to get back to, she had a new job in Australia to look forward to.

Time to start looking to the future, and chalk up this incredible encounter to a fate she didn't believe in.

'Thank you,' she said, brushing a hasty kiss across his lips before slipping out of bed, clutching the bottom sheet around her. 'You have a plane to catch in a few hours, so I'll leave you to it.'

'Kris?'

She paused, wishing she could skip the farewell and fast-forward to when she'd be back on solid ground, away from the seductive powers of a virtual stranger in an exotic place, caught up in the type of magical romance she knew didn't exist in the real world.

'Yes?'

Nate stared at her, his dark, intense gaze trying to send her a message she couldn't fathom. Once again his sad mask had slipped into place, and for a split second she wondered if their impending goodbye had anything to do with it.

Yeah, like he'd be heartbroken over a woman he barely knew.

'I wish things were different.'

For one heart-stopping moment, she felt the same zing, the same spark she'd felt back in the bar when they'd first met, the same tenuous connection that this was right, was meant to be, and she almost ran back to the bed and flung herself into his arms.

But that wasn't the sensible thing to do, and right now logic was about all she had left.

'I do too,' she finally said, opting for honesty, yet knowing it wouldn't make a difference as she slipped into the bathroom to get dressed and head back to her well-organised life and out of his.

CHAPTER THREE

KRIS strode up to the shiny chrome desk of Channel RX, feeling every bit the new kid on the block and hating it. No matter how confident she was, or how carefully she chose her clothes, she always felt the same terrifying insecurity she'd felt every time she'd started a new school or been introduced to a new foster family. And that had been way too many times for her liking.

Pasting her sparkly toothpaste-smile on, she leaned on the desk and fixed the young receptionist with a confident stare. 'Hi, I'm Kristen Lewis, the new executive producer.'

The receptionist, a young version of Julia Roberts, held up her hand as she fielded what looked like five calls at once as the switchboard lit up, and Kristen relaxed, feeling at home straight away.

At least this wasn't any different. She could walk into any television studio around the world and find the same harried receptionist, the same flood of incoming calls from irate or scandalised viewers, and a buzz out on the studio floor you just couldn't beat.

She loved working in television: the drama, the rush, the constant push to be better and strive higher than the competition. She was good at what she did, which was why she'd been lucky enough to land this plum job at Melbourne's premier station.

She couldn't wait to take up the challenge, something new to take her mind off Singapore, and that fateful night she couldn't forget no matter how hard she tried.

'Right, sorry about that. I'm Hallie, general dogsbody around this place. Would you like to head on through, or shall I call the boss and let him know you're here?'

'I'll find my own way, thanks. Give me a chance to look around.'

Hallie sent her a relieved smile as she cast a frantic look at the switchboard which had lit up like a Christmas tree again. 'No worries. If you need anything, holler.'

Kristen waved and headed for the imposing black swing doors.

This was it.

The start of a new job, life in a new city without the complications of memories of a guy with unforgettable dark-chocolate eyes.

'Kristen?'

She stopped and swivelled to face Hallie. 'Yes?'

'The boss man just buzzed through to ask if you'd arrived. He wants to see you in his office asap. Through the doors, down the corridor on your left, last office on the right.'

'Thanks.'

Kristen pushed through the doors and into the swankiest studio she'd ever seen. Polished floorboards lined the endless corridors stretching left and right, with countless doors off each one, while straight ahead lay a huge auditorium-like space enclosed in glass with a small army swarming around a mock-kitchen set.

No one stopped to stare at the new girl, not even to give the odd curious glance. She knew what it was like. Once the cameras were set to roll it was heads down, bottoms up, as everyone performed their roles to perfection. The cameras didn't lie, and the slightest mistake could cost a whole take or, worse, be aired live to an unforgiving audience.

A tingle raised the hackles on her skin, and she shivered. Damn, she loved her job.

Feeling more confident with every passing second, she headed off down the left corridor as instructed, resisting the urge to peek into every office. Many doors were wide open, the hum of voices and the smell of brewed coffee heavy in the air, and she hoped her new boss would offer her a cup. She'd kill for a caffeine hit right now, what with the move to Melbourne on top of her recent sleepless nights—courtesy of Mr Handsome, who she really hoped would turn into Mr Forgettable any time now.

She knew nothing about her new boss. After having been headhunted by a producer here at RX, she'd barely had time to study the channel's prospectus as she'd rushed around like a maniac, wrapping up her work and life in Singapore, let alone learn who the head honcho was.

Thankfully, she rarely dealt with the CEOs of outfits like this: slick, go-get-'em types who were focussed on the bottom line and little else. She'd much rather concentrate on the enjoyable task of creating great TV than counting the behind-the-scenes wheeling and dealing.

Reaching the final door on the right, she pulled up short.

'Nathan Boyd, CEO'.

She blinked, hating the irrational surge of heat the name Nathan sent through her.

Damn it, she should be over this, over him.

It had been one night, nearly three months ago, for goodness' sake! One incredible, amazing night when she'd connected with a guy whose surname she didn't even know.

Yeah, really connected.

Shaking her head, she wiped her damp palms against her skirt, tugged at her jacket hem and, swinging her bag over her shoulder, she rapped sharply at the door.

However, as the door opened and she willed her legs to stay upright, Kristen knew forgetting Nate and that one eventful night would be impossible.

Totally impossible considering Nathan Boyd, CEO—Nathan Boyd, her new boss—was her Nate.

The guy who had rocked her world.

Nate's smile faded as Kristen tried her best not to reel back in shock.

'Kris?'

Not the smoothest of opening lines, but then considering she couldn't think let alone form words at that moment he was faring a damn sight better than her.

Looking way too calm, he stepped aside and gestured her in. 'Please come in.'

She ignored his invitation, her legs rooted to the spot. Wasn't he the least bit rattled to find her on his doorstep? How could he look so cool, so unflappable?

Suddenly, white-hot anger shot through her as she studied his composed face, knowing exactly why she'd been headhunted for this job, and by whom.

'I don't believe this!' she finally blurted, years of professionalism deserting her as she stared at him in growing horror, heat surging to her cheeks.

'Come inside and we'll discuss it,' he said, his voice as deep and steady as she remembered as he opened the door wider and waited for her to step inside.

Marching through the door like a woman sentenced to the gallows, she collapsed into the nearest chair on the visitor's side of his desk, and took several calming breaths before she exploded.

'Did you know about this?'

Taking a seat behind his desk, he sat back, shoulders relaxed and arms resting comfortably on his fancy leather director's chair, while she could barely keep a lid on her growing temper.

'About you working here? No.'

'Really? I'm guessing there aren't a lot of executive producers named Kristen. Were you behind me being headhunted?'

'Why would you think that?'

Rolling her eyes, she said, 'Come on, you're a smart man. Do I need to spell it out? Singapore—the night we were together?'

His lips thinned into a compressed line as he ran a hand through his hair, the first sign he was anything other than on top of the situation.

'Look, I had no idea who the new exec producer was till I opened that door and saw you standing there. I've been in charge of this operation less than twenty-four hours, and have spent most of that time out on the studio floor. I haven't studied employee lists, haven't had the time. Instead, I've asked Hallie to send along everyone from the top down at half-hourly intervals so I can get acquainted face to face rather than studying boring CV's.'

'Uh-huh,' she said, her anger somewhat deflating at the sincerity in his voice as the reality of the situation finally hit her.

She'd just barged into her new boss's office with the finesse of a wounded rhino, flinging wild accusations and acting like the injured party, when in fact this was her dream job and she could've just botched it with her erratic behaviour.

'I'm surprised you didn't do your homework. You know, study up on who you'd be working for.'

Nate fixed her with a stare she found disconcertingly familiar, a gleam of challenge in the dark depths of his eyes, and she bristled, hating his implications that she wasn't professional.

'I did. Though I guess the contract I signed or the prospectus I read didn't mention your name.'

She snapped her fingers, not willing to give him an inch, her latent anger taking little to reignite. 'Then again, I wouldn't have made the connection, not knowing your surname and all.'

He stiffened, the faintest red staining his tanned cheeks. 'You're overreacting. You don't see me throwing around allegations, like maybe you knew I was CEO here and wanted to give me a shake-up by walking in here today as my newest employee?'

'Overreacting?'

She leaped from her chair before she could think twice, planting her hands on his desk and leaning forward.

'Aren't you the least bit thrown by this nightmare situation? Don't you feel awkward? And do you honestly think I'd go to the trouble of faking a shocked reaction just to get a rise out of you?'

Shaking her head, she plopped back down in her chair, suddenly embarrassed by her outburst. 'Look, I'm sorry if I did overreact, but honestly finding out you're my boss has thrown me.'

Though, in all honesty, not half as thrown as how attracted she was to him even in a crazy situation like this.

While she wanted to rant and rave at the injustice of having to work with a guy she'd rather forget, she couldn't help but admire his charcoal-grey designer suit and the way it fitted the great body she'd already had the pleasure of exploring in intimate detail.

As for his eyes… They had a mesmerising quality, their darkness a fathomless pool of mystery which begged to be explored, and her pulse raced at the memories of how far she'd taken that exploration…

Sitting back, he clasped his hands behind his head, every bit the consummate professional, while she struggled to refocus her wandering attention and come to terms with her new employer.

'A coincidence over which I had no control. Now, what do you want to do?'

She wanted to walk out of his office and never look back.

She wanted to stop noticing the way his business shirt stretched across his chest as he leaned back, the same hard, muscular chest she'd had one-on-one contact with.

But most of all she wanted to forget how he'd made her feel on that one incredible night.

Taking a steadying breath, she said, 'I want to be the

best damn executive producer RX has ever had. But this is still uncomfortable.'

She waved her hands between the two of them, wishing he wouldn't look at her like that, the intensity of his dark gaze resurrecting memories she'd rather forget, her mind still reeling from the fact they'd be working together.

'It doesn't have to be. We're professionals. I'm sure what's happened in the past doesn't have to affect our work.'

'Professionals. Right.'

Suddenly her shoulders relaxed, and she sat back in the chair, knowing she'd faced a lot hairier situations and come out on top. Besides, how hard could working with Nate be?

'You're right. We both didn't mind the anonymity that night, and it's in the past. Done. Forgotten. So, Nathan Boyd, what's your vision for Channel RX and how do you see me fitting into it?'

Straight to the point and no bull. She liked that in the people she worked with, and hoped he did too, especially considering her rather emotional outbursts since she'd first set foot in this office.

Thankfully, he accepted her switch back to professionalism and, gathering a stack of papers in front of him, he shuffled a stapled bundle into a glossy navy folder and handed it to her.

'My vision's in there, laid out in black and white. I want Channel RX to ultimately be number one in Australia. I want ratings in prime-time slots to soar, I want innovation, I want a fresh slant on old faithfuls such as the news and current affairs. In a nutshell? I want it all.'

'You're aiming big,' she said, a tiny thrill of excitement shooting through her at the thought of working with a boss who had a clear vision. 'I like that.'

Nodding, he clasped his hands and leaned forward. 'As I haven't had a chance to find out from other sources yet, tell me what you bring to RX.'

'That's easy. I'm the best.'

She shrugged, knowing now wasn't a time for modesty. She needed to impress Nate, to wow him, to show him that what they'd shared really was in the past, and she could give one hundred percent to the job despite her earlier uncharacteristic tantrum.

His lips twitched, resurrecting instant memories of how they'd felt, how he kissed, and she quickly subdued that train of thought.

'You're very confident.'

'You have to be in this business,' she said, fixing him with a direct stare designed to convince him of her sincerity. 'I love my job. I'm prepared to put in the long hours, to do whatever it takes to make the shows I work on successful. I demand respect, and I treat co-workers the same way I'd like to be treated. I won't settle for second best. I deserve more than that.'

His lips curved upwards into a genuine smile as he stood and held out his hand. 'I think you'll be a great asset to this station. We're going to make a good team.'

'Thanks.'

She shook his hand quickly, dropping it before she had time to register the quick surge of heat from his palm to hers. 'I'll go find my office and get acquainted with the rest of the gang.'

'Great. I'll see you later.'

She headed for the door, wondering if this surreal experience was a dream and if she'd wake up as soon as she stepped out into the corridor.

'Kris?'

'Yes?'

Her hand stilled on the doorknob as her heart thudded at the way he said her name, at the memories of how many times he'd murmured her name that night in Singapore.

'It's good seeing you again.'

Managing a half-strangled smile, she bolted out the door.

Kristen willed her legs to move at a sedate pace from Nate's office, when in fact she wanted to bolt down the long corridor and keep running till she reached the massive front doors and beyond.

Seeing the guy she'd spent countless sleepless nights trying to forget open that office door had been like a slap in the face, a swift, sharp wake-up call that she hadn't forgotten him at all. Or, more precisely, hadn't forgotten how he'd made her feel: feminine, desired and special.

How could he elicit those feelings when she barely knew him?

How could she face him on a daily basis knowing he had that sort of power over her?

Rounding a corner, she pulled up short as Hallie held up her hands to prevent a collision. 'Hey! You okay?'

Schooling her face into a practised confident mask, she nodded. 'Sure.'

By Hallie's raised eyebrow, she didn't believe her. 'Didn't the meeting with the boss go well?'

'It was fine.'

Yeah, right.

'You look like you could use a coffee. I'm heading to the cafeteria. Want to join me?'

Kristen would've preferred to find her office and get settled in while getting her emotions under control, but the lure of caffeine proved too strong. She needed something to jolt her out of the trance-like shock at finding Mr Handsome was none other than Nathan Boyd, her new *boss!*

'Love to,' she said, falling into step with Hallie, who stood a head shorter than her but moved with the speed of light despite her three-inch stilettos.

'What did you think of the boss?'

Kristen chose her words carefully. 'Nathan seems like a man with a vision. The channel should go far.'

'Nathan, huh?'

Hallie sent her a wink, and Kristen battled a rising blush and failed, speaking quickly to cover her gaff. 'He's very informal for a CEO. Actually, I didn't expect to meet him on the first day. The CEOs of stations I've worked at before didn't get too hands-on, but I get the impression he likes to be quite involved, especially on the creative side.'

'The boss only started yesterday, and if you want my opinion he can get hands-on with me any time.'

'That's not very professional,' Kris blurted, wishing she'd bitten her tongue as Hallie stared at her in wide-eyed confusion.

Thankfully, a group of cameramen greeting Hallie like a long-lost friend defused the moment. Besides, she wasn't jealous. She had to care to be jealous, and she didn't, she couldn't.

'Okay, here we are. Welcome to the Ritz,' Hallie said,

waving off the boys and holding open the cafeteria door for her. 'Come on, the coffee isn't bad, if you don't mind the odd dreg or two.'

Smiling at the receptionist's sense of humour, Kristen followed her into a cavernous room filled with stainless-steel tables and chairs, chafing dishes piled high with hot food lining one wall, and a huge selection of crisps, chocolate bars and sodas nearby.

From what she'd seen so far, Channel RX did things on a grand scale, and if the quality of their current shows that she'd managed to watch so far was any indication she'd made a good decision.

'What'll it be? They do a mean latte and, seeing as it's your first day, my shout.'

'Latte's fine. And thanks,' Kristen said, feeling like a chick being pushed around by a mother hen.

'Right, here you go. Let's sit over there, and you can tell me the Kristen Lewis story,' Hallie said, handing her a steaming latte in record time and making for a table in the farthest corner.

'Not much to tell,' Kristen said, unable to resist Hallie's open friendliness, but wary all the same. 'Besides, if I tell you all my deep, dark secrets on the first day, you'll think I'm a gossip.'

Hallie rolled her eyes. 'As if. I've only been here a couple of months, you're new, and so I'm bestowing you the great honour of being my work buddy.'

Kristen didn't know what to say, and before she could come up with something Hallie held up her hand. 'Uh-uh. Don't thank me. I know it's a highly coveted position to be on the good side of the receptionist. I know you're probably shell-shocked but, trust me, I'll be nice.'

Staring into Hallie's guileless blue eyes, registering her wide, friendly smile, Kristen knew that at least she had one ally at RX.

Taking a sip of her surprisingly good latte, she said, 'Are you always this upfront?'

Hallie nodded, her auburn curls bouncing around her face. 'Yep. Only way to be. I know you're an exec and will probably blow me off after this, but hey, no harm in trying, right?'

Kristen fought a rising blush and lost. 'Actually, I've always been a bit of a loner on the job. Too tied up in my work, I guess. But, hey, I appreciate the coffee. If you buzz me any time you're having one, and I'm free, I promise not to blow you off. Deal?'

'Deal.'

Hallie settled back into her chair as if snuggling into a comfy sofa, when in fact Kristen knew the hard, cold steel chairs were there to discourage occupants from getting too cosy and encourage them to get back to work pronto. 'So, what's your background?'

'I've worked in Singapore the last four years, London for a while, brief stint in LA, and before that Sydney, which I guess I call home. Worked my way up to executive producer through those jobs, loved every minute of it.'

'Wow, sounds glamorous.' Hallie's eyes lit up, and Kristen wondered when she'd last had that wide-eyed interest in anything. 'But you've basically given me a run-down of your CV. What about your personal life? Any goss there?'

Determinedly ignoring a fleeting image of a naked Nate which flashed across her mind, she forced a laugh and made a grimace. 'Not so much, I'm afraid. I'm a confirmed workaholic. Single and loving it.'

Hallie sent her a dubious look, but continued her grilling anyway.

'Why Melbourne? Why RX?'

'The station has a stellar reputation in the industry. I wanted to come back to Australia, and the opportunity knocked on my door so I took it. Now, if you could spare me a minute in this interrogation, I'd like to have this latte before it goes cold.'

She'd meant it as a joke, but it looked like her buddy skills were on a par with her maintaining-a-relationship skills, as Hallie's face fell.

Darn it; she knew there was a reason she didn't do the friendship thing. Being direct was the only way she knew, and treading around bruised feelings was foreign to her.

She guessed she'd better learn fast if she didn't want to alienate the one person who'd been genuinely nice to her in the last week.

'Sorry, didn't mean to sound so harsh. I'm a bit strung out with the move to Melbourne and starting the new job.'

'No worries,' Hallie said, her resident cheery smile slipping back into place. 'I have to get back to work anyway. I'll save the rest of the interrogation for later.'

'Later?'

She'd envisaged a long day getting acquainted with the running sheets, her co-workers and the station in general. She'd have no time for further coffee breaks, especially ones fraught with probing questions from a girl just trying to be friendly.

Hallie snapped her fingers. 'I forgot, you probably don't know about Manic Mondays.'

'Actually, I think I do,' Kristen deadpanned, knowing the frantic rush of a new working week all too well.

She usually grabbed a bite to eat at her desk for dinner, working all hours to get the week's scheduling on track. It had been the same at every station around the world, and it was comforting to know things weren't so different around here.

'Bet you don't.'

Hallie's sly grin piqued her curiosity, and she grabbed her latte, falling into step beside the petite receptionist.

'Okay, enlighten me.'

'Every Monday everyone stops work at eight and convenes to our local bar for a bit of team bonding and boosting of morale. It's great.'

Taking time out of her busy schedule to have a drink at a bar with co-workers on a Monday night? As if.

'I'm sure it is, but I'll be tied up tonight.' And for every Monday night while she worked here.

She didn't do the casual socialising thing well, preferring to maintain a distance with work colleagues. Sharing a coffee with Hallie was a first, and if the girl knew she'd probably label her a freak.

Not that she cared. She'd been labelled a heck of a lot worse growing up, and she'd survived.

'I'm betting you're not.'

Hallie held open the door and Kristen walked through, sending her one of her characteristic 'don't mess with me' looks. 'Why's that?'

Hallie leaned forward as if about to impart a trade secret. 'Because Manic Mondays are company policy. Everyone goes, from the janitors to the CEO. It really does keep everyone happy. The first drink is on the house, and if people want to stay around they do, but mostly everyone has a drink or a coffee, a bit of a chat, then heads home. It isn't a super-late night, and the powers that be find it works as well as a bonus scheme for morale.'

'Right,' Kristen said, feeling like she was in quicksand and floundering.

Since when did the powers that be sanction weekly social get-togethers for employees, let alone make it mandatory? And *everyone* had to attend?

She'd have a chat to the CEO about this. Just as soon as she plucked up the courage to face him without wanting to fall into his arms.

CHAPTER FOUR

NATHAN sipped at his espresso, content to lean against the bar away from the RX crowd and watch. You could learn a lot about people by the way they interacted with others, and seeing his employees mingle and chat spoke volumes.

Like Hallie, the young receptionist, whose bubbly personality won over everyone within two feet. And Alan, his second in command, who alienated everyone with his pompous ramblings, yet nobody moved away for fear of offending a bigwig.

Then there was Kristen, a fish out of water if ever he saw one. The erect posture, the fixed smile, the glazed look in her striking blue eyes, and the fact she kept casting furtive glances at the door told him she didn't want to be here.

He'd picked her as a fellow loner in Singapore, but he'd expected a confident career woman like her to be more outgoing, more extroverted, yet right now she looked like she'd rather have teeth pulled than stand around and mix with her new workmates.

Draining his coffee, he set it on the bar and made his way towards the door. He'd done his duty, putting in an appearance when all he'd wanted to do was head home and read the pile of reports tucked into his briefcase.

However, getting to the door put him straight in the path of the one woman he'd rather avoid and had done a good job of doing so far.

'Kristen.'

'Nathan.'

Their polite nods and flat tones grated on his nerves, especially when she'd previously called him Nate. In Singapore he'd shocked himself when he'd told her his name was Nate, when it had been an abbreviation reserved for Julia and close family, yet once it had slipped out he hadn't minded. He'd liked how it had sounded on her tongue, how natural it had seemed, lending a familiar quality to what should've been a once-in-a-lifetime chance meeting.

Instead, here they were again, trying their utmost to act like they hadn't spent an incredible evening chatting and joking before indulging in the surprising passion which had consumed them both.

'Heading home?'

'Loads of work to do. You know how it is.'

'I sure do,' she said, a spark of understanding in her blue eyes creating an instant bond between them. 'I guess we're both finding our feet in a new job, huh?'

He nodded, torn between escaping while he still could and staying a while longer in the hope of getting their relationship—their working relationship—back on an even keel. 'It's tough at the start, but I actually love walking into a new place and starting fresh. It's a challenge.'

Kris smiled, the first time he'd seen a genuine expression since their inauspicious beginning earlier that day. 'And, let me guess, like any male you thrive on a challenge?'

'Nothing wrong with that.'

He returned her smile and their gazes locked. He should've looked away first, but he couldn't, riveted by the tiny flecks in her deep blue eyes, remembering how they'd glowed and sparked when she'd been warm and eager in his arms.

Thankfully, she finally broke the deadlock with a little laugh. 'No, there's nothing wrong with enjoying a challenge. I'm all for it myself.'

'The go-get-'em businesswoman, huh?'

'That's me.' She raised her glass in his direction. 'Don't say I didn't warn you.'

'I stand duly warned,' he said, looking forward to seeing what this dynamic woman could bring to his life. To his *working* life.

She sipped at her drink, a teasing glint in her eyes as she lowered it. 'Good. Because I intend to put in the long hours, do the hard yards, whatever it takes to take RX to the top, just as my pushy boss wants in his vision statement.'

He chuckled. 'So you read the documents already? I'm impressed.'

'You ain't seen nothing yet.'

Suddenly, her smile faded, and he wondered at the turnaround, wishing he could recapture some of the easygoing camaraderie of the last few minutes.

'It's great to have an employee with a vision too. But won't long hours interfere with your family?'

Being involved with anything other than business

came at a cost, and he should know. He was still paying a steep price.

If her smile had faded moments before, the shutters well and truly came down now as her expression blanked. 'I can't remember if I told you in Singapore, but I only have two sisters. Carissa's based in Stockton, just north of Sydney, and Tahnee's in Sydney. They're both overseas travelling with their families at the moment, so don't worry, I won't have any distractions.'

'Sorry for being nosy,' he said, the coldness in her voice sending a chill through him. So much for camaraderie. 'Just trying to foster good employee relations.'

'Don't worry about it,' she said, waving off his apology, but her flat tone told him he'd botched whatever inroads he'd made in getting her to unwind tonight.

'On that note, I'm definitely heading off.' Before he put his foot in it again, and this time set her off like the wild woman who'd stormed into his office this morning.

'Actually, I think I'll head off myself. If it's good for the boss, it's good enough for me,' she said, her fragile smile creating a pocket of warmth deep within, and he fell into step beside her, heading for the door.

She waved to Hallie, who cast them a curious glance, and he held the door open for her, savouring the light rose scent he remembered all too well. It had lingered on his sheets after she'd left his hotel room, just as imprinted on his brain as the memory of what they'd shared.

'Would you like me to walk you to your car? Innercity Melbourne can be a bit dodgy at night,' he said, surprised by a strong surge of protectiveness.

He hadn't felt that way towards a woman since Julia, what seemed an absolute aeon ago now.

'My car's right here, so I'll be fine, but thanks.'

'Right. I'll see you tomorrow, then.'

She nodded and crossed the road, an elegant, tall figure in a fitted houndstooth suit, sheer black stockings and towering heels. Dressed for business, she looked incredible, but as hard as he tried he couldn't forget how much more incredible her body was underneath the clothes.

Blinking away that unforgettable image, he waited till she got into her snazzy two-door car, started the engine and pulled away from the kerb, returning her brief wave as she drove by.

He watched till he could make out nothing more than her tail-lights glowing red in the distance, like two glittering eyes pinning him with an accusatory glare.

'Kris, can you come in here now?'

Throwing down her pen on the stack of scripts in front of her, Kris glared at the intercom phone on her desk, hating the thing more than her mobile phone, considering both had become an instant connection to Nate and his demanding ways.

Sighing, she hit the answer button. 'Be right there,' she said, pushing away from her desk and grabbing her personal organizer, a writing pad and the latest updates on new shows, knowing that no matter how prepared she was her new boss would find something to faze her with.

Heading down the long corridor to his office, she smiled at several co-workers, amazed that she'd only been here four days when it felt like a lifetime.

Familiarity bred that feeling. It also bred contempt,

which she was fast heading towards if Nate didn't lighten up a bit.

'Come in,' he barked, a second after she knocked on his door and, fixing a sickly-sweet smile on her face, she strode into his office.

'You wanted to see me, boss?'

His head snapped up like she'd called him something far worse—which wouldn't be entirely out of the question, considering how grumpy he'd been the last few days—and he frowned.

'Take a seat. I need to discuss something with you.'

'No problems.'

She slid onto the chair opposite him, stacking her pile of paper on her lap, and doing her best to appear perky and upbeat, hoping it would highlight how grouchy he was being.

Sitting back in his chair, he crossed his arms, and she struggled not to notice the way his biceps bulged beneath his pale-blue business shirt. In a way, having him act like a pain in the ass was better than having him joking around with her, like on Monday night when it had felt way too comfortable standing in a crowded bar with the man she couldn't forget no matter how hard she tried.

'I want to run an idea past you.'

'Shoot,' she said, clicking her pen and automatically sliding her writing pad to the top of the pile on her lap.

'You remember we discussed a new travel show on Tuesday?'

'Uh-huh.'

How could she forget? They'd been holed up in his office talking over a few ideas for new shows and she'd pushed her own barrow, determined to impress on her second day on the job, well aware of her expertise in the travel-show area. However, what she hadn't been prepared for was the host of memories which had continually scattered across her mind at the most inopportune moments, talk of travel resurrecting Singapore moments, Grand Hyatt moments, long, hot, exquisite moments with Nate…

'I've given it a lot of thought, and I want us to run with it. See what you can come up with and we'll meet to discuss it on Monday.'

'Fine,' she said, unable to keep a huge self-satisfied smile off her face, only to find him glaring at her like she'd just thrown a glass of cold water over him. 'What time?'

Reaching for his personal organiser, he keyed in a few numbers and frowned.

'The earliest I can do is four-thirty. I'm in Brisbane till then.'

'Sounds good,' she said, making a show of checking her own gadget, but knowing she'd shift a meeting with Elvis himself to show her uptight boss what she could do. 'Anything else?'

Okay, so maybe she was laying it on a little thick with her sweeter-than-honey smile and saccharine voice, but the more intimidating he got the more she wanted to push him.

After all, she did enjoy a challenge. And she had warned him!

He stared at her, his dark eyes revealing nothing, but she could've sworn she saw the corners of his mouth twitch. But that meant he wanted to laugh, and there was no way her serious boss would actually crack a smile during work hours.

Shaking his head, he said, 'No, that's it. See you Monday.'

'Have a good trip.'

Striding to the door, she put an extra swivel into her hips, grateful she'd worn her tightest black skirt today.

If Nate wanted to treat his new exec producer with cold indifference, she'd give him a bit of a shakeup and show him that he hadn't always been so impervious to her.

Swivelling at the door, she caught him staring at her butt a split second before his gaze snapped up to meet hers, and his residual frown slipped into place.

'Was there something else?'

Fighting a triumphant grin and losing, she said, 'Never mind. We'll discuss it further on Monday,' and sauntered out the door.

'This is it?'

Kris gritted her teeth to keep from snapping at Nate as he flicked through the documentation she'd prepared, his expression carefully schooled into a blank mask that gave nothing away.

'That's what I've come up with so far. I wanted to outline the gist of the show, run through a few preliminaries with you before getting too involved. What with budgets being the be-all and end-all, I'd like to see what you think before taking it further.'

He nodded and rubbed his chin absentmindedly, flicking the last page shut and finally looking up at her.

'It looks good. I particularly like the reality-show slant you've put on it. It's something new, innovative and exactly the direction I want RX to be heading. Great job, Kris.'

She smiled, instantly forgetting how less than five minutes earlier she'd wanted to pick up the fancy letter-opener on his desk and stab him with it, considering he'd been an hour and a half late, had waltzed in here with his usual sore head and proceeded to read her proposal in silence without giving her a clue as to what he thought.

'I'm pretty excited about it, as you can probably tell,' she said, pointing at the giant stack of paper she'd prepared to wow him with.

Tapping his pen on the stack, he said, 'I'm amazed you did all this since Thursday.'

'Once I got going I couldn't stop.'

Wasn't that the truth, considering she'd spent her entire weekend preparing this presentation rather than enjoying the Melbourne sunshine.

'When you said long hours, you meant it.'

He made it sound like a fault, and she bristled.

'Of course. I'm a professional. I thought you'd gathered that by now.'

A spark of awareness flared in his eyes as he registered her dig.

'Your work speaks for itself,' he said, staring at her for longer than was comfortable before slamming the stack of paper in front of him and making her jump. 'And, speaking of which, I want to nail some of the prelims of this tonight. Are you happy to work back?'

'Sure,' she said, not happy in the least.

Most of the employees had already left for Manic Monday at the local, and while Nate hadn't given her the slightest indication he saw her as anything other than an employee—bar the butt-ogling incident, but she'd basically incited that, and he was only male!—the thought of being cocooned in his cosy office for the next few hours suddenly seemed too intimate when she'd rather keep her distance.

'Good. I'll order in dinner. Chinese okay?'

She nodded mechanically, instantly transported back to that night in Singapore when they'd feasted on fried rice and other Asian delicacies, before feasting on each other.

'Any preferences?'

'I'm not fussy.'

Taking a peek at him from beneath her lashes as he ordered, she wondered if he ever thought about that magical night. Though he was civil to her, he'd gone cold since her first day, almost as if he'd deliberately erected a barrier she couldn't breach.

'Right, that's done. Let's get to it.'

They worked steadily for the next half hour, with Kris making frantic annotations on her paperwork as the ideas flowed between them fast and furious.

She'd worked with some of the best around the world, but bouncing ideas with Nate took creativity to a whole new level, and Hallie's knock on the door almost came as a welcome reprieve as her mind spun.

'Hey, guys, your dinner's arrived.'

Hallie dumped it on the table, took one look at the stack of work in front of them and grimaced. 'I take it you won't be making it to Manic Monday?'

'Afraid not,' Nate said, leaning back in his chair, clasping his hands and stretching, the simple action creating a strange flurry in Kris's gut and bringing a broad smile to Hallie's face.

'Well, then, I'm off.' Hallie turned her back on Nate

and sent Kris a huge wink as she headed for the door. 'Don't work too hard, guys. And don't spend all night with your noses to the grindstone.'

'I'm not that dedicated,' Kris mumbled, the spicy aromas from the takeaway boxes making her nose twitch and her tummy rumble as Hallie closed the door, leaving her all too aware of exactly how good it was to actually spend all night with Nate.

'I think you are,' Nate said, gesturing towards her presentation. 'And your boss is suitably impressed, but why don't we take a break and dig in?'

'Sounds good to me.'

She placed her pen and pad on the table and worked the kinks out of her neck, surprised to find Nate hadn't moved a muscle when she finally looked up.

Instead, a slow-burning heat turned his eyes to molten chocolate as he smiled, the first time she'd seen him send her anything other than a frown for the last week.

'What?'

If his cold treatment left her flustered, it was nothing on how she felt basking under the warmth spilling from his eyes now.

'We're both very driven,' he finally said, reaching for the takeaway cartons and handing her chopsticks, as if the loaded moment had never happened.

'Uh-huh,' she mumbled, shovelling Singapore noodles into her mouth with gusto.

She'd skipped lunch trying to put the final touches to her presentation, and was now starving. By the hungry gleam in Nate's eye and the way he kept staring at her, it looked like she wasn't the only one. Though somehow it seemed she'd morphed from a professional employee, to be kept at arm's length at all times, to an exceedingly tempting morsel.

Okay, maybe that last part was in her own head, but it had a nice ring to it.

'Good?'

He'd barely touched his Kung-Po chicken, while her chopsticks were perilously close to scraping the bottom of her noodle box.

'Fabulous.'

'Almost as good as in Singapore?'

Her heart skipped a beat. Surely Mr Professional hadn't just referred to the one night they'd vowed to ignore?

She could just take the easy way out and opt for a nice, safe answer, the type of answer he'd expect.

But where would the fun be in that?

'Nothing could be as good as that night,' she said, staring him straight in the eye.

He didn't blink.

He didn't look away.

Instead they sat there for what seemed like an eternity, the air crackling between them, bound by the same tension which had made them lose their heads that one magical, balmy night a couple of months ago.

'You're right,' he murmured, taking a stab at a piece of chicken with his chopsticks, unsurprisingly coming up empty considering his eyes hadn't left hers.

In that moment Kris knew that, no matter how cool Nate pretended to be, he hadn't forgotten what they'd shared. Not any of it.

'Well, we better eat up and get back to it,' she said, the false brightness in her voice almost making her cringe.

But she had to do something to get them back on

track, away from the touchy subject of that incredible night and how much she'd like to re-create the same magic again the longer he stared at her with fire in those hypnotic eyes.

'Right.'

In an instant, the heat evaporated, only to be replaced by Nate's cool indifference, and Kris stifled a sigh.

After all, she'd got what she wanted.

Hadn't she?

'Kristen, where are we at with the casting for *Travelogue?*'

Kristen fixed Nate with a glare, convinced he was doing the whole 'let's pick on the new girl' thing on purpose. What with his condescending tone, she could quite easily have throttled him.

'We're on schedule. The final screen tests are done, and we're expecting visa clearance for the last cast member as we speak.'

A tiny frown appeared between his brows and, seeing it combined with his compressed lips, she knew what came next couldn't be good.

'That's all well and good, but what's the actual time frame? Are we talking days or hours here? I need direct answers, not vague platitudes.'

Stiffening, Kristen twirled a pen between her fingers, refraining from stabbing it into her notebook, or better yet stabbing it into the man who had made her working life miserable for the two weeks since she'd started.

She didn't get it.

He'd been fine on her first day, had been the epitome of a chivalrous gentleman, waiting till she'd reached her car after Manic Monday before leaving. Most guys took her confident persona as a sign she could take care of herself—and she could—but it had been nice to feel protected for that brief moment.

However, since that night he'd closed off, and, if she didn't count the slight aberration during their working dinner when he'd thawed for all of two seconds, their conversations had been cold and clipped, his demeanour bordering on antagonistic and she'd had a gutful. Once this meeting was over, she'd confront him.

'The embassy doesn't work to your stopwatch and they can't give me precise times. As soon as the visas come through, I assure you, you'll be the first to know.'

She shouldn't have spoken to him like that, not with Alan watching their sparring with avid interest, but there was only so much she could take and Nate had crossed the line about a week ago with his surly attitude and frigid tone.

'Fine. Let's adjourn till we have more.'

If looks could kill she would've curled up her toes on the spot, but she didn't flinch from his glowering stare.

He could say things were fine, but she knew differently, and she had every intention of finding out what was going on. What had happened to his holier than thou 'we're professionals' speech he'd given on the first day?

Gone as quickly as the special spark she'd imagined they'd once shared.

'Keep me posted,' Alan said, gathering up his paperwork and heading for the door in record time.

Maybe her poker face needed some work, for he cast her several concerned glances on his way out, obviously not wanting to get caught in the crossfire when she let Nate have it.

'Thanks, Alan, shall do,' she said, forcing a smile which quickly faded once the door closed and she turned to face the boss.

'We're finished here,' he said, sliding documents into clear plastic sleeves and shoving the lot into a box he hefted onto his hip.

'On the contrary, we're just getting started.'

She planted her hands on the conference table and leaned forward, fixing him with a glare that had wilted lesser men than him.

'I want to know what's going on.'

'We had a business meeting as far as I can tell,' he said, replacing the box on the table, his exasperation audible.

'Don't patronise me,' she said, hating the tension between them, hating the fact she cared even more. 'You've been giving me a hard time ever since I started. I've done everything you've asked of me and more, yet you can't be civil. What's with that?'

He froze, his expression icy. 'I treat you like any other employee. If you expect special treatment, forget it.'

'Special treatment? Why would you think I'd expect that?'

She knew, though, and the thought sent raw anger spearing through her. Would he ever let her forget the mistake she'd made in Singapore?

'Look, this is getting us nowhere. I'm sorry if you think I've been too pushy or tyrannical or whatever, but it's how I do business. If you don't like it, maybe we need to come to another arrangement.'

'Are you threatening to fire me?'

She gripped the table, her blood pressure soaring and spots dancing before her eyes.

'You're...' The words died on her lips as she swayed, the spots joined by squiggles and stars and quickly followed by darkness as she collapsed onto the table.

Nathan's blood chilled as he watched Kris slump forward in a heap, her head making a god-awful sound as it thumped on the table. He rushed forward in time to catch her before she slid to the floor, struck by two things simultaneously: how scared he was that she'd injured herself, and how petrified he was at how good she felt cradled in his arms.

'Wh-what happened?'

Her eyelids fluttered open, and he breathed a sigh of relief, unaware he'd been holding his breath.

'You passed out,' he said, brushing the strands of hair off her forehead, wishing the lump of fear lodged in his throat would disappear. The longer she stared at him with uncertainty in her wide blue eyes, the larger the lump grew, till he could hardly speak.

'I've never fainted in my life,' she said, her brow creased as if puzzling over what had happened.

'Maybe you've been pushing yourself too hard.'

God knew *he* had, pushing her away every way he knew how.

'I'm used to working at a hectic pace,' she said, shaking her head and wincing as she reached up to feel the growing bump near her hairline. 'Ouch, that must've been some knock.'

'It was. Shook the building, I'd say.'

'Who asked you?'

Her rueful smile faded as her fingers connected with

the bump, and his heart clenched with the fragile glint in her eyes.

'Here, let me check it out.'

He'd expected her to protest, but she surprised him by lowering her hand and closing her eyes as his fingertips skimmed the bump on her forehead and beyond, using gentle pressure to explore her scalp for further damage, relieved he didn't find any.

His relief was short-lived, though, as he registered how damn wonderful it felt to be running his fingers through her hair, just like he'd done that night he'd been trying so damn hard to forget.

Pulling his hand back as if scalded, he gently raised her to a sitting position, needing to get her out of his arms before he did something crazy, like kiss her bump better and follow up with a kiss on her lips to make him feel better.

'You should get to a doctor, get yourself checked out,' he said, propping her against a chair while he reached for a glass of water off the table and handed it to her.

'I hate going to doctors,' she said, taking a sip gingerly before closing her eyes tight again, a pained expression on her face.

'What's wrong?'

'I think I'm going to be sick.'

'Hell,' he muttered, casting a frantic glance around the room for something to act as a sick bag, and coming up empty.

'Just give me a second, it might pass,' she said, taking slow, deep breaths and looking paler by the minute.

Hating the helpless feeling rendering him almost useless, he grabbed one of the clear plastic sleeves containing the month's projection figures and tipped them out in a hurry. It would do as a sick bag at a pinch.

Suddenly, her eyes snapped open, and she fixed him with an accusatory glare.

'Don't think this means we've finished our conversation. As soon as I'm feeling better, you're going to face the music, mister.'

He smiled, relieved to see some of the familiar fire in her eyes, amused that she'd think of chewing him out at a time like this.

'Duly warned,' he said, taking hold of her arm. 'Think you can stand? I'll help you up, then grab a phone so you can call your doc.'

'I don't think—'

'Don't think, just dial. You need a check-up, as I won't stand for having one of my prized employees collapsing on me for no reason.'

Rather than arguing as he expected, she accepted his assistance and he got her onto a chair without further drama, though he should've known she wouldn't stay silent for long.

'If this is how you treat prized employees, I'd hate to see how you treat the ones you don't value.'

Grabbing his cell phone out of the pocket of his jacket draped over the back of his chair, he said, 'Hey, didn't I stop you from falling on the floor in an undignified heap?'

She waved away his response, the colour returning to her cheeks. 'Not that—the way you've been carrying on the last two weeks.'

'We'll talk about that later,' he said, handing her the phone. 'Now, call directory enquiries if you don't know your doc's number off by heart. I'm not letting you out of my sight till you're in a taxi and on the way to see him or her.'

'I don't have a doctor in Melbourne,' she said, thrusting out her bottom lip in a delightful pout which matched her sulky tone.

'Then you can see mine. Doc Rubin is one of the best,' he said, dialling the number and fixing her with a glare that brooked no argument.

'I'm feeling fine now. It was probably the result of long hours and snatched meals.'

'Something tells me you've always worked like that, yet you said you haven't fainted before.'

He waited while the doctor's receptionist put him on hold, hoping he wasn't overreacting.

Maybe she was right and this was a one-off. However, seeing her so helpless lying there with her eyes closed, and cradling her limp body had resurrected stark memories of holding Julia in a similar way. He'd been too late to save her, and he'd be damned if he dismissed Kris's fainting spell out of hand when it could indicate something more serious than overwork.

'You're being awfully bossy,' she muttered, her arms crossed over her chest in an action he'd come to associate with her stubborn side several times during meetings over the last week or so.

'Funny, that, considering I'm your boss.'

He held up his hand as the receptionist came on the phone again, and he took the first available appointment which happened to be in half an hour, courtesy of a cancellation.

Thanking the receptionist, he snapped the phone shut. 'Right. We're all set. Let's go.'

'You're not coming with me!'

Her horrified glance told him exactly what she thought of the idea of his accompanying her, and he stopped short, suddenly struck by how inappropriate it might look for the boss to be seen mollycoddling an employee.

She's more than that and you know it.

Ignoring his inner voice, he said, 'Actually, I was thinking Hallie could ride with you.'

He held up his hand as she opened her mouth to protest. 'Don't even think about arguing. You can't be alone in case you collapse again, so Hallie is riding with you, okay?'

'Okay,' she said, her meek tone telling him exactly how scared she was, but trying to hide it. 'But this doctor better be good.'

Hiding a triumphant grin, he said, 'You'll be in good hands with Doc Rubin. And make sure you head home straight from the surgery. I don't want to see you back here, got it?'

'Is that *ever*?'

He ignored her jibe at their earlier conversation, aware he'd have to do some fast talking once she was better. Anything rather than tell her the truth.

'I'll call you later to see how you went,' he said, offering her a hand to help her up from the chair, which she ignored now she had some strength back.

He should've known her dependence wouldn't last long. She'd never accept a helping hand from him unless desperate.

'Do you need a hand to the front door?'

'I'm fine.' She stopped short of rolling her eyes, and he grinned, holding his hands up in surrender.

'Don't think this lets you off the hook. I'll be back to bust your butt faster than you can say "that's a wrap".'

'I'll look forward to it,' he said, thinking that for a woman who acted so tough she had a delightful sense of humour, and he much preferred being on the receiving end of a funny barb than the killer glare she did all too well.

Then again, he'd done such a good job of alienating her, maybe busting his butt wasn't a joke!

Keeping her at arm's length was proving to be more difficult than he'd anticipated.

Perhaps he had to try a whole lot harder.

CHAPTER FIVE

'YOU'RE pregnant.'

Kristen stared in horror at Dr Rubin, who was a dead ringer for Santa Claus. Ironic, considering she'd never believed in fairy tales or the jolly fat guy himself, especially as he'd never brought her what she wanted. No surprise that his lookalike delivered shocking news she didn't believe.

'There has to be some kind of mistake,' she said, folding her arms and fixing him with a withering stare.

The doctor shook his head, a kindly smile on his rotund face. 'No mistake, Miss Lewis. Can you tell me the date of your last period so I can calculate your due date?'

Right then, the first flicker of doubt set in.

Last period…

When had that been?

She'd attributed her missed periods to changing time zones, the move to Melbourne and the stress of a new job. It wouldn't have been the first time she'd missed a period or two at a tough time in her life.

Never in her wildest dreams—or nightmares—had she considered she could be pregnant.

Racking her brain, she said, 'Over twelve weeks ago? I'd have to check for the exact date.'

'We can go into that later, but right now let me give you a rough estimate.'

While the doctor twirled a cardboard circle peppered with numbers, she sank into the chair and furiously tried to marshal her thoughts.

She couldn't be pregnant.

She didn't know the first thing about being a mother, let alone caring for a child.

How on earth had this happened?

Suddenly, an icy shiver spread cold, clammy fingers through her body. She hadn't slept with anyone apart from Nate, which meant...

'Your due date is December the first.'

'Oh no,' she sighed, squeezing her eyes shut and shaking her head from side to side in a futile attempt to vanquish the logical explanation as to who the father of the baby was. 'No, no, no...'

'I hate to state the obvious, but this pregnancy is unexpected?'

Her shocked gaze met the doctor's understanding one, and she hated the anger bubbling within her at the futility of her situation.

A baby had never been in her grand plan. She had a career, a successful life, she didn't need the complication of a child and all the responsibility he or she entailed.

Darn it, they'd used protection. How could this have happened?

Rubbing a hand across her eyes, she tried to erase the all-too-vivid image which flashed across her mind in response to that particular question.

'We can discuss options if you don't want this baby,' Dr Rubin said, his voice devoid of emotion or judgement.

She didn't want to discuss options.

She wanted to run screaming from his office, head home, dive under her duvet and hide away from the truth: pregnant, to her boss!

Taking a deep breath, she slid a protective hand over her flat belly. She needed time to think, time to absorb the shock, time to figure out what she wanted to do, though in reality she knew it would take a lifetime to get used to the idea of herself as a mother—and Nate as her child's father.

Lifting her chin, she met the doctor's concerned stare. 'That won't be necessary.'

'Good. In that case, let's discuss obstetricians. You'll need to have your first review and ultrasound asap, as you're probably nearing the end of your first trimester.'

'Fine,' she said, knowing it wasn't.

Making the decision to be a mother was one thing, facing up to specialists and ultrasounds and goodness knew what was another.

Apart from knowing next to nothing about kids, she didn't have the faintest idea about what pregnancy entailed—apart from the obvious, like nausea and swollen ankles and a belly the size of a basketball. She had no friends to ask, and the thought of going through this alone hit, and hit hard.

Though there was Nate…

Nate, the father of her baby, who could barely bring himself to look at her these days, let alone acknowledge that the one night he'd made clear meant nothing to him had resulted in a baby.

How could she tell him something like this?

How would he react?

God, what a mess.

'Right. Here's a list of obstetricians, and the multi-vitamins I recommend you commence immediately. Any other questions?'

Kristen stared at the doctor. Was he crazy? She had a heap of them, starting with *how bad will the labour be?* and ending with *how will I care for a baby?*

However, she swallowed her questions and shook her head. If she spent one more minute in this doctor's office, with his twinkly eyes and benevolent smile, she'd start blubbering and never stop.

'No, I'm right for now. Thanks for your help.'

She stood quickly, grasping the information he'd thrust at her to her chest like a shield, and made for the door.

'Miss Lewis?'

She paused and turned back. 'Yes?'

'Congratulations. Bringing a baby into this world is a truly wonderful experience.'

Easy for him to say. He was a man.

She managed a grim smile, which must've come out more like a grimace, and tore out of the room, stuffing the information into her handbag, desperately craving fresh air and a reality check.

'Hey, wait up!' Hallie called out, and she forced her feet to stop.

She needed time to compute what the doctor had just told her, and if her overzealous friend got wind of her predicament the news would travel around RX with the speed of a film on fast-forward.

'What's wrong? Are you all right?'

Kristen nodded, knowing nothing would ever be right again. 'Some viral bug.'

Hallie's eyes narrowed as if she didn't believe a word of it. 'Why were you tearing out of here like a bat out of hell?'

'Fresh air.'

Kristen fanned her face, pretending a slight stagger, and Hallie made a 'be right back' sign at the medical receptionist and hauled Kris outside before she collapsed.

Taking in deep breaths, and feeling like the worst kind of fraud for deceiving the closest person she had to calling a friend, Kristen braced herself against a stubbly brick wall.

'Must be some virus to make you faint,' Hallie said, her head cocked to one side like a curious sparrow.

'Mmm,' Kristen mumbled noncommittally, wondering when she legally had to inform RX about her condition.

Her condition.

She'd hated hearing pregnancy labelled that way in the past, like it was an illness and not a natural part of life. The women she'd worked with had been having babies, not suffering from some debilitating sickness, yet colleagues had blamed the slightest thing—from a missed meeting to a late memo—on their 'condition'.

She hadn't fought it back then, not deeming it relevant, but boy did she have a different outlook now. The first person to label her with a 'condition' would get slugged. Though that could just be the irrational hormones kicking in and making her want to slug anybody, including the infuriating guy who'd got her into this predicament in the first place.

'Ready to go back inside? I'm sure that beady-eyed woman thought we were running out of there without paying. Typical receptionist!'

Hallie rolled her eyes, and Kristen laughed for the first time in hours.

Hopefully, she could be that self-deprecating when the time came for her to face the inevitable sly comments about her pregnancy.

Suddenly grateful for Hallie's presence, she reached out and squeezed her hand. 'Thanks for being here. You've done nothing but make me feel welcome since I started at RX, and I really appreciate it.'

Hallie blushed. 'No worries. For an uptight exec, you're okay.'

'Enough with the compliments.' Kristen matched her smile, and turned back towards the medical centre before swinging to face Hallie. 'Can you do me a favour?'

'Sure.'

'Let Nathan know I'm fine? I think he kind of freaked out when I fainted in that meeting, and said he'd ring me later, but I just want to head home and go to bed.'

'No worries, I'll tell him,' Hallie said, bristling like a protective feline before continuing. 'He's a great boss, though, isn't he? Not many bigwigs would take an interest in their employees like he does.'

Kristen stilled. Was Hallie fishing for info? Had she sensed a past connection between Nate and herself?

'I've worked with worse,' she said, keeping her voice devoid of emotion, hoping to nip Hallie's possible fishing expedition in the bud. 'Now, let me pay this bill, organise taxis for us and head home. I'm beat.'

'Okay.'

Hallie didn't push the issue, and Kristen attributed her comments to the run-of-the-mill frank statements the receptionist was famous for.

Hallie thought the boss was great?

Well, Kristen would soon find out if that was true once Nate heard that his newest executive was pregnant.

More importantly, that he was the father.

'Though I'll share the taxi to your place, then head home from there.'

Kristen opened her mouth to argue, but Hallie held up a hand. 'It's not open for debate. Besides, this may be the only chance I ever get to boss you around.'

Hallie winked, and in a small way Kristen was happy to have the company home. Chatting to Hallie might keep her mind off her predicament—for all of two seconds.

She paid the bill and called a cab, her head spinning the entire time, and thankfully Hallie kept up a steady stream of conversation until they reached her place.

However, as soon as she laid eyes on her terrace house, a thousand doubts plagued her: could she bring up a child in a place like this? Was it too small? What about the steep stairs—and the split-level lounge? And her totally impractical furniture?

'Kris, are you okay?'

Hallie covered her hand with hers, and with that small, caring gesture Kristen snapped and burst into tears.

Not dainty tears, but huge drops which trickled down her cheeks at the speed of light and plopped onto her cream linen skirt, accompanied by sobbing and hiccups and the works.

'I'll take it from here,' Hallie said, thrusting the fare

at a bemused taxi driver and assisting her out of the taxi like an invalid.

'I'm sorry,' Kristen murmured, trying to stem the tears, only to find they flowed faster as she unlocked her front door and stumbled into the hallway.

'Hey, don't apologise. Viruses can make us do strange things.' By the dubious look on Hallie's face, she didn't believe the virus story for a second. 'Now, sit down and I'll get you something to drink. What would you like?'

'Water, please. Kitchen's through there.'

'I'll find my way around,' Hallie said, casting her a concerned look before hurrying away, giving Kristen valuable time to regain control.

She never cried. Ever.

She'd had plenty of opportunity in the past thanks to her upbringing, but tears had been seen as a sign of weakness by bullies, and she'd soon learned to never give them an inkling of her emotions.

Now, it looked like the floodgates had opened and wouldn't stop in a hurry.

'Here you go.'

Hallie thrust a tall glass of water into her hand and plopped onto the couch next to her, waiting till Kristen had drained most of it and her tears had subsided before speaking.

'You know I'm your friend, right?'

Kristen nodded, surprised to find she did consider Hallie a friend. They'd bonded over a few coffees at work, and she'd almost blurted the sorry tale about Nate's cold treatment several times but had stopped at the last minute, aware that loose lips sunk executive producers' ships.

However, if ever she needed a friend, it was now.

'In that case, why don't you really tell me what's going on?'

Kristen opened her mouth to fob Hallie off, to repeat the virus story, to give her any number of false platitudes.

Instead, 'I'm pregnant,' popped out.

Hallie's eyes widened to the size of dinner plates. 'You're preggers? For real?'

'Oh, yeah, it's real,' Kristen said, rubbing her flat belly in a reflex action, finding it almost impossible to equate herself—the ultimate career girl—with a mother. 'The doc just told me. I had no idea.'

'Wow.'

Hallie collapsed back against the cushions, her stunned look soon replaced by the cheeky grin Kristen had grown accustomed to. 'So, who's the father? Anyone I know?'

Hallie's exaggerated, conspiratorial wink should've made Kristen laugh. Instead, dread shot through her at the thought of anyone at work finding out Nate was the father before he did.

Forcing a nonchalant tone, Kristen said, 'No.' Not a lie, exactly. The Nate she'd known for that one brief, magical night in Singapore was nothing like the Nathan Boyd, CEO that Hallie knew.

'So you're doing this on your own? That's pretty brave.'

'Actually, I have no idea what I'm going to do.'

Hallie's grin faded. 'You're going to keep it, right?'

'Uh-huh.'

Kristen's tentative response encapsulated her doubts. She'd never have contemplated any other outcome than going through with this pregnancy. But not wanting this baby had nothing to do with her lifestyle or job, and everything to do with the gut-wrenching fear which had gnawed at her since childhood; the soul-destroying fear that she'd never be a good mother because she'd never had one herself.

Being shunted from foster home to foster home had taken care of that, where the women so casually labelled 'mothers' hadn't known the first thing about caring or nurturing a child. Instead, their focus had been strictly on the dollars allocated by the government for the care of parentless kids like her, and she'd grown to hate their cold, callous indifference.

'You don't sound terribly convinced.'

Straightening, Kristen said, 'I'm having this baby.'

She might not have the foggiest idea how to be a good parent, but suddenly she knew she could do a darn sight better job than the poor excuses that had raised her.

'Fabulous!' Hallie clapped her hands like an excited two-year-old. 'I can be a surrogate aunt. Though I still think you're super-brave to be doing this alone.'

Kristen shrugged, strangely uncomfortable with an admiration she didn't deserve. 'Not really. There are tonnes of single parents out there. I'm just adding to the statistics.'

'Yeah, but a baby? Man, is that going to cramp your style.'

Hallie's eyes sparkled as she sent a pointed look at her fitted skirt and matching jacket. 'Especially your clothes style. Mind if you throw a few casts-offs my way? Your clothes are to die for.'

Kristen chuckled. Nothing fazed Hallie, even an

unexpected pregnancy, and she hoped Nate took the news as well.

'I hate to tell you, but I won't be the size of a house for long. I plan on getting back into my clothes one day.'

'Too bad.'

Hallie smiled and smothered her in a hug. 'Actually, this is cool. It's the best news I've heard in ages. Congrats, Kris. You're going to be a great mum.'

'Thanks,' Kristen mumbled after disengaging from Hallie's bear hug, gulping the rest of her water to dislodge the lump of emotion stuck in her throat, fervently hoping the tears wouldn't start again.

'You know you can count on me, right?'

Kristen nodded and made a frantic grab for a tissue out of her handbag, dabbing at her eyes before she turned on the waterworks again.

'Stop trying to make me cry,' she sniffled, while Hallie grinned and slid an arm around her shoulders.

'Okay. I'll stop. And, by the way, don't worry. Your secret's safe with me.'

'It better be. I haven't had a chance to tell Nathan yet.'

Hallie gave her a comforting squeeze. 'The boss will be fine about it. He'll hire a maternity-leave replacement for your position, and you'll be back before you can say "pooey nappy".'

'I hope you're right,' Kristen said, sending her friend a watery smile.

She had no qualms about Nate accepting the news of her impending maternity arrangements.

It was sharing the news that he was the father of her baby she had her doubts about.

'What about the dad—are you going to tell him?'

Kristen stiffened. 'I hadn't thought that far ahead,' she said, doing her best to avoid the topic.

'You know it's the right thing to do?'

Hallie's astute stare made Kristen squirm, and she shuffled back on the couch, picked up a cushion and hugged it to her tummy.

'Right?' Hallie prompted.

'Look, I've barely absorbed the news myself,' Kristen said, knowing that no amount of time would make this decision any easier.

'Well, if you don't, I think you're selfish.'

Hallie flopped back and folded her arms, her mouth a ridiculous, sulky pout.

'Tell me what you really think,' Kristen muttered, hugging the cushion tighter.

Mostly she agreed with Hallie, but this wasn't quite that straightforward.

This was Nate they were talking about. The same Nate who had erased that amazing night from his memory banks, the same Nate who had given her the cold shoulder for the last fortnight, the same Nate who was her boss.

Could she really tell him the truth?

Hallie turned to face her, a surprisingly stubborn frown firmly in place. 'Every parent has a right to know if they have a child. One of my closest friends would've given anything to know her dad, but her mum always said he was dead. Well, guess what? Turned out Dad was living around the corner the entire time, and when my friend turned up on his doorstep twenty years later he was ecstatic. Mad as hell at my friend's mum for cheating him of playing a part in her life all those years, but really chuffed he had a kid. So, unless your baby's father is an axe-murderer, which I seriously doubt, you should tell him. It's the right thing to do.'

Kristen had never seen Hallie so serious. Joking around, teasing, flippant, yes. But delivering a stern lecture like that? Uh-uh.

'You're probably right, but I just want some time to think this through, okay?'

Hallie deflated, and her trademark smile returned. 'Okay. But if you don't you know I'll be on your case, right?'

'I know.'

Kristen rolled her eyes, knowing she was lucky to have a friend like Hallie to confide in, especially considering they'd only known each other two weeks.

'Well, you've got some thinking to do, so I'll leave you to it. Ring me if you need anything.'

'Shall do.'

Kristen showed Hallie to the door and gave her an impulsive hug, before realising she didn't have any transport home.

'Hey, come back inside and I'll ring for a cab.'

'Don't worry about it. I'll catch a tram. It'll take me ten minutes to get home, max.'

'Sure?'

Hallie gave her a gentle shove back through the door. 'Go. Sit down. Think.'

'Okay, okay.' Kristen held up her hands in surrender, smiling as Hallie bounced down the path, and waved till she hit the street corner.

However, her smile faded as she closed the door and silence descended.

Sure, she might have to do a lot of thinking, but did that necessarily mean she'd come up with the right answer? The right answer for them all?

She needed time, time to adjust and figure out what to do.

CHAPTER SIX

NATE braced himself as Kris's front door creaked open and her frowning face appeared through the crack.

'Hi, how are you feeling?'

'Better.' She opened the door a fraction further, the frown intensifying as she fiddled with a chain. 'What are you doing here?'

'Sorry to drop by unannounced, but I was worried about you.'

'You don't need to be, I'm fine.'

The chain clattered against the door frame, but she didn't invite him in. Instead, she hid behind the door, only her head visible.

'Hallie said it's some kind of virus?'

'That's right.'

Her lips compressed into a thin line, and she glared at him like he'd diagnosed her with a terminal illness rather than a transient one.

So much for being concerned. He was floundering here, way out of his depth, and he'd made a major mistake dropping by.

'I'm glad you're okay. If you need more time off work, take it.'

'I'll be in first thing in the morning,' she said, her tone softening as she opened the door wider. 'Look, you may as well come in now you're here. I'm just not dressed to receive visitors, and you kind of took me by surprise showing up out of the blue like this.'

'You sure? I don't want to impose or anything.'

Her raised eyebrow told him he already had. 'You better come in before I change my mind and slam the door in your face.'

'Put like that, how can I refuse?'

He stepped into the hallway, quickly averting his gaze when he caught sight of the long, silky, purple kimono draping the gorgeous body he remembered all too well.

'The lounge is through there. Make yourself at home while I get dressed.'

He opened his mouth to protest and snapped it shut again. He didn't want her going to any trouble, especially if she was comfortable, but then having to sit across from her dressed in that sexy robe, wondering if she was naked beneath it, would make him extremely uncomfortable.

She padded up the stairs, her bare feet softly thudding against the worn boards, and he watched her for a moment, admiring the gentle swish of silk around her slim ankles and the way the material draped her toned butt, before heading for the lounge, and not up the stairs like he wanted to.

This was a bad idea.

If seeing her in those sexy suits on a daily basis was bad enough, seeing her in that flowing kimono had set his mind off on tangents he shouldn't be contemplating.

Stepping into the lounge, he did another double take.

The outside of the quaint terrace house had a homely feel to it, with its cream rendering and bottle-green fretwork but this room quickly dispelled that impression with its stark modernistic furniture, all sleek lines and devoid of colour. Beige walls, beige suede suite, and a large beige rug covering the pale floorboards, without a splash of contrasting colour or bright pictures in sight.

Another noticeable absent feature was photos. She'd told him she didn't have much family apart from two sisters, but it looked like they didn't rank highly on her scale of personal importance if their absence was any indication. He didn't have many lying around any more either, but that was because of the painful memories every time he caught an unexpected glimpse of Julia's smile, or the characteristic sparkle in her eyes he'd loved since high school.

He did a slow turn, suddenly chilled by the lifeless ambience of the room. Kris was a vibrant, outgoing woman. What was she doing, living in a place like this? A place built for families and love and warmth on the outside yet cold and indifferent on the inside. What did that say about the woman he thought he knew?

'Would you like something to drink?'

He spun around, forcing a smile to hide his discomfort. 'I'm fine, thanks.'

She hovered in the doorway, her blue eyes stark in her pale face, highlighted by the bright red of her T-shirt worn loose over dark denim jeans.

He was used to dealing with a super-confident woman strutting around the office. This waif-like Kris had him wanting to do all sorts of uncharacteristic things, like cradle her close and stroke her tousled blonde hair.

'Why don't you tell me why you're really here?'

She leaned in the doorway, hands thrust into the pockets of her jeans, her feet bare, and the fire-engine red of her painted toenails a perfect match for her T-shirt. Her pallor should've highlighted her vulnerability. However, nothing could dim the intelligence behind her direct stare, and he knew she'd settle for nothing less than the truth.

'Fine, but only if you sit down. You're making me nervous.'

Quirking a brow, she padded across the room and chose the armchair furthest from him. 'Okay, start talking.'

Rather than curling up and tucking her feet under her, like most people would in their own home, she perched on the edge of the chair as if ready for flight.

'My main reason for dropping by like this was to check up on you, but there's something else.'

'I gathered that.'

She didn't encourage him or set him at ease, her rigid posture indicative of the hands-off approach she'd adopted with him. Not that he could blame her, considering he'd been doing the same.

Sitting opposite, he leaned back on the sofa which felt as stiff as it looked. 'I owe you an apology.'

'Go on.'

He couldn't read her blank expression but the banked fire in her eyes spoke volumes. She intended to roast him over his behaviour and then make him sweat to be forgiven.

'I've been pushing you hard, much harder than anyone else at the station. And I'm having one hell of a guilt attack about the role all the extra work I've hefted on you might've played in you coming down with this bug.'

For the first time since he'd arrived, a crooked smile lit her face. 'Save your guilt. Work had nothing to do with how I'm feeling.'

He paused, staggered that one small, barely-there smile could pack such a powerful punch, slamming into his conscience with the precise hook of a prize fighter.

'Nice of you to let me off so easily, but viruses tend to strike when you're run down and I've been running you off your feet. Why don't you take tomorrow off, rest up and come back next Monday?'

She shook her head, the smile vanishing in an instant, only to be replaced by the stubborn set of lips he'd come to associate with his star executive producer. He'd seen a similar mutinous expression every time he'd brought up an idea at work she didn't agree with, every time he'd questioned her rationale.

'Thanks, but I'm fine. I'll be there bright and early tomorrow. If you ever let me get some sleep, that is.'

She cast a pointed look at her watch and he stood, wishing he could somehow make things better between them.

Sure, he didn't want to get too close, but he'd be damned if they continued in this cold manner.

'I miss the easygoing rapport we had in Singapore,' he said, holding out his hand to help her off the chair, knowing he shouldn't have brought up the night they'd sworn to forget but unable to stop.

He needed to do something to shock her out of the casual indifference shrouding her like armour.

He expected her to ignore his outstretched hand, but

yet again she surprised him, placing her hand in his and allowing him to pull her to her feet.

'I do too,' she said, so softly he had to lean forward to catch her words—which would've been fine if it hadn't brought him scant inches away from her lush mouth, and close enough to smell her faint rose essence, subtle and enticing as a stroll through a rose garden on a warm summer's day.

She stared at him, her blue eyes wide with uncertainty and his heart clenched at the vulnerability behind the tough-girl exterior.

For all her attitude Kris reached out to him on a deeper level, and if he wasn't careful he'd find himself sucked into a vortex of emotion he didn't want.

'Friends?'

He squeezed her hand, wishing he could raise it to his lips and kiss it, wishing he could hold it for ever.

But he wasn't a 'for ever' type of guy, not any more.

The vulnerability in her eyes quickly faded, replaced by her usual tough veneer, and she pulled her hand out of his. 'Friends it is.'

She headed for the hallway and he had no option but to follow, trailing after her like some teenager with a crush.

'Remember, if you need extra time off—'

'See you tomorrow,' she said, holding open the door and scuffing her foot impatiently on the floor.

'Righto.'

He brushed past her, knowing his visit hadn't achieved much more than make a start in broaching the yawning gap between them.

She hadn't bought his false apology.

He'd wanted to apologise for pushing her away, for treating her like a stranger rather than the woman who had woken him out of a three-year stupor, but he'd baulked at the last minute, covering it up by referring to work.

So he wasn't ready to bare his soul.

He'd reached out to her, hadn't he? By referring to their night of passion and the connection they'd shared he'd virtually admitted he hadn't forgotten it. Nor did he want to, and in finally admitting it maybe he could get beyond this obsession gripping him for the woman standing in front of him looking ready to boot him down the front path.

'Was there something else?'

'Actually, there was.'

He paused, searching for the right words, knowing he had to make up for the way he'd treated her. 'You're a smart woman. I guess you've realised I haven't only been pushing you hard, I've been behaving like a bastard as well.'

'Well, I wouldn't put it that strongly,' she said, the corners of her mouth twitching and drawing his attention to the fullness of her lips, those same lips which had prompted him to lose his mind that balmy night in Singapore.

'It's true. And we both know it. I'd just like to say it's going to stop.'

Her lips curved into a full-fledged grin, alleviating some of the tired lines tugging around her mouth. 'About time. Though if I'd known the results a quick-fire faint would produce, I would've tried it last week.'

He grimaced. 'Was I really that bad?'

'Worse!'

Shadows flickered across her eyes, her frailty urging him to sweep her into his arms and never let go.

'I'm sorry,' he murmured, reaching up to cup her cheek, unable to stop himself from touching her, from reassuring her that he'd be doing things differently from now on.

'No worries,' she said, her wide-eyed blue gaze locked on his as she moved her cheek an infinitesimal millimetre and leaned into his hand.

Powerless to resist the urge he'd had since he'd first laid eyes on her tonight, he broached the gap between them, slid his hand around to cradle her head, and lowered his mouth to hers.

She sighed as his lips grazed hers, soft, coaxing, in the barest of kisses. However, he should've known that a gentle kiss wouldn't be enough, not nearly enough with this incredible woman, and the moment she angled her head slightly was the moment he lost it.

Wrapping his arms around her, he pulled her flush against him, relishing their perfect fit as his mouth recaptured hers, deepening the kiss till he could barely breathe for wanting her.

Desire slammed through his body, sending his mind into meltdown as he kissed her with all the pent-up passion which had been steadily building since she'd re-entered his life.

A crazy, fiery, no-holds-barred kiss, sending his libido into orbit and their working relationship up in flames.

Suddenly, Kris braced her hands on his chest and pushed him away, her breathing ragged and her eyes flashing fire.

'That wasn't very professional,' she said, her voice deliberately cool, and in stark contrast to her flushed cheeks.

'No, I guess not.'

Unable to keep a satisfied grin off his face, he turned away from her confused stare and strode down the concrete path away from temptation.

CHAPTER SEVEN

'It's fantastic!'

Kristen turned to Nate and struggled not to fling her arms around his neck as her gaze reluctantly left the TV screen and focussed on the man who had backed her one hundred percent on this exciting project.

Nate tried a mock frown and failed, his answering grin setting her heart thudding. 'Hmm...I'm not sure. Could do with a bit of work.'

'Are you serious?'

She leaped up from her chair and stalked across the conference room, filling a cup with water and wondering when she'd last felt this energised, this alive.

'No, I'm not serious.'

He chuckled and she swivelled to face him, hand on hip. 'Joke all you like, but we both know what we've just seen is going to take Australian TV by storm.'

'That's what I like to see. Confidence.'

He joined her at the water cooler, invading her personal space with his presence, standing so close her body warmed from the heat radiating off his, and she took a subtle step back, needing to re-establish some distance between them.

Exuberance over success in the workplace was one thing; jumping her boss because she couldn't get the memory of that unexpected, scintillating kiss on her doorstep a week ago off her mind was another.

'Tell me it's not the best travel show you've ever seen.'

He drained his water and lobbed the cup in the bin, before turning to face her, the excitement in his eyes a dead giveaway for what he was thinking before he opened his mouth to respond.

'Honestly? It's some of the best work I've ever seen. You've done an incredible job, Kris.'

He touched her arm, an all-too-brief squeeze designed to convey his pleasure in her work, but predictably her pulse raced and her mind took flight, resurrecting the many ways he'd touched her all those months ago on that one special night.

'Thanks.'

She headed back to the table and started gathering up her portfolio, knowing she needed to escape as soon as possible. In her current buoyant mood, spending one second longer with Nate could prove disastrous.

Along with her fertile imagination she had a distinct case of pregnancy hormones sending her libido crazy, and with a sexy guy like Nate around it was becoming increasingly harder to think of him in boss-terms only.

'You know this means I'm going to expect this standard from you all the time, right?'

She jumped, his voice coming from way too close over her right shoulder, and she shovelled documents faster. 'No problems. At least I know if I keep producing work of this standard you'll be nice to me.'

Oops! She hadn't meant to say the last bit, even if she

thought it was the truth. Ever since that unexpected kiss he'd changed for the better in the workplace, and they'd grown closer, developing a strong working bond which was fast moving towards friendship.

She'd attributed his change to her performance, but maybe there was something more behind the turnaround.

'I've already apologised for my earlier behaviour,' he said, reaching out and taking hold of her arm before slowly turning her around to face him.

Determined not to let him see how he affected her, she tilted her chin up and hoped her expression wouldn't give away her turbulent emotions: fear he'd revert back to being cold, fear of this new and improved Nate, but most of all fear of how easily she could fall for him given half a chance.

'I know, I remember.'

How could she forget? She'd been ready to deck him that night on her doorstep; he'd kissed her senseless, undermining all her defences in one swift, scorching kiss.

Something akin to desire flickered in his eyes before he dropped his hands and turned away, intent on stuffing documents into his briefcase.

'Good. In that case, you know I meant what I said. That's all in the past. We're a great team, and I intend for us to have a long and profitable relationship.'

His matter-of-fact tone snapped her out of the sensual fog enveloping her brain as she stilled her hands before they could rub the exact spots he'd touched her a moment ago.

Nate was her boss. She was his star employee. They had a 'long and *profitable* relationship' ahead of them.

That's all she was to him, a great worker. It was all

she'd ever be, and no matter how much she analysed that kiss it had obviously been an aberration, a spur-of-the-moment apology from a guy feeling bad about how he'd treated her.

Nothing more.

'Right. See you tomorrow,' she said, shrugging into her jacket, its tight fit reminding her of something else that would potentially bind them in a relationship, though this time it would have nothing to do with work.

She still hadn't made up her mind about telling Nate about the baby though the closer they grew, work or not, she knew the time was fast approaching where she had to make a decision one way or the other.

'I'm really thrilled this is working out, Kris.'

He finally straightened and glanced at her, an inscrutable expression in his dark-chocolate eyes, and for a moment an irrational spark of hope flared to life that maybe, just maybe, he was referring to something other than work.

'Me too.'

Forcing a cheery smile, she waved and sailed out the door, silently praying he had no idea of the giant crush she'd developed.

'Oh, my.'

Kristen stared at the big, flat LCD screen in the corner while the doctor moved a detector over her stomach, skidding through the cold gel as he moved it every which way, showing her in startling clarity that she was pregnant.

'The bub is a perfect size for fourteen weeks,' the doctor said, whose name she'd forgotten the instant she'd stepped into the room, her scared gaze riveted to the monitors and screens crowding the single bed in a makeshift cubicle in his office. 'I'll just take a few more measurements and we'll be done here.'

She nodded, barely aware of anything bar the tiny baby on the screen, its knees tucked up to its chest, cosy and secure with not a care in the world, while her heart raced and her palms grew damp with the enormity of what she was doing.

That little, defenceless baby was hers, from its ten tiny, perfectly formed fingers to its miniature toes. Tears stung her eyes and she blinked rapidly, unwilling to blubber in front of a stranger. Time enough for that at the birth.

As her eyes stayed riveted to the screen the baby's hand moved towards its face as if waving, and Kristen's heart clenched with a surge of instinctual love. In that moment, the fact this pregnancy was real hit her in a tidal wave of emotion, leaving her breathless with joy, fear and anticipation.

'Almost there,' the doctor said, taking snapshots of the baby by hitting a few keys on the elaborate keyboard linked to a monitor.

She wanted to say *take all the time in the world,* because for this one significant moment in time she realised something. Coming face to face with her baby, seeing the hard evidence she was carrying a real, live little person inside of her, hammered home the enormity of the situation.

She hadn't created this tiny miracle all by herself. And, as much as she'd prevaricated over the dilemma of whether to tell Nate or not, seeing the living, breathing evidence of the life they'd created left her with no choice.

She had to tell him.

It was the right thing to do.

Though now she'd made the decision her stomach somersaulted at the thought.

Since the night he'd dropped by her place a fortnight ago they'd forged a strong working relationship. He'd let go of whatever hang-up he'd had the first two weeks and they had become closer than she'd dared hope, considering their capricious start. Not that they were best buddies or anything, but it was nice to consider the boss a friend rather than an enemy.

However, how friendly would he be when she dumped her pregnancy surprise on him?

Most guys would run a mile. Then again, Nate wasn't most guys.

For a CEO who owned a substantial percentage of Australia's entertainment interests, he didn't have a mean bone in his body and, though he hadn't shaken the inherent sadness which seemed to be a part of him, he smiled most days, a smile which lit up her world if she were completely honest.

'All done.' The doctor wiped the gel off her tummy and handed her a small picture. 'Here. One for your album.'

Grinning like an idiot, she traced the baby's outline with a fingertip, unprepared for the surge of fierce, intense love which arrowed through her body and lodged directly in her heart.

Though she didn't have a clue about parenting, she would be the best mother if it killed her. She'd buy a library full of books, take parenting classes, do whatever it took to ensure her baby had the best mum in the world.

'Thanks,' she murmured, raising tear-filled eyes to see the young doctor smiling at her.

'Really hits home right about now, huh?'

She nodded, clutching the small photo like Charlie holding onto the golden ticket to the chocolate factory.

'Make sure you schedule another ultrasound for twenty weeks on your way out,' he said, helping her down from the table. 'I'll see you then.'

'Okay.'

Placing the photo on the bed, Kristen zipped up her trousers and slipped her stockinged feet into stiletto pumps, her gaze never leaving the first picture of her child.

Her child?

Sighing, she picked up the picture and slid it into her handbag. *Their* child. Nate was the father, and he deserved to know no matter how protective she might feel towards her unborn baby.

Whether he wanted anything to do with the baby or not, it should be his decision to make, not hers.

This baby was real.

This baby was theirs.

Suddenly, Kristen knew it was time to give Nate the news. This wasn't only about her, and a good mother always put her child's needs first.

Starting now.

Kristen opened the door to her dinner guest, her breath catching as she caught sight of Nate standing on her doorstep wearing dark denim, a navy designer T-shirt and a smile.

The guy was seriously gorgeous, and she could easily fall for him given half a chance.

But that was out of the question. She had a baby to care for, a life to build for them both, and her needs would come a far second to that of her child.

'These are for you.'

He handed her five large blocks of Swiss chocolate with the gooiest fudge-caramel centres, her favourite, and she welcomed him in.

'How did you know?'

'I've seen you devouring the odd block or two at your desk.'

The odd block or two? She reckoned she'd bought out the local chocolatier with her intense cravings for the creamy, smooth chocolate that melted on her tongue. So her baby would have a sweet tooth. If that was the worst trait he or she inherited from its mother, she'd be lucky.

'Have you been spying on me?'

He grinned. 'Of course. I always keep an eye on my best exec producers. James Bond has nothing on me.'

'You could give James a run for his money,' she said, ushering him into the cosy dining room set for two and handing him a bottle opener. 'In the successful stakes, of course.'

Uh-oh, had she actually said that, the bit about him giving James Bond a run for his money? Going by his cocky smile she had, and he probably knew exactly how she was comparing him—in the sexiness stakes. Her cover-up for her gaff had been pathetic at best.

She bustled about the table, handing him the wine to uncork while she topped up her glass with sparkling mineral water.

'Wine?'

'No thanks,' she said, the mere fumes sending a wave of nausea crashing over her.

She hadn't been too bad with morning sickness, but

come six p.m. her hormones surged, and the faintest of smells set her off and running for the loo.

Indicating he take a seat, she slid into the chair opposite. 'I'm not having wine, though I thought you might like some. It's the one you ordered in Singapore, your favourite, I believe.'

'You remembered?'

His expression relaxed as he sat down, though the wariness never left his eyes. He had no idea what he was doing here, and it was time she enlightened him.

'Uh-huh,' she said, barely refraining from adding *how could I forget anything about that evening?*

He poured himself a glass of wine, his steady stare never leaving her for an instant.

'I must say, this dinner invitation came as a pleasant surprise.'

She almost choked on her mineral water. Not half as much a surprise as it would be before the evening ended.

Replacing her glass on the table for fear of sloshing the lot, she clasped her hands to stop from fiddling, and looked him straight in the eye.

'I wanted us to have some quiet time together away from the office.'

'Really?'

She couldn't fathom the expression in his eyes. Confusion? Interest? Fear?

Nodding, she said, 'I have something to tell you, and it's important.'

Curiosity replaced confusion in his coal-dark eyes, and he leaned forward, all his attention focussed on her.

'Go ahead, shoot. Though, if you're gunning for a raise, forget it.'

Her nervous laugh sounded hollow. 'I'm pregnant and you're the father,' she blurted, horrified at the inane way the words flew out of her mouth, grateful he finally knew the truth.

The smile died on his lips as he stared at her, blanching, his pallor matching the sickly beige of the walls.

'What?'

'I thought the chocolate gorging might've been a dead giveaway?'

Her false bravado petered out quickly as he didn't move a muscle, stunned into immovability, staring at her in wide-eyed shock.

'But we used protection.'

'Condoms are only ninety-seven percent effective,' she said, watching him compute the figures, but the information not really sinking in. 'I know this must be pretty shocking for you. I felt the same way when I found out—'

'How long have you known?'

She looked away, pretending to study the elaborate table setting. 'Since that day I fainted.'

'And you've waited till now to tell me?'

She wouldn't have been surprised if he'd exploded or lost his temper or jumped up from the table. Instead, his cold, icy control terrified her more than any of the reactions she'd anticipated.

Reaching a hand across the table to comfort him, she flinched as he leaned away from her and out of reach.

'I wasn't sure if I wanted to tell you or not. It was a big decision to make, so I wanted to take my time, think about it and make sure I made the right one.'

If he'd been pale before, he turned positively ghostly now.

'And have you? Made the right decision, I mean? After all, it must've been real tough working out if you think I'm the kind of guy who can handle being told he's about to become a father.'

He pushed away from the table so fast his chair slammed onto the floor, fury etched into every tense line of his body.

She shook her head, hating how this was going. She should have led up to the news, broken it to him gently, tried to formulate some answers to the inevitable questions he would have.

Instead, she'd spilled the news quicker than she'd dropped her guard around him that night in Singapore.

Hating the surge of tears at the mess she'd made of everything, she said, 'Look, Nate, it wasn't like that. It took me a while to absorb the news. I just wanted to make sure I was doing the right thing in telling you.'

Clenching his fists, he turned to face her, his frigid glare freezing her heart.

'You should've told me earlier.'

'Maybe,' she said, sipping at her mineral water in an effort to buy some time, to give him an opportunity to calm down.

Not that she could blame him for reacting like this. She'd bawled, he'd ranted. Everyone handled life-changing news in their own way and, boy, was his life in for a major change if he wanted to be a part of their child's life.

'But I can't turn back time or change the way I've gone about this, Nate. Believe me, I've really thought about this long and hard, and once I'd made the decision I really wanted you to know.'

He grunted, fixed her with another icy glare, before shaking his head, righting his chair and sitting back down.

'The baby's doing fine, by the way,' she said, hoping to focus his attention on the real issue here—their child— and away from how much he'd like to throttle her.

His hand shook as he reached for his wine, and he quickly took a healthy swig before replacing the glass and dropping his hand out of sight, as if embarrassed by a physical sign of his obvious shock.

'That's good. And how are you?'

'Okay, apart from the usual stuff like morning sickness.'

'How far along are you?'

'About fourteen weeks.'

His gaze flickered to her belly, strategically disguised behind a loose, flowing peasant top.

'You can't tell.'

'I'm not that big yet,' she said, grateful they'd moved onto discussing the baby and away from his rage, but wishing they could fall back into their natural camaraderie rather than speaking in these stilted syllables.

'A baby,' he muttered, draining half his glass of wine before shaking his head.

They lapsed into silence, his eyes round, dark orbs in his pale face, stark in their bleak expression, her gaze darting to his to ascertain the slightest change in mood.

After thirty tension-fraught seconds which felt like a lifetime, she knew she had to get the rest out before she bolted upstairs and let the waterworks flow.

'I told you because I believe you have a right to

know, not because I expect anything from you. Whether you want to be involved or not is entirely up to you…' She trailed off, horrified by the pain which jagged across his face, his striking features almost collapsing into a crumpled heap.

'I don't believe this,' he muttered, running a hand over his face, rubbing his eyes as if trying to erase the memory of the last few minutes—maybe erasing the memory of the night that had landed them in this parenting role together.

You better believe it! she wanted to scream.

In fact, in the face of his reaction, she wanted to jump up and down and throw a tantrum to end all tantrums.

She'd worked so hard to stay calm, to tell him in the right way, to understand the roller-coaster of emotion he'd just stepped onto, but as he raised stricken eyes to her she wanted to shout, wave her arms about, do anything to snap him out of it.

Struggling to keep her voice steady, she said, 'What part don't you believe? The part about being a father, being involved or the role you played in all of this?'

Some of her anger must've been audible, because he sat back and folded his arms, pinning her with a stare that could turn her to stone.

'Don't patronise me,' he snapped, his lips compressed in a thin, rigid line. 'I'm well aware of my *role* in all of this. As for being involved, what do you want me to say?'

Suddenly, the fragile hold on her temper broke. 'Tell me what you're thinking. Tell me how you're feeling. Tell me what I can do to make this easier. Tell me whatever you damn well please, but for God's sake stop blaming me for something that isn't my fault!'

She thought he'd really lose it then, but her tirade had an unexpected effect, as his shoulders softened and he reached across the table as if to take her hand before thinking better of it.

'This isn't your fault.'

'Damn right it's not,' she muttered, downing the rest of her mineral water and topping up, anything to keep her hands busy and away from strangling him, or touching him, whichever was worse.

'I can't tell you what you want to hear because I have no idea what I'm feeling, let alone what I'm going to do about any of this.'

She heard the sincerity in his voice but it didn't make this any easier. The man she'd hoped would stand up and be counted the moment he found out about his unborn baby wasn't feeding her the reassuring lines she'd wanted to hear.

Sighing, she pushed away from the table.

'Look, I know this is a big deal, and I'm well aware you probably need some time to absorb what I've just told you. Why don't we skip dinner?'

Gratitude flickered through his eyes, the first sign of any emotion other than shock or pain.

'You sure?'

Hating the way her heart sank at his first instinct to bolt, she nodded.

'Go ahead. If you want to talk some more, you know where to find me.'

With as much dignity as she could muster, Kris headed up the stairs. She needed to get away to process her disappointment, to rationalise the disillusionment that, despite the faint hope that Nate would be as thrilled as she was about this baby, he wasn't.

It didn't surprise her, yet she couldn't help the wave of sadness which washed over her as she realised what a delusional fool she'd been for hoping her wretched crush could morph into something more, something they could build on and strengthen in time for the baby's arrival.

Blinking against the tears burning her eyes, she padded up the stairs, hating the finality of the front door slamming as Nate left.

Nate staggered from Kris's house like a drunk, the half glass of wine he'd had sloshing around his stomach till he thought he'd throw up.

Kris was pregnant.

He was the father.

Straightening, he glanced back at the house, his heart clenching at the sight of the woman carrying his child silhouetted against an upstairs window before she quickly closed the blinds.

He'd known something was different lately.

She'd been too withdrawn, too accepting of his proposals the last couple of weeks, agreeing to practically everything he'd put forward without so much as a minor skirmish or argument.

He'd attributed it to their new-found truce, and in a way he'd been too happy to question it. Building a strong working relationship with her had been rewarding, fostering a friendship even more so.

He loved the way they were on the same wavelength. He'd have an idea, she'd put the finishing touches on it.

He'd propose an amendment, she'd sanction it. They were a great team, and he could envisage RX moving forward into the upper echelon of Australian TV at a rate of knots.

But it was more than that.

He loved her quicksilver smile, the triumph in her deep blue eyes when they made an idea happen, her loud laugh when RX's latest comedy series hit the top of the ratings. He loved her fierce independence, and now all that was about to change, courtesy of him.

She was carrying *his* child.

Hell.

Bracing himself against the front fence, he took a deep breath, the crisp, bracing Melbourne air filling his lungs, hopefully clearing his head.

He couldn't do this.

No matter how much he liked Kris, he couldn't be the man she wanted.

Taking a chance on fatherhood was a risk he wasn't willing to take.

Releasing the fence, he turned away from her house and strode down the street towards his car, his long, angry steps eating up the pavement.

If hearing Kris's news had shocked him, it had nothing on the bolt of disappointment when he'd realised he couldn't be the father she wanted for her child—yet for one brief, crazy moment when she'd first told him he'd had a startling vision of the two of them together, his arm around her while she cradled their baby.

Irrational, stupid and beyond belief, the absurd surge of hope that their one incredible night together could've resulted in a baby had thrilled him before he'd bolted, running from his demons.

He didn't want to be a father.

Reaching his car, he slammed a hand against the bonnet, hating the painful memories slashing through the fog of confusion caused by Kris's revelation.

Could he take a risk again?

No, he couldn't do it.

With his head pounding with unanswered questions, Nate gunned the engine and slid away from the kerb.

He needed time to think, time to get his head around the fact he'd fathered a child, and what on earth he was going to do about it.

CHAPTER EIGHT

'You wanted to see me?'

Nate nodded and beckoned Kristen in, scribbling furiously on a notepad while he mumbled a string of 'uh-huhs' into the phone squeezed between his ear and shoulder.

She stepped into his office, wishing she had the guts to quit. It had crossed her mind several times since he'd left her place two nights ago. It would be so difficult to work with him, seeing him on a daily basis, trying to pretend that everything was okay, when as a matter of fact she wanted to clobber him over the head for being a cold, callous cretin.

And she'd thought her string of lousy foster mothers had been bad!

At least they'd feigned interest in her at the start, whereas Nate didn't seem interested in his son or daughter at all.

He hadn't tried to contact her, hadn't phoned or visited when she'd called in sick to work yesterday. Nothing, and his silence spoke volumes.

Some people were cut out to be parents and some weren't, and till a few months ago she'd fallen into the latter category herself. But that was before she'd woken up and smelt the ginger tea—a godsend for her nausea. In a way she should be grateful he'd shown his true colours now and hadn't strung her child along, promising birthday visits and ponies only to renege on every vow at the last minute.

She'd hated the false promises more than the lack of affection from her numerous foster parents, and she'd be damned if she sat back and let her child go through the same heartache.

Cupping his hand over the mouthpiece, he murmured, 'Sorry, this will only take a minute.'

She nodded, not caring if he took an eternity on the phone and never spoke to her again.

Being here, sitting across from him like nothing had happened, grated. She couldn't quit no matter how much she wanted to. She'd made a vow to be the best mum she could, and for her that meant staying at home for the baby's first year at least, which meant she needed to scrounge and save every penny she could now. Besides, who would employ a pregnant woman for the next few months only?

She had no choice.

She had to act the model employee, while eyeing the steel letter-opener within arm's reach and imagining creative ways she could make her heartless boss squirm.

Hanging up the phone, Nate threw down his pen and said, 'Sorry about that. Interstate conference-call took longer than expected.'

She ignored his apology, eager to get straight to the point. The less they saw of each other, business arena or not, the better.

'What did you want to see me about?'

'This.'

He handed her a gilt-edged embossed invitation and she opened it, scanning over the words with little interest. 'An invitation to the Logies. So?'

'We're going.'

The stiff cardboard invitation to the Australian television awards crumpled in her clenched fist like tissue paper, and she forced herself to relax.

'You might be. I'm not.'

It took every ounce of willpower to place the balled invitation on the desk and not throw it in his face. Now, if she could manage to hold onto her temper for the few steps between the desk and the door, she'd be doing well indeed.

'Actually, we both have to go. Una and Alan are both interstate this weekend, so that leaves us to represent the station.'

'Take someone else,' she said, shifting her weight from foot to foot, enjoying standing over him, but hating the way the straps on her stilettos cut into her ankles.

Maybe it was time to forego fashion for comfort now that she was retaining a bit of fluid. The joys of motherhood...and this was only the start!

He shook his head, reaching for the invitation and smoothing it out.

'No can do. We're the head honchos of RX at the moment, we have to attend. It wouldn't look good if we didn't go, not to mention giving the rumour-mill fodder for the next few months. You know we're launching an all-out attack on the ratings soon. For the sake of good PR we have to be there, no excuses.'

Kristen mustered her worst intimidating glare, knowing she had no choice but to go along to television's biggest awards night—with him!

Damn him for being right.

Damn him for putting her in this predicament.

Most of all, damn him for eliciting the faintest thrill of pleasure at the thought of accompanying him, especially when she was supposed to be hating him right now.

'Fine. E-mail me the details and I'll meet you there.'

She turned on her heel and headed for the door without a backward glance.

'Kris?'

She bit her tongue to keep from responding and kept moving. Only a few more steps...

'We need to talk about the baby.'

She stopped dead, swivelling so fast her head spun. 'Now?'

'I didn't want to have this conversation here,' he muttered, running a hand over his eyes as if to obliterate a host of memories. She knew the feeling. 'Poor form on my part, but I can't let this wait till later. I don't know about you, but I can't function with the two of us like this.'

'We're professionals, Nate,' she said, wondering if he remembered using similar words on her first day when he'd belittled what they'd shared in Singapore, negating it to nothing with his nonchalance. 'We need to function as best we can regardless of our personal situations.'

'I deserved that, but can we talk?'

He crossed the space between them in a flash, gripping her upper arms so she couldn't move, and darn if her pulse didn't leap and jump and thud all over the place.

Stupid pregnancy hormones.

Trying to ignore the warmth seeping into her body from his touch, she said, 'Do you really want to talk about the baby here? Now? That's what the other night was about, you know. If you hadn't run scared, that is.'

His dark eyes widened, and all colour drained from his face as his grip on her arms tightened, his fingers biting into her tender flesh till she squirmed.

'You don't know anything about me.'

Yanking free of his grasp, she sent him a scathing look. 'Too right I don't. Funny thing is, I thought I did. I never thought you'd be the type of guy to turn tail and run and then give me the cold shoulder when you finally see me again.'

'You're right, I'm sorry...' He trailed off, rubbing the bridge of his nose as if he had a thumper of a headache, closing his eyes for a second before they snapped open and fixed her with a stare that could have frozen nitrogen. 'My reaction has nothing to do with you.'

Raising an eyebrow, she tried to match his cold stare and failed. She couldn't do it when she glimpsed the devastation behind the forced coolness in his eyes, and wondered what or who had put it there.

'You're wrong. It has everything to do with me. We're in this together.'

She reached out and gripped his hand, giving it a quick squeeze before letting go. Touching him, even for something as innocuous as a comforting squeeze on the hand, felt way too good. 'If you want to be, that is.'

Shaking his head, he perched his butt on the back of the chair, his steady stare never leaving her face. 'Honestly? I don't know what I want right now.'

'Oh.'

'I know this is hard for you, but I need some more time,' he said, his grave expression imploring her to understand something she had no idea about as she wondered how her life had got so complicated.

A few months ago the hardest decision she'd had to make was which suit to wear to work, and now, thanks to one amazing night, they'd woven an intricate web of parenthood which had them both confused and scared.

'Time. Right.'

She nodded, hating how high and tight and squeaky her voice sounded, hating the threat of tears prickling the back of her eyelids more.

'Hey, it's okay,' he said, enveloping her in a hug before she knew what was happening, and though her first instinct was to pull away she ignored it, relaxing into his embrace, wondering when she'd last been held like this, comforted like this.

Probably that night in Singapore, when the same man had wrapped his arms around her, though back then there had been nothing but passion and heat and an overwhelming attraction.

Her skin tingled at the scorching recollection, and she placed her hands on his chest and pushed away, albeit reluctantly.

She needed to get out of here before she blubbered. Being held by Nate, enveloped by his purely masculine scent, cradled in his strong arms, did nothing but short-circuit her brain and make her forget every logical reason she had for pushing him away.

'It's okay to be scared, you know,' she said, knowing most guys would be blown away by news of impending fatherhood, yet unable to shake the feeling there was more behind Nate's reaction than simple fear.

He wavered between anger, coldness, fear and warmth, vacillating all over the place when he was usually so commanding and in control.

'Scared? I'm terrified,' he said, the serious expression on his face telling her far more than his honest words did.

There *was* something more at play here, but she couldn't push him. If he hadn't made a decision about being involved with the baby yet, what right did she have to push him for answers to questions she could barely formulate?

'Hey, I'm scared too. I know it's a big deal, and besides, I've had longer to absorb it all than you have.'

Cupping her cheek, he brushed his thumb along her skin, sending shivers skittering through her body. 'Thanks for being so understanding.'

'Yeah, that's me.'

She stilled under his touch, her breath catching as his thumb rasped across her cheek for a brief moment before dropping away. 'I don't even know if you like babies.'

Some guys did, some would run a mile at the barest hint of a goo-goo or ga-ga, and she'd wondered where Nate stood ever since she'd discovered the pregnancy.

He sighed and looked away, and her heart plummeted. From the moment Nate had said he wanted to talk about the baby, she'd built an elaborate fantasy in her head, one where Nate loved the baby and grew to feel half of what she felt for him, wrapping them all up in one neat family package.

However, with his crestfallen expression and guilty gaze, he'd ripped the bow off in a swift, painful action, exposing her fantasy for what it was: an empty dream without all the trimmings.

'It's complicated,' he said, finally raising his eyes to meet hers again.

'Right now, complication is my middle name,' she said, forcing a brittle, hollow laugh which echoed eerily around the room.

'Look, I want to explain it to you, but I can't get into it right now. This isn't the time or place.'

'Maybe later?'

Her voice came out soft, small, shy, like a coy teenager asking a boy out on a date, and she felt just as uncertain and gauche, hanging on his answer with hope in her heart.

His face fell along with her hopes. 'I can't. I'm flying to Brisbane in a few hours to one of the other divisions. I'll be there all week, getting back late Sunday afternoon before the Logies.'

'Oh.'

Could this get any more convoluted?

Maybe she and Nate weren't meant to sort things out. Maybe she'd be better off pinning her hopes on winning the lottery?

A million-to-one chance, about the same odds she had as ever getting on the same page as Nate.

'Hey, I promise we'll talk after the Logies, okay?'

He tipped her chin up, his gaze warm and steady, imploring her to trust him.

Like she knew anything about trust.

She'd had her scant personal belongings stolen by the foster family's own kids at the first foster home she'd been dumped in, she'd been let down at parent-teacher interviews by her second foster mum on no less than three occasions, and the third, fourth and fifth foster homes she'd lived in had been rife with verbal and psychological abuse.

What she knew about trust equalled what she knew about babies—next to nothing.

'I don't expect anything of you,' she said, stepping away, glad to re-establish some control over her personal space, hating the bereft feeling when his arms fell to his sides. 'You know that's not what the other night was about. I just thought you had a right to know.'

'Thanks. It means a lot.'

However, he didn't look grateful. In fact, he looked downright uncomfortable, as if being a dad was the last thing he wanted.

Well, she'd make it easy for him.

'No one needs to know about this,' she said, fiddling with the edging of her jacket. 'I won't name you as the father on the birth certificate.'

She'd thought she was doing him a favour.

By the angry crimson flush creeping up his neck, and his thin, compressed lips, she'd thought wrong.

'I'm not ashamed of this child or being recognised as the father. I just need some time.'

Time for what?

Time to invent excuses why he couldn't be around?

Time to make himself scarce?

She could've asked him, but she wouldn't give him the satisfaction of knowing how much his answers meant to her.

For some strange reason, it suddenly mattered why he needed time. A lot.

After the other night she'd resigned herself to being her baby's sole parent, yet now having Nate take responsibility seemed paramount.

She wanted to know what was driving him, what was behind the fleeting guilt she glimpsed at times. Because maybe, just maybe, if she understood more about what motivated him, she'd have a chance of making him see how great being a parent to their child could be.

With her thoughts swinging as wildly as her emotions, courtesy of her hormones, she knew she'd better leave before she did something crazy—like fling herself back into his comforting arms.

'More time? Sure. We're not going anywhere.'

She patted her tummy, a never-ending sense of awe flooding her body at the bump already there, while his panicked glance flickered between her belly and her face.

Whoa! How could a capable, take-charge CEO look like he was about to faint at the thought of being a father? Maybe he wasn't half the man she'd thought he was.

And maybe you need to give the guy a break.

He'd said he would explain on Sunday and she had to give him the benefit of the doubt. She had no other option.

'I'll pick you up at seven?'

'Fine,' she said, wondering how she'd get through the rest of the week knowing that they would be discussing their baby's future after some silly, flash awards-night. 'See you then.'

She spun on her heel and opened the door, needing some air, needing some distance between her and the man who made her dream and want and crave things she had no right believing in.

'Kris?'

'Yeah?'

She glanced over her shoulder, unable to fathom the intense expression casting shadows over his handsome face.

'Thanks for giving me a chance.'

Flashing him a wan smile, she headed out of his office, wondering if he meant a chance at being a father, a chance at explaining, or something else entirely.

CHAPTER NINE

THE brass knocker clanged noisily against Kristen's front door, and she slipped on her shoes, grabbed her evening bag and made a mad dash for the stairs, forcing herself to slow when she reached the top.

'Sorry about the bumpy ride,' she murmured, caressing her belly as she descended the stairs to greet Nate, filled with uncertainty and fear and longing, the latter a terrible, desperate yearning for a man she knew could never be hers.

For if Nate hadn't wanted her before she was pregnant there was no way she'd fall for any sudden change of heart.

She wouldn't put it past an upstanding guy like him to want to do the right thing and include her in his grand plans for giving his child the perfect life—if he wanted an involvement with his child, that was.

Pity he hadn't realised they could've had the perfect life before the baby had obligated him to her.

Opening the door with a welcoming smile, she said, 'Hi, you're back.'

Not the most scintillating line, but not bad considering her mind had shut down the second she'd caught sight of Nate in a designer tuxedo, his dark eyes sparkling, a sexy smile playing about his mouth, and his hands filled with a giant box covered in adorable teddy bears.

'You look beautiful,' he said, the banked heat of his top-to-toe glance setting her body alight, his admiration thrilling her. She'd spent an inordinate amount of time with her make-up, hair and adjusting the exquisite A-line empire-style dress of mauve chiffon, gathered over her nicely expanding bust and falling in loose folds to her ankles.

She wanted Nate to see her as an attractive woman.

She wanted him to see her as more than the mother of his child.

Stupid, foolish, crazy?

Definitely but she couldn't help but wish her baby would have more than she'd ever had—a father to protect her, to give her advice, to beat off randy teenagers like those who'd treated her as trash because she'd had no parents and no one who particularly cared.

Not that she was completely delusional. She didn't expect Nate and her to be a couple, but she wanted them to establish a bond, a close friendship which would envelop her baby in love and security. Two things she would've given anything for growing up.

'And this is for you.'

'Thanks, come in.'

She stepped aside, inhaling deeply as he brushed past her, the heady scent of his signature aftershave sending her receptors into meltdown. She'd never forget that smell, its tangy freshness a lingering reminder of the incredible night they'd shared and the way his skin had pressed up against hers in so many delightful ways, branding her own with his exotic scent.

'Aren't you going to open it?'

He laid the box down on the dining table and she nodded, suddenly shy at the way he devoured her with his eyes, the glint of desire she glimpsed there a potent reminder of what they'd shared, what they could share again if he threw caution to the wind and she lost her mind.

I'll blame the hormones again, she thought, remembering how she'd swiftly flipped past the chapter in one of the books where it had stated that expectant mothers often found their libidos out of control.

That had to be true considering all she could think of right at this minute was ripping that stuffy bow-tie off Nate's neck, tearing open his snowy-white shirt and burying her face against his amazing rock-hard chest.

'Kris?'

Heat flushed her cheeks—she could easily have skipped the blush—and she opened the box, her heart expanding with emotion as she lifted out a giant, purple hippo wearing a goofy smile.

'He's gorgeous,' she said, blinking back sudden tears at Nate's generosity, hoping this was the sign she'd hoped for, the sign that he wanted to be a part of their child's life and, if so, knowing this would be the first of many presents for their lucky child.

'There's something in there for you too,' he said, gently taking the hippo out of her hands when she didn't move, brushing away the lone tear that trickled down her cheek. 'Though, if you cry I might have to take it back to the store.'

She chuckled, dabbing under her eyes to prevent further spillage, and delved into the box, her hands searching amongst a sea of tissue paper until she encountered a small, square box.

It felt suspiciously like jewellery, and she hesitated, suddenly nervous.

What could this mean?

Surely Nate hadn't taken his obligation to extremes and bought her a ring? He wouldn't be crazy enough to propose…?

'You're one of those infuriating go-slow people on Christmas Day, aren't you? The kind who never rip off the wrapping paper all in one go to get to the good stuff.'

She flashed him a haughty stare. 'Good things are worth waiting for.'

'Damn right,' he said, sending her another trademark sexy smile which notched up the temperature in the room by ten degrees at least.

With shaking fingers she flipped open the box, breathing a sigh of relief and wonder as she poked at the tiny gold booty nestled in white satin.

'It's gorgeous,' she said, marvelling at the intricate work, the perfection of it.

He cleared his throat, and she wondered if he felt half as choked up as she did as the enormity of what they were doing hit home.

They were going to be parents.

There would be many more opportunities like this for giving and sharing gifts with their child: birthdays, Christmases, graduations and beyond.

Special moments to be captured like a still photograph and pressed into her heart, never to be forgotten, made extra special for sharing it with a man like Nate.

'I thought you might clobber me with your laptop if

I gave you jewellery, so this way you can choose to keep the charm for the baby's bracelet if it's a girl or add it to one of your own.'

His tone, husky with emotion, had her avoiding his gaze. If she looked up and saw those dark eyes studying her, she'd burst into tears without a doubt.

'And if it's a boy?'

He chuckled. 'Okay, you got me. I really want you to have the charm. Maybe one day you'll let me buy you the bracelet to go with it?'

'Don't push your luck,' she said, sending him a mock-scathing look that withered under the intensity of his stare.

'How about a charm for every milestone of the baby's life?'

'Yeah, that sounds good. I can see it now. A dummy for the first month, a teething ring for the sixth, and a potty around two?'

Actually, she liked the idea. It was sweet and thoughtful and totally Nate.

'Though I draw the line at miniature gold forceps to commemorate the birth, okay?'

He laughed and slipped an arm around her waist. 'Come on. We have some serious schmoozing to do.'

'And later?'

His hand felt way too good resting on her hip, its warmth branding her skin through the thin chiffon, sending a powerful wake-up call to those crazy hormones which had dozed off for the last few minutes.

'I promise we'll talk,' he said, dropping an all-too-brief, too-chaste kiss on her cheek before guiding her out the door.

Resigning herself to an interminable evening of

back-slapping and fake smiles at equally fake people, she focussed on what really mattered about this evening: Nate by her side, their baby nestled safe within her belly, and the conversation with the potential to make or break her future.

'Are you having a good time?'

Kristen nodded, and tried for the umpteenth time that evening not to get lost in the dark depths of Nate's eyes.

'Actually, I am. Usually these functions are kind of dull, but with lemon-meringue pie for dessert, it's taken the evening into the next realm.'

Nate chuckled and pushed his dessert plate across to her. 'And here I was, thinking I was the reason you were having such a good time.'

'Now why would you think that?'

She batted her eyelashes at him, loving every minute of this unexpectedly enjoyable night as he laughed and pointed to the plate.

'Eat up. It's good for you,' he said, dropping his voice low as he sent a pointed stare at her belly.

'Okay. If you insist,' she said, needing little encouragement to devour a second serving of her favourite dessert.

However, she almost choked on the first mouthful as Nate's gaze stayed riveted to her lips, his expression hungry, though she had a sneaking suspicion it wasn't for food.

'Do you want some?'

His gaze stayed focussed on her lips a tad longer before slowly drifting upwards. 'No thanks. Besides, it's much more fun watching you enjoy it.'

'Uh-huh,' she said, taking her time with the next mouthful, savouring the sweet tart exploding on her tongue, her pulse racing at the hungry gleam in Nate's eyes.

Looked like her boss wanted to have his cake and eat it too!

'So, what's your favourite dessert?' She needed to say something, do something to break the sexual tension which had enveloped them in a cosy cocoon, before she did something crazy like offer him a taste of the pie...from her lips!

'Tiramisu.'

'Not bad. But not as good as this.'

'I'm starting to believe it,' he said, reaching across to dab at a meringue crumb which clung to the corner of her lips.

'Thanks,' she murmured, expecting him to deposit the crumb in his napkin, shocked when he lifted his finger to his mouth and ate it.

'You're right. Delicious,' he said, his hypnotic stare never leaving hers for an instant as his lips curved into a knowing smile.

Kristen didn't know how long they sat there, staring at each other like a couple of moonstruck teenagers, but if it hadn't been for the band starting up she knew without a doubt she would've leaned into him and kissed him.

It had been that kind of night.

A night for flirting, for chatting and for learning new things, like favourite desserts.

A night for growing closer, for fighting a losing battle with the escalating attraction sizzling between them.

A night for doing crazy things, like throwing herself at her boss.

'Would you like to dance?'

She shouldn't.

If sitting next to him was sending her body into meltdown, what hope would she have wrapped in his arms?

'I'd love to,' she said, happily ignoring her own logic and placing her hand in his.

They strolled hand in hand to the dance floor, or, more precisely, Kristen floated alongside Nate, grateful for his strong grip. The way her knees trembled, she wouldn't have made it two feet without his support.

'It's been ages since I've done this,' Nate said, taking her into his arms and cradling her close, while she struggled not to kiss the pulse point in his throat beating at her eye level.

It was so tempting...the rhythmic throb, throb, throb a beacon to her overstimulated imagination.

It would be so easy...

'Let me guess. Favourite song?'

She tore her gaze away from his throat and tried to focus on what he was saying.

'This song? You were humming it under your breath.'

Kristen had been oblivious to the music till now. In fact, they could've been dancing a polka and she wouldn't have known, wouldn't have cared, as long as she was wrapped in this incredible man's arms.

'It is a favourite. It's an Elvis classic—*Are You Lonesome Tonight.*'

His eyes widened ever so slightly. 'Is that an offer?'

She held her breath, wondering how far she could tease him, wondering if she could handle the fallout.

And there would be—she had no illusions about that. They hadn't discussed the baby yet. In fact, this evening was a mere prelude to the main event, and she shouldn't get caught up in the romance of it.

So Nate was flirting a little.

It probably didn't mean anything, and she'd be better off recognising that.

'You know it's the song title,' she said, reluctantly disengaging from his arms as the song came to an end and heading back to the table.

'My favourite's *It's Now or Never*,' he said, falling into step beside her, the laughter in his voice audible.

She rolled her eyes and smiled as he pulled her chair out and she sat down, feeling every inch a princess yet aware her Prince Charming could well turn into a frog by the end of the evening.

'I've had a good time tonight.'

Nate captured her hand, the tender expression in his eyes bringing a lump to her throat, and in total contrast to the suave, confident guy who'd been teasing her all evening.

'Me too,' she said, trying not to get too caught up in the moment, but fighting a losing battle when he interlaced his fingers with hers.

'Want to get out of this place and go have that chat?'

'You bet.'

However, as they left the Grand Ballroom with their hands intertwined, Kristen wondered if she'd have been better off living the fantasy a little longer.

After all, reality had a funny way of letting her down.

* * *

'Where are we?'

Nate turned into his street, pulled into the first house on the right and killed the engine, turning to face Kris.

'There are advantages to you not being a Melbourne girl. I can take you anywhere and it's like an adventure every time,' he said, smiling as her eyes widened with curiosity, their dazzling blue a more muted midnight in the dim car.

'Right now, this intrepid adventurer needs to use the bathroom desperately, so unless this is your house or the house of a very good friend who'll let a crazy woman bash their door in I suggest you get me to a convenience store pronto.'

He smiled, enjoying her sense of humour. It was one of the things he remembered from their brief liaison in Singapore, her dry sense of humour and the ability to laugh at herself even in the face of adversity.

'Rather than have you terrorise the good folk of Middle Park on a Sunday night, I'll let you use the bathroom. Come on.'

She almost ran all the way to the front door and he unlocked it, disarmed the alarm and pushed it open in record time, barely having time to say, 'Down the hall, last door on the left,' as she pushed past him and dashed down the hallway, her heels clattering along the boards.

Wondering what she'd think of his place and hoping she'd go for his plan he flicked on the lights, illuminating the lounge, his favourite room in the house. With its soaring ceilings, elaborate cornices and marble fireplace, the room captured the period feel of the house perfectly, and he often spent his limited own-time in here, working from his laptop in front of the fire or reading a book while stretched out on the Chippendale sofa.

Julia had loved this room too. In fact, they'd both walked into the house and known this place was perfect, making an offer to the surprised estate agent on the spot.

Battling the wave of sadness which swamped him whenever he thought of her, he picked up a picture, his favourite, depicting the two of them in the Whitsundays: smiling, joyous, without a care in the world.

Life had been pretty simple back then—work, play, live for the moment. Buying this house had been a big step towards their future, and now maybe it was time to start thinking about a future of a different kind.

'Who's that?'

Kris had slipped off her shoes and come up behind him, her eyes fastened on the picture frame.

'My wife,' he said, replacing the photo on the granite mantelpiece and quashing his old memories, knowing it was time to explain, and eager to get to the point of this evening.

However, before he could say another word, Kris paled and slumped onto the sofa, her mouth a surprised O, before her eyes clouded in confusion and flicked between the photo and his face.

'Your *wife?*'

She shook her head, bewilderment etched across her beautiful face.

CHAPTER TEN

KRISTEN struggled to process Nate's revelation, knowing there had to be a perfectly logical explanation behind this.

Nate couldn't be married. She'd worked with him for months and he spent all his time at the office. Besides, he wasn't that sort of guy, the sort that played around on his wife, having one-night stands in foreign countries, getting other women pregnant...or was he?

She knew next to nothing about him, and coming to his house accentuated the fact.

Though her knowledge of Melbourne wasn't extensive she knew Middle Park was an upper-class suburb and period homes like this cost a small fortune.

Throw in the fact that the house was the epitome of a family home, with a sprawling front lawn complete with rope and tyre hanging from an old oak tree just waiting for some child to swing from it, and the sheer size of the rooms she'd seen to date, and she knew that Nate had some explaining to do. Big-time.

'Julia died three years ago,' he said, sitting next to her on the sofa and reaching across for her hand before thinking better of it.

She scuttled away from him to the furthest corner of the sofa and folded her arms. She needed to absorb his words and touching him, indeed any kind of proximity, didn't help.

'I'm sorry,' she said softly, her trite words echoing in the cavernous room. She felt ashamed for jumping to stupid conclusions a moment ago but still annoyed she knew nothing about him.

Admittedly, it wasn't his fault. They'd agreed to forget their one night of passion, to move on to a professional footing once she'd started working at RX, but the game plan had changed thanks to the little life inside her, and the closer they'd grown at work despite all intentions otherwise.

'We were the clichéd high-school sweethearts,' he said, studying his hands clasped in his lap as if they held the answers to the world's problems. 'We dated for an eternity, taking a break once to see other people before realising we were meant to be together.'

She remained silent, biting on her inner lip to stop crying out from the pain lancing her heart. Sure, she'd wanted to know more about Nate, but this wasn't quite what she'd had in mind—listening to him offload about the love of his life.

'We got married eight years ago. That picture with Jules was taken on our honeymoon.'

Kris's folded arms tightened as she tried to give herself a comforting hug, trying to ignore the tender expression on Nate's face at his cherished memories, hating herself for being insanely jealous of a dead woman.

Right then, it hit her.

She could never compete with a ghost and, as much

as she'd tried to deny that having Nate in her life wasn't an issue, she'd been lying to herself since the moment she'd walked into his office and discovered the guy she hadn't been able to forget had re-materialised in her life.

'You must miss her very much,' she said, needing to fill the growing silence, desperate to say something before she let out an anguished groan.

He nodded, finally lifting his gaze to meet hers, and what she saw there shrivelled up any last residual hope she might have harboured of being anything more to him than his child's mother.

'I loved her like nothing else,' he said, his gaze bright with adoration. 'But she's gone, and I've had to move on.'

Kristen didn't want to dwell on how much Nate had obviously loved his wife, but she needed to know what had happened, if only to satisfy some weird curiosity to discover everything that made this enigmatic man tick.

'How did she die?'

Nate's expression hardened, his dark eyes turning glacial. 'A haemorrhage.'

'How awful,' she murmured, aware that sudden, unexpected brain haemorrhages were on the rise in young people, often with no preceding signs or symptoms.

Little wonder Nate wore an invisible cloak of sadness wrapped around his shoulders, and had since the first minute they'd met. Losing his wife so quickly, so tragically, must've really hurt and hurt deep.

Suddenly, a light bulb flashed in her head. The guilt she'd sensed after they'd slept together, the way he'd flirted with her one minute then pulled back the next, his swinging moods when they'd first started working together—it all made sense now.

He loved his wife despite the years since her death, then she'd entered the picture and thrown him for a six. Sleeping with her must've really been a big deal for him, and he'd probably tried to put it behind him only to have his night of guilty pleasure rubbed in his face when she'd walked through the doors of RX.

Trust her to fall for a guy still wrapped up in the memory of his beloved dead wife.

'It's over. It's in the past.'

He spoke softly, as if reassuring himself, and she waited, knowing that whatever she had to say next would sound inadequate.

'But that's not relevant to what I want to discuss with you tonight,' he said, louder this time, and back in control. 'Before we get into any of that, would you like something to drink?'

'No, I'm fine,' she said, wishing he'd get to the point so she could high-tail it out of here with what was left of her tattered dignity intact.

If she stayed a minute longer in this elegant room, with pretty *Jules* smiling down on her, she'd start bawling.

'I've been thinking,' he said, scooting closer to her, invading her personal space with his powerful body. 'This place is too big for one person. It's designed for a family. So what do you say to moving in? Let me take care of you during the pregnancy, and when the baby comes we can take it from there.'

She shot bolt-upright, her lower back twinging as it had been for a while now—more of those hormones, apparently, softening her spinal ligaments.

'You're kidding, right?'

He shook his head, his expression deadly serious, and she wondered if the hormones were affecting her lucidity too.

'It makes sense, Kris. Your place has all those steep stairs, and the larger you get the harder it will be to drag yourself up and down them. There's a master bedroom on the ground floor here, with a sitting room attached which would make a perfect nursery.'

'Master bedroom, huh?'

He had this all figured out.

Up until that instant she'd assumed his offer had stemmed from concern for the baby and doubts in her ability to care for it, but now he'd drawn another picture, one which involved the two of them reneging on their deal to remain platonic, and for one ridiculous second her traitorous body leaped at the idea.

'My room's upstairs, so you'll have use of the whole ground floor if you want.'

Okay, so he didn't want her body. Not that she could blame him, what with her expanding waistline, thickening ankles and the first hint of cellulite dimpling her previously toned thighs.

But that still didn't make his offer any more appealing.

It didn't make sense.

Why would a workaholic, successful guy at the top of his game want to take care of her? She wasn't exactly helpless, far from it, and though she wanted to tell him where he could shove his offer a small part of her loved him for making it.

Loved him?

Like the sun rising slowly over the horizon and

bathing the earth with an illuminating glow, the first rays of realisation filtered through her, creating warmth and amazement and havoc.

She loved him?

How could that be possible when she'd never experienced the nebulous emotion first-hand, let alone knew what it felt like?

Besides, it wasn't supposed to happen like this.

They were supposed to be two ships passing in the night, colliding for one brief interlude before moving on. However, it looked like not only had their ships docked but they'd taken on an extra passenger, one who made them both contemplate crazy things.

He wanted her to move in, and she suspected she felt more for him than the crazy crush she'd previously harboured.

Time to cast away and set sail for destinations unknown before her ship along with her dreams sunk like a stone.

'So, what do you think?'

'I think you're nuts,' she said, resisting the urge to reach out and comfort him when his face fell. 'First you ask for more time to absorb the fact you're going to be a dad. Then you give me presents which hint at your intentions to be involved but don't actually spell it out, and now you jump to this? It's crazy.'

'It's the best solution for everyone.'

She raised an eyebrow, wondering if some of her irrational hormones had taken a flying leap and landed on him.

'Thanks for the offer, but we can't live together. I've never lived with anyone, and I value my independence, as I'm sure you do. It would never work.'

His jaw tightened, a stubborn set to it. 'We'd make it work. For the sake of the baby.'

Suddenly, the pieces of the puzzle slid into place like the rumblings of tectonic plates moving into place.

'You don't think I'm capable of caring for this baby myself?'

'Don't be ridiculous,' he said, his quick look-away glance speaking volumes. 'I only want what's best for you.'

'Cut the crap, Nate. We both know you want what's best for the baby. I'm just the incubator,' she said, anger turning her words into sharp barbs intended to wound him like he'd wounded her.

'That's not fair. I care about you.'

He reached for her hand, gripping it tightly when she tried to tug away, using his other hand to tilt her chin up.

'Listen to me. I know this pregnancy is the last thing either one of us expected, but it happened and we're responsible. You wouldn't have told me about the baby if you didn't want me involved, and like it or not I'm here to stay. I'm sorry it took me a while to get my act together, but I'm one hundred percent committed now. This baby means more to me than you could possibly know, and I intend on doing everything in my power to make sure the both of you are cared for. Understood?'

The vehemence behind his impassioned words startled her. It sounded like he meant business—and a huge part of her was grateful that her baby would have a father who would love and cherish and protect it, something she'd never had after her parents had died.

'You're pretty hell-bent on this, aren't you?'

'Damn right,' he said, his fingers warm against the

tender skin under her jaw as his thumb brushed her bottom lip.

Sighing, she finally relaxed, taking hold of his hand—she couldn't take much more of that lip stroking—and squeezing both of them in hers.

'Okay, here's how it will be. I'm not moving in here, no matter what you say, but you can have full involvement in the pregnancy. Ultrasounds, obstetrician visits, antenatal classes, the works. How's that for a compromise?'

'You drive a hard bargain,' he said, his smile warming her right down to her toes. 'Sounds good. For now.'

She ignored his addendum, too tired to ram her point home. She'd never move in with Nate no matter how hard he pushed or how many logical arguments he laid out.

She wasn't a fool, and raising a child in a home where two parents didn't love each other would do much more damage than visitation rights and planned holidays.

With a weary smile, she said, 'Okay, then. Let's see some of this caring attitude starting with you taking me home. I'm beat.'

And if she didn't establish some much-needed distance between them in the next few minutes she'd be curling up on his sofa—or, worse, checking out the *upstairs* master-bedroom.

Being with Nate felt too comfortable, too cosy, too right, and hot on the heels of her startling realisation that she actually might love him it threatened to undermine her very existence.

No matter how much he cared for her, no matter how close the baby brought them, she could never compete with Julia. He'd virtually said she'd been the love of his life, and she had no intention of coming in a poor second.

She'd had enough of that feeling growing up, always playing second fiddle to a foster mum's biological kids, always the new kid on the block as she moved from school to school, always the outsider.

Never again; she'd make sure of it, even if it meant breaking her heart in the process.

'Come on, I'll take you home,' he said, gently pulling her to her feet, clasping her hands like he'd never let go.

More of that wishful thinking.

'Thanks, Nate. For everything,' she said, knowing how lucky she was to have a dependable guy as the father of her baby, a part of her wishing there could be more between them.

'You're welcome.'

He dropped a chaste kiss on her cheek, the type of kiss indicative of their relationship.

Or was it?

No matter how platonic they tried to keep their relationship, there'd been the shared moments in the office working on *Travelogue,* and as for the Logies tonight…

Nate had been at his charming best, and she'd had a hard time separating her rational side, which told her he was just being nice to her at a work do, and her emotional side, which replayed every touch, every intimate smile. And that spectacular dance where their bodies had been so very close…

She should be ecstatic they'd ironed out some major issues where the baby was concerned.

Instead, as she followed him out the door of his beautiful home and to his car, she couldn't help but wish for it all.

CHAPTER ELEVEN

'WOULD you like to know the sex of the baby?'

Nate's coal eyes clashed with Kris's, a wonder-filled smile spreading across his face.

'What do you think?'

Kris didn't know what to think.

She hadn't known what to think for a while now. Since their chat after the Logies, Nate had showered her with attention, doing considerate things like dropping by with groceries, accompanying her on walks around Albert Park Lake, even bringing her the chocolate milkshakes she craved at all hours.

A girl could get used to this sort of treatment, and with every passing week she fell deeper for the man with a knack for lavishing some much-needed affection on her.

'I'm not sure. Would you like a surprise at the end?'

A shadow crossed his face, but before she could interpret it he said, 'Honestly? I think we've both had all the surprises we can take. I'd like to know.'

'Me too.'

She clasped his hand and turned to the doctor. 'Okay, let us have it.'

The doctor beamed as he wiped the ultrasound gel

from her belly. 'Congratulations. You have a healthy baby girl growing in there.'

'A girl,' Nate said, his voice barely a whisper as he clutched her hand.

'Wow.'

Kris let the tears flow as she sat up and thanked the doctor, who grinned at them like a generous benefactor as he handed her a photo of the baby and left the room.

'Bet she's as gorgeous as her mother,' Nate said, tracing the baby's outline with a fingertip before leaning over and placing a soft, lingering kiss on her lips.

Kris blinked, but the tears flowed heavier as he gathered her in his arms, strong and protective as the rest of him, as she tried to figure out what that tender kiss had been about.

'I take it this means you're happy?'

He drew away from her and brushed a strand of hair out of her face, his hand warm against her cheek for a brief moment.

'Very.'

She sniffled, gratefully grabbing a few tissues from the box he held out to her, wondering if she'd ever get over the urge to bawl at the slightest provocation. 'We're having a girl...'

'Pretty amazing, huh?'

Amazing? Nothing came close to the overwhelming intensity of emotions flooding her body: pride, awe and blinding love filled her till she could barely see.

Knowing the sex of the baby made it all the more real, and she could now chat to her baby girl, labelling her a 'she' rather than an unknown entity.

'This is all so unbelievable,' she said, gripping his

hand like she'd never let go, gazing down at her protruding belly with a growing sense of wonderment. 'I have a little girl in there.'

Nate reached out and rubbed his hand over her belly, like a hopeful man with an old lamp wishing for a genie.

'My girls,' he said, the sheen of unshed tears in his eyes as he looked at her, pride overpowering the momentary sadness she could've sworn she'd glimpsed earlier.

'Well, at least one of us is,' she said, pushing up to a sitting position and patting her tummy. 'Is it too early to start talking about names?'

He smiled and helped her off the bed. 'No. How about we do it over dinner?'

Kris hesitated. So far, all of the time they'd spent together had been centred on the baby, and she preferred it that way. No use fuelling her useless fantasies of Nate seeing her as anything other than the mother of his child. Having a cosy dinner for two wouldn't help her fertile imagination, especially an imagination which took his caring words 'my girls' and turned it into something more meaningful.

'I'll cook.'

He saw that as an enticement, whereas the thought of spending time holed up in his perfect house waiting for the perfect family intimidated her more than the thought of eating with him.

Darn it, she'd known falling for him would complicate matters, but she hadn't expected to feel this out of her depth all the time—lending weight to words which were meaningless, imagining more than friendship behind every touch or casual peck on the cheek, wishing he'd feel more for her.

'Sounds good,' she said, forcing a smile, when her less-than-enthusiastic tone obviously hadn't convinced him of her enthusiasm for his plan if the tiny frown between his brows was any indication. 'As long as you don't feed me Brussel sprouts and broccoli. I'm taking a vitamin supplement, and if I have one more green leafy vegetable this week I'm going to barf.'

'I thought the morning sickness had stopped ages ago?'

The teasing glint in his eyes soon had her chuckling along with him as she padded over to a screen, clutching the back of the hospital gown which threatened to give him an eyeful with every step, and slipped behind it to get dressed.

'Would you like me to bring anything?'

'Just my favourite girls.'

His voice drifted over the top of the screen, and her fingers fumbled with the last button of her blouse as she wondered if he had any idea the impact of his casual words had on her.

She couldn't see his expression, therefore couldn't ascertain whether he was serious or joking, especially as his tone gave little away.

Silently chastising herself for reading too much into his comments, she stepped out from behind the screen after sliding the last button home.

'Okay, then, let's get back to work. Alan should have the first tape of *Travelogue* ready for viewing.'

She headed for the door, brisk and businesslike, the only mode which kept her focus diverted from Nate and the mixed signals he was sending her.

'Speaking of which, are you going to announce your pregnancy today?'

She nodded, glancing down at her flowing geometric-patterned top in turquoise, black and camel. 'I'm surprised nobody's guessed yet with the loose clothes I've been wearing.'

'You look sensational as always,' he said, his admiring glance sweeping from her top to her fitted black trousers with the elasticated waist and back again. 'With a gorgeous body like yours, no one can tell you're pregnant unless they've seen your belly.'

She fidgeted under his intense stare, flattered by his words, wishing her overactive imagination wouldn't conjure up the glint of desire in his eyes.

'Well, until now you're the only one who has had that privilege, so let's spread the word before the rumour-mills start up.'

He laid a hand on her arm as she opened the door. 'You know I'm proud to be the father?'

'Uh-huh. But we've both agreed to keep the paternity a secret at work. It's nobody's business but ours, and I don't want it affecting our professional lives.'

'You sure?'

'Positive.'

It was tough enough climbing the corporate ladder, without having to fend off snide barbs from co-workers insinuating she was getting ahead because she was sleeping with the boss.

Ha!

If they only knew it had been a one-off, a distant, cherished memory she replayed at will, especially in the long, lonely hours of the morning when her bladder woke her for frequent trips to the loo and she couldn't get back to sleep for thinking about Nate.

'There is one thing you can bring to dinner tonight.'

'What's that?'

'A hat.'

She stared at his deadpan face, the corners of his mouth twitching with barely concealed amusement.

'A hat?'

'That's right. Now, let's get back to work before the boss fires your cute butt.'

Sending him a mock-angry glare, secretly thrilled about his butt comment, she followed him out of the clinic, wondering if he would ever stop surprising her.

'One hat, as requested.'

Kris placed a misshapen red beanie on the dinner table, smack bang between the silver candlestick-holders and the crystal glasses. 'Now, are you going to tell me what on earth it's for?'

Nate smiled and pulled out her chair, gesturing for her to sit.

'Well, you strike me as being a woman of firm opinions, so I thought the only way for us both to decide on a name would be to draw one out of a hat.'

She laughed, the loud, genuine sound of a woman who was happy, something he'd heard more of lately, and he hoped she'd still feel that way after he dropped his little bombshell on her tonight.

'Are you saying I'm stubborn?'

'Interpret it as you will,' he said, grinning as he filled her glass with her preferred sparkling mineral-water and lemon, increasingly grateful they could joke around like this.

They'd grown closer, had settled into a comfortable

friendship, the type of friendship he valued, the type of friendship he could easily see developing into something more given half a chance.

She sipped her mineral water and replaced it on the table, her cheeky glance alerting him to another of her trademark quick remarks. 'There won't be a problem as long as you agree with me.'

He chuckled. 'Tell me you're not into the way-out Hollywood-style names. I'm a conservative kind of guy, and I don't think I can cope with my daughter being called Apple or any other types of fruit.'

'You sound like an old man.'

'I am,' he said, feeling every one of his thirty-six years.

Gut-wrenching grief did that to a man, robbing him of optimism, joy and hope. But the remarkable woman sitting in front of him had changed all that.

Courtesy of the little miracle she was carrying, he suddenly had hope for the future. And it felt great!

'You're right. I can see quite a few grey hairs amongst all that black,' she said, pointing to the area around his temple. 'Hope you haven't passed on the premature-ageing gene to our daughter.'

'You'll keep,' he said, grinning as he pointed a finger at her before heading for the kitchen. 'Just for that, I'll serve your favourite sprouts and broccoli first.'

He half expected her to follow him into the kitchen, but as he returned with plates piled high with steaming stir-fry, and saw her sitting on the edge of her seat and fiddling with cutlery, he had to admit it would take more than a few teasing words and a home-cooked meal to get her to relax.

She'd seemed on edge the last time she'd been here,

but he'd put that down to discovering he'd been married and the strangeness of the situation. However, it looked like she hadn't loosened up at all, and if he didn't get her to unwind he had no chance of convincing her to see the wisdom of his plan.

Setting a plate down in front of her, he took a seat opposite.

'This smells fantastic,' she said, inhaling the fragrant aroma of sautéed garlic, ginger and lemon grass, the three staples he used in any stir-fry.

It was too long since he'd cooked, preferring to eat at the office or grab a quick bite on his way home.

He'd missed this, missed seeing the appreciative expression on someone's face as they took the first bite, the low 'Mmm' resonating from them as they forked more into their mouths.

Jules had loved his cooking, though with her long hours at the Playhouse he'd often ended up eating alone over the years.

However, seeing Kris's obvious enjoyment as she slurped up noodles, smacked her lips and shovelled the food into her mouth with surprising speed, more than made up for any reticence on Julia's part in the past.

A painful niggle of guilt wormed its way into his heart. He shouldn't compare the two women.

They were very different, and he'd already come to terms with the fact he needed to move on with his life.

Over the last weeks he'd wondered if Kris's unexpected pregnancy wasn't the catalyst he needed, forcing him to compartmentalise his memories and set about creating a new future.

However, to do that he'd have to tell her the whole

truth about Julia's death, and now that her pregnancy was advanced he couldn't do it.

He didn't want to scare her, and the stress of hearing the truth now couldn't be good for her or the baby. He'd have to bide his time and hope she'd understand once he told her everything.

And he would, there was no doubting that.

He'd been torn up inside for too long, guilt-ridden over possibly letting another woman into his life to usurp Julia's position. However, after long nights of soul-searching, he knew Julia wouldn't have wanted him to put his life on hold, to wallow in grief and self-pity. She'd always lived life to the full, throwing herself into their relationship with as much passion as she'd done for her roles on stage.

'Life is meant to be gobbled like a scrumptious chocolate-cake, not nibbled around the edges,' she'd used to say, and he could almost sense her now, silently egging him on to set aside the past and focus on the future.

'You haven't touched yours,' Kris said, pointing to his plate while she dabbed at her mouth, her apologetic glance flicking between her plate and him. 'Meanwhile, I've just entered the *Guinness Book of Records* for scoffing a meal in two seconds flat.'

'You know there was broccoli in that?'

Her hand flew to her mouth in mock horror. 'Really? Is that what those little green tree-shaped things were?'

He laughed, pushing his noodles around the plate before giving up and resting the fork down. No use pretending he had an appetite. Besides, he doubted he could force a mouthful of food past the giant lump stuck in his throat.

'What's wrong?'

Realising there was no time like the present, he swapped seats, sliding into the stiff-backed chair next to her. 'Nothing's wrong. But I want to talk to you about something.'

'Uh-oh. By the look in your eye, it sounds serious.'

'It is.'

He took hold of her hand, small and soft, hoping she felt one iota of what he felt for her. It was the only way he could convince her to go through with this.

'I was planning to wait till later, but I can't concentrate on anything else.'

Her eyes widened, depthless blue pools a man could drown in. 'You're starting to scare me.'

'Sorry, that's the last thing I want to do.'

Taking a deep breath, he tried not to blurt out the words he'd silently rehearsed for the entire afternoon in one go.

'I know this is going to sound crazy to you, especially after you refused my offer to move in, but I want you to consider this carefully. It's the best thing for the baby, to surround her with both parents, especially in the early formative years. She needs to feel loved and I think we can give that to her. Together.'

Gripping both her hands, staring into her incredible eyes and hoping to God he was doing the right thing for them all, he said, 'Kris, will you marry me?'

CHAPTER TWELVE

KRIS stared at Nate in horror, certain she'd heard a proposal spilling from the lips she'd spent way too much time fantasising about, her brain having a problem computing it.

'*Marry* you?'

Shaking her head, she took shallow breaths, trying not to hyperventilate at a time when she needed her wits the most.

He squeezed her hand, his voice steady when she felt like screaming. 'I know it's out of the blue, and probably the last thing you expected, but I really want us to make a go of this. To try and be a family for our daughter.'

Kris gritted her teeth so hard her jaw ached. She couldn't believe he was doing this to her—again! First the 'move in and let's play happy families' scenario and now this!

Hating the quiver in her voice, she said, 'Do you love me?'

The widening of his eyes and quick look away spoke volumes.

'I care about you, Kris. Surely you know that?'

Numb with pain, she said, 'It's not enough. I know

you care, but a marriage needs more than that. And I know you mean well, but you've just presented your proposal with all the flair of a business deal, and it's not enough. You want to take care of me and the baby? Fine. You want to lavish our daughter with love? Fine. But we don't have to be married or live together for you to do that.'

'We'd have a solid foundation for a marriage. We could build on it. We could—'

'I can't marry you, Nate. I'm sorry.'

She stood, not surprised he released her hands and moved across to the fireplace, staring into the flames while she blinked away tears before turning to face him again.

'I know you want what's best for the baby. I do too, but children pick up on emotions around them, and I don't want our daughter realising the only thing keeping her parents together is her.'

'It wouldn't be like that,' he said, his tone low and imploring as he crossed the room to stand beside her. 'Surely you feel something for me? Enough to take a chance on building a future for our daughter? To take a chance on seeing what develops?'

Pain ripped through her at the bleakness in his eyes.

Feel *something?*

She felt everything for him.

Shaking her head, she picked up her denim jacket lying on the back of the sofa and shrugged into it.

'I'm sorry, Nate. Feeling something just isn't enough. And I'm not prepared to sit around waiting for whatever we feel for each other to maybe or maybe not develop into something more. Respect, admiration, attraction, whatever we've got right now, isn't enough. I deserve more than that. We both do. I need more and I won't settle for anything less.'

Willing her legs to move towards the door, she half expected him to stop her.

Even with the empty ache spreading through her heart with every step taking her further away from him, she wanted him to stop her, to tell her this was all some huge mistake, that he did love her, and that marrying her, becoming a real family, was the most important thing in his life.

He didn't stop her, and the hollow slam of the door echoed the slamming door in her heart as she shut away her love for the man who'd broken it without trying.

'What's this?'

Nate looked up from the pile of documents on his desk and held up a letter the minute Kristen entered his office and closed the door.

Damn, she'd decided to play this cool, to be professional to the end. But seeing him sitting behind his fancy desk, with a smug expression on his face and a raised eyebrow, as if he didn't quite believe her letter was serious, spiked her temper in a second.

'Have you read it?'

'Uh-huh.'

To her annoyance, he screwed it up into a ball and lobbed it into the bin three metres away.

Forcing her hands to unclench, she marched over to his desk.

'You really should keep important documentation like resignation letters for the HR department. They'll want stuff like that for employee files.'

Folding his arms, he leaned back in his chair and fixed her with a benevolent smile.

'I'm not accepting your resignation.'

'You have no choice!'

Her voice rose and she calmed it with effort, the same effort it took not to lean over the desk and wipe that grin off his face.

'Look, I don't want to get into this with you,' she said, wishing he was more rattled, hating that he wouldn't take her seriously.

She'd thought long and hard about this since his proposal. Working with him on a daily basis with that hanging between them had made her life unbearable. She couldn't stand another second of it, let alone the remaining time left before she went on maternity leave.

'What about your maternity leave?'

Squaring her shoulders, she said, 'What about it? If I leave it doesn't matter, does it? I'll be on permanent maternity leave till I find another job.'

His eyes narrowed, and she saw his right hand flex. At last, she'd scored a reaction.

'You don't have to do this, Kris.'

'Damn right I do,' she said, finally taking a seat. It was hard to maintain a tough stance when her feet were killing her courtesy of swollen ankles.

'Is it so hard working with me?'

Her gaze snapped to his, surprised by the hint of vulnerability she glimpsed in the dark depths, and hating how her heart thawed at the sight of it.

'Honestly? Yeah, it is.'

'I thought we'd moved past the proposal?'

'You might've,' she muttered, hating the lurch of her

heart as she recalled that fateful evening, the evening where for one tiny second she'd almost believed all her dreams had come true.

However, remembering his businesslike proposal rankled, no matter how much he cared, no matter how many different ways he showed it.

Seeing him on a daily basis was exhausting emotionally, and she just couldn't do it any more.

'Let's just call it quits, okay?'

Nate pushed out of his chair and moved around the desk in a flash to squat next to her and grab hold of her hand. 'Are you just talking about the job?'

'Of course,' she said, surprised by the devastation in his eyes, the sad twist to his mouth.

'Then why? Why walk away from a job you love and are great at if you're still going to see me anyway?' Shaking his head, he grabbed her other hand till she had no option but to face him, to listen to him. 'Obviously I'm the problem here, the problem you're trying to escape, but I'm not going anywhere. I'm still going to be a part of the baby's life, so why run away? Why now?'

Because I love you.

Because it hurts too much seeing you every day, thinking about what we could have if you'd give us a real chance—not some marriage based on obligation.

Because I want us to be the family you spoke about, for real.

Hating the treacherous warmth seeping from his grip through her body, she pulled her hands out of his.

'Because it's too hard,' she finally said, her voice barely above a whisper as she stared at her folded hands lying in her lap.

'It doesn't have to be,' he said, placing a finger under her chin and gently tipping it up till she had no option but to meet his eyes.

'I don't want you to go, Kris. You mean too much to me.'

'Don't you mean the *baby?*'

He didn't deserve her bitter response, not when she could see the genuine tenderness in his eyes.

To his credit, he didn't back down, even when she pushed away his finger and broke the tenuous contact binding them.

'I'm not talking about the baby. I'm talking about you and me.'

Straightening, he stalked to the bin, pulled out her resignation letter, smoothed it out and laid it on the desk in front of her.

'I've tried to be as honest as I can with you, about everything. And I'm not letting you leave here without a fight. So, here's your letter. If it's gone by the time I come in tomorrow, I'll take it you've come to your senses. If not…' he shrugged into his jacket and picked up his briefcase '…be prepared to do battle. I'm not letting my star exec producer walk out of here no matter what she thinks.'

'You're…you…'

He silenced her indignant sputtering with a swift, fierce but all-too-brief kiss on the lips before sending her a smug grin and strolling out the door.

Nate entered the conference room carrying a huge goodie-basket filled with baby stuff, pasting a smile on his face as he fought his way through the crowd surrounding a radiant Kris.

'For the mum-to-be,' he said, placing the basket on the table, wondering how long before he could make a run for it.

Having a baby shower before Kris left had been Hallie's idea, but now that the day had arrived he couldn't be less happy if he'd tried.

He'd miss her.

A lot.

Feeling something just isn't enough.

Her words from the night he'd proposed haunted him, taunting him with their finality, implying she might feel a bit for him but that it was nowhere near enough to get her to marry him.

Until her refusal he'd had no idea how badly he wanted to provide a stable home environment for his daughter, how much he was willing to risk in perhaps opening up to the possibility of more than a platonic relationship with Kris.

Being married would've given him the opportunity to take things slow, to break down the carefully erected barriers around his heart and maybe, just maybe, take a chance on more than just caring for a woman again.

But Kris didn't see the logic in his proposal, or didn't feel enough for him to take a chance and no amount of wishing things could be different would change that fact.

She'd said she deserved more than he was willing to give—and sadly she was right—but he couldn't lie to her. He had no idea what would happen if he opened his heart to another woman, and he'd been as honest as he could.

For Kris, it wasn't enough.

'Thanks,' she said, smiling up at him, the familiar twinkle in her eyes.

Ever since he'd called her bluff over her resignation a month ago, they'd entered a weird impasse in their relationship.

He'd challenge her, she'd fire back.

She'd tease him, he'd want to kiss her senseless, till he remembered he had to keep things in the office professional.

If she'd wanted to bolt after his proposal, it didn't take an Einstein to figure out what she'd do if he hauled her into his arms as he'd wanted to do almost on a daily basis.

'Hey, boss. How about you propose the toast?'

Hallie thrust a champagne flute into his hand and he blinked, annoyed by the coy little smile playing about Kris's sensual mouth, as if she could read his thoughts.

Straightening, he addressed the room, as he'd done many times over the last few months.

'Since I've taken over here at RX I've been constantly impressed by the work ethic and camaraderie shown by all of you, as demonstrated today in this great turnout for Kristen's farewell and baby shower. As you all know, she's agreed to take a year's worth of maternity leave, and I'm hoping to lure our star executive producer back to the fold then.'

Cheers greeted his announcement, and he smiled at Kris, his heart pounding as she returned it.

'She's been a great asset to the RX team, and I know you'll all join me in wishing her and her bundle of joy all the best.'

He raised his glass in her direction, watching her throat move almost convulsively as she sipped at her apple juice, her expression stoic.

'Since you're so impressed with our work ethic, boss, does this mean you'll be shouting the bar at Manic Monday tonight?'

Several people cheered Hallie's cheeky question and he held up his hand to quieten them.

'While our impossible receptionist seems to think this station has a bottomless pit of funds, I'm willing to shout each of you a drink tonight if you get back to work within the next five minutes and actually get something done in the next two hours before knock-off time.'

As expected the conference room cleared within the prescribed time, people draining champagne and taking their cake plates with them. His staff may be the most productive, loyal lot around, but boy did they love a drink to unwind after work on a Monday.

Once Hallie, the last straggler, had given them a final cheeky smile and closed the door behind her, Nate sat next to Kris and topped up her glass with juice.

'How are you doing?'

'A little tired,' she admitted, sitting back and resting her folded arms on her belly.

Exhausted, more like it, he thought, noting the dark rings of fatigue around her eyes despite the careful use of cosmetics.

'You sure you're up for the pre-natal class tonight?'

'Positive.'

She nodded, her blonde hair falling around her shoulders, longer and softer now than when she'd first started work. 'They're going over the birth options, and I really want to be there for that.'

'Want me to pick you up?'

He threw out the offer, expecting her to refuse as

she'd done on the previous five occasions, but to his surprise she nodded.

'That would be great. I've been feeling pretty lousy today. For a while there I thought I'd have to miss my own baby shower.'

'Nothing serious?'

His calm voice belied the surge of worry within. Now that she'd mentioned it, she didn't only look exhausted she looked downright ill. Despite the sassy look she'd sent him earlier, her eyes now appeared dull, and could be indicative of something more serious such as a virus. Her pallor wasn't disguised by blush.

She rubbed her belly and grimaced. 'No, I'm okay. Just the odd Braxton-Hicks contraction.'

Suddenly, it hit him.

She was scared, probably petrified, by the fake contractions that sometimes preluded the real thing.

He reached for her hand instinctively, desperate to reassure her. 'It's going to be okay. Trust me.'

Her gaze settled on their hands, her body inert, before she finally turned her hand over in his and hung on for dear life.

'I do.'

Two little words, whispered into the fraught silence, encapsulating every hope and dream he'd had for the two of them.

He'd wanted to hear her utter those words in a different context, but for now this would have to do.

He needed to be there for her, to shunt aside his own fears as her due date grew near, and concentrate on being strong for the both of them.

'You stay here and I'll load this stuff into your car then drive you home, okay?'

She nodded and slowly withdrew her hand from his. 'Nate?'

Resting a basket filled to the brim with soft toys on his hip, he said, 'Yeah?'

'I couldn't have done this without you.'

He smiled, sensing the vulnerability underlying her words, knowing he needed to reassure her now more than ever.

'Yeah, you could. You're superwoman. You just hide away your cape and wear that dodgy underwear on the inside.'

He headed for the door, thankful he'd made her smile, hoping it stayed there for the weeks ahead leading up to the birth.

Kristen tried to concentrate as the nurse facilitator droned on and on about epidurals, forceps, episiotomies and a host of other not-so-fun things she might have to look forward to at the birth of her baby.

Women in the group winced and crossed their legs for most of the talk, which she found incredibly funny, considering it was way too late for that.

As for the men, most had paled when the nurse had passed around the forceps, and some had left the room when the actual birth video had been screened.

Nate had stayed by her side through it all, his expression focussed and resolute, as if he didn't want to miss a second. She could've admired him for it if it weren't for the constant nagging ache in the middle of her back and the fact she blamed him for putting it there.

Irrational? Maybe, considering she'd been more than a willing participant in their unforgettable night in Singapore. But as the birth grew closer and her fears escalated accordingly it only seemed fitting to blame every little thing on the guy who had put her into this predicament.

'How're you holding up?' he murmured as the nurse passed around lifelike dolls to the couples, along with a bundle of cloth nappies each.

'So far so good,' she said, handing him the doll with all the finesse of a rugby player making a pass. 'Though I think it's your turn for nappy duty tonight.'

'No worries.'

Sending her a confident grin, he whipped off the doll's threadbare clothes and folded a nappy as they'd been taught at the last class. However, his skilful demonstration came undone as he attempted to fasten the nappy, involving some slick manoeuvring of the doll's leg which resulted in the leg detaching from the body.

'Oops. I better keep a close eye on you when it's time for you to look after the real thing.'

She'd meant it as a joke, but Nate didn't laugh. In fact, he didn't move or do much of anything apart from stare in horror at his hand holding the leg.

'Hey, it's no big deal. These dolls are worn out. You'll be great with our daughter.'

They had briefly discussed some names, but still hadn't got round to naming the baby yet, and she knew they'd have to tackle that potentially touchy subject in the coming weeks. Though she hadn't told him yet, she did favour slightly alternative names in favour of the stodgy old-faithfuls, and it looked like another battle loomed on the horizon.

'I need to get out of here,' he said, thrusting the doll's leg at her, his dark eyes stark and haunted. 'I'll meet you outside in half an hour.'

'Nate, it's okay—'

She didn't get to finish her sentence, as he fled the room like a man with a million demons on his tail, leaving her holding a one-legged doll and trying to ignore the ten pairs of curious eyes focussed on her.

So he'd run out on her.

It wasn't like it hadn't happened to her before. Though Nate had never abandoned her or let her down, unless she counted the crucial fact he didn't love her.

They'd pretended his proposal had never happened, but as the baby had grown and it had been increasingly difficult to sleep, she'd often thought back to that night and played the 'what if' game.

What if he'd felt more for her?

What if the proposal had been fuelled by love and passion rather than caring and obligation?

What if she was the type of woman to not give a damn anyway, and take what he offered?

Many couples had marriages based on a lot less than the mutual respect and caring she and Nate shared, but she couldn't do it. She couldn't tie herself to a man who didn't love her, no matter how solid and dependable he was.

Besides, she'd promised to be the best mother she could, and that meant being happy and content—two emotions she'd have to fake if forced to live in a sham marriage with the man she loved.

'Is everything all right, dear?'

Kristen nodded at the kindly nurse who had concern in her eyes. 'Yes. I'm fine.'

The nurse looked doubtful as she moved on to the next couple, casting the occasional glance over her shoulder as if Kristen might follow suit and bolt—okay, waddle—out the door after Nate.

Sorely tempted, she settled back in her seat, constantly wriggling as the pain in her back fluctuated from bearable to agonising, not hearing a word the nurse said as her thoughts centred on Nate and the way he'd reacted to the doll breaking.

That was no ordinary reaction.

He'd practically freaked out, so much so that he wouldn't have been able to stay for the rest of the class. She might've expected that reaction at the actual birth, but losing it over a doll's leg?

There was something drastically wrong and, though she couldn't fathom his reasons for bolting like a dad who'd just discovered he had quadruplets rather than twins, come the end of the class she'd find out.

CHAPTER THIRTEEN

'Do you mind telling me what your vanishing act was all about?'

Kristen barged right up to Nate in the hospital foyer, just stopping short of stabbing his chest with her finger. 'Because, the way I see it, there's no way you'd get that upset and miss the rest of the class over breaking a doll—so what's the deal?'

'Let's talk somewhere more comfortable.'

He took hold of her arm and, rather than pulling away as was her first instinct, she let him lead her to his car. No use letting pride get in the way of a little support, especially considering her back chose that moment to remind her it didn't fancy her carrying around the extra fourteen kilos or so.

'Don't you dare think about starting that engine till you've explained everything,' she said, turning to face him once they'd settled in the car.

'We can talk at your place,' he said, running a hand over his eyes as if to block her out.

Fat chance.

'No way. Start talking. Now.'

'It's complicated.'

He fiddled with his keys, jiggling them in his hand till she reached out and grabbed them.

'You've tried that one on me before, and I've got to admit it's sounding about as tired as I feel.'

Sighing, he closed his eyes for a moment and rested his head against the headrest.

'When I told you Julia died, I didn't tell you everything.'

Kristen's heart stilled at the audible pain in Nate's voice.

'She was pregnant at the time.'

'Oh, Nate.'

Kristen reached out blindly, wanting to touch him, to comfort him, to do whatever she could to take away half the agony he must be going through.

Opening his eyes, he turned to face her, his expression unreadable in the darkness of the car.

'I know I overreacted back there. Stupid, isn't it? How such a small, insignificant thing like that can ram home how inadequate I felt over Julia's death and the fact I couldn't save her or our child.'

Grasping his hand tightly, her heart aching for him, she injected as much warmth, as much love, as she dared into her voice.

'You can't blame yourself for what happened. I can't begin to understand the heartache you must've gone through over losing your wife and your child, but medical stuff happens. Stuff you can't explain or change or fix, no matter how much you want to. And, for what it's worth, I'm here for you, and I know you're going to be a great dad for our daughter.'

'Thanks.'

She caught a glimmer of his smile in the wan light and squeezed his hand, wondering what else he had to say when he opened his mouth before quickly shutting it again.

'Is there something else?'

'I'm worried about the birth,' he said, his voice unsteady as he raised worried eyes to hers. 'I hate feeling out of control when I can organise the rest of my life with ease. It's tough.'

Her heart turned over at his honest response. She understood exactly what he was feeling. For a girl who bordered on being a control-freak herself, she wasn't so rapt about the whole 'unexpected scenarios' thing the nurse had stressed in the birthing class.

'So you're admitting you're scared?'

She thought he'd lie, do the macho thing and fob her off with some lame platitude. Instead, he surprised her by taking hold of her other hand, his grip tight.

'Terrified,' he said, his expression matching the feeling perfectly.

'What happened to you being the solid one for us both? What about all those "she'll be right" pep talks you've given me?'

He shrugged, a hint of a smile playing about his mouth.

'As I remember, you told me to be quiet the last time I tried to give you a confidence boost, though in much more blunt terms.'

She smiled, releasing his hands before she did something stupid like haul him over the console and hug him to death. 'Must've been the hormones talking.'

'We're going to get through this. You know that, right?'

She rolled her eyes, determined to lighten the mood.

She had enough to worry about, without Nate freaking out and turning into a reedy sap rather than the strong oak she'd grown to depend on.

'Of course we will. As long as you don't buy our little girl any dolls for Christmas, we'll be fine.'

He finally smiled, a rueful expression erasing the lines fanning from the corner of his eyes like a worry map.

'You're not going to let me forget that episode ever, are you?'

'Nope.'

'If you bring it up at her twenty-first, I may have to ensure you never work in the TV industry again.'

She waved away his remark with a smirk. 'I'll be a millionaire by then, living off my name alone, consulting for the best producers in town.'

'Yeah?'

'Yeah,' she said, realising they hadn't traded banter like this in way too long.

They'd been too busy treading on eggshells around each other, all their conversations focussed on the baby and little else.

This felt good. Way too good, and the baby kicked at that precise moment as if reminding her it couldn't last.

'I like a confident woman,' he said, holding out his palm for the keys.

'And I like a man who admits to a doll phobia,' she said, plopping the keys into his hand and chuckling when he snatched them away, inserted them in the ignition and started the car with a roar.

'I'm never going to live this down, am I?'

'You said it,' she said, settling back into the plush leather seat, content to concentrate on the inner glow fuelled by the thought of them being together at their daughter's twenty-first.

A lot could happen in that time—including convincing the gorgeous man beside her what he was missing out on by not giving them a chance.

A real chance, based on love and sizzle, rather than an obligatory proposal reeking of old-fashioned chivalry.

Time would tell, and right now it was enough to hope and dream and look to a future filled with a bouncing baby girl and Nate by her side.

Nate knocked on Kris's door for the second time, pounding the brass knocker longer and louder before peering through the sheer curtains lining the front window.

A strange sense of foreboding crept through him as he scanned the empty room, wondering why she wasn't answering the door.

She'd been expecting him, had chewed him out for five minutes about installing the car seat in her car before her due date next week, and he'd hurried over, the slightly hysterical edge to her voice filling him with concern.

When he rapped on the window and got no response, he vaulted the side fence and ran to the back door, relieved to find the flimsy catch unlatched.

'Kris? You in here?'

He entered the kitchen, trying to keep a lid on his skyrocketing blood pressure. There could be a perfectly logical explanation why she hadn't answered the door: she could be taking a bath to ease her back pain, or making another of her frequent toilet stops.

However, as he entered the hallway and spied her

inert form slumped over the bottom stair, sheer unadulterated panic shot through his system and he ran towards her, haunted by a terrifying sense of *déjà vu*.

'Please, God, no,' he muttered, reaching for her, feeling for a pulse in her neck, almost sagging with relief when he found one.

Gently turning her into the recovery position, he fumbled for his mobile and dialled an ambulance, praying harder than he ever had in his life.

Brushing back her hair, he bent over her, whispering in her ear. 'Kris, I know you can hear me. Everything's going to be fine. We have a precious baby girl waiting for her mum to wake up and give me another verbal spray about something, so come on. Wake up, you hear me?'

Her eyelids flickered, and for a second hope overrode the adrenalin surging through his body. But she didn't open her eyes. She didn't do anything apart from lie there, looking too still, too lifeless.

He knew he should check for blood, but he couldn't do it. Seeing her like this was tearing him apart; he couldn't face the possible evidence that she was losing their baby too.

Sirens grew closer, and he dropped a kiss on her lips before rushing to the door and opening it for the paramedics.

'She's in there.'

He pointed to the woman he loved, frozen like a statue as they went to work on her, their precise movements calming yet terrifying at the same time.

Right then, it hit him as he watched the paramedics fiddle with pressure cuffs and stethoscopes and a whole host of intimidating medical paraphernalia skimming over Kris's body.

He loved her.

Wholeheartedly. Unreservedly. Terrifyingly.

And, as much as he loved their unborn daughter, even if the unthinkable happened and she didn't survive he would still love Kris and everything she'd become to him.

'How many weeks is she?'

'Thirty-nine,' he said, knowing the baby could be delivered safely now.

If the baby was still alive.

At that moment, Kris's eyelids fluttered open, her bright blue eyes fixing on him.

'What's going on?' she said, struggling to sit up, confusion clouding her beautiful features.

'I'm guessing you fainted,' the older paramedic said, casting Nate a look between exasperation and congratulation.

'Not again,' she said, rolling her eyes and sending a horrified look at her dress hiked up around her waist. 'Is the baby all right? Did I do any damage in the fall?'

The female paramedic laid a reassuring hand on her arm. 'The baby is fine. The heartbeat is steady and strong.'

'Thank God.'

Kris's whisper slammed into him, reinforcing his own overwhelming relief. He crossed the short distance separating them, crouching down to her level, torn between wanting to bundle her into his arms and hug her breathless, and shaking her silly for scaring him like that.

'Do you have gestational diabetes?'

The female paramedic squatted down next to him and

took Kris's blood pressure, while the other paramedic repacked the emergency case.

Kris shook her head, and he forced himself not to reach out and smooth the tousled blonde waves back from her face.

'No, though my blood sugar has dipped a few times. The doc told me to pop a jelly bean or barley sugar every time I felt woozy. I was just heading to the kitchen when I must've passed out.'

'Well, your blood pressure's fine, as are the rest of your vitals.' The paramedic slid the pressure-cuff off her arm and tucked it away in her jacket of a hundred pockets. 'You should be fine, but take it easy, okay? This bub wants its mum in tip-top shape when he or she makes its grand entrance into the world.'

'She,' Nate and Kris said in unison, their eyes meeting, hers luminous, his relieved.

He'd never known relief till she'd opened her eyes a few minutes ago, the relief backed up by the paramedics pronouncing the baby was fine.

Whatever the cause of her collapse, he knew one thing for sure—he wasn't going to let her out of his sight ever again.

She could kick, she could scream, she could threaten to tell every media outlet in Australia about the infamous doll incident, but he wasn't taking no for an answer this time.

They belonged together, now and for ever.

'Right, we'll leave you folks to it,' the male paramedic said, flanking Kris's other side as they helped her to her feet and to the nearest chair. 'Take care.'

'Thanks,' she said, colour returning to her cheeks as

he sent her a glare which read 'sit there and don't move a muscle', before escorting the paramedics out the door and returning to the lounge.

'You look mad.'

She pointed to the chair next to her, and he marvelled at her resilience while smiling at her bossiness.

Nothing kept this woman down: a move from one country to another, discovering the man she'd probably wanted to forget was her new boss, an unexpected pregnancy, and the odd collapse here or there thrown in for good measure.

She was remarkable. Little wonder he'd fallen for her, even if it was the last thing he'd wanted to do.

'I'm not mad,' he said, taking a seat next to her, wondering if he should go for the direct approach—which he'd tried and failed before—or lead into it gently.

She leaned across and placed a hand on his forearm, her palm cool against the heat of his skin.

'Look, I know I must've given you a scare when you came in and found me like that. But I'm fine. The baby's fine. No use getting that look.'

'What look?'

The corners of her mouth twitched, and he could hardly restrain himself from closing the short distance between them and covering her lips with his. 'The same look you got before you asked me to move in with you, the same look before your proposal.'

Her other hand reached up and she traced a slow, sensuous path between his brows. 'You get this funny little frown-line right here. It alerts me to the fact you're about to say something profound.'

'I am.'

He missed her touch as she sat back and folded her arms, resting them on her swollen belly.

'Okay, let me have it. What is it this time—you think I should have a water birth? You've hired a police escort to take us to the hospital when the time comes? You—'

'You talk too much,' he said, leaning across the chair-arm and kissing her, angling his head for better access, his libido firing on all cylinders as she melted under him, opening her mouth to him.

He could've kissed her like this for ever, her lips warm and pliant, her hands clutching his shirt like she'd never let go. If he had his way, she wouldn't.

The fire they'd created in Singapore had been nothing like this mind-blowing, raging inferno which spread like wildfire and threatened to consume them both.

He'd tried denying the sizzling attraction back then, and his good intentions had ended up like his discarded underwear on the floor of his hotel room.

He'd never believed in fate. Yet some indefinable force had led him to this woman, to this shattering moment when his heart unfurled and swelled with love, a feeling he'd shunned for too long.

Whatever had brought this amazing woman into his life, he couldn't believe his luck, and he'd make sure she knew it every day.

'Whoa!' Her fingers relaxed from their death-grip and her palms splayed across his chest as she pulled back slightly, her lips rosily plumped and her sparkling eyes wide with shock. 'What was that all about?'

'Would you believe I thought you needed mouth-to-mouth?'

She smiled. 'Try again, wise guy.'

'Would you believe I've just eaten a jelly bean and thought you could use the sugar boost?'

She arched an eyebrow. 'Come on, you can do better than that.'

'Would you believe I love you, I want to marry you and I want us to be a real family—you, me and our daughter?'

Her face fell, her eyes hardening to icy blue as she dropped her hands into her lap.

'That's not funny.'

'It's not a joke,' he said, desperate to make her see how genuine he was, how much she meant to him. 'I want us to be together.'

He'd known she'd be a hard sell, but her frigid expression could have frozen him solid if he'd been wet.

'You'd do anything to protect this baby, wouldn't you?'

'No…yes… Hell.'

He rubbed a hand over his face, wishing this were a bad dream and he'd wake up to find Kris nestled in his bed, smiling up at him with love and affection.

'Yes, I'd do anything to protect our baby, but this isn't about that. This is about us. This is about me first falling under your spell in Singapore. This is about me being unable to sleep at night for thinking about you, for missing you, for wanting more for us but being too scared to grab it, too scared to face up to my feelings.'

Her glacial expression thawed to semi-cold. 'I don't get it. Why didn't you tell me any of this before? Why did you let me walk away after I knocked back your last proposal?'

He sighed, having known it would come to this.

Having known he'd have to tell her the whole truth if he wanted to win her love.

'You know that suitcase you had when I first met

you? Well, I carry around enough baggage which would make that look like a thimble.'

Sadness flickered in her eyes. 'This has to do with Julia, doesn't it?'

He nodded, regret filling him that he hadn't told Kris everything. It would've saved him a lot of trouble and a lot of heartache. He'd loved Julia with all his heart, but what he felt for Kris went way beyond that.

In a way the depth of his feelings for her had scared him beyond belief, but now that he'd come to his senses he couldn't stand for them to be apart a second longer.

Before he could speak, she placed a finger on his lips and shushed him.

'You don't have to say it. I know she was the love of your life. I know you'll never get over her. You say you love me, but can you look me in the eye and say it's the same love you had for her?'

'No, it's—'

'Aaahh!'

Her groan filled the air, chilling his blood as she doubled over and gripped under her belly, all colour draining from her face.

'The baby?'

She nodded, her lips turning blue from being compressed so hard, before another guttural groan tore from her throat.

'Damn it, I wish those paramedics had stuck around,' he muttered, kneeling in front of her and capturing her face in his hands. 'Kris, look at me. Is your hospital bag upstairs in your bedroom?'

'Yesss,' she gritted out, pain contorting her features while he attempted to smooth away the lines.

'Okay, I'll grab it and then we'll head to the hospital. I need you to breathe through the contractions and try to relax.'

'Just get the bloody bag,' she said, every ounce of her pain concentrated into the killer look she sent him.

He ran up the stairs, knowing her language might get a lot more expressive before the birth was over.

The birth… He was going to be a dad…hell!

Sprinting into her room, he grabbed the small wheelie-suitcase near the door and headed down the stairs, taking two at a time.

Not surprisingly, she hadn't moved, gripping onto the arms of the chair so hard her knuckles stood out.

'How far apart are they?'

'I don't know! I'm not wearing my watch,' she said, her petrified gaze locking with his, and he dropped a quick kiss on her head before bolting to his car, shoving her case in the back and running back to the house.

It was the damnedest thing, almost as if he were having an out-of-body experience, watching this crazy man running all over the place, yet totally focussed on the woman waddling down the path, leaning heavily on his arm and doubling over as they reached the car.

'Come on, sweetheart. We'll be at the hospital in five minutes,' he said, handing her into the car as another contraction hit and she almost broke his wrist with her grip.

'Make it two,' she said, resting her head back and closing her eyes, one hand rubbing the top of her belly while the other circled beneath.

Nate considered himself a careful driver, but when Kris let out the loudest groan yet he floored it, cutting lanes, copping two-finger salutes and tooting horns left, right and centre as he screeched into the hospital and pulled up in front of Emergency.

'Hurry!' she moaned, her head thrashing side to side and he made a dash for the entrance, grabbing the first nurse he could find and pointing to his car. 'The baby's coming! Now! Do something!'

To the nurse's credit, she made efficient hand-signals at the receptionist, who summoned an orderly with a wheelchair and a doctor within two seconds.

'Calm down, sir. Everything's going to be all right.'

Was it?

He had no idea.

Everything was happening so fast, and he hadn't even had a chance to tell Kris how much she meant to him. What if something happened to her? What if she went through this daunting experience thinking he loved her less than Julia?

'Naaate!'

Kris's ear-piercing scream had him sprinting after the wheelchair and into a small room off the emergency room.

The next five minutes happened in a blur as a grim-looking doctor bustled in, checked Kris's dilation and pronounced her two-centimetres dilated.

Only two? *Two?*

A little piece of Nate curled up and died deep inside as he held her hand, watching her grunt and sweat and moan her way through the next contraction, knowing there would be many more before their daughter was born, as the stuff he'd absorbed in pre-natal class came back.

The cervix needs to be dilated ten centimetres before the next phase begins.

He distinctly remembered the midwife conducting the classes teaching them that, the figure particularly sticking in his head because ten centimetres had sounded awfully big to him.

Kris whimpered and he squeezed her hand, wishing he could do more, wishing he could take away her pain, wishing he could do something other than sit here like a big, useless dummy.

As if reading his mind, she fixed him with an angry stare. 'You being here is enough, so don't go getting any ideas to bolt on me, you hear?'

He smiled, trying not to wince as pain contorted her beautiful features. 'I'm not going anywhere, even if you call me every name under the sun.'

She gritted her teeth and gripped his hand tight as another contraction rippled through her belly, her pallor and perspiration-covered face combining to leave him feeling like he'd been kicked in the gut.

'You better remember that,' she bit out, relaxing back onto the pillows and easing her death grip on his hand as the contraction passed. 'If this is only the beginning, I feel a lot of swearing coming on—most of it directed at you for getting me into this predicament in the first place.'

There was no malice behind her words. If anything, the cheeky glint in her eyes surprised him.

'As I recall, we were both pretty involved at the time.'

Their gazes locked and held as memories of their night in Singapore washed over them, notching up the temperature in the birthing suite in an instant.

'We never got to finish our talk,' she said, a small, serene smile playing about her lips, begging him to reach forward and cover them with his own.

However another ripping contraction vanquished that urge in an instant, and their shared moment of intimacy was lost.

Nate had never been a clock watcher, putting in the required hours at work without giving it a second thought. But over the next eight hours he couldn't tear his gaze away from the large, ugly kitchen-clock stuck on the wall in front of him as he rubbed Kris's back, offered her ice chips to suck and bore the brunt of her increasingly fraying temper.

'Nate, I don't think I can do this any more...'

Her whispered plea for reassurance slammed into him, and his gut turned over as he leaned forward and stroked her forehead, needing the physical contact for reassurance as much as she did.

'You're doing great, sweetheart. You're amazing. Hang in there. Our daughter is on her way.'

He hated how inadequate he sounded, how totally pathetic, and he turned in desperation to the midwife as she entered the room, silently imploring her to give them good news.

The midwife, way too calm and cheery, bustled about with ferocious efficiency, pronounced Kris ten-centimetres dilated and instructed her to push.

'There is a slight problem, dear.'

Nate's heart stopped as he stared in open-mouthed horror at the midwife, who so casually delivered news that could be catastrophic. As he'd already learned, there were no 'slight' problems with birthing; they tended to be major ones, and he hoped to God this wasn't anything serious.

'Though the baby is head down, her head is facing

the wrong way. In these cases, usually with a bit of pushing, the little mite will automatically turn and come out quickly. So we'll give it a go, shall we?'

'What's with the "we" business?' Kris muttered, sending the midwife one of the dangerous looks she'd been reserving for Nate up till that point.

In the midst of his anxiety she managed to ellicit a smile out of him, albeit a weak one, and he copped an angry glare for his trouble too.

'You're almost there, sweetheart.'

He leaned over and kissed her on the cheek, half expecting her to push him away or whack him for his trouble. Instead, she surprised him by cupping his cheek for an all-too-brief instant before the next contraction took her breath away and the roller-coaster of pain began again.

And again… And again…

Minutes stretched into hours, hours into an interminable stretch of moans and groans as he helplessly watched the woman he loved go through unbearable agony.

He barely remembered the midwife hooking up a foetal monitor over Kris's belly; he barely remembered passing Kris the nitrous oxide to help with the crest of the increasingly painful contractions. But when the baby's heartbeat started to slow with every push he rocked out of the chair and marched across to the worried midwife, who was in deep conversation with the obstetrician who'd just entered the room.

'You've got to do something now!' he said, casting frantic glances back at Kris lying in a sweaty, pale heap on the bed, hating his helpless frustration more than anything.

'We're taking her to Theatre shortly,' the obstetrician said, giving him a comforting pat on the arm which came across decidedly condescending. 'An anaesthetist is on their way up.'

'What's going on?'

Kris's shout made them both jump, and he followed the obstetrician back to the bed, his eyes glued to the foetal monitor, petrified when the heartbeat slowed yet again.

'We're taking you to Theatre shortly. We don't let our mums go longer than twenty-four hours, and you've done a mighty job, Kris. However, this little girl of yours isn't turning, so I'll try forceps, and if that doesn't work we'll be doing a Caesarean, okay?'

Nate expected Kris to protest, remembering how pro-natural she'd been about the birth throughout the antenatal classes, but she merely nodded and slumped back, exhaustion rendering her speechless.

'Let's do it, Doc,' he said, grateful for some positive action, not quite believing Kris had been in labour for almost a day.

The rest happened in a blur: the trip down to Theatre, gowning-up himself, the obstetrician smiling when the forceps worked, and asking Kris to give one last, almighty push.

Suddenly, his breath caught as the doctor held up a red-faced, screaming little girl covered in white gunk, and he would've forgotten how to breathe if Kris hadn't burst into noisy tears at that moment.

'She's beautiful, just like her mother,' he whispered, tears filling his eyes as he pushed away the damp strands of hair stuck to Kris's face and kissed her on the mouth.

'Oh, Nate.'

Her sobs subsided but the tears continued, flowing down her cheeks and plopping softly on the bed, as their bundled daughter was placed in her arms and he found his own tears falling softly on the baby's blanket.

'She's incredible.'

Leaning forward, he cuddled them close, filled with an indescribable love for his girls.

'We never did get around to choosing a name,' Kris said, nuzzling the top of the baby's head with her nose, while he traced the soft curve of his daughter's cheek.

'Later,' he said, wanting to capture this moment in time for ever. 'I love you both so much.'

Thankfully, Kris didn't argue as they formed a protective circle around the baby with their linked hands.

CHAPTER FOURTEEN

Kris pretended to sleep as Nate crept into her room and over to the cot, his voice barely a whisper as he greeted his daughter.

'Hey, little one. Hope you're being good for Mummy. She needs her rest, and so do you.'

He had that right.

She hadn't had a moment's peace since the birth, what with midwives teaching her to breastfeed, trying to express a nonexistent milk supply and learning how to bathe her gorgeous girl.

Then there was Nate—always hanging around, doting over her and the baby, reminding her of how amazing he was and of what she couldn't have.

'You know, I bet your half-brother is looking down on you right now. He's your guardian angel.'

She stiffened, wondering if the analgesia they'd given her for the episiotomy stitches had affected her comprehension.

'I never got to hold him like I have you. Guess I was too scared, but I've regretted it every day since. Babies need to be held, and I promise to cuddle you every single day.'

Kris opened her eyes, unable to lie there and pretend she hadn't heard the gut-wrenching pain in Nate's voice.

'You had a son?'

Nate jumped and swivelled to face her, his face cloaked in shadows.

'I never got to that part, did I?'

He sat on the edge of the bed and took hold of her hand, glancing across at the cot with love radiating from his eyes.

'Tell me now,' she said, happy to have her hand held, enthralled by the emotional bond created from having had the man she loved stand by her every second of the labour ordeal.

Meeting her eyes directly, he said, 'You know Julia was pregnant when she died. I wanted to tell you the rest, but I didn't want to scare you, what with the way she died. I'd been away with work and came home to find her bleeding on the kitchen floor. She'd had a placental abruption, where the baby dies and she haemorrhaged quickly. They were both dead.'

'Oh, my God. I'd assumed it was a brain haemorrhage.'

Now she understood the stricken look on his face when he'd hovered over her after she'd passed out on the stairs. He'd probably thought he was walking in on the same tragic scenario all over again.

He shook his head. 'I blamed myself. If I'd been there for her, hadn't gone to work that day, maybe I could've done something, prevented their senseless deaths in some way—but I wasn't, and I'll never forgive myself for that.'

He looked away, his glassy stare fixed on some point

over her left shoulder, and she remained silent, unsure what to say, knowing whatever words she mumbled out loud would sound trite and inadequate.

'I've lived with the guilt for a long time, shutting myself off from everything but work, focussing all my energy on business, numbing the pain of feeling. Then you came along.'

She shook her head, dread creeping through her exhausted body. He'd said he'd loved her before the birth, and now she finally understood.

Nate had shut down emotionally since losing Julia and their child. Kris had given him what he wanted most, another child, and he'd confused his awakening emotions with love.

He didn't love her—he couldn't.

How could he love her when he was still grieving? He'd just said he could never forgive himself; how did he expect to move on?

'You don't have to explain anything to me, Nate. I get it.'

'No, you don't. Sure, I've been battling the daily guilt of not being there for Julia, but I've been fighting an added guilt too. The guilt of moving on, of letting Julia go, of possibly loving another woman, of acknowledging that I love you more than I loved her.'

Kris's jaw dropped, and she didn't resist when he reached up and tipped a finger under her chin to close it.

'I already told you, Jules and I were high-school sweethearts. It's only now I realise that our love was based on friendship, rather than the inexplicable connection you and I've had since we first met. What I feel for you is richer, deeper, more profound than anything I felt for Julia, and I've been beating myself up over it till I realised something. It's okay to love you, to feel good again, to start living my life, rather than using my guilt as an excuse to push you away.'

Hope unfurled in her heart, uncertain and fluttering and making her head feel lighter than any pain relief could have.

'I love you, Kris. You're everything to me.'

His kiss slanted across her lips, a gentle kiss of persuasion, and she responded as if someone had lit a rocket under her, sliding her hands around his neck and pulling him up the bed, desperate to get closer, throwing all her pent-up emotions into the kiss she'd been awaiting for ever, the incredibly special, once-in-a-lifetime kiss of a man who truly loved her.

'You know I love you too?'

She traced his bottom lip with her fingertip, enjoying his blatant shock.

'Actually, I thought we had a few sparks, and I hoped you'd grow to love me.'

'Too late. It's already happened,' she said, snapping her fingers and injecting all the love she had in her heart for him into a dazzling smile. 'Seems like I've loved you for ever.'

'For ever, huh?'

Capturing her face in his hands, he brushed a tantalising kiss across her lips. 'Sounds good to me. That's how long we've got to love each other, to create the happy family we deserve.'

He'd said the magic words—love and happy family—and Kristen melted into his embrace, knowing there could be no better place than in his protective arms. The safeness he made her feel finally banished the shadows left on her soul by her childhood, a childhood she had yet to tell him about, but the lack of love in her past seemed less important now than the love being offered to her here and now. And there would be time, time to fill each other in on the past, in a future that they would now share.

'You're going to marry me, right?'

Kristen pretended to think about it as Nate kissed his way very, very slowly up her neck, stopping to lavish some extra attention on the sensitive spot there.

'You can't keep me dangling for ever, you know. I don't want to be proposing at Maeve's twenty-first.'

'You know I love that name, right?' She smiled; choosing the name had been easy once they had met their daughter. 'And it's so perfect to have our little girl named after your mum, especially as she'll never get to meet her granddaughter.'

A shadow flickered across Nate's dark eyes. 'Mum would've loved her as much as we do. Now, stop trying to distract me by getting all sentimental and tell me your answer.'

'I thought I'd already answered you.'

She leaned down and rubbed noses with him Eskimo-kiss style, loving their closeness, the teasing, the one hundred percent security being with a guy like him brought.

For a girl who'd craved stability her whole life she'd finally found it, all wrapped up in one incredible package.

He tightened his arms around her waist, squeezing the breath out of her till she could hardly breathe.

Or was that sexy glint in his dark-as-coal eyes telling her she was pushing her luck?

'You haven't given me an answer. What with you threatening to walk out on me after my first proposal, then scaring the life out of me by collapsing, closely followed by Maeve's birth just as I'm professing my undying love to you, we haven't got around to discussing the important stuff—like weddings.'

She arched a brow, sending him the sassy look he loved so well.

'So you're pretty confident there's going to be a wedding, huh?'

'You bet.'

His fingers skimmed her spine, his feather-light touch scattering goose bumps all over, and she shivered, preening under his touch, wishing this could go on for ever.

'In that case, who am I to stand in the way of your pushy nature?'

They grinned at each other like a couple head over heels in love, knowing there'd never been any doubt about them getting married once they'd declared their love, enjoying playing the game.

'Is it kosher to marry the boss?'

'You're not my boss any more,' she said, slanting a long, slow kiss across his lips, the type of kiss guaranteed to light a fire between them. 'I'm on maternity leave as of now, remember?'

His hands framed her face as the kiss ended, his dark eyes glowing with passion in the surreal dawn light. 'I love you so much.'

'Right back at you.'

Her eyes filled with tears, and he wiped them away with a gentle fingertip. 'Still those damn hormones, huh?'

'Yeah. They make me do crazy things.'

'As long as you don't fall out of love with me when they wear off, I'll be happy.'

'Not a chance, my love. Not a chance.'

'So do you want to wait till Maeve's walking so she can be flower girl at our wedding?'

'Hell, no! I need to make an honest man out of you asap.'

'How soon?'

He traced her cheek, toying with a strand of hair, twisting it around his finger in the same way he'd done to the rest of her since the first moment she'd met him.

'I'm a busy mum. You're the high-flying CEO who plans everything to the nth degree. How long do you think it will take to organise our wedding?'

His eyes glittered with intent as he tugged gently on the strand of hair, bringing their lips mere centimetres apart.

'You'll be in hospital for five nights. So is a week from today too soon?'

'To start the rest of our lives together? Never,' she said, closing the tiny distance between them, and kissing him till they were both panting and breathless.

'I'm kidding,' he said, desire clouding his eyes in a dark fog. 'I'll give you a chance to catch your breath.'

She smiled and dropped a kiss on his lips. 'Soon is fine. A small ceremony with you, me and Maeve. Perfect.'

'Perfect,' he echoed, sliding his arms around her till she had no option but to snuggle tight against his chest, knowing she'd found what she'd always wanted.

Love, respect and validation, made all the more special by Maeve, their adorable baby girl sleeping peacefully by their side.

A family of her own.

Perfect indeed.

Boardroom Baby Surprise

Jackie Braun

Jackie Braun is a three-time RITA® finalist, three-time National Readers Choice Award finalist and past winner of the Rising Star Award. She worked as a copy-editor and editorial writer for a daily newspaper before quitting her day job in 2004 to write fiction full time. She lives in Michigan with her family. She loves to hear from readers and can be reached through her website at www.jackiebraun.com

For my boys, Daniel and Will

CHAPTER ONE

Seated in the tastefully decorated reception area at Windy City Industries, Morgan Stevens gripped the upholstered arm of the chair and panted as discreetly as she could.

Breathe, she coached herself. In…out…and again.

The jagged edge of the contraction was just beginning to wear off when the secretary returned through one of a trio of doors on the opposite wall.

The name on the woman's desk plate was Britney. It suited her to a T. She was young, attractive, model-slender and crisply fashionable in a fitted black suit, bold-print silk blouse and a pair of killer heels. In comparison, Morgan felt decidedly dowdy in her pastel-colored maternity tent and the comfortable flat sandals that were the only shoes that would accommodate her swollen feet.

"I'm sorry, but Mr. Caliborn is busy and can't see you," Britney said, working up a smile that looked about as sincere as a shark's. "Might I suggest you make an appointment before coming by next time?"

Why? So he could be conveniently gone when she got there? No way. Morgan had been trying to reach Bryan Caliborn for months. She laid a hand on her protruding midsection. Nearly nine of them. The only correspondence she'd had in return, if it could be called such, was a letter from his legal counsel advising her that Mr. Caliborn disputed her allegation of paternity. In fact, he disputed knowing her. He considered her claims nothing less than extortion, and he would sue for damages if she continued to make them.

More than hurt and insulted by his threat, Morgan was outraged. If he didn't want to play a role in their child's life, fine. He should just say so. But to say they'd never met, well, that was beyond defense, legal or otherwise. She never would have taken Bryan Caliborn for such a ruthless, heartless man. Nor had he seemed slow, but he had to be if he wasn't aware that all it would take was a bit of DNA to confirm Morgan was telling the truth. She'd hoped, apparently in vain, to avoid that sort of ugliness.

Rising awkwardly to her feet, she returned the young woman's smile with one that was equally insincere. "Fine. Please pencil me in for his earliest availability."

"Let me just check his calendar and see when that might be," Britney said.

Morgan saw no sense in arguing with the secretary. She would deal with the elusive businessman herself. And she would do so now. While Britney walked behind her desk, Morgan headed to the door through which the woman had appeared a moment earlier. She assumed it was Bryan's office. Opening it, however, she found it was a conference room, a conference room that was filled with suit-clad professionals seated around an oblong cherry table. File folders were open in front of them, not that they were looking at the pie charts and bar graphs. They were gaping at Morgan. But it was the man at the far end of the room who held her attention.

Handsome? No. A better word would be *arresting*. He had dark, almost black hair and eyes of the same fathomless hue. His face was angular with sharp cheekbones and slashing brows that, at the moment, were pulled down in a frown. The nose above his sculpted, flesh-toned lips was thin and just crooked enough to give it character.

Morgan swallowed. Even seated, it was obvious he was tall and powerfully built. Never in her life had she been attracted to the dark and brooding sort, but something about this man was definitely appealing. She told herself it was only because he seemed oddly familiar.

That thought shattered when he spoke. She'd never heard a voice like that before. He didn't break the silence so much as pulverize it. His words boomed through the room like a thunderclap when he demanded, "What is the meaning of this?"

"Sorry," she began, backing up a step only to bump into the secretary, who took Morgan's arm. The gesture seemed more like an effort to detain rather than to steady her, which irritated Morgan enough to prompt her to say, "I need to speak with Bryan Caliborn, and I need to speak to him right now. I thought he might be in here."

"He is." All eyes turned to the big man at the end of the table, who was now rising to his feet. He was every bit of six-four, maybe six-five, and every inch of him radiated power and authority. Again she had the odd feeling that she knew him, but it came as an utter shock when he said, "I'm Bryan Caliborn."

"No." Morgan shook her head, sure that she had heard him wrong. "You're n—"

She didn't finish the sentence. Her water broke, releasing in a gush to form an unbecoming puddle on the polished parquet floor. The secretary let go of Morgan's arm and jumped back, anxious to protect her Marc Jacobs pumps from harm. The people seated around the table gasped in unison, pulling back in their seats, as if Morgan's condition were contagious. Only the man who claimed to be Bryan moved. Swearing richly half under his breath, he stalked around the table toward her.

"Sorry," Morgan whispered, though she felt more mortified than apologetic.

She would have left then, turned and run away— or waddled as the case may be—but as her luck would have it, another contraction began to build. She angled away from him, hoping to make it to the reception area's couch to wait out the worst of it. She made it only one step before grabbing the door frame and sagging against it. Using the other hand to support her abdomen, she fought the urge to whimper. Nothing was going as planned. Nothing *had* gone as planned in a long, long time.

"Britney, call an ambulance," the big man barked. To Morgan he said, "I take it you're in labor."

Labor? She was being wrenched apart from the inside out. None of the books she'd read, none of the classes she'd taken had prepared her for this kind of pain. But she nodded, worried that any attempt at speech would release not only a whimper but a wailing shriek. God, she hurt.

She needed to sit down. She needed some of the drugs she'd learned about in her birthing class. She needed her mother. Only one of those things was an option now, but before Morgan could wilt to the floor, she was scooped up in a pair of powerful arms and carried into the office that was one door down from the conference room.

He settled her on the leather couch and returned a moment later with what looked to be a balled-up trench coat and a glass of water. He positioned the trench behind her head on the arm rest and then thrust the glass at her. Morgan wasn't interested in water. For that matter, she doubted she could keep it down.

But she dutifully took it and pretended to sip from the glass. His rigid demeanor told her he wasn't the sort of man who stood for being defied. And while she generally wouldn't stand for being bullied, she was in no shape to put him in his place.

"The ambulance will be here any moment," the secretary said, peeking around the semi-closed door.

"An ambulance really isn't necessary," Morgan began. Not to mention that it would be expensive for someone who had just lost her health insurance along with her teaching job when the school year had ended a week earlier. The economy being what it was, the district didn't have the funds for extras like music.

The worst of the contraction had passed, so she swung her legs over the edge of the couch and planted her feet on the floor. She would go now, exiting as gracefully as her condition allowed. Her car was in the parking ramp adjacent to the building and she could be at Chicago's Northwestern Memorial Hospital in less than twenty minutes, assuming the traffic lights and her finicky compact car cooperated.

What stopped her wasn't the big man, even though he took a lurching step in her direction, but the framed picture on the wall just to the right of the door. In it two men stood arm in arm, one dark and brooding, the other fairer and far less serious. Morgan blinked. She knew those smiling eyes, that windblown brown hair and carefree expression. By turns sweet and silly, this was the man with whom she'd spent seven lovely and, for her, uncharacteristically reckless days in Aruba.

Bryan.

She must have said the name aloud because when she glanced over, the man's gaze also was on the photograph, his mouth compressed into a line so tight that it was hard to tell where his top lip ended and the bottom one began.

"You do know him," she accused, pointing to the photograph. "You do know Bryan Caliborn."

"*I* am Bryan Caliborn," he proclaimed a second time. "That's Dillon, my younger brother."

Dillon…

Brother…

The words registered slowly, poking through a haze of disbelief. Though a part of her wanted to dispute them, the proof—all six-feet-something of it—was literally standing before her, his arms crossed, his expression ominous and intractable.

Bryan…rather, Dillon—the man who'd fathered Morgan's baby, hadn't given her his real name. This wasn't exactly the kind of revelation a woman needed to hear with motherhood a few centimeters and a couple of hard pushes away. It made Morgan wonder what else he had lied about. What other truths he had obscured with his beguiling kisses and those impeccable manners she'd found every bit as seductive as his smile.

In her best schoolteacher's voice, she demanded, "I want to see him." For good measure, she added,

"And don't you dare tell me I need to make an appointment. As you can see, I'm not in any condition to wait an hour let alone a week or two."

"It's not possible," the real Bryan had the audacity to say. She opened her mouth, intending to let loose with a blistering retort. Before she could, though, he said, "Dillon's dead."

Anger abandoned her, evaporating like water on hot asphalt. Bewilderment took its place—bewilderment and a couple dozen other emotions that swirled around in a dizzying mix. Since her legs threatened to give, Morgan backed up to the couch, sinking onto its cushions.

"He's dead?"

Bryan's head jerked down in a nod.

"But how? When?" She asked the questions, needing to know even though the answers really didn't matter. What would they change? Not only was she about to become a single mother, her baby would never know his or her father. She swallowed a fresh wave of nausea. For that matter *she* hadn't known her baby's father.

"Six months ago. A skiing accident in Vail, Colorado." The words came out stilted, made curt by grief. Or was that some other emotion lurking in those onyx eyes?

"I…I didn't know."

"Neither did I." He glanced meaningfully at her stomach. "Where did you and Dillon meet?"

"Aruba. Last August."

She'd gone there alone, using the tickets she'd bought her folks for their thirtieth wedding anniversary. They'd never had a honeymoon. Morgan had wanted to give them one as a surprise. Before she could, though, they'd died in a fluke carbon monoxide accident at their home. Though she wasn't one to make excuses for her behavior, her grief helped explain why someone as levelheaded as she usually was had fallen for the faux Bryan's advances in the first place. She'd been lost, lonely. He'd been charming and a distraction from bitter reality.

"And you...spent time with my brother?" One brow arched in disapproval as Bryan once again glanced at her abdomen.

"Yes."

If she'd felt awkward and conspicuous before, she felt doubly so now. She stood, intent on leaving this time, though where exactly she would go beyond the hospital she hadn't a clue. She was between jobs, between homes and in a strange city without family.

A pair of emergency medical technicians arrived before Morgan could get to the door. They carried black bags and were pushing a gurney.

She held up a hand. "Oh, this really isn't necessary. I can get to the hospital on my own steam. My contractions aren't that close together."

Even as she said this another one began. Just how

many minutes had passed since the last? She didn't dare chance a glance at her wrist now.

"It is necessary," Bryan objected. "Assuming what you say is true, that child is a Caliborn."

"Assuming—" She gritted her teeth, and not because of the contraction. She would have stalked out then, but one of the technicians, a kind-faced man with salt-and-pepper hair and a bushy mustache, laid a hand on her arm.

"Let's have a look at you first, okay? We wouldn't want you to have that baby while you're stuck in traffic on Michigan Avenue."

He reminded Morgan of her father, which was the only reason she let him lead her back to the couch.

Once she was seated, the EMT knelt in front of her and pulled a blood-pressure cuff from his bag. As it inflated over her upper arm, she glanced at Bryan, who stared back at her stone-faced. She was coming to know that expression. She could only imagine what he was thinking.

Damn Dillon! Damn him for doing this. And damn him for being dead!

Bryan wanted to throttle his little brother, pin him in a chokehold like he used to do when they were kids and pound some sense into him. Only he couldn't. Knowing that reopened a wound that had just barely begun to heal. Why did Dillon have to go and get himself killed?

Bryan still couldn't quite wrap his mind around the fact that Dill was gone, buried in the family plot at Winchester Memorial Gardens alongside their paternal grandparents and a spinster great-aunt. How was it possible for someone that vibrant and full of life to die? Half the time Bryan wanted to believe that his younger brother was simply off on another one of his irresponsible jaunts, charging his good time to Bryan's accounts.

He'd done that often enough after burning through his own trust fund by his late twenties, Vail being the last wild excursion. Bryan had been furious when his credit card company had called to confirm the charges. Only the best accommodations and restaurants for his little brother. He'd dialed Dill at the luxury hotel where he was staying in a suite that was costing Bryan a few grand a night, and left him a blistering message.

"Grow up, already!" he'd shouted into the receiver. "You're thirty, for God's sake. You have a position at the company if you'd ever deign to work. You need to start earning your own way and stop mooching off me. You do it again and I swear, Dill, I'll call the police."

Of course, he wouldn't have. But he'd been so furious.

Now, sitting in his office looking both terrified and lovely as she answered the EMT's questions and cringed her way through another contraction, was one doozy of an example of his little brother's foolishness. As per usual, it would be up to Bryan to clean up the mess. He'd done that Dill's entire life. Apparently, that applied posthumously, too.

He scrubbed a hand across his eyes. This mess was going to be harder than the others, assuming Morgan wasn't lying about her baby's paternity. That was a possibility given the Caliborn family's net worth. She probably thought she had a big payout coming. Given the state of his brother's finances, she was in for a rude awakening. Unfortunately, determining the truth wasn't as easy as requesting a DNA test. It wasn't because the father in question was deceased. Bryan's DNA could be used to confirm a biological link between the baby and the Caliborns. That was precisely what had him hesitating. He was in no hurry to go through that…again.

He had to say, Morgan Stevens wasn't Dill's usual type. His brother had always gone for flashy women—bombshell blondes, busty brunettes and sassy redheads whose idea of keeping up with current events was to leaf through the tabloids while they had their hair styled. One of the dates Dill had brought to a family dinner last year had actually thought Austria was an abbreviation for Australia.

Morgan appeared to be intelligent and well-spoken, if her phone messages and letters were any indication. She was wearing conservative, if hideous, attire and, despite her advanced pregnancy, didn't appear to be built like a Playboy centerfold.

So, just what had Dill seen in this woman?

Bryan didn't have to wonder what Morgan had seen in Dill. His brother had been good-looking, charming and exceptionally free with his money, which he could afford to be since the money was actually Bryan's.

Gold digger.

It was an old-fashioned term, but Bryan had met enough of those sort of women over the years to know it still applied. Rock stars weren't the only ones who had groupies. Power brokers attracted them, too, though admittedly they were more refined and they tended to be looking for a ring and a Bergdorf charge card.

His ex-wife came to mind. She was remarried to a Texas oil tycoon whose fortune made the Caliborns' look paltry by comparison. And she'd borne the tycoon a son, a son who, for a brief time, she'd allowed Bryan to believe was his.

The scandal had been the talk of Chicago for months after the news broke. The DNA test results had been leaked to the media—even before Bryan had seen them. The gossipmongers had had a field day and they would again if they caught wind of this.

Morgan's moan brought him out of his bitter musings. Her lips parted and she began to pant. Her eyes were pinched closed, her face drawn and dotted with perspiration. She looked incredibly young and scared, especially when she whispered brokenly, "I don't…think I can…do this."

Bryan didn't like weakness. In business, he considered it a character flaw. Oddly, her vulnerability touched him. It made him want to go to her, hold her hand, stroke her cheek and offer reassurance. Absurd reactions, all. He folded his arms across his chest and leaned against the edge of his desk instead.

"Sure you can. You're going to be fine," the EMT told her. "Lie back on the couch now. I'm just going to check to see how far you've dilated."

That brought Bryan upright. He was no expert on labor and delivery, but he'd heard that term before and knew what it meant. On his way to the door, he said, "I'll be outside."

In the reception area, he paced uncharacteristically. He was used to taking charge of any given situation and then taking action. At the moment, he wasn't sure what to do. Should he call his folks, who were currently vacationing abroad, and tell them… what? What exactly could he say? *Congratulations, you may soon be grandparents.*

Dill's death had been so hard for Julia and Hugh Caliborn to accept. The death of a child, no matter how old, was wrong. It flouted the natural order of things. Parents were not supposed to bury their offspring.

Bryan pictured his mother upon hearing about Morgan's baby. She would be excited and weepy about reclaiming a precious bit of her younger son. No doubt, she would lavish the child with every comfort and amenity. And Morgan, too, by default. She'd done the same with his former wife and the baby she'd been cruelly duped into believing was her first grandchild. Four months before the due date his mother had already made over one of her home's guest rooms into a nursery. Then she'd thrown her daughter-in-law a lavish shower, buying everything left on gift registry afterward. She'd been at the hospital for the birth, crying the happy tears women cry at such occasions. And, eighteen months later, when they'd learned that Caden Alexander Caliborn was not a Caliborn at all, she'd shed more tears, nearly as devastated as Bryan had been.

He clenched his fists. Until he knew for certain this young woman wasn't pulling a very convincing con, he had to protect them. That meant keeping news of Morgan not only from his parents, but from the press.

"Britney," he called as he stalked to her desk. "Not a word of this leaves the building. If anyone in the conference room has questions about who this young woman is or why she came here looking for me today, you direct them to me. Understand?"

"Of course, Mr. Caliborn. You know you can count on me…for anything." Her smile was a just a little too personal for his liking, but he ignored it. In all other aspects, Britney was an efficient and loyal employee.

Her apparent crush on him would wane in time, especially if he kept doing nothing to encourage it.

When he turned around, the EMTs were wheeling Morgan out of his office on the gurney. Her head was elevated. Her face was as white as a sheet.

"Will you be coming with us?" the older EMT asked. "We have room in the ambulance if you want to accompany your wife to the hospital."

Wife? He heard Britney gasp and gritted his teeth. Another rumor to dispel.

"She's not my wife," he bit out as the old bitterness returned. He glanced at his ring finger, recalling the gold band he'd once worn. To him, it had been a symbol of his love and fidelity. It wasn't until Camilla had asked for a divorce that he'd learned neither had been returned.

Whatever the EMT thought of Bryan's blunt denial, he masked with his professionalism. "Maybe you could make some calls for her then. It would be nice for her to have some support in labor and delivery, even if it doesn't look like she'll be in there long."

Bryan nodded and glanced at Morgan. In a gentler tone, he asked, "Who should I contact for you?"

Her eyes remained closed and though she was no longer panting; her voice was a breathy whisper when she replied, "No one."

"What about your family, your parents? Give me their number and I'll have Britney call them. They'll want to know."

Moisture had gathered at the corners of her closed eyes. It leaked down her temples now, blending into her perspiration-dampened hair. Weakness, he thought, once again drawn by her vulnerability. Before he realized what he was doing, he reached out and dried her tears.

Morgan's eyes flicked open at the contact. Green, he realized. A rich and vivid green. Like precious twin emeralds. He pulled back his hand and cleared his throat. "Your parents' number?"

"They're gone."

"Where can we reach them?" he asked.

"You can't." Bryan experienced an unfamiliar ache in his chest when Morgan whispered brokenly, "I have no one. No one at all."

CHAPTER TWO

SEVEN hours later, Bryan paced the length of the waiting room, sipping tepid coffee from a disposable cup while his gaze strayed to the large clock on the wall. It was after six, but Morgan remained in labor. So much for the EMT's assertion that the delivery would be accomplished quickly.

What was he doing at the hospital? He didn't have an exact answer, though duty ranked high on his list of choices. Given Morgan's claims, he felt a certain sense of obligation to follow up on the situation. Of course, that didn't explain why the minute the EMTs had wheeled her into the elevator he'd told Britney to clear his schedule for the afternoon, then he'd hopped in his Lexus, arriving at the hospital in record time. The entire way, he'd recalled Morgan's pinched features and heart-tugging vulnerability.

She needed someone. Bryan was the only someone available.

He finished the remainder of the coffee and tossed the cup into the receptacle. If he'd known the birth was going to take this long, he would have lingered at the office or at the very least brought his laptop with him. Duty, he thought again. As Windy City Industries' Vice President of Operations and soon to be CEO, he had plenty of work to keep him busy.

"Mr. Caliborn?"

He turned expectantly at the sound of the nurse's voice. The woman stood in the doorway, a smile lurking around her lips, which he took as a good sign. He hadn't realized he was holding his breath until she said, "The baby is a boy."

Another Caliborn boy. Was this one the real thing? He pushed aside that question and asked, "Is everything…okay?"

"Fine. The baby is perfectly healthy and a respectable seven pounds, eleven ounces."

He cleared his throat. "And Morgan?"

"She's doing well, all things considered. It was a difficult labor, especially toward the end. For a while the doctor thought he might have to take the baby by caesarean section, but it all worked out."

Because he didn't know what else to say—a rare occurrence for him and not an entirely pleasant one—he offered a curt nod. Then he went to collect his suit coat from the back of one of the chairs. If he hurried, he could catch a couple of members of his management team before they left their offices for the day and maybe go over some of the plans for the company's overseas expansion. But even as he was shoving his arm into a coat sleeve, he was changing his mind. Leaving seemed wrong.

"Excuse me!" he called out to stop the nurse. "I know it's late, but would it be possible for me to see…the baby?"

That's all he wanted, a glimpse at this child who might very well be his brother's legacy and the sole Caliborn heir, as Bryan certainly had no desire to put his heart on the line ever again. For him, marriage and fatherhood were a closed chapter.

"I think that can be arranged." The nurse smiled again before slipping out of the room.

Unfortunately, seeing the baby wasn't as simple as taking a quick peek in a nursery window so Bryan could assuage his curiosity while maintaining his distance. The newborn was with its mother, the nurse told him when, forty-five minutes later, she led him down the corridor to Morgan's room.

"Don't stay too long," she advised. "Morgan really needs her rest."

He raised his hand to knock. Even as his knuckles grazed the door he wondered what he would say. In a business setting he could hold his own, but he'd never been good at casual conversation with virtual strangers. That had been Dill's specialty.

After his knock, he waited for Morgan to call for him to come in. Instead, the door was flung wide by a bleary-eyed man decked out in wrinkled green scrubs and wearing a sappy grin.

"Have a cigar," the man said, thrusting a cellophane-wrapped stogie into Bryan's hand.

Bryan pegged him to be about thirty, and, given his attire, he'd been at the hospital for some time. So much for Morgan's Oscar-worthy claim that she had "no one." Disgusted with himself for falling once again for a woman's lies, he turned to leave.

"Hey, wait!" The man grabbed his arm. "I take it you're here to see the other new mom."

Other new mom? Bryan shifted back and glanced into the room. A brunette, presumably the man's wife, was holding a blanket-wrapped infant in the first bed. Beyond her, a drawn curtain partitioned the room.

"Maybe I should come back," Bryan said. He already felt awkward and now he was going to have an audience.

"Nah. Come in," the man coaxed, tugging on Bryan's arm. Lowering his voice, he added, "I think she could use some company. The nurses said she went through labor alone and I overheard them say she doesn't have a husband or anything." His cheeks turned red. "You're not the baby's—"

"No."

Bryan shook off the man's hand and walked to the far end of the room. When he peeked around the curtain, Morgan's eyes were closed. He used the opportunity to study her in a way that would have been rude if she were awake. Matted blond hair and a blotchy complexion offered proof of the hours she'd spent in labor…all alone. It wasn't guilt he felt. He had no reason for that. But something else nudged him. Admiration? She'd certainly shown a lot of grit when she'd burst into the conference room, demanding to see him. As she slept, her brow wrinkled and what he was experiencing shifted, softened. Once again he felt the odd desire to touch her and offer comfort.

From the other side of the curtain, he heard the man talking softly to his wife. Though Bryan couldn't hear the actual words, the tone was intimate. He recalled seeing a bouquet of fragrant flowers and a congratulatory helium balloon bobbing toward the ceiling. When Bryan's wife had given birth, he'd bought out the hospital's floral shop and had lavished her with gifts, including a diamond pendant necklace and matching earrings.

Morgan's side of the room was stark. No flowers, no balloons. No man whispering soft words of love and encouragement. No expensive gifts from a proud father. Bryan swallowed. He tried to picture Dill in the role of new dad. He tried to picture his brother being supportive and taking responsibility. But he couldn't. Even in a situation like this.

What was it Dillon had said upon learning Bryan was to become a father? After offering his congratulations, he'd added, "Better you than me."

How bitterly ironic.

From the bassinette beside the bed came a faint sound, more like a mewling than a proper cry. Morgan might have been exhausted but her eyes opened immediately at the sound and a smile tugged at her lips.

"I'm here," she crooned softly as she shifted somewhat awkwardly to sit on the edge of the bed. "Mommy's here."

It was then that she noticed Bryan.

He cleared his throat, feeling as if he should apologize for intruding. Instead, he said, "Hello."

"Hi. I didn't realize you were here. I must have dozed off for a minute." She attempted to run her fingers through her hair, only to have them snag in a knotted clump of pale gold. Her cheeks grew pink.

"I won't stay. If I'd known you were asleep…" He shrugged. "I just stopped in to see the baby and… Do you need anything?"

"No." Then she shrugged. "Well, the little suitcase I had packed and ready for the hospital would be nice. I have a hairbrush in it, among other things." Her smile turned wry.

"Where is it? I'll send someone for it."

"At my hotel." When she mentioned the hotel's name Bryan's lips must have twisted in distaste, because she said dryly, "Apparently it's not up to your high standards."

No, it wasn't. The place was little more than a flophouse. He kept that opinion to himself, though the idea of her and the baby—of any young, single woman and helpless infant—staying there bothered him tremendously.

"I'll have Britney bring it by first thing in the morning."

"Thank you." When he backed up a step, she said, "Don't you want a closer look?"

He did. That was why he'd come to her room when good sense had told him to be on his way. Yet he hesitated, oddly more afraid of what he might *not* see than what he might.

The baby was lying on its back. Bryan remembered from Caden's infancy that doctors recommended the position to prevent Sudden Infant Death Syndrome. When Caden had learned to roll over onto his stomach, Bryan had woken up at all hours of the night to check on him, watching his tiny back rise and fall in the low light of the nursery.

"He has hair under the cap," Morgan said.

Bryan spied a few dark brown wisps poking out. Puffy eyes, that deep sea-blue ubiquitous to newborns, were wide open, and though the baby probably was merely trying to focus, he seemed to be regarding Bryan. Finally, one side of his tiny mouth crooked up in a fair imitation of a smile.

Dillon.

Bryan felt as if he'd taken a sledgehammer to the solar plexus. He saw his brother in that little face, not in obvious ways, for the baby's features were too small. But taken in total, they reflected familiarity. Bryan's heart ached again, this pain bittersweet because he couldn't be completely sure he was seeing things as they were or as he wished them to be.

That had been the case once before. And how it had cost him to believe and later find out he'd been deceived.

"What will you name him?" he asked stiffly.

"Brice Dillon Stevens."

He nodded, not surprised that she'd worked his brother's name in somehow. But he wondered if Morgan had chosen to give the child her surname because she was unmarried or because she knew the baby wasn't really a Caliborn. Of course, that hadn't stopped Bryan's ex-wife. She'd tossed the child's paternity in his face when their marriage had splintered apart. She'd stayed with Bryan for all the months it took her to convince the oil tycoon he was the biological father.

Bryan's lips twisted at the memory.

"I suppose you listed my brother as the father on the birth certificate?"

"I did. Is that a problem for you?" Morgan's voice held an edge that belied her otherwise fragile appearance. She looked so young and vulnerable in that hideous hospital-issue gown that snapped closed at the shoulders. Yet her direct gaze and even more direct query hinted at steel.

He ignored her question. "I'll be going. You need

your rest." Before he did, though, he removed a business card from his wallet and handed it to her. "If you require anything else, my private number is on the back."

"Thanks, but I won't be calling. I'm..." She glanced down at the baby, her expression softening in a way that tugged at him. "*We're* going to be just fine."

After Bryan's departure the doubts Morgan had been experiencing for the past several months once again began circling like vultures, picking away at her usual optimism and determination.

We're going to be just fine.

Were they?

What had she been thinking, packing up and crossing state lines without a firm plan in place? That wasn't like her. Of course, nothing about her current situation fell within her personal range of normal. What was she going to do for a job, a place to live?

She hadn't come to Chicago expecting Bryan—er, Dillon—to help out financially, though their child certainly was entitled legally and morally to monetary support. But she had hoped he would offer to pitch in on some expenses, such as the hospital bill. After that, she'd planned to leave up to him how much or how little he wanted to be involved in his son's life both physically and financially. Morgan wasn't a charity case. She had a small settlement from her parents' estate. Unfortunately, the higher cost of living in Chicago was chewing through it more quickly than she'd anticipated.

And now she'd discovered that Dillon not only had lied to her about his identity, but he had been killed in an accident every bit as unforeseeable as the one that had claimed her parents. Gazing at the son they had created together in Aruba, she wasn't quite sure how to feel. Being angry over his betrayal served no purpose. He was gone. She wanted to mourn the man she had known as Bryan, and she did, in the abstract way one mourns any life that is snatched away too soon. And, of course, she mourned him as her baby's father. Morgan had been lucky enough to enjoy a close relationship with both of her parents, but she'd been especially tight with her dad. She'd wanted the same for Brice. God knew her son had precious few relatives as it was, with her parents gone.

As for mourning Dillon as someone significant to her, she didn't. She couldn't. It simply wasn't possible since she hadn't known him well. Indeed, beyond physically, she hadn't known him at all, she realized again, and experienced another wave of shame. She wasn't the sort of woman who engaged in a vacation fling, which perhaps explained why she'd gotten pregnant the one and only time she'd been foolish enough to throw caution to the wind. Or maybe subconsciously she had wanted a child, someone to love and nurture and to help fill up the yawning emptiness she'd felt since her parents' deaths.

Whatever the reason, looking at her newborn son now she had no regrets.

"I love you," she whispered, leaning over to stroke his cheek.

Indeed, Morgan had loved him from the time she'd learned he was growing inside her. But love, even a love this grand and expansive, wasn't capable of obliterating her concerns. And she had plenty of those.

From the other side of the curtain, she could hear the couple discussing who they wanted to act as their newborn's godparents. Judging from the number of names they tossed around, they had a lot of people to choose from. Morgan wasn't completely without relatives, though none lived in the midwest. She did have a small circle of friends back in Wisconsin. A couple of them had urged her to stay in town even after she'd lost her job.

Jen Woolworth, another teacher, one with more seniority who had weathered the latest round of cuts, had been particularly vocal against Morgan leaving the state.

"Hon, you're due soon. You shouldn't be traveling, let alone moving. Stay here with us," she'd urged.

The offer had been tempting. Jen was a dear friend and the two of them often grabbed a cup of coffee after school or hooked up on the weekends for a little shopping and girl talk. But Jen shared a small bungalow-style home with her husband, two rambunctious prepubescent boys and an incontinent miniature poodle they had named Puddles for obvious reasons.

They had enough chaos and no room for another adult, let alone an adult and an infant, even if Jen claimed it would be no big deal to make her boys bunk together in one of the small bedrooms, freeing up the other ten-by-eleven-foot space to serve as Morgan's living quarters and nursery.

The baby fussed. Morgan pulled down her gown, recalling the instructions she'd received in her prenatal classes. Nursing should have been easy. It was the most natural thing in the world, right? But Brice seemed as baffled by it as she was, and he grew fussier by the minute. Finally, he all-out wailed. It was a pitiful sound, heartbreaking. As tears brimmed in Morgan's eyes, she felt demoralized.

We're going to be fine.

The words mocked her now. Had she really said them to Bryan less than half an hour ago? Had she, even for a moment, really believed it herself?

She wanted to join Brice in crying, but she didn't. She'd never been a quitter and she wasn't about to become one now. Her son needed her. He was depending on her. She couldn't let him down. The luxury of tears would have to wait.

"Let's try this again," she murmured resolutely.

He finally latched on after a couple more false starts.

The flowers—a huge vase full of festive daisies,

lilies and delicate irises—arrived as Morgan was putting Brice back in the bassinet. She couldn't imagine who would have sent her such an expensive bouquet. No one back in Wisconsin knew Morgan had given birth and she didn't know anyone in Chicago. Well, no one except for... No way.

She plucked the little white envelope from its holder among the blooms and tore it open. Sure enough, written in slashing bold cursive under the card's pre-printed congratulatory message was the name *Bryan Caliborn*.

The *real* Bryan Caliborn.

She blinked. Who would have guessed that hard, brooding man could be so thoughtful? An hour later, when a couple of orderlies came to move her and the baby to a private room down the hall, Morgan added the word *accommodating* to his attributes. This room was far more spacious and included amenities such as a plush rocking chair, cable television, a padded window seat and framed reproductions of museum-quality art on the walls.

Just about the time Morgan was beginning to think she'd completely misjudged him, Bryan ruined it with his edict.

That's what the typewritten missive amounted to. It was delivered the morning she was to be released from the hospital by the same snooty receptionist who'd brought Morgan's suitcase by the day before: Britney. The young woman arrived just as Morgan finished dressing in a shapeless, oversize dress. Of course, Britney looked slender and runway chic in a fitted jacket, flirty skirt and peep-toe high heels.

"This is for you." Britney set a large shopping bag on the bed and handed Morgan a note. It was from his highness.

Though Morgan was curious about the contents of the bag, she was even more so about the note.

Morgan,
I have sent a car to deliver you and the baby to new accommodations that you may use for the rest of your stay in Chicago. Your bill at the hotel has been settled in full and I've taken the liberty of having your belongings collected and moved.

I have asked Britney to accompany you. I will be in contact later this evening to ensure you have everything you need.

Bryan

Relief came first. This was the answer to her prayers. Just the thought of taking Brice to that dingy hotel room that reeked of stale cigarette smoke made her nauseated. And housekeeping and laundry services were included. What new mother wouldn't appreciate help with those time-consuming chores? But Bryan's motive puzzled her. Was he doing this because he believed her or was he merely interested in keeping a closer eye on her? She read the note again, but still was unable to decipher any clues. This time, however, relief wasn't all she felt. It chafed her pride that he'd made the arrangements and moved her things without at least running his plan by her first. She didn't like being told what to do.

Nor what to wear, she added, when Britney scooted the bag closer and said, "Mr. Caliborn told me to pick up an outfit suitable for your trip home from the hospital."

"I have clothes," Morgan objected.

Britney eyed her dubiously before going on. "Yes, well, I brought a couple of selections for you to choose from. I had to guess your size, but I went with loose-fitting styles," she added, her gaze straying to Morgan's midsection.

Morgan knew she still looked pregnant. Not the ready-to-pop balloon she'd appeared to be at her first encounter with the svelte Britney, but a good four or five months gone.

"I have clothes," she said a second time. The words came out forcefully, causing the baby to rouse from his slumber.

"Mr. Caliborn felt you would be more comfortable in fresh things," Britney clarified.

"You can tell Mr. Caliborn—" Morgan began, fully intending to decline the offer, but that was as far as she got before Britney pulled a subtly printed dress from the bag. Then Morgan's only concern was, "God, I hope that fits."

Britney's brows arched. "I can tell Mr. Caliborn what?"

"That I said thank you. And that I will reimburse him."

It did fit. Morgan had to hand it to Britney. The woman not only had a good eye for fashion, she had a good eye for what would look best on Morgan's post-pregnancy body. While nothing could completely camouflage her tummy, the dress Britney had picked certainly minimized it, while accentuating a couple of assets that also had been enhanced by pregnancy. She just hoped Brice wouldn't need to nurse between now and the time they reached wherever it was they were going, because the dress, which zipped in the back, wasn't made for that function.

"Much better," Britney said when she saw Morgan.

Her tone bordered on astonished, but it was hard for Morgan to be offended when she agreed.

"Thank you."

With a curt nod, Britney glanced at her watch. "I've called for an orderly to bring a wheelchair. You've signed your discharge papers, right?"

"I did that before you arrived."

She nodded again and pulled out her cell phone. "Noah, it's Britney. Have the car waiting at the main entrance in fifteen minutes."

Morgan might have felt a bit like Cinderella then,

except Britney was hardly fairy-godmother material and, of course, she had no Prince Charming.

Then Britney said into the phone, "If you see any photographers, call me back immediately and we'll go to plan B."

"Photographers?" Morgan asked as soon as the other woman hung up.

"Paparazzi. Every effort has been made to keep news of you and your son under wraps, but it pays to be cautious."

"I'm afraid I still don't understand."

Britney huffed out a breath. "The Caliborns are a big deal in this city. They're in the headlines regularly for business and philanthropic reasons, but scandals always sell more papers than straight news."

Great. Morgan was a scandal, her son's birth fodder for the tabloids. No wonder Bryan had been eager to find her "alternative accommodations."

CHAPTER THREE

MORGAN stepped into the apartment foyer behind Britney and gasped. She certainly hadn't expected her new place to be a penthouse that offered views of Lake Michigan and the famous Navy Pier from windows that ran the length of the exterior wall.

In the large living room the color scheme was heavy on beige and other neutrals with nary a punch of color. The furniture was tasteful and obviously top quality, and included a baby grand piano that had Morgan's fingertips tingling to play just looking at it, but the place didn't look lived-in. Indeed, every last inch of it seemed as cold as the foyer's Italian marble floor.

"Who owns this place?" Morgan asked. She swore the question echoed.

"Mr. Caliborn. It's his home," Britney replied with a roll of her eyes.

"He lives here?" That came as a surprise. He had such an imposing personality she'd expected to see it stamped on his belongings.

"Since his divorce three years ago." The secretary arched a brow then and asked sarcastically, "What? It's not up to *your* standards?"

"It's not that. It just seems a little…impersonal." Yes, that was the word. It looked more like a showroom in a high-end furniture store than a home. "There aren't even any photographs."

"Mr. Caliborn isn't the sentimental sort."

Morgan wasn't sure she agreed. He kept a picture of Dillon in his office. And she also recalled seeing one of an older couple, most likely his parents. And then there were the flowers he'd sent to her hospital room. She said as much to Britney.

"Don't be so naive, Miss Stevens. Appearances are important to someone in his position. Precautions have been taken just in case the press ever gets wind of you and your…situation. Hence the flowers." Her gaze lowered. "And the new frock he had me select in case some industrious photographer managed to snap a shot of you leaving the hospital. Think of it as damage control."

Damage control? Morgan felt as if she'd been doused in ice water, yet for all that she was steaming mad. Before she could muster a response, though, Britney was moving past her, high heels clicking purposefully on the marble floor before she disappeared through an arched doorway off the living room. Morgan was left with little choice but to trail behind her. After passing through the formal dining room, Morgan caught up with Britney in the kitchen.

"The pantry is fully stocked and so is the refrigerator." The young woman opened the stainless-steel behemoth's double doors, revealing shelves lined with staples including milk, juice, cheese, eggs and butter. The crispers were bursting with a mouthwatering assortment of fresh fruits and vegetables. "Mr. Caliborn said to help yourself and to make a list of anything else you need. He has a housekeeper who comes in twice a week to do the cleaning and laundry. Hilda also takes care of buying his groceries."

So he'd mentioned in his note. But that brought up a most pertinent question. "Where will Mr. Caliborn be staying?"

"His parents are abroad for the summer. He's moved to their residence in Lake Forest for the time being." Britney cast Morgan a quelling look. "It means he'll have a longer commute to work, but apparently he felt you would be more comfortable here than in a hotel."

Some of Morgan's anger dissipated. She *would* be more comfortable here. That went without saying, but Morgan didn't want to displace Bryan from his home and disrupt his routine. She would call him after Britney left. Maybe they could come up with a different solution.

"Besides, the doorman here is vigilant in guarding Mr. Caliborn's privacy, and as such he'll be sure to keep any reporters from slipping up to see you."

Ah, yes. Damage control.

Brice stirred in her arms then. She lifted him to her shoulder and pulled off the little cap he was wearing. Dropping a kiss on his crown, she murmured, "Hey, sleepyhead, are you finally waking up?"

Britney's gaze shifted to the baby. She was a career woman, emphasis on *career*, but surely she wasn't immune to the allure of a newborn. Rather than softening, however, her expression hardened. Apparently, she was.

Still, Morgan asked, "Would you like to have children someday?"

Britney wrinkled her nose. "God, no! Though I suppose *accidentally* getting pregnant can wind up being the ticket to the good life."

Morgan felt sucker punched. "What do you mean by that?"

The other woman snorted. "Take a look around and you'll figure it out."

"You think I'm after money?"

"Yes," Britney said baldly. "And I doubt I'm the only one to reach that conclusion. I suggest you don't get too comfortable with the Caliborn lifestyle. Bryan's noble sense of obligation aside, ultimately, you're not his type."

Two things occurred to Morgan then. First, Britney didn't know that the baby was Dillon's, and second, the young woman had a serious crush on her boss.

Well, Morgan wasn't going to clarify the situation

if Bryan hadn't. Though she longed to assure Britney the brooding businessman wasn't her type either, she kept her mouth closed.

"The bedrooms are this way." Britney click-clacked out of the kitchen, once again leaving Morgan to follow in her wake. "The one at the end of the hall is Mr. Caliborn's. You'll be using the guest suite."

Britney swung open the first door they came to, revealing a large and neatly furnished room. The queen-size bed was outfitted in a taupe duvet. The walls were a couple of shades darker in the same color. A crib, changing table and glider-rocker were set up against the far wall. The pastel-blue bumper pads and comforter provided the only color.

Before Morgan could ask about the nursery furniture, Britney said, "Mr. Caliborn ordered furnishings for the baby. They're top-of-the-line, of course."

"But I have a crib and changing table." They'd belonged to her friend Jen, who had given them to Morgan as a shower gift. For the time being they were in storage with the rest of her belongings.

Britney shrugged. "Now you have two. You'll find diapers, wipes and all that sort of thing in the drawers of the changing table."

"He's thought of everything," Morgan murmured, finding it impossible not to be touched by his efforts, no matter what their motivation.

"Yes. He always does." Britney glanced at her watch, clearly eager to be gone. "My cell phone number is programmed into the telephone. You may call me at any time."

"Oh, that's not necessary."

"Mr. Caliborn thinks it is." With that, Britney left.

Mr. Caliborn thinks...

Mr. Caliborn feels...

Mr. Caliborn has decided...

Under other circumstances, Morgan would have screamed. But as irritatingly high-handed as he could be and as independent as she'd always been, the fact was, she needed someone and he was the only someone available. As she laid Brice down in the brand-new crib in a room that smelled of fresh linens she couldn't help but be grateful they were not back in the claustrophobic hotel room breathing tainted air.

As soon as she could manage it, she would find a job and another place to live. In the meantime, she would suck up her pride and do what was best for her son.

The knock on the door surprised her. It was after eight o'clock that night and Morgan was curled up on the living room couch. The television was on, though she wasn't really watching it. She had too much on her mind to follow the sitcom's quick-paced dialogue.

Britney's confidence in the doorman's abilities aside, Morgan checked the peephole before flipping open the dead bolt. A grim-looking Bryan stood in the hallway, arms folded across his broad chest.

"Hello," she said after opening the door.

Dark eyes surveyed her, no doubt taking in the oversize shirt and unflattering sweatpants. "I hope this isn't a bad time. I forgot my shaving kit when I packed up my things earlier."

"Oh. Sure. Come in." She stepped back to allow him entry.

"The baby sleeping?"

"For the time being," she said wryly. If she got lucky, she would have another hour before Brice roused and demanded to be fed.

Bryan nodded. "Britney said she showed you around. I take it everything is to your liking."

"Yes." She laced her fingers together. "She mentioned that you're staying at your parents' home in Lake Forest and that they are out of the country."

"They keep a villa in the south of France. Now that my father is getting closer to retirement, they've been spending large blocks of time there," he said matter-of-factly, as if everyone's folks had a second home on the French Riviera.

She pictured the elder Caliborns, pampered, snobbish and every bit as laconic and dictatorial as their eldest son. Heaven help her. Morgan had wanted Brice to have extended family, loving relatives to help fill in the gaps a single mother couldn't. Now she wasn't so sure she would be doing him any favors.

Still, she said, "I had hoped to meet them and to have them get to know Brice. He is their grandson, after all."

"Perhaps on another visit to Chicago," he suggested with a shrug.

She didn't bother to correct his assumption that she was just visiting. It was fast becoming apparent that moving here had been a huge mistake, even if she still felt strongly that she should live in closer proximity to the only family her child had.

"They don't know about me," she guessed.

"No."

"And you're not planning to tell them."

"Not yet."

No need to ask what he was waiting for. Obviously, he required proof of Brice's parentage. She expected him to request a paternity test then. When he didn't, Morgan decided to change the subject.

"I want to reimburse you for the groceries and, of course, for the amount you've had to spend on damage control."

Dark brows tugged together. "Pardon?"

"The bouquet of flowers, the private room and the new dress purchased for me to wear home from the hospital," she clarified. "Britney mentioned that the baby and I would make excellent tabloid fodder and, as such, appearances had to be maintained."

Bryan scowled, but he didn't deny it. Instead, he said, "No reimbursement is necessary. I wanted you to have those things."

"Well, I insist on paying for my lodgings. When you get right down to it, I'm subletting your apartment." She swallowed, knowing a Chicago penthouse with this incredible view and a rooftop patio far exceeded her limited budget, but she wasn't going to stay here long and pride wouldn't allow her to freeload, especially since Bryan clearly expected her to do just that. "If you'll have a contract drawn up, I'll pay the full rent and utilities for the next month."

"I own it."

Of course he did. "Then, whatever you feel is fair."

"When the month is up, will you be returning to—Cherry Bluff, Wisconsin, isn't it?"

"No, I don't think I'll be going back." Other than her friends, there was nothing for Morgan there. As much as she missed Jen, she could no more freeload off her than she could off Bryan.

"What about your job?"

"I lost it."

"I see." Almost instantly, his dark eyes lit with speculation, suspicion.

Both stung. "I wasn't fired. I was pink-slipped."

"Another word for the same thing, I believe."

"Not from my point of view. I loved my job and I was good at it. The principal hated to see me go, but the school district had to make cuts." She folded her arms. "Perhaps you've noticed that the economy isn't as strong as it once was. Well, in bad times, the arts are the first thing to face the ax."

He appeared surprised. "You're a teacher?"

"A music teacher, yes." She nodded her head in the

direction of the baby grand. Her own upright was sitting in storage. "You have a lovely piano. Do you play?"

"Not really."

"Oh." It seemed a waste for an instrument like that to go unused.

He apparently read her mind. "I assume that you do." When she nodded, he said, "Feel free to use it, although it probably needs a good tuning."

"If it does, I'll pay for it."

He sighed, shook his head. Was that amusement she spied in his gaze or exasperation? "Fine, but I'll hear no more talk about contracts and subletting. That subject is closed."

Morgan didn't argue. When she moved out, she would leave a check to cover her expenses. Bryan Caliborn would discover she could be every bit as stubborn as he was. Still, she had to know, "Are you still worried about appearances just in case I'm found out?"

"Among other things," he answered evasively. The enigmatic response as well as the way he was watching her made her wonder what those other things might be.

"Well, for the record, I do appreciate your kindness, even if I feel funny about taking over your home."

"Don't."

One word uttered resolutely. Another edict. It grated against her already raw pride. "You know, you have a very annoying habit of telling me what to do and, now, what to think."

A pair of dark brows shot up, telling her she wasn't the only one who was annoyed. No doubt he wasn't used to being talked to in such a manner. She waited for a blistering retort. Instead, he bowed mockingly.

"My apologies."

Damn him! He was humoring her. "I'd accept them if I thought they were sincere."

"You're questioning my sincerity?"

In her stocking feet Morgan was a full head shorter than Bryan. Even so, she squared her shoulders and raised her chin. "Yes, I am."

"God, you're so damned—" he was frowning when he finished with "—refreshing."

The description threw her, as did the momentary confusion she'd glimpsed in his eyes. "I don't know what to make of that," she replied honestly.

He snorted out a laugh. "Good. We're even then, because I don't know what to make of you."

And he didn't. Bryan usually could read people easily enough. Morgan, however, remained an enigma despite her blunt talk. Interestingly, the more time he spent with her, the more baffled he became. And the more curious. With that in mind, he said, "I'll just get my shaving kit and be on my way."

When Bryan returned to the living room, she was seated at the piano playing softly in deference to the infant sleeping down the hall. In the room's low light, she looked almost ethereal, though the sound emanating from the piano was anything but heavenly. Even to his untrained ears he could tell it was off-key.

"How bad is it?"

She glanced up. "Abysmal. It's a crime what you've allowed to happen to an instrument of this quality."

He nearly smiled at her damning words. She certainly wasn't one to pull punches. "I'd apologize, but I'm pretty sure you'd only accuse me of being insincere again."

"You're mocking me." She plunked out more of the discordant melody.

"Only a little."

She wasn't amused. "I find that almost as intolerable as the fact that you don't trust me and yet feel the need to clothe and shelter me as if I'm some sort of helpless waif."

"Oh, I wouldn't call you helpless. I'd say you've managed quite nicely up till now."

Her eyes widened at the jab.

"Stop it! Just stop it!" she shouted, looking angry and exhausted enough to make him feel petty. "I don't know what your problem is, but it's *your* problem. Not mine. I'm not after the precious Caliborn fortune."

"If I had a dime for every time a woman has said that—"

She slammed the lid down over the piano keys. "And to think I was starting to feel grateful for all of your help. I'd get Brice and leave right now if my car wasn't still parked across town in your company's lot."

He knew he'd regret it later, but he couldn't stop himself from adding, "And if you had someplace to go. But you don't, Morgan. No place to go and no job. Which is why you came to Chicago."

Her eyes turned bright. Her voice became hoarse. "How is it possible that you and Dillon were brothers? I've asked you for nothing. You're the one who insisted on moving me into your apartment, yet you're so suspicious."

I have good reason to be, he thought, calling on bitter memories to make him immune to her tears. He wouldn't be played for a sucker a second time.

"You're right, Morgan. Dill and I are very different men. You'd do well to remember that." He lowered his voice to a more intimate level and added, "Although I can assure you there are certain things I am every bit as skilled at as you found my brother to be."

She shot to her feet, shaking with justified outrage as she poked a finger in the direction of the door. "Out! Get out of here right now!"

Bryan didn't question her right to order him from his own home. He did as she asked, already hating himself for the cheap shot and not at all sure why he'd taken it.

Bryan sat at his desk staring sightlessly out at the Chicago skyline as he levered a gold fountain pen between his fingers. He was too keyed up to concentrate on work, though he had plenty of it to occupy his attention. His agitation had nothing to do with the fact that Windy City's last quarter's earnings were not what he'd hoped they would be. He was thinking about Morgan.

It had been almost a month since he'd last seen or spoken with her. And though part of him knew he owed her an apology for the unforgivable comment he'd made, he couldn't force himself to do so. In fact, just yesterday, after uncharacteristic foot-dragging, he'd hired a private investigator to probe her past. It was time to find out a little more about Morgan Stevens than what could be gleaned at face value. It wasn't just that he couldn't bring himself to trust her, though that was part of it. He didn't trust himself and this odd desire he had to believe she was exactly what she claimed to be.

Now she'd thrown him for a loop again. She'd called half an hour ago and left a message with Britney that she would be moving out of the penthouse later that day.

That didn't make sense. Nor did the fact that even though Bryan had a meeting with his management team in forty-five minutes, he was pushing himself away from his desk and preparing to stride out of his office. He needed to get to the bottom of this.

When he arrived at the apartment door twenty minutes later, he didn't knock. He let himself in only to stumble over the luggage that was stacked in the foyer. She was packed and ready to go. But she was leaving a bit of herself behind, he noticed. His beige sofa now sported a pair of plump red pillows, and a throw of the same hue was tossed over the chair. Three weeks in his home and she'd infused it with more vibrancy and life than he'd managed in three years. But then, this was just a place for him to lay his head at night. He'd stopped wanting a home the day he'd learned he didn't really have a son.

On the coffee table he spied an envelope with his name on it. He opened it to find a check made out to him. The sum had him shaking his head. She was either a clever actress or had too much pride for her own good. Though it wasn't large by his standards, it was probably far more than Morgan could afford. With an oath, he tore it in half before stuffing it into his pocket.

From down the hallway came an infant's shrill cries. He followed the sound, stopping outside the open door to the guest suite. Morgan was at the changing table with her back to him. She'd lost weight. That much was obvious despite the oversize clothing she wore. Her hair was pulled into a ponytail that made her look deceptively young. She was talking in soothing tones as she put a fresh diaper on the screaming baby.

"Hey, hey. Come on now, Brice. It's not as bad as all that," she said. "We're going to be fine, you and me. We're a team, remember?"

The baby quieted, almost as if he understood. More likely, though, the reason was because his bottom was dry and he was being lifted into the security of his mother's arms. The baby eyed Bryan over her shoulder. Brice had more hair now. It stood up on end at the crown. And he'd acquired another chin. He and Morgan made quite a picture, the perfect snapshot of everything Bryan had held dear.

Before learning it was a lie.

He cleared his throat. Upon hearing the sound, she whirled around. The warmth that had been in her tone when she'd spoken to Brice was absent when she told Bryan, "I'll be out in less than an hour."

"It's hardly necessary for you to leave."

"I think it is," she replied.

"Where are you going?"

"Does it matter?"

It did—for reasons he couldn't explain to himself, much less to her. He should be happy she was going. Glad to be rid of her. Except…

"Look, Morgan, I want to apologize. What I said to you the last time I was here, it was…crude."

"Insufferably so," she agreed with a nod. "But your appalling lack of manners is not the reason I'm leaving. My plan was to stay here until I found employment, and I have."

This came as a surprise. "You've been looking for a job?"

She rolled her eyes. "I know you'll find this hard to believe, but I've always been self-sufficient and I prefer to remain that way."

"What kind of job?"

"I'll be turning tricks in the blue-light district. I hear I can set my own hours," she deadpanned. "A teaching job, of course."

"Were you called back to the school in Wisconsin then?" Oddly, his stomach clenched as he awaited her reply.

"No. I'll be staying in Chicago, at least for the time being."

He ignored the relief that had him wanting to sigh, perhaps because a new worry surfaced.

"Which school will you teach at?" Some of the public ones could be kind of rough. Though he admired Morgan's spunk, it made his blood run cold to think of her going toe-to-toe with some young gang recruit.

"Actually, I won't be in a school." She lifted her chin. "I've been hired by a south-side community center to give lessons as part of an after-school program that's being funded through a Tempest Herriman Foundation grant."

His eyes narrowed. "That doesn't sound long-term or, for that matter, very lucrative. Is it even going to cover your expenses?"

"I don't see how that's your concern," Morgan snapped irritably.

He shrugged. And though it was far from the truth, he reminded her, "Appearances."

"Appearances!" she spat. "If I wasn't holding

Brice right now, I'd describe to you, in minute detail, what you can do with your appearances."

"Please, don't hold back. He's too young to grasp words. It's tone that babies this age understand."

"Now you're an expert on children?" She expelled a breath, but then continued in a voice suited to a nursery rhyme, "Maybe it's a good thing you don't believe he's a Caliborn. I don't want my son raised around someone as superficial and self-important as you are."

Bryan ignored the insults. He was a firm believer in quid pro quo, so he figured she was entitled to fling them. Besides, she looked absolutely lovely, with her color high and those emerald eyes flashing in dangerous fashion as she put him in his place.

Stepping fully into the room, he commented conversationally, "I never would have taken you to be the sort to cut off your nose to spite your face."

"That's not what I'm doing."

"No? You're going to move your son, who's barely a month old, out of the safety and comfort of my penthouse and take a job on the city's south side making peanuts. What about health insurance?"

Morgan said nothing, but she swallowed hard and he had his answer.

"No benefits," he scoffed with a shake of his head and then drew closer. "And where are you going to live, Morgan? In some fleabag apartment on a par with that hotel where you were staying before the baby was born? Be reasonable."

"Being reasonable hasn't gotten me very far with you." She abandoned the sweet tone. "You've done your level best to make me feel unwelcome, yet now you have the audacity to act amazed that I'm leaving. What do you want from me? Just what do you want?"

She'd shouted the last question and now the baby began to wail. She looked on the verge of losing it herself. That had him panicked, both because he knew Morgan's tears were the real thing and because the bullying he typically reserved for the boardroom was the primary cause.

"God, don't cry."

"Don't tell me what to do," she countered on a sob. "I've had it up to here with your edicts. I've had it up to here with you. Go away, Bryan. Just go away."

He ignored the directive. In fact, he stepped closer. Close enough that he could smell the scent of baby powder. Close enough that he could have run his knuckles along the underside of her quivering jaw if he'd wanted to. And, God help him, he wanted to.

"Stay, Morgan. Not for the sake of appearances."

"Why then?"

Because I want you to, he thought. I want to get to know you, figure you out. How nonsensical was that? So, he said, "Because it's the right thing to do for Brice."

The fight went out of her. Her shoulders slumped

and she lowered her chin. Bryan leaned closer until her forehead was resting on his chest. Brice quieted, too, cocooned between them.

After a moment she sighed. "That's so low."

He laughed without humor. "Yes, but we've already established that I'm a bastard."

She lifted her head and, without heat, admonished, "Don't swear in front of the baby."

"Sorry."

"I'll stay, but only until your parents return. They still don't know about Brice, do they?"

"No."

She shook her head. "Why am I not surprised?"

"They've been through so much pain." The loss of what they believed to be their first grandchild as well as the death of their younger son.

"And you're sure I'll cause them more," she said sadly.

He stepped back, turned away. "I have reasons for being the way that I am," he said slowly. It was as much of an explanation as he could bring himself to give her and more of one than he would have offered anyone else.

"Well, unless you want to live a very lonely life, you're going to have to get over those reasons."

CHAPTER FOUR

BRYAN sat across from his date in the upscale French restaurant, sipping a nice pinot noir and pretending to listen to his date while he replayed the conversation he'd had with Morgan that day three weeks earlier in his apartment.

...unless you want to live a very lonely life, you're going to have to get over those reasons.

She was wrong. He wasn't lonely, he assured himself. Far from it.

"Don't you agree?" Courtney said now.

"Of course," he replied, nodding even though he hadn't a clue as to what had just been said.

All he knew was he had *exactly* what he wanted. Courtney Banks was worldly and wealthy and, okay, every bit as cynical as he was when it came to members of the opposite sex thanks to her own ugly divorce. But that made her perfect. She had absolutely no interest in settling down a second time and absolutely no need for his money. Since not long after his divorce, she and Bryan had gotten together whenever either of them felt the need for a no-strings-attached evening of fun. That's why he'd called her tonight, but now the only woman on his mind was an outspoken blonde about whom he had no business thinking, much less dreaming as he had last night.

"You're not listening," Courtney accused, laughing.

Blinking, he said, "Excuse me?"

"You just agreed with me that the White Sox are a far superior ball club to the Cubs, and we both know what a rabid Cubs fan you are."

He winced. "Sorry. I guess I have a lot on my mind tonight."

"If I didn't know better, Bryan, I might find myself jealous."

He reached across the table and squeezed her hand. "You're not the jealous type." Not to mention the fact that nothing about their relationship warranted the emotion. They weren't exclusive. They weren't committed. Neither one of them had spouted words of love, because, quite frankly, neither one of them wanted to fall in love again.

Courtney's shoulders lifted in a delicate shrug. "I may not be jealous, but I am greedy. When I'm with a man, I want to be the only thing on his mind."

"That's no less than you deserve," he agreed. And more than he was capable of this night. "Would you hate me if we ended the evening early? I'm not fit company."

"*Hate* is the wrong word. I'll be disappointed, though, and so will you. I had plans to model new lingerie." She sent him a smile that in the past had sent blood pumping through his veins. He waited, hoping it would this time, but it had no effect on him.

"It's my loss," he said graciously.

"Yes, it is, and I'm glad you understand that." Her brows rose meaningfully.

He paid the bill and they left the restaurant. After he dropped Courtney off at her Lake Shore Drive address, he should have continued north on 41 to Lake Forest, but Bryan found himself driving south instead. Back into the city. To his penthouse and Morgan.

It was past nine when he arrived at the door. He hesitated before knocking, oddly nervous. Maybe he should have called first. Hell, he shouldn't even be here. What was he thinking? Even as he asked himself this, he raised his fist and rapped three times. If she didn't answer right away, he would go.

The door swung open a moment later. Morgan was dressed in jeans and a T-shirt that she'd left untucked. Her feet were bare, her toenails painted a sheer pink. She'd pulled her hair into a messy ponytail that was a nod to necessity rather than style. Other than a faint sheen of gloss on her lips, her face was free of makeup.

Bryan wasn't sure what to make of the intense

awareness that had him sucking in a breath. He only knew it didn't bode well for him.

"This is a surprise," she said.

"It's late and I should have called first," he replied, echoing his earlier thoughts. "Sorry."

"That's okay. I'm up."

"I wanted to pick up a few shirts." Which was a complete lie. "Mind if I come in?"

"It's your home." She shrugged and stepped back. "Don't tell me you're just getting off work."

"No. I was…out with a friend for dinner."

Her brows rose at the same time her lips twitched. "Is that code for a date?"

He didn't know whether to laugh or sigh. She saved him the trouble of having to decide by asking, "Can I take your coat or won't you be staying that long?"

He shrugged out of his suit jacket by way of an answer and handed it to her. While she hung it in the foyer closet, he reached up to loosen his tie. He was unbuttoning his collar when she turned. She averted her gaze.

"Am I making you uncomfortable?"

"No. Well, not as long as you stop with that button," she said bluntly.

"That was the plan." He laughed self-consciously, and then changed the subject. "How's Brice doing?"

"Oh, he's great." Her expression softened at the mention of her son. "And growing like a weed. He's packed on another two pounds since our last visit to the pediatrician."

"And it looks like you've lost that and then some." His gaze meandered down and when interest sparked he told himself it was a natural reaction that had nothing to do with Morgan personally.

"I've been trying," she admitted. "I have an entire wardrobe I'm eager to fit back into. You may not believe this, but I do own more than baggy shirts." She tugged at the hem of the one she was wearing.

"You look good even in that."

Her cheeks turned pink. "Can I get you a drink or something?"

"I wouldn't mind a Scotch and soda." When her brow wrinkled, he said, "I'll get it myself."

He walked to the wet bar tucked to one side of the room. Though he wasn't much of a drinker, he kept it fully stocked. After filling a glass with ice and soda, he added a shot of Scotch. When he turned, she was seated on the sofa, feet tucked up beneath her, some papers spread out in front of her. Sheet music.

"What are you doing?" he asked, coming around the side of the couch.

"Trying to come up with song selections for a couple of my more advanced students."

That had him puzzled. "You're working?"

She glanced up. "At the south-side community center I told you about."

"But I thought you agreed not to take the job?"

"No. I agreed not to leave your apartment until your parents arrive home from Europe."

"But what about the baby?" he asked.

"Brice comes with me. It's only a few hours in the afternoon." She smiled. "He tends to sleep through most of it, even my beginner students. But when he doesn't there's no shortage of people eager to hold him. The kids adore him and so does the staff."

Her explanation baffled him even more. "I don't understand why you're doing this. You shouldn't be working right now, Morgan."

"I need to. My bank account isn't as flush as yours, which is why I'm still sending out résumés looking for a full-time teaching position."

"But you just had a baby."

"Even women whose jobs afford them a paid maternity leave would be back to work by now," she pointed out. As the soon-to-be head of a Fortune 500 company, he knew this, of course. "If I were still at a school, of course, I would have the rest of the summer off. But working at the community center isn't so bad. Actually, I find it quite satisfying, even if the instruments could all use an overhaul."

"No baby grands?"

"Nope. Not a one. The grant money the center receives only goes so far. I moved my upright piano from storage to the center just so I would have something decent to play."

"Why go to the trouble?"

"The kids." Her eyes lit up. "I've never had such interested students. Some of them come from really disadvantaged backgrounds and dysfunctional homes and yet they are every bit as enthusiastic about music as I am. That makes them a joy to teach."

"You really mean that."

She frowned. "Of course, I do." The baby began to cry then. She rose with a sigh. "Excuse me."

While Bryan waited for her to return, he sipped his drink and paced around the penthouse, noting the new touches she'd added. A floral arrangement sat on a richly patterned runner in the center of his dining-room table. He'd never eaten dinner in that room, he realized. When he ate in the penthouse, he'd either sat on a stool at the kitchen island or taken his meal into the living room to watch television. He missed family meals, the kind where everyone gathered around the table and actually communicated. He hadn't had that with his wife. After Caden was born, Bryan had thought maybe things would change. Of course, they *had* changed, just not how he'd expected or hoped.

Back in the living room he noticed a trio of fat scented candles on the fireplace mantel. They weren't just for show. Their wicks had been burned. He imagined how the room would look, awash in only their light. Cozy. Intimate. Romantic.

He took another sip of his beverage and moved on. A framed picture on one of the side tables caught his eye. In it Morgan was flanked by an older couple. She was wearing a black robe and mortarboard, clutching a diploma and grinning madly. He picked it up to study it. She looked ready to conquer the world.

"That was taken at my college graduation."

He turned to find her standing behind him. He hadn't heard her return. Instead of feeling awkward about snooping—could one snoop in his own home?—he was curious.

"Are these your parents?"

"Yes." She took the photograph from his hands, swallowing hard as she stroked their faces with the pads of her thumbs. In contrast to the radiant woman in the picture, the one standing in front of him was sad. "They were so proud of me."

"You mentioned that they were gone."

"Yes, both of them."

"Sorry," he said as she put the photo back in its place. Then he motioned with his hands. "You've added a few things to the room since you've been here, I see."

"I hope you don't mind."

"No. I like what you've done. It looks nice." In fact, it looked inviting, which was why even though he should be going, he found himself in no hurry to leave.

"Why haven't you?" At his baffled expression, she added, "Made this space more personal."

He shrugged. "I don't know. I guess I just don't see the need."

"But you've lived here for three years. Ever since

your divorce." At his raised eyebrows she said, "Britney told me that."

He walked over to the couch and took a seat. He'd have to have a talk with his secretary. "What else did Britney say?"

"Not nearly enough to satisfy my curiosity," she admitted baldly. "Why don't you tell me the rest?"

"There's really not much to tell. I was married for a few years, but in the end it didn't work out, so we went our separate ways." He shrugged, even though it was hardly that simple.

Morgan settled onto the cushion next to his. "Is she one of those reasons you spoke of before? For being the way you are today?"

He sipped his drink before answering. "Yes." A single word, yet he felt as if he had just bared his soul.

"She hurt you," Morgan said. It wasn't a question, but a statement. "I'm sorry."

Bryan wasn't comfortable with her sympathy, especially because, when one got right down to it, his brother had done quite a number on her as well.

"I've gotten over it."

"Have you?"

Where a moment ago he'd been in no hurry to leave, now he stood. "I should be going. You…you're probably tired."

"Too close for comfort?" she asked. "You only need say as much. You don't need to run off."

"I'm not running." He forced himself to sit

again. Then, feeling ridiculous, admitted, "Okay, I'm not comfortable talking about it. It wasn't a pleasant experience."

"I don't imagine the end of a marriage ever is, regardless of the circumstances involved. Are you sure you don't want to talk about it? I've been told I'm a good listener."

God help him, he almost did. He'd kept it bottled up inside for so long. But he shook his head, unnerved by this sudden desire to share. "No. Thanks."

"Okay, but the offer stands."

Out of the blue, he heard himself ask, "Did you love him?"

She glanced away, her cheeks turning pink even before she admitted, "I only knew him for a week."

Seven days and as many nights. Bryan's stomach clenched.

"Some people fall in love at first sight, or so they claim."

Her gaze reeled back to his. "Is that what you want to hear?" she asked. "That I saw Dillon across a crowded room and—*bam!*—lost my heart to him?"

"Yes. No!" His hands were fisted at his sides. He loosened them, shrugged. "It doesn't matter. Your relationship with Dill is no more my business than the relationship I had with him is yours."

That was the end of it, he thought. Discussion over. But Morgan said quietly, "Just for the record, I'm not…promiscuous."

Her face flamed red, giving her words even greater credence. Guilt nipped at Bryan as his thoughts turned to the probe he'd initiated into her background a few weeks back. Call it off, his gut told him. Get the facts, his head insisted. It wasn't like him to be so damned indecisive.

He shoved a hand through his hair. "Dill could be irresistible," he allowed.

"Yes, well, I'm usually pretty good at resisting, but I was at a low point in my life. A really low point. It's not an excuse for my behavior," she said quickly. "But it is a fact."

"Do you regret it?"

"How can I? I have Brice," she reminded him. "If I regret my actions, I'd have to regret him. And I don't. He's the best thing that's ever happened to me."

He swallowed, nodded. "I'll go now."

"Your clothes."

"I'll get them another time." As he started toward the door, he admitted, "I shouldn't have come in the first place."

"Why did you, then?" Morgan asked.

In the foyer, she retrieved his coat from the closet and handed it to him. Their fingers brushed, the contact fleeting. It sent shock waves through him just the same. Need built, both dangerous and exciting. Why had he come? Suddenly, he knew.

"I shouldn't have," he said again.

But she was just as persistent. "Why?"

"You don't want to know, Morgan."

"Yes, I do."

"Because of this."

He dropped the coat to the floor and cupped her face in his hands, drawing her to him even as he leaned down. His mouth was impatient, greedy. Hers was pliant, giving. So much so that even though the kiss began as an almost furious assault, it was an apology, an entreaty by the time it ended.

They stared at one another, their labored breaths seeming to echo off the marble floor. And because all he wanted to do was reach for her again, he scooped up his jacket, yanked open the door and left.

Morgan couldn't believe he'd kissed her. For that matter, she couldn't believe the way she'd responded. How could she expect him to accept her claim that she wasn't promiscuous when she'd welcomed—indeed, reveled in—every second of their intimate contact?

But while she stood in the empty foyer and waited for shame to wash over her, it never came. And when she lay in bed later that night, still too keyed up to sleep, the only regrets she felt were that Bryan still didn't completely trust her and that she hadn't experienced this kind of white-hot attraction for her baby's father.

CHAPTER FIVE

THE following week passed without a word from Bryan, and then a second one did, too. She wasn't sure whether to be grateful or disappointed. She still grew warm every time she recalled that kiss, and, God knew, she thought of it often enough.

Did he?

She managed to push that question to the recesses of her mind only to have it spring front and center again when he called her on Friday evening.

"Morgan, it's Bryan," he said unnecessarily. It wasn't as if she had many callers, let alone a male one with such a deep and sexy voice. "Are you free tonight?"

The question startled her, so it took her a moment to answer. In fact, she didn't answer. She asked a question of her own. "Why?"

"There's something we need to discuss."

That sounded ominous and made her only a little more nervous than the thought that he might be asking her out. Maybe her reaction to his kiss had finally prompted Bryan to seek a paternity test.

"Have you eaten yet?"

She glanced at her watch. It was nearly seven o'clock. "Two hours ago. If a bowl of cereal can be considered dinner."

There was a slight pause. Then he said, "I could pick up Chinese food on my way over. There's a great place just around the corner from the penthouse. Interested?"

Though she wasn't quite sure what to make of his offer, she said, "I like chicken and peapods, skip the egg roll and fortune cookie, and make sure to get white rice instead of fried."

She thought she heard him chuckle. "I'll see you in half an hour."

Unfortunately, he was as good as his word, arriving on her doorstep just as she finished feeding Brice, who'd sent up a squeal almost as soon as she'd hung up the phone. That meant she hadn't had a chance to do anything with her appearance. She was still wearing the loose-fitting tank-style dress she'd put on to go to the center. Her hair was pulled back in a clip at her nape, although several curls had made their escape and whatever makeup she'd put on that morning was long gone.

The baby was in her arms when Morgan opened the penthouse door. Bryan's gaze drifted to the infant, the tight line of his mouth softening. Was it because he saw his brother there? More and more, Morgan thought she caught glimpses of Dillon or some trait that surely was more Caliborn than Stevens.

Or was Bryan recalling that the last time the two of them had stood in the foyer, they'd kissed? His gaze was on her now—specifically, on her mouth. She waited, certain he was going to bring it up. But he didn't and she didn't know whether to be relieved or disappointed. Did that mean she was the only one who'd spent time obsessing over that earth-shattering lip-lock?

He ended the potent silence by holding up a brown paper bag. "Shall we eat in the kitchen?"

She nodded. "No sense breaking out the fine china for takeout."

Morgan retrieved Brice's bouncy seat from the bedroom and joined Bryan as he set the granite-topped island with two plates and cutlery.

Glancing up, he asked, "Can I get you something to drink?"

"That's all right. I'll get it." She set Brice in the seat and poured herself a glass of milk. "Do you want some or would you prefer—what was it?—Scotch and soda?"

"I'll just have water tonight."

She waited till they were seated to say, "So, what did you need to discuss?"

"A couple of things, actually." He selected one of the cartons and forked out some white rice. "First,

Windy City Industries would like to make a donation to the community center."

She blinked in surprise. "That's very generous. They'll be thrilled with any amount, I'm sure."

"Not money. Well, not directly anyway. Your supervisor will be notified, but basically you'll need to make up a list of the instruments you require for the after-school program you teach. We'll see to it that whatever is on the list is purchased and gets delivered as soon as possible."

"Bryan, I don't know what to say. Other than thank you, of course." She beamed at him. "You have no idea what a tremendous gift you're giving these children."

He brushed her gratitude aside. "It's not me, Morgan. The donation is coming from Windy City Industries. We believe in being community-minded and supporting worthwhile causes. I thought an after-school music program for at-risk kids was just such a cause and passed the recommendation to the appropriate people at the company to make the final judgment. They notified me today of the gift."

"Well, pass my thanks along to Windy City then." She smiled at him. He might try to distance himself from the donation, but they both knew he was responsible.

"And now to the other matter." He cleared his throat. "Unless their plans change, my parents will be returning from France the Friday after next."

"Oh." She gulped and a peapod nearly stuck in her throat. The hour of reckoning would soon be at hand.

"I'll make the appropriate arrangements once they arrive and settle in," he said.

Then Morgan's eyes widened as another thought crossed her mind. "You'll need your apartment back."

That had been the deal they'd struck when she'd agreed to stay. She'd been paying him for the privilege, not that he'd cashed the checks she'd made out to his name.

"There's no hurry," he said.

Morgan set her fork aside. She'd been looking for a new place, and had a couple of leads on efficiencies that were in her price range. It was time to get off the fence and put down a deposit.

"When do you need me to leave?"

"Whenever," he answered vaguely.

"Don't tell me you're enjoying staying in your boyhood room?" she teased.

He merely shrugged. "Actually, my parents have a guest house at the back of their property. Dill lived there on and off. I've been using it while you've been here. It's quite comfortable, especially since there's a pool and hot tub practically outside my door."

"Well, as long as you're sure I'm not putting you out." She picked up her fork again and pushed a piece of chicken around on her plate. "Britney mentioned the commute when Brice and I first moved in here."

He frowned. "Britney talks too much."

"I probably shouldn't say this, but she's got a serious case of the hots for you."

It might have been a trick of the lighting, but she thought he blushed. Regardless, he didn't look comfortable. "Beyond the fact that I'm her boss, and not in the market for either a sexual-harassment suit or a serious relationship, she's not my type."

"She said the same thing about me." Morgan wanted to kick herself as soon as the words left her lips; instead she plowed ahead. "What is your type?"

His gaze was steady, piercing, actually. It probably scared most people witless, but Morgan didn't blink. He was good at pushing people away, but she was even better at hauling them close. She came by the talent naturally. Her father had been a pro at getting her to open up and share her feelings.

After a moment, he picked up his napkin. Folding it into smaller squares, he said quietly, "I used to know what I wanted. Now I'm not so sure."

She knew exactly what he meant. Tall, dark and brooding had never been her ideal. Although lately…

He pulled her from her musing by saying, "About the penthouse. Don't worry about packing up for the time being. You're not putting me out. As for my parents, I'll get together with them as soon as they've recovered from jet lag, explain everything and set up a meeting."

"I'd prefer that you set up a visit," she corrected. "A meeting implies business. Business, to me anyway, implies money. I want it to be clear that's not what I'm after. I want a family for my son. Specifically, grandparents, since both of my folks are gone." She tilted her head to one side. "I also wouldn't mind an uncle, since as an only child I can't provide Brice with one of those. Do you understand?"

God help him, he was starting to. More of the old distrust melted away. Morgan was so real and pragmatic. Her feet were planted firmly on the ground. She took on the yoke of responsibility without complaint. He couldn't help wondering, he couldn't help asking, "What in the hell did you see in my brother?"

Her eyes widened. "I…I…"

"Don't answer that question!" Bryan stood so quickly he knocked over his water. The glass cracked and water sloshed across the granite before spilling over the edge and forming a puddle at his feet.

Morgan was up in an instant, grabbing a dish towel to mop up the mess on the island. When she bent down, he knelt beside her, his hand over hers on the towel. "Don't answer the question," he said again, this time more softly. "It came out wrong. For all of my brother's faults, he was a good man."

And Bryan missed him. God, how he missed him.

"I believe that, too." They both stood. "And, since I would love to hear you talk about him more and, you know, share the kinds of things I can pass along to Brice, I'm relieved you feel that way."

He waited until she returned from dumping the

soaked towel and broken glass in the sink, to ask, "Why wouldn't I?"

She settled back onto her stool. "Well, the name thing for one. Some people would have been upset about that, especially since I get the feeling it wasn't a one-time occurrence."

"No, it wasn't." He sighed and sat as well. "When he was killed in Vail, the police first notified my parents that I was dead. Since I was having dinner with them at the time, we all realized what must have happened. Still, we held out hope that it was all just a big mistake and that Dill would come waltzing through the door."

"I'm so sorry."

"I flew to Vail to make a positive ID." His chest ached as he recalled the shock of seeing his brother's body on a cold metal slab at the morgue.

"My God! How horrible."

"Yeah, but better me than my mother or father. No parent should have to go through that."

"No parent should have to lose a child, period."

The ache in his chest intensified. There was more than one way to be robbed of that joy. She laid a hand on his arm. How was it possible that such a simple touch could offer so much comfort?

"You're probably wondering why Dillon did what he did." When Morgan nodded slowly, he decided to tell her. She had a right to know. "He was pretty much broke."

If the news disappointed her, it didn't show. Her expression never wavered.

"He had a trust fund, a sizeable one, left to him by our grandparents, same as I did. I invested most of mine. He spent his. Most of it was gone by the time he got out of college."

"Didn't he work?" She did look disappointed now.

"He had a position at the company." Their father would have gladly made Dill a vice president if he'd shown any interest or initiative. "He showed up sometimes, but he didn't put in regular hours. Dill was… He never really grew up."

"And so you let him use your identity and spend your money?" Her tone held an odd mix of disbelief and censure.

"He was my brother. I looked out for him." Guilt nudged Bryan as he recalled that final phone message he'd left. Perhaps that's why his voice was hoarse when he added, "I'd been looking out for him since we were kids."

"Maybe that's why he never grew up," Morgan answered quietly. "He never had to deal with the consequences of his actions."

Anger came fast. Bryan welcomed it since it not only chased away the grief and guilt he felt over his brother, it corralled his wayward interest in this woman who was off-limits to him. She was his late brother's conquest. The mother of Dillon's child.

"I don't recall asking for your analysis," Bryan

snapped, even though he knew she'd merely said aloud what he sometimes thought. That between his parents and himself they'd made it too easy for Dill.

"I'm sorry," she said. "You're right. I didn't mean to be judgmental. We all have flaws and, as you said, despite those, Dillon was a good man." Her gaze veered to Brice. "That's what I'll make sure my son understands about his father."

"Thank you."

"You've never held him, you know."

Bryan didn't feign ignorance, rather he ignored the question, forking up a bite of sweet and sour pork instead.

"What is it about him that makes you hold back?" Morgan persisted.

God, the woman was blunt. He knew hardened dealmakers who weren't as adept at going for the jugular. Brice came to Bryan's aid. Without any fussing at all, he spat up all over his pajamas.

Morgan crinkled her nose. "Sorry about that. We're working on his table manners."

"That's all right."

She tipped her head to one side. "You're really not grossed out."

"He's a baby."

"A lot of men would be, unless they're dads themselves." Morgan used her napkin to mop up what she could before scooping the baby out of the seat. It was just as well she wasn't looking at Bryan. Her offhand comment had landed a direct hit.

After she left the kitchen, Bryan picked up his plate and dumped his uneaten dinner down the garbage disposal. His appetite was gone, obliterated by a powerful and confusing mix of emotions. He decided to leave before she started asking more questions that he didn't want to answer. Questions whose answers he was no longer sure he knew.

He was on his way to the bedroom to tell her goodbye when a knock sounded on the door. He could hear Morgan talking to Brice in the nursery. Since she was busy and this was still his penthouse, he decided to answer the door.

Courtney was on the other side, wearing a low-cut black dress and stiletto heels. Just what the doctor had ordered in the past, but seeing her crimson lips bow with promise now did nothing for him.

"The doorman said you were home. Hope you don't mind my popping by. I'm celebrating the fifth anniversary of divorce." She held out a bottle of Dom. "Want to join me? I hate drinking alone."

He glanced over his shoulder, nervous for no reason that made sense. "I'm…I was just on my way out, actually."

"Let's stay in for a little while," she coaxed, walking past him into the foyer.

"I can't stay here." He expelled a breath.

"Okay. We can go to my place," she suggested.

Take her up on the offer, he ordered himself. Go and forget about everything for a few hours. That was what he'd done in the past. But he shook his head. "Not tonight."

"Oh? Not in the mood?" There was nothing Courtney found more exhilarating than a challenge. Her brows rose and she set the bottle of champagne and her handbag on the entry table. "Perhaps I can change your mind."

She reached for him, but before her arms wound around his shoulders Bryan trapped her hands in his. He brought them to his lips for a kiss. The gesture wasn't intended to be seductive. It was a goodbye. He could tell she knew it even before he said, "I'm sorry."

She stiffened for a moment, but then was laughing huskily. "Who is she, Bryan? Please tell me it's not that snooty little secretary that glares daggers at me every time I stop by your office."

He really had to do something about Britney. But back to the matter at hand. "She's no one you know."

Courtney pulled away and turned, regarding him in the foyer mirror. She sounded genuinely interested when she asked, "Is she worth it?"

He glanced toward the bedroom. "It's not like that."

Courtney, of course, didn't see it that way. Turning, she said, "It's exactly like that, Bryan, or you'd still be interested in what I have to offer."

"You do have a lot to offer," he replied in lieu of an answer to her initial question.

Taking Courtney's bejeweled hands in his, he raised them to his lips again. This time the kiss he dropped on her knuckles held an apology.

Morgan, however, was the one who said the words aloud. "I'm sorry."

Both he and Courtney turned. Morgan was holding a freshly changed Brice, her eyes wide and assessing, her expression disappointed. In him?

"Oh, my," Courtney told Bryan. "Now I can see why you said 'not here.'"

"Courtney Banks, this is Morgan Stevens. She's my…she's my late brother's…." He motioned with his hand, not sure what word to use to fill in that last blank.

The baby in Morgan's arms apparently clarified things for Courtney. "Ah. I see."

"I didn't mean to interrupt," Morgan said. She would no longer meet Bryan's eye. "I just wanted to tell you that I'm going to put Brice down."

"I was just going anyway," Bryan said. Why did he feel like such a heel? He had nothing to hide. He'd done nothing wrong. The kiss he and Morgan had shared came to mind. *Liar*.

"Well, thanks for the takeout. It was nice to meet you, Courtney."

"The same here." Courtney gathered up the champagne and her handbag.

He wasn't leaving with her, but Bryan knew that was exactly what it looked like. Maybe that was for the best. "I'll call you when I hear from my parents," he told Morgan.

Her forced smile was the last thing he saw before closing the penthouse door.

"I'll see you to your car," Bryan said to Courtney as they stepped into the elevator.

She was quiet during the ride to the lobby. He appreciated her silence. He didn't want to answer questions right now. He walked her to her car, a sleek red foreign number that was parked in the fire lane.

"You're lucky you haven't been ticketed or towed," he remarked.

"I like to live dangerously," she said with a delicate shrug of her shoulders. Then, more seriously, she added, "Take care, Bryan. Don't let her hurt you."

"She's...we're not in the kind of relationship that allows for one to be hurt."

"But you'd like to be."

He opened the car door for her and ignored the comment. "I can't be hurt, Courtney."

"Sure you can. We both can be. By the right person. And we were in the past, which is why we've sought out one another's company these past few years. It's been safe."

"It's been more than *safe*," he pointed out in an effort to soften their goodbye.

Courtney's laughter was bawdy as she slipped into the driver's seat. "Well, that goes without saying. We've had some good times. I may even miss you."

She pointed back toward his building. "If things don't pan out the way you're hoping, be sure to call me. The Dom will be gone by then, but I'll spring for a new bottle."

He smiled, but made her no promises. After his divorce he'd stopped making promises to women. Or maybe he just hadn't met a woman who'd changed his mind. Until now.

CHAPTER SIX

Morgan grew anxious waiting for Bryan to call. Not, she assured herself, because she felt he owed her an explanation as to how he could kiss her so passionately and fail to mention he had a girlfriend—a gorgeous, perfectly coiffed, perfectly proportioned girlfriend who looked as though she'd just stepped out of the pages of a fashion magazine. No, she wanted to know if he'd spoken to his parents and how they had taken the news about Brice.

Already she'd been apprehensive about meeting the Caliborns. She was doubly so now. She'd conceived a child with one of their sons during a brief fling in Aruba, and now, just months after giving birth, she found herself disturbingly attracted to the other one.

What would they see when they looked at her? A conniving gold digger? An opportunist? Someone of low moral character?

What would they see when they looked at her son? Would they too question Brice's paternity, perhaps even demand a test? It still surprised her that Bryan hadn't done so yet, because even though his attitude seemed to have softened, he remained detached from the baby.

By the time the following Friday rolled around, she was a bundle of nerves, though it helped to be busy at the community center, so she'd stayed late to help a young girl practice scales. Carla was ten and had just signed up for the program the week before. She was shy and introverted, but, like the other kids, eager to learn.

The girl's fingers stumbled over the keys of Morgan's old upright. Carla missed a couple of notes, went back to find them and winced when the wrong ones came out.

"Sorry."

"Don't apologize. Just do it again. Practice is the only difference between you and me. I've had years of it."

"You think I can be as good as you someday?"

"Maybe even better if you stay with it. Remember to invite me to see you play Carnegie Hall."

"Have you played there?"

"Twice. Now play."

The girl flashed Morgan a grin and started again, this time finishing with only a couple of minor mistakes. In his car seat on the floor next to the piano, Brice let out a delighted squeal when Carla was done.

"See, even the baby thinks you've improved."

"Thanks, Ms. Stevens. I appreciate the extra help."

"Don't mention it. It's been my pleasure. Is someone coming to pick you up?"

"My mom. She told me to wait for her at the front door so she doesn't have to find a parking space."

"Okay. Have a good weekend."

Morgan stood and gathered up some sheet music from a nearby stand. When she turned, Bryan was leaning against the jamb of the door through which Carla had exited. His suit coat was slung over one shoulder and he was watching her with dark, unreadable eyes that left her feeling far too exposed.

"How long have you been standing there?"

"Long enough. Carnegie Hall twice, hmm? You must be very good."

She lifted her shoulders in lieu of an answer. "Are you here for a lesson?"

"That depends."

"On what?" she asked.

"On what you're offering to teach me."

His reply raised gooseflesh on her arms. Morgan cleared her throat and glanced away. "In addition to the piano I play the oboe and clarinet. I'm passable on sex—*sax*."

His brows rose at the Freudian slip, but Morgan noted thankfully that he let it go without comment. He pushed away from the doorjamb and came fully into the room. "My parents are home. I spoke to them last night. They're eager to see Brice and to meet you, too, of course."

Nothing like being tacked on as an afterthought to make one feel welcome, Morgan groused internally.

Brice cooed and Bryan's gaze shifted to the baby, who was batting his chubby fists against a string of colorful rings that Morgan had draped over the carrier's handle. Bryan's expression softened. She saw him swallow hard before glancing away. Did he see his brother in the baby? Was he missing him? Could it be that that was why he sometimes seemed so sad when he looked at Brice? Now wasn't the time to ask such questions, though. Other ones needed to be answered first.

"When do your parents want to meet me? And where?"

He laid his coat on top of the piano and sat down on the bench. "They're leaving that up to you."

That news had Morgan slumping down next to him. The bench was small. Their hips bumped. She could smell his cologne. It was the same scent he'd worn the day he'd kissed her. She was inhaling deeply, even as she tried to focus on the matter at hand.

"The sooner—"

"The better," he finished for her. His gaze was locked on her mouth. She swore he leaned closer for a moment, before he pushed to his feet and took a few steps away. "That's what my parents said, too."

"How about next Saturday?" That would give her

a week to rehearse what she was going to say and to find something suitable for her and Brice to wear.

"That leaves where."

"Well, I can't very well invite them to your apartment. Of course, they probably know I'm staying there since you're living in their guesthouse."

"Yes. They think I'm chivalrous."

"I can only imagine what they think of me," she remarked dryly. She turned on the bench and played the opening chords to one of her favorite concertos. "I suppose we could have dinner at a restaurant, although that seems a little impersonal. Not to mention that we wouldn't be able to talk freely without the risk of being overheard." She sent a smile in his direction and added, "My name may not be as well known as your family's, but I'm every bit as eager as you are to keep it out of the tabloids."

"In that case, I suggest that you and Brice come to my parents' estate."

She stopped playing. "You want me to invite myself to their home? Gee, should I tell your mother what to serve for lunch, too?"

He surprised her with a chuckle. "If you'd like."

"I'm serious, Bryan."

"So am I. Outside of my penthouse, the location makes the most sense."

She sighed, because he was right. "Okay."

"I'll set it up." He tucked his hands in his trouser pockets. "Are you heading home now?"

She nodded. "You?"

"I was thinking of stopping off for dinner first. Meal preparation isn't included with my new accommodations."

She smiled. "Mine either. But I've enjoyed having someone to do the grocery shopping for me. Not to mention the laundry and the housework. I'm getting spoiled."

"Somehow, I doubt that," Bryan replied.

He meant it. A woman who would work for peanuts in a community center teaching underprivileged kids the joy of music wasn't spoiled. That conclusion didn't surprise him as much as the fact that he felt Morgan deserved to be pampered and he wanted to be the one doing it.

His gaze dropped to her lips and he recalled that kiss. He didn't like the feelings that had begun to take root. They were the kind that held the potential to grow, spread and blossom into something that terrified him. His dealings with Courtney had been blissfully straightforward. No ties. No lies. No talk of a shared future. Which was why parting the other night had been managed so easily and so affably. There were no messy emotions to get in the way. No explanations required.

But he heard himself offer one to Morgan now.

"Courtney and I…we're not seeing one another any longer."

"Oh?" Her brows notched up. "I'm sorry."

"Do you mean that?" he asked quietly.

She glanced away. "Of course I do. She seemed... nice. And she's very pretty. You made a handsome couple."

"Did we?"

"Yes. You're both very..." She lifted her shoulders. "You turn heads."

He wasn't a vain man. Nor was he one who required his ego to be stroked. But he asked, "Turn heads?"

"You have a commanding presence."

He laughed. "Some people just call me intimidating."

"Do you try to be?"

"Sometimes," he admitted. "It has its uses."

She shook her head. "I think it gets in the way of real relationships. How long were you and Courtney together?"

Bryan thought back. "Since just after my divorce was finalized."

"So a few years. It sounds like it was serious."

"No. It wasn't like that. Actually, it was...pretty casual." He frowned.

"Well, I hope my being in your penthouse had nothing to do with your split."

"No." But it did. It had everything to do with it, Bryan realized, because suddenly *pretty casual* wasn't enough. His frown deepened. "I can't figure out what it is about you that..."

"What?"

He left his previous thought unfinished and said instead, "You don't fit into any mold."

"Then why do you keep trying to force me into one?" she asked.

"Habit."

"It's a bad one. Break it." Her gaze held a challenge.

"I don't know if that would be a good idea." He tilted his head to one side.

"Why?"

A million reasons came to mind. The one he offered rose from his subconscious. "You're dangerous, Morgan."

She blinked in surprise. "Dangerous. Me?"

Yes, he thought. From the moment he'd met her she'd been a blight on his peace of mind. He wanted it back. Even more, though, he wanted... her.

He shot to his feet. He should go. Hell, he shouldn't have come. He could have called Morgan with the information about his parents. He could have had Britney call her, for that matter. But he'd wanted to see her and he'd figured a public place was safer than stopping in at his penthouse.

And so was a restaurant, his libido offered slyly. What could happen in a restaurant with a table between them and waiters and other patrons around?

"Would you and Brice like to have dinner with me?" he asked.

"Now?"

"Now."

"I can't. Sorry. I'm nearly out of diapers and he's going to need to nurse soon."

He nodded. "I understand." Just as well, he decided. Just as well.

"May I have a rain check?"

Bryan shrugged. "Sure."

It was hot when he arrived home an hour later. He'd been hungry when he stopped at the community center. He was starving now and it had nothing to do with the fact that he'd skipped dinner.

He bypassed the main house, even though he knew his parents would welcome a visit from him and would gladly ask their cook to whip up a meal. Instead, he headed to the guesthouse and changed into his swim trunks.

A moment later, he was diving into the deep end of the in-ground swimming pool, powerful strokes taking him to the far side in a matter of seconds. Just before reaching it, he flipped and pushed off the wall with his feet. The water was cool on his heated skin and the exertion took the edge off his frustration. When he hoisted himself out of the water twenty minutes later, his mother was holding a towel, which she handed to him.

Julia waited till he'd dried off and caught his breath before asking, "So, did you talk to her?"

"Yes. I suggested that she come here."

His mother nodded. "Good, good. Well, as long as she won't find that too intimidating."

Rough laughter scraped his throat. "I don't think *anything* intimidates that woman."

"Oh?"

He cleared his throat. "We set it up for next Saturday. I didn't pin down a time. I figured I'd ask you what worked best first."

"See if one o'clock is acceptable and tell her we would like her and the baby to come for lunch." She rubbed her hands together in an uncharacteristic show of nerves. "Do you know what she likes to eat?"

His mother's question had him chuckling since it echoed Morgan's earlier comment. "I can ask her if you'd like."

"Yes. Do that. I want everything to be perfect. Oh, my God." She covered her mouth with her hand for a moment. "I still can't believe it."

"Mom," he began, not sure how to proceed. "There's no concrete proof that she's telling the truth."

"Yes, so you mentioned when we first came home and learned that she'd been here since the end of May." Her tone held censure and more than a little hurt. Julia hadn't been happy that he'd kept Morgan and Brice a secret. His father wasn't pleased either, though Hugh at least understood and accepted Bryan's reasoning.

"Why haven't you sought that proof?" she asked now.

All it would have taken was a swab from the inside

of Brice's mouth and one from Bryan's. Since Dillon was dead, short of having his body exhumed, that was the only way to establish a link between the baby and the Caliborns.

"The last thing we need is for the press to get wind of our family requesting *another* paternity test," he said tightly. "The slowing economy is already giving our investors enough reasons to worry."

"Very well, but you've met her, Bryan. You've spent time with her and you've seen the baby. Tell me, do you really think she's lying about Dillon being the father of her child?"

"No. Not lying."

"But you think she could be wrong about…the circumstances," Julia allowed.

I'm not promiscuous.

Morgan's words echoed in his head. Nothing about her suggested otherwise, so why hadn't he called off the investigation? Why wasn't he just accepting she was exactly what she said she was and Brice was who she claimed him to be?

Perhaps because he was scared to death of the attraction he felt for her.

With a muttered oath, he shoved the wet hair back from his forehead. "I don't know what I think anymore, Mom."

Julia laid her hand against his cheek. It was the same hand that had soothed his hurts when he was a kid. As comforting as he still found it, he knew it wasn't going to set things right this time.

"This must be especially hard for you, Bry."

"It's dredged up a lot of memories," he admitted. "None of them very pleasant to recall. Caden turned five a few weeks ago. I still think about him, you know."

"I know."

"The happiest day of my life was the day he was born." He'd been in the delivery room, gaping like a fool as he'd watched the miracle unfold. "I was the first person to hold him when he came into this world," he whispered hoarsely.

And he'd been among the last to learn of his wife's duplicity thanks to the DNA test results that were leaked to the media.

"We loved him, too," his mother reminded him. Julia's voice was filled with the same tangle of emotions that had Bryan's throat aching and his eyes stinging. "What Camilla did to you—what she did to us all—with her lies, it was wrong. More than wrong. It was cruel. But at some point you have to let go of the past and move on. It pains me to see you so lonely."

"I'm not lonely," he protested.

This was the second time in recent weeks that he'd been labeled as such, the second time he'd been told he needed to move on. He didn't like it.

His mother patted his cheek again, smiling sadly, and even though she didn't say a word, it was clear she didn't believe him.

CHAPTER SEVEN

For the next week, Morgan dragged poor Brice into half the stores in Chicago looking for an appropriate outfit to wear when meeting the Caliborns. Nothing in her closet would do. Well, except for the dress that Britney had selected for Morgan to wear home from the hospital in case a picture got snapped. She was averse to it for obvious reasons.

Besides, she'd lost more weight and a few more inches from her waist. She wanted to make the most of it. She owed her improved figure to yoga and running. Not the kind of running that involved lacing up high-performance shoes and heading out into the late August heat. Rather the kind involved in being a single, working mother whose car had decided it needed a rest. The ancient compact had started stalling out regularly a couple weeks earlier.

Usually, after a couple of minutes, it was kind enough to start back up, so she'd put off taking it in. Today, the engine had whined copiously and refused to switch on again. Now it was at a garage being worked on by a mechanic named Vic, whom Morgan hoped wasn't going to try to pad out the price of repairs just because she was female.

She shoved that thought from her mind. She had more important things to worry about, such as what she was going to wear to meet the parents of the now-dead man who had fathered her child. Outfitting Brice had been easy and affordable. As a shower gift one of the other teachers had given her an adorable sailor suit. It was in a bigger size, but he'd grown enough to wear it. Finding something for herself was proving far more frustrating.

All she knew from her brief conversation with Bryan earlier in the week was that his parents were expecting her and Brice at one o'clock on Saturday at their Lake Forest home. Lunch would be served in the garden, weather permitting. Somehow she doubted they were going to gather around a picnic table and eat franks and beans. More likely, the Caliborns would serve fancy little finger sandwiches stuffed with things like cucumbers, alfalfa sprouts and watercress.

"I don't think I like watercress," she muttered as she rummaged through the clearance racks in Danbury's.

It was the third department store she'd been to this day and it would be the last since she had to work later that afternoon. Without her car, she and Brice would be taking the El before transferring to a bus and then hoofing it three blocks to the community center.

From the final rack, Morgan pulled out a yellow sundress. Holding the hanger just below her chin, she asked Brice, "What do you think? The price is right at half off."

He yawned up at her from the stroller before smacking his lips together, clearly unimpressed.

"You're right. The color will make my skin look sallow."

Sighing, she put it back. Another two hours wasted. Or maybe not, she thought, spying the moss-colored suit on a mannequin in the department across the aisle. The jacket was short and fitted with three-quarter-length sleeves and double rows of mother of pearl buttons. The skirt flowed slightly away from the body for a fit that was sure to flatter her post-pregnancy curves without drawing too much attention to the ones she was still working to erase. She steered Brice over to it and then held her breath as she reached for the price tag.

"Oh, my God!" She swallowed. She almost prayed she was right when she said, "They probably don't have my size anyway."

They did.

"It probably won't look good on me," she said.

"Can I put that in a fitting room?"

Morgan turned to find a saleswoman standing behind her. "I—I—" With a sheepish smile, she nodded.

Not only did it fit, it looked fabulous, if she did say so herself. Even Brice gurgled happily as she modeled it in front of the changing room's trifold mirror. Of course, his exuberance may have been the result of gas since he belched loudly afterward.

"How are you doing in there?" the saleswoman asked from outside the door.

"Great. It fits and I love it. But I have one problem." Other than the price tag. Morgan stared at her reflection. "I need shoes."

She wound up walking out of the store with more than the outfit and a pair of pricy peep-toe heels. She also purchased a new handbag and had made an appointment in the store's salon for the following day. She wasn't even going to think about how much she'd just put on the charge card she kept for emergency purposes.

But late that night, as Brice slept in his crib, Morgan sat at the kitchen table sipping a cup of herbal tea and balancing her checkbook. She'd come home to a message from the mechanic working on her car. The repairs were going to total just a little less than the amount she'd plunked down in Danbury's, meaning she would have to tap the emergency credit card again.

With a sigh, she ran the numbers a second time. In the very near future she was going to have to get a real job, a full-time position that included benefits and a pension. That made her sad. She really enjoyed sharing her love of music with the kids at the center and she felt they got something out of the experience, too.

* * *

Normally, Bryan wouldn't answer his cell phone during dinner, but when he noted the call-back number he excused himself from the table with an apologetic glance toward his mother and walked to his father's study. It was Gil Rogers, the private detective he'd hired to look into Morgan's background. He'd left a message for the man earlier in the day.

"Gil, thanks for returning my call."

"You said it was important."

"Yes. I—I decided I don't need a background check on Ms. Stevens after all. It goes without saying that I'll pay you for your services so far."

"Are you sure?" The detective chuckled then. "Never mind. I guess it makes sense. If it weren't for the baby I'd wonder if the woman wasn't a candidate for a convent. Other than a couple of boyfriends in college and an occasional date, she doesn't appear to have been involved in any serious relationships."

"So she wasn't seeing anyone else around the time the baby was conceived?"

"Not according to the people I spoke with." Gil paused. "I did learn something else, not that it has much bearing on her child's paternity, but I thought you might find it interesting."

"Go on."

"Both of her parents are dead."

"Yes, I know."

"They died together at their home in Brookside. Carbon monoxide poisoning, according to the news clips I was able to dig up. Investigators blamed it on a faulty furnace vent."

"God." The information came as a shock. He sank onto the sofa as he processed it.

"Miss Stevens found them," the detective was saying. "Her folks were still in their bed. Apparently they'd gone to sleep the night before and just never woke up. The story I read included a photograph of her collapsing in the arms of one of the firefighters who'd arrived on the scene. She looked pretty distraught."

Bryan closed his eyes, imagining how it must have been for Morgan and aching on her behalf.

I have no one.

She'd said that all those months ago when she'd gone into labor in his office. How horribly true her statement turned out to be.

"When did this happen?"

"A year ago last spring," Gil replied.

The information jogged Bryan's memory. More pieces of the puzzle fell into place. She would have been in Aruba just months after burying her parents. Alone, sad…vulnerable.

I was at a low point in my life. A really low point. It's not an excuse for my behavior. But it is a fact.

Bryan recalled her words that day in his penthouse. Unlike Dill, who had made excuses for everything, Morgan wasn't willing to fall back on one, even a very good one. Just as she hadn't claimed to have fallen in love with his brother, nor had she tried to gain Bryan's sympathy. Rather, she'd taken full responsibility for winding up pregnant and alone.

He thought about the check she'd written him for the use of his penthouse. Although he'd destroyed it, she'd sent him two more since then, presumably to cover each month's rent. His brother had used Bryan's name and charged his good time to Bryan's accounts. Morgan wasn't even willing to accept his hospitality.

Perhaps because she sensed his reticence.

"No more," Bryan murmured.

"Excuse me?"

"As I said, I no longer require your services," he told Gil.

"I understand, sir. But I've still got inquiries out with several people. The community where she taught in Wisconsin is pretty close-knit. It's been hard to get many people to talk. Do you want to wait until I've heard back from them?"

"No. As I said, I'll pay you for your time and trouble."

"All right." Gil's tone was reluctant. "I'll mail you a written report along with an invoice."

Bryan flipped his phone closed and tossed it on his father's desk. Then he poured himself a drink from the decanter of Scotch on the adjacent credenza. He drank it in a single gulp, closing his eyes as the liquor burned its way down his throat.

"Bryan?" His mother stood in the doorway, her concern obvious. "What is it? What's wrong?"

He was wrong.

He'd felt that way for a while now, but he had been too stubborn to admit it. He'd allowed the lies of the past to blind him to the truth of the present.

He stared at his empty glass in his hand, an idea germinating. Finally, he said, "Nothing that can't be put right."

Morgan didn't expect Bryan to come into the city to collect her and Brice on Saturday, but when he called Friday evening to tell her when he'd arrive at the penthouse, she didn't argue. Her car supposedly was repaired, but she wasn't willing to press her luck on this day of all days. Besides, she was too nervous to drive.

When the doorbell pealed, her heart was racing. Then she opened the door, saw Bryan and she swore it stopped beating. She'd always found him imposing and dangerously handsome. Today, in place of the corporate attire she associated with him, he wore tan slacks and a white oxford-cloth shirt open at the throat. He looked younger and far less formidable than he did wearing his usual pinstripes and power tie.

He smiled. She wasn't sure she'd ever really seen him do that. And the word *sexy* got tagged on to her description.

"Wow."

His brows rose in question and she realized she'd

uttered the word out loud. As cover for her foolishness, she added, "You're right on time."

"I'm always on time."

"Yes." But she'd been hoping he would be late.

She stepped back to allow him in. When she turned after closing the door, he was watching her. Indeed, he was looking at her as if he'd never seen her before.

"The outfit is new," she said, in case that was the cause for his bafflement. "I felt the occasion called for it. Does it look okay?" Before he could respond, she added, "And just let me say, given what I spent on it, your answer had better be yes."

He didn't smile at her joke. Instead, he said most seriously, "Turn around, Morgan."

Feeling a little ridiculous, she nonetheless managed a slow twirl. "Well?"

"You've done something different with your hair." He made a vague motion with his hand.

"I had it cut. I was due for a new style." The result was a sleeker look that framed her face before flipping up slightly at her shoulders.

"It looks…you look… You're beautiful, Morgan. Stunning, in fact."

He said it the way he said everything: definitively and in a tone that allowed no argument. Not that he was going to get one from her. If the man wanted to call her stunning, who was she to quibble? Unlike Dillon's profuse flattery, Bryan's statement was all the more touching for its rareness. Something stirred in his dark eyes and for a moment she thought—and God help her, hoped—he was going to kiss her again. But then he took a step backward and glanced away.

"We should be going."

The Caliborns' home in Lake Forest boasted more square footage than the elementary school where Morgan had taught in Wisconsin. Given its columned portico and lush landscaping, *grand* was an apt description for it. At the moment, so was *imposing*.

Bryan came around and opened her car door. The gesture wasn't only gentlemanly but practical since she'd made no move to get out. She wasn't a coward, but she briefly considered feigning illness and asking him to take her back to the city. He seemed to understand because he offered his hand to help her out and then gave hers a squeeze of encouragement before releasing it.

"They're good people," he said quietly. "Good people who have suffered some unbearable losses."

Losses. Plural. Before she could ask what he meant, a slender woman of about sixty, wearing work gloves and carrying a trowel, came around the side of the house. She let out a squeal of excitement when she spied them and hurried forward. This was certainly a warm welcome from the gardener, Morgan thought.

"Mom." Bryan's face softened and he leaned down to kiss her when she reached them.

Mom? Morgan had been expecting a Chanel-wearing, diamond-sprinkled matriarch, not this warm and vibrant woman whose lovely face was finely etched from a lifetime of smiles that she apparently had no interest in erasing with Botox. Her hair was solid silver, not white or gray. She wore it short, in a style that flattered her oval face. Eyes every bit as dark as Bryan's dominated that face.

"Here are Morgan and Brice," Bryan was saying. "Morgan, Dillon's and my mother, Julia Caliborn."

"Hello, Mrs. Caliborn." Morgan shifted the baby to the crook of her other arm so she could extend her right hand.

"Call me Julia, please." She extended the trowel before drawing it back with a flustered laugh. "Oh, my. I'm afraid I'm not making a very good first impression. Forgive my appearance," she said to Morgan. To Bryan, she accused, "You're early."

He shook his head, looking mildly amused and all the more attractive for the smile lighting up his eyes. "We're exactly on time, Mom. You just got caught up in your garden again."

"Guilty as charged." She sent Morgan a smile. "I find playing in the dirt a good way to relax. I've been out pulling weeds and pruning plants since breakfast. Being abroad, I missed almost the entire growing season this year. I had someone looking after things here, but my flower beds are in a shambles."

"Unlikely," Bryan said. To Morgan, he added, "My

mother is being modest. She's a master gardener and the estate's grounds have been featured in a couple of national publications." His pride was obvious.

Julia waved away his compliments and smiled at Morgan. Then her gaze lowered to the sleeping baby. Her voice was barely above a whisper when she said, "I'd ask to hold him, but I'm a mess at the moment."

She wasn't only referring to her stained clothes, Morgan realized, when Julia's eyes began to fill with tears. One spilled down her cheek and she swiped one away, leaving a smudge of dirt in its place. Morgan's own eyes grew moist. She'd expected this encounter to be emotionally charged for her, but she'd failed to realize how much more so it would be for the Caliborns, given Dillon's death.

"Let's go inside, Mom. Dad can keep us company while you…clean up." He handed her his handkerchief before putting an arm around her shoulders and hugging her to his side as they walked to the front door.

"Your father is probably in his study. Go visit with him while I freshen up. I won't be long."

After Julia excused herself and disappeared up the staircase that curved off from the foyer, Bryan led Morgan through the house, past the living room and formal dining room. Both rooms were every bit as lovely as she'd imagined they would be. They were filled with fine furnishings and stunning artwork, most likely pricy originals rather than reproductions. The rooms didn't appear to be showplaces, but actual living spaces. They exuded comfort and warmth and, Morgan suspected, reflected the home owners' personalities. Very different from Bryan's sterile penthouse.

More of her uneasiness melted away, but it was back in an instant when they entered the study. A man stood at the window with his back to them. He was every bit as tall as Bryan, though not quite as broad through the shoulders. Still, he was physically fit for a man in his sixties. His hair was steel gray and, when he turned, his eyes were the same tawny color Dillon's had been.

"Dad, this is Morgan Stevens. Morgan, my father, Hugh Caliborn."

"It's nice to meet you, sir."

"Morgan." The older man nodded as he stepped forward awkwardly as if not certain whether he should shake her hand or kiss her cheek. Ultimately, he did neither. To Bryan, he said, "Does your mother know you're here?"

"Yes. She came around the side of the house just after we pulled up. She'd been gardening." The two men exchanged knowing looks. "She's upstairs now changing her clothes."

Hugh nodded. Then his gaze dropped to the infant in Morgan's arms. "Bryan tells us that you named the baby Brice Dillon."

"Yes." She held her breath, waited for what, exactly, she wasn't sure.

"It's a nice name." He swallowed.

"I thought so, too."

One side of the older man's mouth crooked up. "He's just a little thing, isn't he?"

"Not so small that he hasn't already managed to take my heart hostage," Morgan mused. She still felt awed by the unprecedented wave of love she'd experienced the first time she'd held him…and every time after that.

"You'll never get it back, you know." Hugh's smile was tinged with the sadness of a father who has outlived a child.

"No," Bryan agreed. The source of his sadness had her puzzled. He cleared his throat then and suggested, "Why don't we all sit down?"

In addition to an expansive desk built of the same wood as the cherry-paneled walls, the room offered seating clustered around a fireplace. Bryan selected one of the oversize armchairs; his father took its twin, leaving Morgan to the sofa. For the next fifteen minutes they talked about inconsequential things such as the weather until Julia, fresh from a shower, joined them.

"Hugh, goodness' sakes, haven't you offered our guest anything to drink?" she chided.

Morgan shook her head. "Oh, no thanks. I'm fine."

"I wouldn't mind a glass of iced tea," Bryan said.

"A fresh pitcher is in the refrigerator. Why don't you bring enough glasses for the rest of us just in case Morgan changes her mind."

Morgan blinked and it took an effort not to allow

her mouth to fall open when Bryan rose to do his mother's bidding. Her shock must have been apparent, because after he was gone Julia turned to Morgan and said, "Everything all right, dear?"

"I didn't think anyone told Bryan what to do." She felt her face heat and she cleared her throat. "I mean, it's just that he's so adept at giving orders, I never thought—"

God, she was digging herself a hole. But Bryan's mother was smiling as she sent Hugh a knowing look.

"Bry is much better at giving orders than taking them, which is why I try to give them on a regular basis. Someone has to keep him from becoming too dictatorial." She plucked at the buttons on her blouse as her tone turned nostalgic. "He's always been like that. Not Dillon, though. Instead of making demands, he charmed people to get what he wanted."

Didn't Morgan know it.

"Bryan and Dillon were such different personalities," Hugh agreed. "Sometimes Julia and I wondered if they'd made a pact to be polar opposites just to drive us insane." He chuckled. "Despite their differences, they were thick as thieves. There wasn't anything they wouldn't do for one another."

"It's still so hard to believe Dill's gone." Julia fell silent.

They all fell silent, except for Brice. Before the mood could become too maudlin, he began babbling happily and pumping his fists.

"Looks like you might have a prizefighter on your hands," Hugh said with a chuckle.

"He's an active baby."

"Can I… Would you mind if I held him?" Julia asked.

"Not at all."

Bryan returned to the room just as Morgan was placing Brice in his mother's arms. Morgan wondered what he was thinking as he watched Julia press her cheek to the baby's and close her eyes with a sigh. A moment later, his father was leaving his chair to perch on the arm of the sofa.

"God, it's like looking at Dill all over again, isn't it, Jule?" Hugh's voice was rough with emotion.

"Right down to the little swirling cowlick on his crown." She traced it with a fingertip.

They believed her. Their voices held no doubt, only awe and excitement. Morgan's relief was immense. She'd worried about coming here today and encountering skepticism or at the very least a cool reception. They'd welcomed her and Brice. And now they were accepting them.

From the doorway, the cook announced, "Lunch will be ready in fifteen minutes. Will you still be eating outside?"

"Yes. Thank you, Mae," Julia said. "Bryan, bring the tray of iced tea. It's too nice outside to stay cooped up in here."

She and Hugh set off with the baby, leaving

Morgan and Bryan to follow. On the patio, a scrolled wrought-iron table was already set for lunch with fine china and cloth napkins. Shrubs and plants, many of them past their flowering stage, bounded the sides of the patio and spilled out into the yard. Flagstone paths led from one lush oasis to the next, as well as to a large in-ground pool. Morgan guessed the building beyond it to be the guesthouse where Bryan was staying.

"Your home is beautiful, but this—" She motioned with her arms. "This is breathtaking."

"Thank you," Julia said. "Too bad you missed it when my plants were at their peak." She shot an accusing look in Bryan's direction.

"There's next year," he said quietly.

"Yes. Next year." Julia nodded. "Do you garden, Morgan?"

"No. I lived in an apartment back in Wisconsin. I tried growing geraniums in a pot on my balcony one summer, but they only lasted until the end of June."

"I killed my share of plants, too, before I got the hang of it," Julia commiserated. She shifted Brice from one arm to the other.

"I can take the baby if you'd like," Morgan offered. "He's small yet, but he gets heavy after a while."

"Oh, no. I'm delighted to hold him." Julia laughed then. "In fact, you might have to pry him out of my arms when you and Bryan leave. You know, if you ever need a night out with friends or a little time to pamper yourself, I'll be happy to watch him for you."

"That's a generous offer."

"There's nothing generous about it. I want to spoil him rotten, as is a grandmother's prerogative." She leaned down to nuzzle Brice's cheek. The baby gurgled in response.

The sweetness of the moment had a sigh catching in Morgan's throat. This is how it would be if her own mother were alive. For the first time since coming to Chicago, she not only felt that she'd made the right choice, but that everything was going to work out. She glanced at Bryan, wondering what he thought of his mother's remark. The pain she saw in his dark eyes came as a surprise.

"Bryan tells us you've been living in his penthouse since the baby was born," Hugh said.

"Yes. I told Bryan it wasn't necessary for him to move out." She colored after saying it, realizing his parents could interpret the statement a couple of ways. "I mean, it's been kind of him to let me stay there, but I could have found another place to live. And I will, of course, now that you're home."

"What does that have to do with anything?" Julia asked. "We've enjoyed seeing so much of Bryan. It's hardly been an imposition for him to stay in the guesthouse."

"I'm relieved to hear you say that, but I think it

probably has been an imposition for Bryan, what with the commute and all." Morgan sent him a wry look.

"She's right."

"Bryan!" Julia admonished.

He talked over his mother's objection. "I would prefer to be back in the penthouse, but you needn't look at me as if I'm proposing to throw Morgan and my nephew out on the streets of Chicago to fend for themselves."

Morgan's mouth dropped open. For the first time, he'd called Brice his nephew. For a moment she thought she might have heard him wrong, but when she looked at him there was no mistaking the apology in his gaze. What had prompted his change of heart?

She was so caught up in her thoughts that she missed what else Bryan said, and so it made no sense when Julia clapped her hands together and exclaimed, "That's a great idea! I don't know why I didn't think of it first. What do you say, Morgan?"

"Wh-what?"

"I said, I think you should move in to the guesthouse when I move back to the city," Bryan told her.

"Oh, no. No. I can't do that. You've already been so kind. All of you." She glanced around the table, her gaze lingering on Bryan. "I can't impose on your family's hospitality any longer. It's…it's not right."

"Don't be silly. We'd love to have you and Brice here," Hugh said. "For as long as you want to stay."

"And it will reduce my commute time," Bryan reminded her with a crooked smile.

Julia's argument, however, was the most poignant. "Besides, it's not an imposition. You and Brice are family."

Morgan's mouth fell open as the word embraced her with all the comfort of a hug. She'd felt so alone, she'd *been* so alone, since losing her parents. Now here were people who had known her for less than an hour offering her not just a place to stay, but a place in their lives.

"Oh, that's…that's so…" Her eyes began to fill, and because she knew it was only a matter of time before she made an absolute fool of herself, Morgan shot to her feet.

She had no idea where she was going, only that she needed a moment of privacy to get hold of her emotions. She followed one of the flagstone paths through a rose-covered arbor, drawn by the soothing sound of rushing water. The pathway opened up to a small waterfall that emptied into a koi pond. Morgan sank down on the nearby stone bench and dropped her head in her hands, giving in to the tears that begged to be shed. When she pulled her hands away, Bryan was standing there.

"I came to see if you were all right."

As he had for his mother earlier, he offered Morgan his handkerchief.

She blotted her eyes—so much for the morning's

careful application of mascara and liner—and worked up a smile. "Sorry. I just needed a minute."

"No need to apologize."

"Your mom is very kind and…" She shifted her gaze to the pond. The sight and sound of the water had a soothing effect. Bryan's presence did too. "It's incredibly lonely to be without family. I've got some aunts and uncles and a few cousins I exchange Christmas cards with. But it's not the same."

"No, I don't suppose it is."

Turning toward him, she said, "I never felt cheated to be an only child. My parents were great. Fun, funny. I could tell my mom anything, and my dad, he and I…" Her voice trailed off and it was a moment before she could continue. "When my parents were gone it was as if my whole world just stopped having any order. Suddenly, I had no place to be on Sunday afternoons. I had nowhere to go for holidays, no one to call for advice or pep talks."

"That must have been hell."

She swiped away fresh tears. "When I found out I was pregnant with Brice, my first reaction wasn't shock or desperation." She shrugged. "Oh, sure, I wasn't all that excited to become an unwed mother, especially when I found out I was about to lose my job and my health insurance. But part of me was just so relieved that I wasn't going to be alone any more."

"You're not alone, Morgan."

"I know. I have Brice."

"You have more than that." He offered his hand to help her to her feet. Afterward, he didn't let go. His fingers curled through hers. Their palms met. "If you don't want to stay and eat lunch, I'll take you back to the city. My parents will understand."

"No. I'll stay. I finish what I start."

"I've figured that out about you."

The way Bryan was studying her made Morgan feel exposed and self-conscious. Maybe that was why she asked, "What else have you figured out about me?"

"Not nearly enough to satisfy my curiosity," he admitted. "But enough to know I owe you an apology."

"Thanks."

"Shall we?"

He was still holding her hand, the gesture friendly but somehow intimate. Though he merely led her back to the table, Morgan felt a bridge had been crossed.

On the patio, lunch was being delivered. As Mae served grilled salmon sliced over beds of crisp greens and passed out freshly baked hard-crust rolls, a younger, similarly clad woman brought a bassinet out from the house and set it between Morgan's and Julia's seats. It was white and though the wicker appeared somewhat yellowed, the bedding was obviously new.

"Thank you, Carmen." To Morgan, Julia said, "Bryan and Dill slept in this when they were infants. And Caden, too." Julia's face colored and she flashed an apologetic look in Bryan's direction.

Who was Caden?

Morgan didn't ask. Even if she'd wanted to, she didn't get the chance. She and Brice were the topics of interest in this conversation, and so, for the next forty-five minutes she answered Julia and Hugh's questions. It could have had the feel of an interrogation, but it didn't. Indeed, the Caliborns made it easy for Morgan to open up, perhaps because they'd accepted without reservation that her baby was Dillon's son.

The only time she felt awkward was when she talked about what she did for a living. Morgan didn't want her limited financial reserves to color their opinion of her.

"I'm a teacher. Unfortunately, I'm between full-time jobs right now," she admitted.

Bryan had been quiet, though whenever she'd glanced his way, he'd nodded encouragingly. Now he inserted, "Morgan teaches music. She worked in a public school district in Wisconsin, but lost her job due to budget cuts."

"That's a shame, for you as well as for the students. The arts are so underappreciated." Julia's mouth puckered in disdain. "Do you play an instrument then?"

"A few, actually, but mainly the piano."

"And she's passable at the sax." Bryan said it with a straight face, but amusement was evident in his eyes.

God, she hoped she wasn't blushing. Clearing her throat, she said with as much dignity as she could muster, "I was classically trained. My parents had dreams of me becoming a concert pianist, especially after they'd scraped together every penny they had to send me to Juilliard."

"Juilliard?" This from Bryan, who then told his parents, "And she's played Carnegie Hall twice."

"We'd love to hear you play sometime," Julia said.

"I'm afraid I'm pretty rusty at giving concerts. These days, rather than playing Beethoven or Mozart, my time in front of the piano is largely spent helping kids learn notes and scales. I'm working a few hours each weekday afternoon in a community center." She sent a smile in Bryan's direction. "In fact, Windy City Industries recently announced it is making a generous donation of instruments to the center."

Hugh nodded in approval. "Bryan mentioned that at dinner the other evening."

Julia looked puzzled when she added, "He neglected to tell us that you worked there."

"It's a good cause," Bryan said, shrugging.

"A very good cause," Julia agreed. "I'd imagine there are a lot of struggling families for whom private music lessons and quality instruments are beyond reach."

"Exactly. I love it, too. The kids are great, and if it helps keep them off the streets and out of trouble or harm's way, all the better."

"It doesn't pay much, though," Bryan said.

"Bryan, don't be rude," Julia chastised.

Morgan sipped her iced tea. "I'm afraid he's right, which is why I'm still sending out my résumé."

"To schools in the Chicago area?" Julia asked hopefully.

Morgan exhaled slowly. "And elsewhere. The cost of living here is a little more expensive than some of the other communities where I'm applying."

"I have a solution to that," Bryan surprised her by saying. Setting his fork aside, he reached into the back pocket of his pants and pulled out a crinkled envelope. "This is yours."

"What is this?"

"Open it."

Perplexed, Morgan did as he said, and then blinked in shock. Inside the envelope was a check. A check made out to her for the sum of two million dollars.

Bryan watched Morgan's brow wrinkle and confusion infused her expression. Glancing up, she said, "I don't understand."

"It's from Dillon's life insurance policy. He named me his beneficiary."

Shaking her head, Morgan told him, "I can't accept it," and attempted to hand back the check.

He closed his hand around hers. "Yes, you can."

"But it's yours. I don't want money." Her gaze veered to his parents then. "I didn't come here for money. Honestly, that's not…that's not…"

When Bryan squeezed her hand, she stopped talking.

"Morgan, we know that."

"Do you?" The question, dagger-sharp, was directed at him.

"Yes, I do."

Her eyes grew bright and she nodded. "But I still can't take your money."

"It's not my money. By rights, it belongs to Brice. It belongs to my brother's son."

"Bryan's right, Morgan," Julia said.

Hugh was more direct. "Dill was irresponsible when it came to his finances. Money passed through his fingers as quickly as water. Where Bryan invested the trust fund my parents left him, Dillon squandered his. In truth, I'm surprised he thought to take out a life insurance policy. He probably only did it because the father of a girl he dated in college was the principal owner of a large Chicago insurance firm." He coughed, embarrassed. "But whatever the reason, I'm glad he did it. And I agree one hundred percent with Bryan that it should go to Brice."

Morgan turned to Bryan. He was still holding her hand and could feel that she was shaking. "But Dillon named you his beneficiary. He left the money to you."

"He should have left it to Brice. I have to believe if he'd known you were pregnant, he would have. His son is entitled to that money, Morgan."

Put like that, he figured she would agree. Finally, she nodded slowly.

"Okay. For Brice."

"Good. I'll be happy to offer some advice on investments," he told her.

"Investments. Yes. I'd appreciate that." A smile loosened her lips. "I guess I don't have to worry any longer about his college fund."

"It's a wonderful idea to secure his future," Julia said. "But there's nothing wrong with also using some of it in the meantime for day-to-day living expenses, housing, trips and that sort of thing. You won't be spending it on yourself. You'll also be spending it on him."

Bryan could tell she was still struggling with the notion. Most likely because the money in question was to come from his bank account, he decided, when she asked quietly, "Are you sure you're okay with this?"

"Yes." In fact, at that moment, he'd never been more sure of anything.

CHAPTER EIGHT

MORGAN visited with the Caliborns far longer than she'd anticipated. It wasn't obligation that found her there late in the afternoon. It was their warmth and kindness. And, of course, the way they doted on Brice.

"We probably should be going," Bryan said, pushing back from the table.

"I wish this day could last forever." Julia's tone was wistful as she glanced at the baby cooing in the bassinet. "We've enjoyed this visit so much."

"I have, too. We'll get together again soon," Morgan promised.

"We'll look forward to it. It's been a pleasure getting to know you, dear. You're a very nice young woman. Exactly the sort a mother would want for her son."

Morgan smiled, but said nothing. If Dillon were still alive, would they be together now? She doubted it. Before his death, he'd made no effort to contact her. They'd made love, but they'd never spoken of a relationship. Would they have fallen in love, brought together by the shared duties of parenthood? Or, would she have come to Chicago and still wound up damningly attracted to his brother?

"Now that Bryan has given you Dillon's life insurance money, you'll probably want to invest in a home of your own," Hugh said. "But while you're looking, Julia and I still would love for you to stay in our guesthouse."

"Oh, yes. Please say you will," Julia added. "I promise not to be popping in unannounced all the time and disturbing you. Maybe just once a day to play with Brice."

Morgan had to admit, the idea of an extra set of hands held almost as much appeal as the opportunity for Brice to develop a relationship with his grandparents.

"Can that once a day be at two in the morning when he decides he doesn't want to go back to sleep?" she asked with a grin.

"Is that a yes?"

"Yes."

The older woman wrapped Morgan in a hug and rocked back and forth. "I'm so glad."

It was a moment before she stepped back. Then she said to Bryan, "Why don't you show Morgan around the guesthouse before you leave. It's in presentable condition, I hope."

"More or less."

"Good." Julia scooped up the baby. "And take your time."

"We'll be lucky to get out of here before midnight," Bryan groused good-naturedly as they crossed to the guesthouse. His tone was more serious when he added, "I'm glad you agreed to stay here for a while. It means a lot to my parents to be able to get to know Brice and have him so near. They're not very happy with me that I kept him a secret for so long."

"You did what you thought was best," Morgan allowed, though she still felt she was missing some pertinent facts. "And it means a lot to me, too, to have them so close by. Every child deserves at least one set of doting grandparents."

"They'll spoil him rotten if you're not careful. Before you know it, toys will start arriving. Big toys like motorized cars and life-size stuffed ponies." He snorted out a laugh. "They're good at that."

Morgan frowned. He sounded as if he spoke from experience, she thought as he opened the door and waited for her to go inside.

The guesthouse was much smaller than Bryan's penthouse, but what it lacked in square footage it made up for in warmth and coziness. The kitchen was outfitted with high-end appliances and warm maple cabinetry. A high counter separated it from the living room. A newspaper was laid out on the counter next to a cup of coffee and a plate dotted with toast crumbs and a small wedge of crust. She pictured him sitting there, combing through the business section as he ate.

"That looks like the breakfast of champions," she teased.

"Making toast is the extent of my culinary abilities." He shrugged. "Don't tell my mother I left dirty dishes out. She'd be appalled."

"Actually, this place is amazingly clean for a bachelor pad," Morgan remarked as he led her down a short hall.

"That's because I'm not here much to mess it up." He opened the first door they came to and switched on the light, revealing a full bath with the kind of tub a woman could do some serious soaking in and a glass-enclosed shower. Pointing to a partly opened door on the other side, he said, "You can access this room from either the hall or the bedroom."

That was their next stop. Once inside, he pulled back the drapes and light flooded in. The room was amply proportioned, although she would have to rearrange the furniture to accommodate Brice's crib and changing table. Bryan read her mind.

"If you take out the desk and move the bed over to that wall, you'll have no problem fitting in Brice's nursery."

The desk in question was piled high with file folders and a laptop computer.

"You're not home enough to mess up this place, but you find time to work here?"

"The company is in the middle of an expansion right now. Since my father is close to retiring, I'm working with the project manager to handle the details and smooth out any wrinkles that develop."

She didn't doubt he was busy, but it still sounded like an excuse to her. "You should be getting out more, spending time with people."

"Who says I don't?"

She folded her arms across her chest. "Does that mean you've found a replacement for Courtney so soon?"

"Would it bother you if I had?"

"Yes." The reply came quickly and left her blinking. It *would* bother her, she realized. A lot. In fact, just thinking about Bryan kissing another woman the way he'd kissed her that one time in his foyer made Morgan want to scream at the top of her lungs. Fortunately, her tone sounded normal when she continued. "You told me that things between the two of you were pretty casual."

"Yes. That's what I want."

Because of his divorce? It had to be. Had he been hurt that badly? "Well, I think you deserve more than that."

He looked mildly amused. "Oh, you do?"

"You're a good man, Bryan."

"Are you sure about that?"

She hadn't been when they first met, but she was now. Oh, he tried to hide it, for reasons that remained a mystery to her. But he was sensitive and fair. The instruments for the community center and the transference of Dillon's life insurance money to Brice were proof of that.

"Yes, I am. And it doesn't hurt that you're also drop-dead gor—"

She ended the description abruptly, but not before he'd figured out where she was heading with it. One side of his mouth crooked up.

"By all means, go on."

When she didn't, Bryan turned the tables on her. "What about you? You're a good person. Drop-dead—et cetera. Don't you deserve more?"

"I stopped thinking about what I deserved the moment I had Brice. I have responsibilities and obligations. I'm a mother now."

"Even mothers can get dressed up and go out on a date now and then, Morgan."

She shook her head. "Not this one."

"Why?"

The way he was watching her made it hard to think, especially since they were standing on opposite sides of an unmade bed whose tangled sheets had her mind straying into decidedly inappropriate territory. "Brice needs me."

Bryan's voice dipped low. It was a seductive whisper when he asked, "Don't you have needs?"

The question was dangerous. The answer that echoed in her head was even more so. Her gaze dropped to his mouth. What she wanted was off-limits and had to remain that way. Morgan couldn't afford to be reckless again. What if things didn't work out? Then what? She would still have to see him. Morgan might not be related to the Caliborns, but her son was. She couldn't afford to jeopardize things.

So she told him, "I have everything I need."

Bryan watched her swallow after making that declaration. She'd sounded resolute, but the way she'd stared at his mouth told him something else.

"Same here," he said.

They were both liars.

It was growing dark when they arrived at the penthouse. Bryan found a spot in front of the building. It didn't surprise her that he came around to open her door. But it shocked her when he lifted Brice out of the car seat.

"I'll carry him," he said when she reached to take him. "That's if you don't mind."

"I don't mind." Quite the opposite. She liked seeing Brice cuddled in Bryan's capable arms as they walked to the building. "You know, I never noticed it before, but you and Brice have the same shaped eyebrows."

His tugged together. "Really?"

"Well, not when you do that."

He stopped walking. "Do what?"

"Frown." Before she could think better of it, Morgan reached up and smoothed out his brow. Afterward, she drew back her hand quickly. To cover her nerves, she quipped, "You do that a lot."

"Do I?"

"I wonder if he's going to be able to intimidate people with a mere glance when he grows up."

"It takes years of practice to perfect. I'll have to get busy teaching him."

Though his comment was offhanded, she hoped Bryan really planned to play a more active role in her son's life. That was what she'd hoped for when she'd stayed in Chicago. That was all she could hope for now.

When the elevator arrived at the top floor, Bryan remarked, "I think someone needs a change of pants."

"Give him to me. I'll take care of him."

"That's all right. I'll do it."

Morgan was aware her mouth had fallen open, but she couldn't seem to close it as she watched Bryan walk down the hall to the bedroom.

Bryan laid Brice on the changing table and rolled up his sleeves. "Try not to move around too much, okay?"

The baby kicked his legs as an answer.

"Never mind."

For the past few months, Bryan had gone out of his way not to hold the baby or touch him, even though at times he'd been tempted. Just being around Brice had brought back too many memories, and even the good ones had made him ache. He'd reached a conclusion, though. He needed to face his demons head-on and step up to the plate as the boy's uncle. This was his brother's son, Dillon's legacy, which was why Bryan wanted Brice to have the life insurance money. But money was a poor substitute for affection. Morgan and the baby needed him. A little scarier was the realization that he needed them, too.

"You'll be happy to know I'm not a novice at this."

The baby merely blinked at him.

"Hey, don't look so unimpressed."

This time Brice yawned and turned his head to one side. Bryan traced the baby's ear from the folded edge at the top down to the tiny lobe.

"It seems we have more in common than our eyebrows. The Caliborn ears. Mine are a little bigger than yours. Your dad had these, too. If you're lucky you'll inherit his ability to make people laugh. He didn't take life too seriously." Bryan shook his head. "He said I did that enough for both of us."

He swallowed then. Missing Dill. Missing Caden. "I wanted you to be his, you know. From the very beginning I wanted you to be his. Just like I wanted Caden to be mine."

"Bryan?" Morgan stood in the doorway. "I just came to see how you were doing."

He cleared his throat. "Fine."

"I can take over if you'd like."

"No. I've changed a diaper or two in my time." He began unsnapping the blue-striped sleeper, a task made a little more difficult by the baby's flailing limbs. But he finally managed to remove it, along with the soiled diaper. A moment later he was re-dressing Brice, who was now cooing happily.

"I guess you *have* done that a time or two," Morgan commented.

"You doubted me?"

She nodded. "Sorry. It's just that you don't look like the sort of man who's ever pulled diaper duty."

"It has been a while."

"How long?" she asked softly.

"A few years." Rough laughter scraped his throat. "I guess that diapering a baby is like riding a bike. Once you learn how, you never forget." He lifted Brice to his shoulder. "You don't forget this, either. How they feel in your arms."

"Who is Caden?" she asked quietly.

He closed his eyes. "My…ex-wife's son."

"Oh." Morgan frowned. He could see that his reply had raised more questions than it had answered. "I thought…I guess I thought he was your son."

His laughter was harsh. "I did, too."

The story spilled out, haltingly at first as the words were wrenched from deep inside him. Through it all, Morgan said nothing, listening in that patient way of hers, her expression concerned and sympathetic rather than pitying.

"I'm sorry, Bryan," she murmured. Reaching up,

she brushed his cheeks. He'd been crying, he realized. The tears should have embarrassed him. In the past he would have considered them a show of weakness. But they were cleansing and empowering somehow. And he felt stronger.

"I wish you'd told me sooner."

Oddly, so did he. "It's not something I talk about."

"Then I'm glad you shared it with me."

Morgan put one arm around his waist and, pressing her cheek to his shoulder, hugged him. Bryan shifted Brice to his other shoulder so he could hug her back. They stood like that for a long time.

"Can I stay?" he asked quietly. "Just to sleep."

"Yes."

As Morgan sat in the rocking chair and nursed Brice, she could hear Bryan moving around in the bedroom next door. A moment later the shower switched on. The sounds were routine, domestic and oddly comforting.

After burping Brice, she laid him in his crib. He fussed before settling down, grunting as he wriggled around to find a comfortable spot.

Morgan patted his tummy and recalled what Bryan had revealed. Her heart ached for him. To have been deceived that way by someone he'd loved and trusted had left a lasting scar. No wonder he'd been so cynical and distrustful when she'd first arrived. No wonder he preferred casual relationships with women like Courtney. Would he ever be willing to risk his heart again?

Morgan kissed her fingers and touched Brice's cheek before slipping out of the room. She had no business wanting to know the answer to that question.

It was almost nine o'clock when Bryan joined her in the living room. His hair was still damp from his shower. He wore the tan pants he'd had on earlier and a white cotton T-shirt he'd culled from his dresser. His feet were bare.

She'd made a bowl of popcorn and was watching an old movie on cable. "Are you hungry?" she asked. "I can make you a sandwich or something."

He settled next to her on the couch. "That's all right. What are you watching?"

"I'm not sure. I tuned in after it started. Want some popcorn?" When he nodded, she shifted the bowl between them.

"You moved the television," he said. "And the couch."

"Yes. It made more sense over there. And, well, once I moved the television, I couldn't leave the couch where it was. I'll move it back when I leave."

"No. That's okay." He glanced around, nodded. "I like it this way. It's more…homey."

Because she didn't know what to say to that, she asked, "Speaking of moving, when are we going to make the swap?"

He rubbed his chin. "Does next weekend work for you?"

"Sure." She wiped her fingers on a napkin. "Brice and I don't have any other plans."

They finished off the popcorn while they watched the rest of the movie. As the credits rolled, Morgan glanced over at Bryan. He'd been quiet for a while and no wonder. His head was resting on the back of the couch and his eyes were closed. She reached for the remote and switched off the TV. It had been a long and emotionally draining day for both of them. If not for nerves, she wouldn't have lasted this long.

I should wake him, she thought. Let him settle into the comfort of his bed. And seek out the refuge of mine.

Morgan reached over and turned off the light. In the darkness she felt his arm come around her, stopping her from rising to her feet. She sank back on the cushion, allowed him to pull her closer to his side. Though she told herself to go, she stayed exactly where she was until Brice's cries woke her five and a half hours later.

CHAPTER NINE

Morgan was out early Monday morning running errands when the first fat raindrops began to fall. As she hurried to her car with Brice in his stroller the front page of a newspaper caught her eye. The black-and-white photograph of her, Brice and Bryan standing on the street outside the apartment ran four columns wide. She was touching Bryan's face. Smoothing his brow that was so much like her son's, she recalled now, though the photograph made the contact appear far more intimate than that.

It didn't help that the accompanying headline read: Another Questionable Caliborn? This time Windy Cities scion in no hurry to claim child as heir.

Groaning in disbelief, she snatched a copy from the newsstand. Her dread increased tenfold as she scanned the contents of the article. Not only did it debate Brice's parentage and make insinuations about the character of the single mom who'd moved into Bryan's penthouse, it went on to rehash the horrid details of his divorce and the painful revelation that Caden was not his son. Given how violated she was feeling, Morgan could only imagine Bryan's reaction when he learned that his private life had once again been turned into a public spectacle.

She paid for the paper and tucked it into the diaper bag. She had to reach him, talk to him, offer whatever help or comfort she could. Her hair was damp by the time she reached her car. She quickly buckled Brice into his seat in the back and stowed the stroller. Then she swore under her breath when the engine refused to turn over.

"Not today!" she hollered.

Thumping the steering wheel with the palms of her hands, she debated her options. Bryan would be at the office. She needed to find a phone and call him, warn him. Unfortunately, she didn't own a cell. Yet. She would before the day was out, she decided, making a mental note. She remembered passing an El stop a few blocks from where she was parked. She was a good two miles from Bryan's office. Mind made up, she got out of the car and retrieved the stroller. Covering Brice up with an extra blanket from the diaper bag, she took off at a run.

Bryan was in a foul mood when he stepped off the elevator. He usually arrived at the office no later than seven-thirty, but he'd had a Rotary breakfast across town, followed by a meeting with bank officials.

Then he'd run into a snarl of traffic on State Street. It was almost ten o'clock now and in less than fifteen minutes he had a transatlantic conference call scheduled with the site manager and a couple of other managers concerning the London expansion project.

Britney trailed behind him into his office, going over his phone messages as he peeled off his damp coat. It was pouring outside and thunder rumbled in the distance. Everything they said about Mondays was true, he decided, and that was before he saw the tabloid on top of the stack of traditional newspapers he read each day.

At his muttered expletive, Britney said, "I'm sorry, Mr. Caliborn, but I knew you would want to see this."

No. He didn't. But he read the headline anyway and that alone had him shouting, "Get my attorney on the phone."

The young woman nodded, but hesitated in the doorway.

"Is there something else?" He almost hated to ask.

"Yes." Her tone cooled considerably when she said, "Miss Stevens phoned you. Twice in the past hour. I'm guessing she saw the newspaper as well."

Bryan closed his eyes and sighed. To think he'd believed this ugliness was finally over and forgotten. Not only had his past been dredged up, Morgan and Brice had been dragged into it. That just plain ticked him off. Somebody's head was going to roll.

"Get her on the phone first."

"I would, but she didn't leave a call-back number."

He frowned. "She wasn't at home?"

"No. She was calling from a pay phone." Britney tugged at the hem of her jacket. "Not that it's any of my business, Mr. Caliborn, but do you think Miss Stevens could be one of the unnamed sources?"

"What?"

"In the story. It relies heavily on them."

"What on earth would Morgan have to gain by making herself the center of a scandal?" he snapped.

"I don't know. Some people enjoy notoriety and the attention. I mean, she showed up here in labor, burst in on your meeting." She coughed delicately then. "And it can pay well."

"You think Morgan sold this story to *City Talk* for money?" He wasn't angry, but incredulous.

"I hope not. For your sake, Mr. Caliborn. You've been through enough of this kind of thing. If there's anything I can do to help you, anything at all, I'll be glad to do it. But I felt the need to raise the possibility since so much of what is printed here is, well, inside information. Who else would have known that you were so generously allowing her and her baby to live in your penthouse, even though obviously you were suspicious of her claims about the baby being yours?"

"What do you mean by that?"

"You hired a private detective to investigate her sexual history." At his raised eyebrows, she said, "I put through the invoice Gil Rogers sent with his report last week."

She also had to have read the report to know what the man had been investigating.

Bryan held up a hand. "Stop right there. I can think of a few people wise to those details, which, by the way, aren't exactly the facts. That's why I know Morgan didn't plant this story. She wouldn't have gotten things wrong. As for needing money, Morgan is a wealthy woman in her own right these days."

"She...she is?"

"Yes. But I agree this information came from an inside source. When I find out who's responsible for this story, and I will, that person won't be working here. In fact, it would be better for that person altogether if they resigned their position and cleared out their desk before I had to ask them to do it."

Her face paled beneath her blusher. He had a sick feeling he'd just found his Judas.

"If Morgan calls back, put her through immediately."

"But the conference call..." Britney began.

He meant it when he said, "Interrupt me, if need be. She's more important."

When the conference call from London came, he still hadn't heard from Morgan. Bryan didn't like it. Where was she? Had she seen the story? Was she being hounded by reporters? Unfortunately, he had no choice but to wait.

Bryan's mood didn't improve as he listened to the site manager rattle on about cost overruns and a couple of snags the construction crew had encountered with local officials.

Rubbing his forehead, he asked, "How much extra are we talking?"

The sum had him swearing. From the doorway, Britney cleared her throat. "Hold on a minute, John." He covered the mouthpiece with his hand. "Do you have Morgan on the line?"

"Actually, she's here."

Relief flooded through him. "Get her a cup of coffee or tea if she prefers and tell her I'll be with her in a few minutes."

It was nearly half an hour, though, before he was finally able to wrap up the call. He'd found it difficult to concentrate on the site manager's concerns with Morgan just outside his office, especially when he heard Brice start to fuss.

When he finally hung up and stepped out into the waiting area, his mouth fell open at the sight of her.

"My God! Are you okay?"

"I'm fine." She didn't look fine. Her hair was soaked and plastered to her head. Her clothes were equally soggy. Brice had fared better thanks to the stroller's hood and an extra blanket. Now that he was sipping from a small bottle of juice, he was perfectly content.

"What happened?" Bryan asked once they were alone in his office.

"I had to see you."

"Morgan, you're soaked to the bone." And cold, too, he thought as he watched her shiver. He helped her out of her wet coat and put his suit jacket around her shaking shoulders. Together they sat on the leather couch, the same couch where she'd once writhed in labor.

"I got caught in the r-rain. My car broke d-down again."

"That thing is a hazard," he said as he rubbed her back.

"Agreed. It's gone to the scrap heap as of today. But that's not why I'm here, Bryan." She shifted so she was facing him, green eyes filled with concern. "I don't know how to tell you this, but—"

"You've seen the article in *City Talk*."

She winced. "You know."

"Britney brought in a copy." He frowned. "That's why you rushed here in the rain?"

"I tried calling from a coffee shop and again at the El stop, but this seemed the sort of thing you should be told in person anyway. I'm so sorry."

She meant that, he knew. "It's not your fault. Hell, you and Brice are as much victims as I am. More so, when you get right down to it. You only got dragged into this because of the Caliborn name."

She tilted her head to one side. "It's a good name. One worth standing up for. Fight back, Bryan."

"Oh, I plan to. I've already spoken to my attorney about bringing a libel suit against the publisher. He thinks we have a good case, despite my standing as a quasi-public figure. They printed half truths and outright lies without making any effort to verify the facts."

"Tell me about it. They make me out to be some sort of…" She shook her head, left the sentence unfinished.

It was his turn to apologize. He pulled her against him, dropped a kiss on her temple. "I'm sorry you got thrown under the bus with me."

"That's okay. I'm pretty resilient."

"I know." But she didn't deserve this. He stood and helped her to her feet. "Now let's get you and Brice home so you can get out of those wet clothes."

Morgan didn't expect Bryan to stay after he delivered her and the baby to the penthouse. Especially after they spotted a photographer hanging around outside and the doorman told them a couple of reporters had tried to sneak into the elevators. But he didn't leave. Instead, he offered to change and entertain the baby while she took a hot shower and put on fresh clothes.

She did so quickly, pulling her still-damp hair into a ponytail and not bothering with makeup. She didn't want to keep him waiting too long. Surely he had to get back to the office. But when she joined him in the living room, Brice was asleep in his swing and Bryan was in no hurry to leave.

He was sitting on the couch with one foot propped

on the coffee table. He'd removed his suit jacket when they arrived. His tie was loosened now, too, the sleeves of his crisp white shirt rolled halfway up his forearms.

"It's almost lunchtime. Are you hungry?" she asked.

"Not really. You?"

"No." She'd felt queasy since seeing that headline. She plunked down next to him on the couch.

"I called my parents to let them know. A neighbor saw the paper in the grocery store and had already given them the news."

Grimacing, Morgan asked, "What did they say?"

"Well, they weren't happy about it, but they were more worried about me." He sent her a smile. "And you. They're especially glad you're going to be moving into their guesthouse. You and Brice will have more privacy there. They'll see to it."

"But isn't my moving there likely to raise more speculation? The last thing I want to do is cause your parents to be hounded by reporters or have photographers camped outside their front door."

He leaned forward, rested his elbows on his knees. "They have a suggestion for how we can prevent that. They want to call a press conference, Morgan." One side of his mouth rose. "Steal the gossipmongers' thunder, as my dad put it."

"A press conference?"

"They want to make it clear to everyone that Brice is a Caliborn. They don't want it to seem as if we're hiding something or are somehow ashamed of the situation." He turned, touched her face, his fingers lingering on the curve of her cheek. "But it's your decision. They're leaving it up to you."

She glanced away. "The details make it all seem so sordid."

"You don't owe them details. Just the basic facts. Brice is Dillon's son and you came here to connect with your baby's family. There's no shame in that."

"No shame in that," she repeated. Being an unwed mother wasn't as big a deal as it used to be, but that didn't mean Morgan was eager to have all of Chicago discussing her situation over their morning coffee.

"None."

She nodded as she rose and crossed to her sleeping son. Lifting him out of the swing, she dropped a kiss on his forehead. "I'm going to put him in his crib."

Bryan was still on the couch when she returned. "We don't have to say anything," he told her. "You don't owe anyone any explanations. My parents will understand."

"No." She shook her head. "I told you to stand up, fight back. I need to, too. Your parents are right. In the absence of the facts, the lies will just continue being spread."

He stood, crossed to her. Hands on her shoulders, he asked, "Are you sure?"

"Yes. I won't let my son be the subject of rumors."

Bryan pulled her close for a hug. He intended the gesture to offer reassurance, but it morphed into something else as the seconds ticked by. She fitted perfectly in his arms, soft curves molding against him. He turned his head slightly so he could breathe in her scent. It was nothing overpowering, a hint of citrus and soap. His lips brushed her temple as his hands stroked her back, and just that quickly, the need he'd tried to keep banked was stoked to life.

"Morgan." He sighed her name. "God, I wish…" He covered her mouth with his to prevent the words from slipping out. They were too frightening, too damning to utter.

Her arms came up, her hands gripped his shoulders. He felt her fingernails dig into his flesh through the fabric of his shirt, letting him know that this need wasn't one-sided. Bryan took everything she offered and still wanted more. He'd never been this greedy or felt half this desperate. His fingers brushed her cheek, stroked the column of her neck and then found the buttons of her blouse. As he nibbled the sensitive skin just below her ear, he slipped the first one through its hole. When the last one gave way and his fingertips brushed the valley between her breasts, he was rewarded with a moan of pleasure.

"You're in—"

"Insane." Morgan finished as she pushed away, pulling her blouse together. Her hair was mussed, half of it hanging free from the ponytail.

The breath sawed in and out of Bryan's lungs. Actually, he had been thinking intoxicating, incredible.

"I— We can't do this!"

He almost argued the point. He thought they could do it, very well and to both of their satisfaction. But he knew that wasn't what she meant.

"Can we pretend this never happened?" she asked.

They'd done that after the first time he'd kissed her. It hadn't worked for him then. It wouldn't work now. But Bryan nodded anyway. "If that's what you want."

"I think it's for the best, given everything that's involved here."

Bryan retrieved his coat. Though his body was burning with need from their all-too-brief encounter, he said, "It never happened."

After he left, Morgan flopped down on the couch. She was mortified by her behavior. The way she'd kissed him. The thoughts that had gone through her mind at the time. Just thinking about them now had goose bumps prickling her flesh, heat curling through her…tears blurring her vision.

A year ago, confused and in mourning, she'd allowed Dillon to seduce her. She was every bit as confused now, but no seduction was necessary on Bryan's part. She wasn't sure when or how, but the fact was irrefutable. She'd fallen in love with him.

CHAPTER TEN

THE Caliborns called the press conference for the following afternoon. It made no sense to put it off, Morgan knew, especially now that the mainstream media had started sniffing around, too. But given what had transpired between her and Bryan twenty-four hours earlier, she was a nervous wreck. How was she going to stand in front of a crowd of probing reporters and explain that her relationship with Bryan was strictly platonic?

She wore the outfit she'd purchased to meet the Caliborns just the weekend before. Though she'd deposited the check Bryan had given her, she'd hardly had time to shop for something new. Vaguely, she wondered if someone would notice it was what she'd had on in the photograph that had been snapped. As for Brice, it didn't really matter what he wore. Morgan planned to have him wrapped up tightly in a blanket, allowing only minimal exposure. She wasn't about to let her son's image be exploited so they could sell more papers.

Bryan sent a car for her. The conference was slated to begin at ten o'clock at the Windy City offices. She arrived just after nine and was quickly ushered inside the same conference room where she'd first encountered the real Bryan Caliborn. He was at the end of the same long table, standing rather than sitting, and instead of a file folder, a bank of microphones was in front of him. He looked every bit as handsome and authoritative as he had that day. The only difference was that instead of scowling when he spied her, his eyes lit up and he smiled.

Julia and Hugh were there, too. Julia gave Morgan a hug and took Brice, who had fallen asleep on the car ride over. Hugh hugged her as well.

"Damned vultures," he muttered. "For all the good things Windy City Industries has done in this city, you'd think they'd show some restraint on private matters."

When Hugh released her, Bryan was there, holding out a cup of tea like a peace offering. He didn't hug her, but he did squeeze her arm when he asked, "Nervous?"

"Yes." For reasons that had more to do with the man in front of her than the throng of reporters assembling outside. "I suppose you're better at this sort of thing than I am. This is my first news conference."

"I've done several, but I'm nervous, too. I'd much rather be talking about business than about my private life," he said ruefully. "Did you read over the notes I sent last night?"

She nodded. He had e-mailed Morgan a set of

questions he felt they were likely to encounter and suggestions for how they should respond. Basically, all she had to be was honest, but brevity was the key.

"Remember, don't offer them anything they don't ask for, and feel free not to answer any question that makes you uncomfortable. They're not entitled to all of the details," he said.

She hoped it wouldn't come to that, because clamming up would defeat the purpose of such a press conference. They wanted the media to get their fill and then go away, otherwise the story would grow legs and keep running.

A knock sounded at the door a moment before a young woman poked her head inside. "The waiting room is full. Should I start sending them in, Mr. Caliborn?"

"Give us five more minutes," he said.

"Who's that?" Morgan asked.

"My new secretary." His mouth tightened.

This came as a surprise. "What happened to Britney?"

"She wisely decided it was in her best interests to resign."

They stood at the end of the room, Morgan holding Brice and flanked by the elder Caliborns. Bryan was just in front of them at the microphones. The long table kept the reporters and photographers at a distance, though close enough that Morgan saw eagerness and speculation in some of their expressions. When the noise died down and everyone had filed into the room, Bryan cleared his throat and gave his prepared statement.

"Thank you for coming here today. As you know, a story about my family recently ran in *City Talk*. It was poorly researched and full of innuendo and outright lies. My attorney will be filing a libel suit on my behalf. In the meantime, we asked you here today to set the record straight.

"First of all, the baby in question is a Caliborn."

Camera flashes popped and a couple of reporters shouted out questions. Bryan ignored them and kept talking. "His name is Brice Dillon Stevens. He is my late brother's son."

The room erupted into a frenzy then. He gave up continuing with his prepared remarks and pointed to a reporter.

"Leslie Michaelson with *City Talk*," the woman began. "I didn't write the original story that appeared in my newspaper."

"Rag, you mean," Julia inserted. The comment, coming as it did from such a demure and usually pleasant woman, had most of the reporters snickering.

The woman cleared her throat and went on, "We were led to believe, by a source very close to you, that the baby was yours. Do you deny that Miss Stevens had been contacting your office for months, seeking an audience with you regarding her pregnancy?"

"Miss Stevens did contact me looking for her

baby's father. Dillon was not here, so I referred the matter to my attorney."

Morgan was impressed. What he'd said was true, he'd just left out enough information to give a different impression—much like the woman's *City Talk* colleague had done in the original story.

"My question is for Miss Stevens," another reporter chimed in. "How did you meet Dillon Caliborn?"

"I met him while vacationing. I found him very charming, and I was very sorry to learn of his death."

The man opened his mouth to follow up on the question, most likely to fill in the gaps left by her response, but Bryan called on another reporter before he could.

"Mr. and Mrs. Caliborn, is there any doubt in your mind that Miss Stevens's child is your grandchild?"

"None whatsoever." Julia beamed.

"He's a Caliborn through and through," Hugh agreed. "If he chooses, he'll be the one standing before you one day, putting you in your place instead of putting up with your nonsense."

That caused a rumble of uncomfortable laughter from their ranks.

The reporter wasn't deterred, though. This time he addressed Bryan. "In the matter of the son your former wife conceived while married to you, a paternity test was performed. Was one done this time?"

Morgan chanced a glance at Bryan. His expression was inscrutable, but she knew the pain the question caused and it was all she could do not to shout for them all to go away and leave him alone.

"No test was necessary. Unlike my former wife, I trust Miss Stevens."

"Is that why you hired an investigator to probe her background and report back on any other men she might have been seeing at the time of the baby's conception?"

Morgan hadn't seen that question coming. It landed like a prizefighter's uppercut. She let out a little gasp, which she camouflaged by clearing her throat. "I'll take this one," she said.

More flashes popped. Holding the baby so his face wasn't visible to the cameras, she stepped to the microphone.

"I requested the investigation." Morgan didn't question why she felt the need to stretch the truth, only that, even though she was hurt by the revelation, it seemed the right thing to do. "The Caliborns accepted my son and me right away. They have shown me nothing but kindness. But given what the family had been through in the past, I wanted them to be assured of my claims. Even though they saw no need for a definitive paternity test, I wanted as many facts as possible on the table."

"Are you still living in Mr. Caliborn's penthouse?" someone shouted.

"I will be moving out today and he will be moving back in. He's been very gracious to let me stay there as long as he has, and I've appreciated his kindness."

"Where will you move to?"

"Do you really think I plan to give the lot of you my new address?" she asked with wry laughter.

The reporters and photographers laughed as well.

More questions were asked, all of them anticipated and as such easily answered. Then Bryan announced, "This will be the final question."

Morgan nearly sagged with relief until she heard what it was. Then she stiffened.

"Mr. Caliborn, what exactly is your relationship to Miss Stevens?"

Had the question been directed toward her, she would be stammering over her words. But not Bryan. Without hesitation and in that tone that brooked no argument, he said, "My relationship to Miss Stevens is obvious. Her son is my nephew and since my brother is no longer alive I feel an obligation to look after both of them."

His words echoed what Britney had told Morgan when she'd moved into the penthouse: *Mr. Caliborn takes his responsibilities very seriously.*

The answer was jotted down in the man's notebook, apparently accepted as the truth, but Morgan didn't want to believe it could be possible that while Bryan was attracted to her and finally trusted her, duty was his main priority.

* * *

Bryan was grateful to see the last straggling queue of reporters file out of the conference room and pile into the elevator.

Once they were gone, Julia wilted onto one of the chairs with a sigh. "I think that went well."

"For a feeding frenzy." Hugh grunted. "But at least it's over and done with now."

Morgan was leaning against the far wall, jiggling the baby in her arms and staring intently at a spot on the carpet. She was quiet, far too quiet for Bryan's liking, and he suspected he knew the reason.

"Mom, would you and Dad mind taking Brice into my office? I'd like to talk to Morgan alone for a minute."

When the conference-room door closed behind his parents, he turned to her. "That was pretty brutal. How are you holding up?"

"I'm fine."

Liar, he thought. But he didn't call her on it. He'd lied as well. By omission, when it came to Gil Rogers, but still.

"Look, Morgan, about the private investigator," he began.

She shook her head to stop his words. "Don't, Bryan. There's really no need for you to explain. I didn't know you'd hired one, but I knew that you didn't trust me. You made that pretty plain."

"In the beginning, yes. But that was before—"

Before he'd gotten to know her and realized what a strong, brave and determined woman she was.

Before he'd kissed her and his ordered world had begun spinning into chaos.

Before he'd fallen in love with her.

The last revelation was too new and staggering to ponder let alone share. Love? Good God! He hadn't seen it coming. Of course, he hadn't predicted any of the recent events that had occurred in his life.

Morgan was watching him, waiting for him to continue.

"I let past circumstances color my judgment. I meant it when I told the reporters you're nothing like my ex-wife. I should have seen that right away. I should have believed you."

"I understand, really." But her arms remained wrapped around her waist, her body language stating quite plainly that something was troubling her... something had hurt her.

"Still, I'm sorry. I made things more difficult for you in the beginning than they needed to be, especially given everything you were already going through. I know what happened to your parents."

"The detective?"

He nodded guiltily. "I can't even begin to imagine how horrible that must have been for you. And then, in my stubbornness, I cheated you and my parents out of months of time together."

That wasn't what he was most sorry for, though. Most of all, he was sorry about Dillon. Not only because his brother had lied to Morgan, charmed and seduced her in Aruba, and then walked away without a backward glance only to die in a tragic accident and leave her child fatherless. No. Bryan was sorry that Dillon had been the Caliborn brother to meet her first.

"It's okay. In the end, things have worked out the way they were meant to." Something in her words struck him as ominous, though he couldn't put a finger on what before she motioned toward the door and asked, "Do you think that's the end of it?"

"God, I hope so." Running a hand over the back of his neck, Bryan added, "I don't want to be dodging reporters' questions and photographers' flashbulbs every time I leave the office or arrive home. That's why I tried to spell out the facts as clearly as possible so they won't look for more."

She offered what passed for a smile. "Well then, I'd say mission accomplished."

Immediately following the news conference, Morgan moved out of the penthouse as planned. Bryan moved back in. Her personal effects were gone, but reminders of her were everywhere. In the red accent pillows and throw, the scented candles and the dining-room-table runner she'd left behind. Even in the rearranged living-room furniture. She'd turned his place into a real home during the short time she'd lived there. But it didn't feel like a real home now that she and Brice were no longer in it. When he came home from work late the first evening she was gone, the penthouse just felt big and empty, and, yes, he could finally admit it, lonely.

He was lonely.

In the weeks that followed, it became clear that his relationship with Morgan had changed along with their addresses. Did she regret the stolen kisses they'd shared? She'd told him they should forget they'd ever happened and apparently she had. Bryan, however, hadn't been successful. He lay awake each night, torturing himself with memories of what had been as well as what he wished had transpired…what he still wished would happen. But none of it seemed possible when Morgan smiled at him so politely and kept him at a distance during visits that she made sure were conducted under the watchful eye of his parents.

It was killing him. She seemed not to notice.

CHAPTER ELEVEN

IN THE middle of November, Morgan found a house. She'd fallen in love with it at first sight. It was a two-story Tudor in a quiet, tree-lined neighborhood of older homes just a few miles from Bryan's parents' place. Compared to that house, it was small, but with four bedrooms and three and half baths spread over two stories, it more than accommodated her and Brice's needs.

It had a big yard with a couple of mature oaks whose fat limbs were perfect for supporting a tree house or a tire swing, and while the landscaping was nice, Morgan was sure Julia could give her plenty of ideas on how to improve it. The owners had already relocated to another state, which meant she could move in as soon as the paperwork was completed. If all went as planned, she and Brice could be in their own home by Thanksgiving or at the very least Christmas. The idea appealed to her. Even though she enjoyed staying in the guesthouse and the Caliborns respected her privacy, she wanted her own home, a place on which she was free to put her own stamp.

Today, Bryan was coming by to see the house. She'd asked him to, wanting his opinion since she would be plunking down a chunk of Brice's inheritance to pay for it. She waited for him in her car in the driveway. The vehicle was new, purchased a couple days after the old one had left her and the baby stranded in the rain. It was nothing flashy, but it boasted all of the latest safety features and had fared the best in a national publication's crash tests.

Leaves swirled on the street when Bryan pulled his Lexus to the curb. Morgan got out of her car and joined him on the brick-paved walk that led to the front door. He was dressed in a dark suit since he'd come straight from his office. His attire was professional, his smile personal. Upon seeing it, her pulse took off like a warning flare.

They hadn't been alone together since the press conference. Morgan had made sure of that. They wouldn't be alone for long now. Her real estate agent was running late, but the woman would be there any time to let them inside and answer his questions during the walk-through. Even so, Morgan wondered if it had been a mistake to leave Brice in the care of Bryan's parents. At least with the baby in her arms she wouldn't be so tempted to open hers to Bryan when he reached her.

"Hello, Morgan."

"Hi." The cool temperatures turned their greetings into white mist. They eyed one another awkwardly before she asked, "So, what do you think of the neighborhood?"

Stuffing his hands into his trouser pockets, he glanced around. "It's very solid. The values here are in no danger of dropping. And there's nothing wrong with the home's curb appeal."

"The mature trees help," she said, pointing to a nearby oak. Its leaves had turned yellow and most of them had fallen, exposing a squirrel's nest high in the thick branches.

"Brice is going to have a field day around here when he gets older."

"Tell me about it. He's already impatient to be mobile. Just this morning he pushed up onto his knees after rolling onto his belly. Any day now, he's going to be crawling and everything at his eye level will be fair game."

He glanced toward her car. "You didn't bring him?"

She shook her head. "He's with your mother."

The real estate agent arrived then. After apologizing for her lateness she unlocked the front door and waved them inside. "If it's okay with you, I'll just stay out here and make a few phone calls while you show Mr. Caliborn around."

Morgan swallowed. She had little choice but to agree. The door closed behind them with a thud that seemed to echo in the empty house.

"The parquet floors are original and for the most part in excellent shape."

"So I see."

She pointed to a room through an arched doorway to the side. "Why don't we start the tour in the dining room?"

Bryan had more on his mind than the house, but he followed her through the rooms, listening patiently and with no small amount of interest to her plans for decorating. It was clear Morgan loved the house. He liked it, too. Even though it was bare of furnishings and its walls were in need of a new coat of paint, it exuded charm and character. No doubt once she took possession of it, in short order and with little effort, she would turn it into a home.

Even now as they walked from space to space he could picture her there. In the living room sitting beside the fireplace and admonishing Brice to keep away from the flames. In the kitchen baking cookies or drinking hot cocoa at a table tucked into the nook. In the library curled up with Brice on an overstuffed couch turning the pages of a picture book.

And in the master bedroom at the top of the stairs, he pictured her in a big bed, wearing white satin and smiling as she held out her hand in invitation.

"What's wrong?"

Her question yanked Bryan from the daydream. "Sorry?"

"You're frowning. Don't you like the house?"

"That's not it. The house is perfect. I can see you here," he told her truthfully.

The problem plaguing Bryan was he could see himself there, too. With Morgan. With Brice. And with the other children he wanted to create with her to fill up the spare bedrooms. He hadn't thought it possible to want a wife and children again after what had happened. He hadn't wanted to risk his heart as either a husband or a father. He knew the reason behind his changed mind. She was standing in front of him. She was also moving on. She didn't need him.

"Then you think I should buy it?" Morgan's excitement was palpable.

"Yes. It's a good investment, although I wouldn't offer the full asking price given the current market."

"I was thinking the same thing," she replied. "Especially since the owners have already left and are motivated to sell."

He couldn't have asked for a better segue. Bryan cleared his throat. "Speaking of leaving, I'll be flying to London next week."

"The company's expansion project?" she guessed. She'd heard him and his father talk about it enough.

He nodded. "We've hit another snag. At this point the new facility won't be operational until next summer, which puts us six months behind schedule and close to three million dollars over budget. I'm hoping that by being there I can help move things along."

"How long will you be gone?"

"A month is the best-case scenario. Three or more if we need to appeal a judge's ruling."

Her expression dimmed. "You'll miss the holidays."

He shook his head, offered a crooked smile. "They have these things called airplanes, you know. But I will miss—"

Bryan couldn't stand it any longer. He had to touch her, even if just to stroke the side of her face, which he did. His hand lingered, turned so his palm could cradle her cheek. He didn't want the contact to end or the connection he felt with her staring up at him to be lost.

"What will you miss?" she asked softly.

"Seeing Brice on a regular basis. Babies change so fast." He swallowed. "And you, Morgan. I'll miss you."

His mouth found hers. The kiss was light, soft, giving her a chance to pull away if that's what she wanted. When she didn't, he infused it with all of the feelings he couldn't yet give voice to. Dillon had been good with words and a master when it came to persuasion. His brother also had been spontaneous, never thinking beyond the moment. Bryan couldn't be like that. He always looked before leaping. But he could be persuasive in his own way.

By the time the kiss ended, a plan was forming. He needed time to put it in place, to perfect his strategy. Twenty-four hours would do it.

"I have to go, Morgan, but can I stop by the guesthouse tomorrow evening?"

"Okay," she said slowly.

"Ask my mother to sit for Brice again. There's something we need to discuss."

Morgan blew out a breath and paced the length of the living room, hoping to wear off the worst of her nerves. Brice was already at the main house with the Caliborns, and Bryan was due to arrive at the guesthouse soon. She'd changed her clothes three times before deciding on a chocolate-brown sweater and tweed pants. She blamed her indecisiveness on the way he'd looked at her after that kiss.

Bryan could be a hard man to read, but as they'd stood in the empty master suite with the late-afternoon sun filtering through the window, she'd sworn a much deeper emotion had stirred in his dark gaze than the sort that went with either sexual attraction or family obligation. It had thrilled her to see it, especially coming as it had after his admission that he would miss her and Brice during his stay in London. But a moment later he'd been his usual contained self when he'd asked to stop by the guesthouse tonight.

She was adding a little more lip gloss when she heard the knock. She glanced at her watch. Bryan was early. Morgan wasn't sure what his eagerness said about the topic he wanted to "discuss."

"Hello, Morgan."

"Hi." She managed the greeting in a casual voice

and stepped back to allow him inside. "Can I take your coat?"

He handed it to her along with the bottle of wine he'd brought. Morgan was still nursing Brice, but she decided to indulge in half a glass when she poured him some of the merlot. She'd expressed some breast milk earlier for Julia to give the baby and she'd begun supplementing his feedings with some formula and cereal so he slept through the night.

When she returned with their glasses, he was standing in front of the sofa. He took his glass of wine, but instead of sipping from it, he set it aside and then squared his shoulders as if preparing for battle. His tone was firm, his words more of an order rather than a request, when he said, "I want you and Brice to come to London with me."

"Wh-what?" Morgan's wine nearly sloshed over the rim at that. He took it from her hand and set it next to his on the side table.

"I know I won't be gone long, a matter of months at most, but I want you with me."

"You do?"

"Actually, I don't just want you with me in London, I want you to marry me, Morgan."

Her heart bucked out an extra beat as she waited for a declaration of love or at the very least a mention of his true feelings, but what Bryan said next was, "It makes sense for a number of reasons."

"Marriage makes sense?" she asked, because she wasn't sure she'd heard him right.

"Absolutely." He nodded, clasped his hands behind his back and began pacing in front of the sofa where she'd taken a seat since her legs threatened to give out. As if addressing Windy City's management team, Bryan began ticking off those reasons in a voice that conveyed plenty of conviction, but lacked the kind of passion a woman hopes to hear from a man asking her to spend the rest of her life with him.

"Brice is a Caliborn. He is an heir to one of the largest businesses in the country. It's not expected, but of course it's hoped, that when he comes of age he will take his place within the company that his great-great-grandfather started in post-fire Chicago."

"I'd never stand in the way of that."

"I love Brice. I know it took me a long time to show it, but it's true."

"You had your reasons," she said softly.

"I'd do anything for him." *Just as he would have done anything for Dillon?* "I want to look after him, Morgan." *Just as he'd always tried to look after Dillon?* "And I want to look after you." *Because Dillon was no longer there to do it?*

Responsibility, obligation, duty. Morgan needed better reasons than those to wed. "But marriage is—"

"The perfect solution."

His use of the word *solution* implied Bryan was addressing a problem. Her heart began to ache. The pain grew worse when he said, "You and I are compatible. I enjoy spending time with you." His gaze dipped to her lips. Longing, was that what she saw? Apparently not, she decided when he said, "We share similar tastes in takeout food and home furnishings."

Her eyes narrowed. "Chinese food and room decor are a good basis for a lifelong commitment?"

"That's not what I meant." He frowned, as if sensing his argument wasn't winning her over. "It's just that a lot of couples I know got married because they were attracted to one another."

"And that's bad?"

"It's not enough. You have to have things in common to succeed long-term."

She agreed with him to an extent, but he still wasn't talking about love. Love was the only reason Morgan would marry.

"I will be faithful to you," he was saying. "Of course, I'll expect the same from you in return. And, as my wife, I will support you in whatever you want to do." He gestured with his arms. "For example, if you want to continue teaching music weekday afternoons at the south-side community center, you may do so."

"Gee, thanks for the permission."

He coughed. "What I mean is you wouldn't be limited to only that. I have the resources that would allow you to create your own center somewhere if you'd like, or do whatever else you feel necessary to bring music into the lives of young people." He ruined that fine speech by adding, "Philanthropy is a Caliborn trait."

"Apparently so is high-handedness." Morgan rose from the sofa. She'd heard enough. More than enough. Her heart couldn't take any more. Crossing her arms over her chest, she shouted, "Where do you get off telling me what I can do and expecting me to settle for compatibility in a marriage? When I marry—if I ever marry—it will be for love."

"But—"

She steamrollered over him. "As for Brice, you have no need to be concerned that I'll somehow deprive him of his heritage. As a matter of fact, I was already considering starting the necessary paperwork to legally change his last name from Stevens. As you said, he's a Caliborn. His name will reflect that soon enough."

"I didn't mean—"

"You didn't mean what? To insult me? To make me feel belittled and bullied? Well, you have. I thought—" She shook her head and shoved hurt behind anger. "It really doesn't matter what I thought now. I was wrong."

"It does matter."

She pointed a finger in the direction of the door. "Go, Bryan. Now. Because while you seem to think we have so much in common, at the moment I can't think of anything."

"Morgan—"

When he made no move to leave, she marched to the door, flung it wide for him.

"Just go. Maybe it's for the best you'll be leaving for London soon. I don't want to see you for a while. When you return, I'll be in my new home and things will be less awkward for all of us."

He stood at the threshold, looking dismayed. "You're angry with me."

The understatement grated. "And hugely disappointed." Hurt came into play, too. "But don't worry that how I feel right now is going to prevent me from allowing either you or your parents to see Brice. I came to Chicago because I wanted my child to have a relationship with his father's family. That hasn't changed. I may be a lot of things, but I can assure you that spiteful isn't one of them."

"I never thought that."

"Good." She nodded.

Frowning, he said, "I handled this wrong."

He was still *handling this wrong* as far as Morgan was concerned.

"Proposing marriage shouldn't make sense, Bryan. I know you've been hurt. I know what happened to you must have made it very hard for you to trust again. But marriage should be about love. You should want to marry the person you can't imagine living without. Not merely the person you feel an obligation to on behalf of your family."

She closed the door before he could respond. She didn't need to hear any more of his cold rationalizations.

* * *

He'd botched it. Screwed it up royally. He sat on one of the lounge chairs beside the pool and reran their conversation. He'd laid out his argument just as he'd planned. It had sounded reasonable when he'd rehearsed it in front of the bathroom mirror earlier that day.

His head dropped forward and he scrubbed a hand over his face. *Reasonable*. God, he was an idiot. He walked to the main house, pausing outside the patio doors. Inside he could see his parents doting on Brice, who was lying on a blanket on the study floor.

They were happy again. Nothing could replace Dillon, of course. But the sharpest edges of their grief had been filed down thanks to the baby. Thanks to Morgan. She'd done the same for his grief, both over his brother and the boy he'd thought was his son.

She'd given them all a chance to get to know Brice when she could have filed a paternity suit and claimed compensation. In return she'd been doubted, dismissed, investigated and libeled.

If I ever marry—it will be for love.

The one thing Bryan had kept from her, even while seeking her hand. How cold it must have sounded, he thought as he climbed into his car and revved the engine to life. Hell, it must have sounded as if he were proposing a business merger rather than marriage.

CHAPTER TWELVE

FOR the next several days, Morgan was determined not to think about Bryan and his heartbreaking suggestion that they marry because it "made sense." She was hurt and angry with him. She also was disappointed with herself, because after he'd left she'd wondered if she should have said yes. She loved him. She wanted to be his wife.

To keep her mind off his proposal and her foolish heart, she immersed herself in the upcoming move. The owners had accepted the offer she'd made, leaving only the paperwork and packing to complete. Morgan was looking forward to retrieving the rest of her belongings from storage and having the new piano she'd purchased delivered. At the penthouse, she'd had Bryan's baby grand to play. Other than at the community center, she hadn't played in weeks.

Before she could move in, however, some work had to be done, thankfully all of it cosmetic and not likely to take very long. She'd hired a painter and was in the process of picking out wall colors, had measured the windows for custom shades and draperies and had made inquires to have the hardwood floor in the living room refinished. If all went according to plan, she and Brice would be out of the guesthouse the first week in December.

Bryan would already be in London. Morgan sat down at the counter with a bundle of paint chips and tried not to think about the fact that he was leaving that day. She wasn't very successful. She could only hope that by the time he flew in for Christmas, she'd have her emotions under control.

When she glanced up and saw him outside the door that led to the patio, she almost thought she was imagining things. But he knocked then and the sound had her scrambling off the stool.

"What are you doing here?" She glanced at her watch. "Your flight leaves for London in less than three hours. Shouldn't you be on your way to the airport?"

"I should be," he agreed. "But I couldn't leave without seeing you."

Morgan's heart, bruised but apparently still foolish, knocked against her ribs. Tell him to go, her head demanded. Her feet didn't obey. Stepping back, she invited him inside. He was, after all, her son's uncle. If he could be pragmatic about their relationship, then so could she.

"So, besides seeing me, what brings you here?"

She gave herself high marks for her casual tone and blasé attitude. They provided a nice cover for her clammy palms and rioting nerves.

"You and I have some unfinished business that needs settling." He shook his head then and grimaced. "Not business. Forget I used that word. What's between us is personal."

"I think we already *discussed* everything we needed to discuss when you were here the other night."

Having picked up on her emphasis on the other offending word he'd used, he told her, "No discussion this time, Morgan. I'm here to apologize."

"Okay." She crossed her arms, a reminder to herself to hold firm. "I'm listening."

He blew out a breath, looking uncharacteristically nervous. "Oh, hell, I'm no good at this."

Genuinely curious, she asked, "At what?"

"Talking." He gestured with one hand. "Oh, sure, with cue cards or memorized responses, I can come off well enough. But when I have to speak extemporaneously—" he cleared his throat "—or from the heart, I don't do so well."

Her eyebrows inched up. "I promise not to grade you."

"Right. The other night when I came here, I knew what I wanted, but my approach was all wrong. I left you with the impression that my ultimate goal was to provide for you and Brice."

"It's not?"

"No. Well, yes. Of course I want to provide for you. But that's not why—" He swore again and then reached for the fan of paint chips. "I want to marry you, Morgan, because I don't want to come home to a beige penthouse any longer. My life is beige. I want color in it. And, before you say it, I'm not talking about home decor here."

When she opened her mouth to speak, he waved a hand to stop her.

"That sounds corny. Forget it. What I meant to say is I'm lonely." He winced. "God, that makes me sound desperate and as if just anyone would do. But that's not true. I am lonely, but I don't want to be alone anymore and you're the reason."

Before she could respond, he blew out a sigh. "I'm making an ass of myself when I'm trying to sweep you off your feet. I need you. I don't want to lose you, because I love you, Morgan. I love you and Brice. And I want us to be a real family."

She put a hand over her mouth, holding in a sob and unintentionally covering up her smile. He loved her. The passion in his tone and his perfectly imperfect proposal made that clear.

"Aren't you going to say anything?" he asked.

She crossed to where he stood. For the first time since she'd known him Bryan didn't look authoritative, imposing or powerful. His expression was unguarded and sincere enough to steal her breath. Maybe that was why it took her so long to speak.

"Well?" he prodded, looking like a newly convicted man awaiting his sentence.

Morgan decided to put him out of his misery. "I have just one thing to say." Going up on tiptoe, she wound her arms around his neck. A moment before her lips touched his, she murmured, "It looks like we're going to have to call another press conference."

* * * * *

Book of the Month

We love this book because...

Alison Roberts' Heartbreakers of St Patrick's Hospital duet should come with a health warning —*dishy doctors: heart palpitations likely!* No one is immune to Dr Connor Matthews and neurosurgeon Oliver Dawson's irresistible charms!

On sale 6th July

Find out more at
www.millsandboon.co.uk/BOTM

Special Offers

Every month we put together collections and longer reads written by your favourite authors.

Here are some of next month's highlights—and don't miss our fabulous discount online!

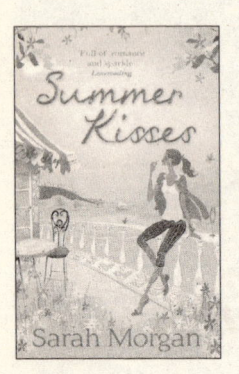

Summer Kisses — Sarah Morgan
On sale 15th June

Champagne Summer — India Grey
On sale 15th June

P.S. I'm Pregnant — Heidi Rice
On sale 6th July

Save 20% on all Special Releases

Find out more at
www.millsandboon.co.uk/specialreleases

Visit us Online

0712/ST/MB3

Happy ever after is only the beginning!

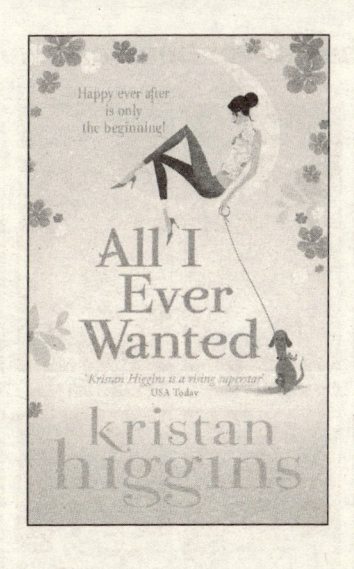

All I Ever Wanted

kristan higgins

'Kristan Higgins is a rising superstar' USA Today

Callie Grey has got a great job, a great man and, fingers crossed, a whopping great diamond—then her boss/boyfriend gives her dream and her sparkly ring to someone else…

She's spent her life reaching for the moon. Now Callie's let go and, falling among the stars, who will be there to catch her?

www.millsandboon.co.uk

The Santina Crown

Save over 20% on the whole collection

Royalty has never been so scandalous!

Cover	Author	On Sale
£2.99	PENNY JORDAN	On sale 20th April
£2.99	SHARON KENDRICK	On sale 4th May
	KATE HEWITT	On sale 18th May
	CAITLIN CREWS	On sale 1st June
	SARAH MORGAN	On sale 15th June
	MAISEY YATES	On sale 6th July
	LYNN RAYE HARRIS	On sale 20th July
	CAROL MARINELLI	On sale 3rd August

Save over 20% on the RRP!

When you buy *The Santina Crown* 8-book bundle

Save over 20% on the complete collection now at
www.millsandboon.co.uk/santinacrown

Visit us Online

0512/MB3

Mills & Boon® Online

Discover more romance at
www.millsandboon.co.uk

- **FREE** online reads
- **Books** up to one month before shops
- **Browse our books** before you buy

...and much more!

For exclusive competitions and instant updates:

Like us on **facebook.com/romancehq**

Follow us on **twitter.com/millsandboonuk**

Join us on **community.millsandboon.co.uk**

Visit us Online
Sign up for our FREE eNewsletter at
www.millsandboon.co.uk

WEB/M&B/RTL4

The World of Mills & Boon®

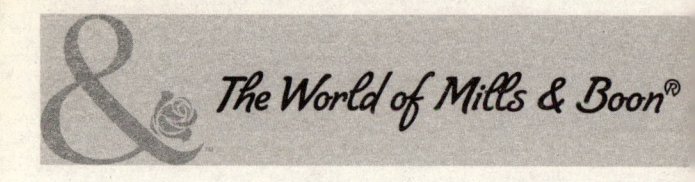

There's a Mills & Boon® series that's perfect for you. We publish ten series and with new titles every month, you never have to wait long for your favourite to come along.

Blaze® — Scorching hot, sexy reads

By Request — Relive the romance with the best of the best

Cherish™ — Romance to melt the heart every time

Desire™ — Passionate and dramatic love stories

Visit us Online — Browse our books before you buy online at **www.millsandboon.co.uk**

What will you treat yourself to next?

HISTORICAL — Ignite your imagination, step into the past…

INTRIGUE… — Breathtaking romantic suspense

Medical Romance — Captivating medical drama—with heart

MODERN™ — International affairs, seduction and passion

nocturne — Deliciously wicked paranormal romance

RIVA™ — Live life to the full – give in to temptation

You can also buy Mills & Boon eBooks at **www.millsandboon.co.uk**

Visit us Online

M&B/WORLD

Have Your Say

You've just finished your book. So what did you think?

We'd love to hear your thoughts on our 'Have your say' online panel
www.millsandboon.co.uk/haveyoursay

- Easy to use
- Short questionnaire
- Chance to win Mills & Boon® goodies

Visit us Online

Tell us what you thought of this book now at
www.millsandboon.co.uk/haveyoursay